T0089088

PENGUIN CLASSICS

DASHING DIAMOND DICK
AND OTHER CLASSIC DIME NOVELS

J. RANDOLPH COX is the editor of *Dime Novel Round-Up* and a professor emeritus at St. Olaf College in Northfield, Minnesota. He is the author of *The Dime Novel Companion: A Source Book; H. G. Wells: A Reference Guide* (with William J. Scheick); *Man of Magic and Mystery: A Guide to the Work of Walter B. Gibson; Masters of Mystery and Detective Fiction: An Annotated Bibliography;* and *Flashgun Casey, Crime Photographer: From the Pulps to Radio and Beyond* (with David S. Siegel). He has contributed to *The Oxford Companion to Crime and Mystery Writing; Mystery and Suspense Writers; Dictionary of Literary Biography;* and other reference books. He lives in Northfield, Minnesota.

Dashing Diamond Dick and Other Classic Dime Novels

Edited with an Introduction and Notes by
J. RANDOLPH COX

PENGUIN BOOKS

PENGUIN BOOKS

Published by the Penguin Group

Penguin Group (USA) Inc., 375 Hudson Street, New York, New York 10014, U.S.A.

Penguin Group (Canada), 90 Eglinton Avenue East, Suite 700, Toronto, Ontario, Canada M4P 2Y3
(a division of Pearson Penguin Canada Inc.)

Penguin Books Ltd, 80 Strand, London WC2R 0RL, England

Penguin Ireland, 25 St Stephen's Green, Dublin 2, Ireland (a division of Penguin Books Ltd)

Penguin Group (Australia), 250 Camberwell Road, Camberwell, Victoria 3124, Australia
(a division of Pearson Australia Group Pty Ltd)

Penguin Books India Pvt Ltd, 11 Community Centre, Panchsheel Park, New Delhi—110 017, India

Penguin Group (NZ), 67 Apollo Drive, Rosedale, North Shore 0745, Auckland, New Zealand
(a division of Pearson New Zealand Ltd.)

Penguin Books (South Africa (Pty) Ltd, 24 Sturdee Avenue, Rosebank, Johannesburg 2196, South Africa

Penguin Books Ltd, Registered Offices:
80 Strand, London WC2R 0RL, England

First published in Penguin Books 2007

LIBRARY OF CONGRESS CATALOGING IN PUBLICATION DATA

Dashing Diamond Dick and other classic dime novels / edited with an introduction by J. Randolph Cox.
p. cm.—(Penguin classics)

Contents: Dashing Diamond Dick / W.B. Lawson—Over the Andes with Frank Reade, Jr., in his new air-
ship / Anonymous—Frank Merriwell's finish / Anonymous—The liberty boys of '76 / Harry Moore—
Dr. Quartz II at bay / edited by Chickering Carter.

ISBN 978-0-14-310497-1

1. Dime novels, American. 2. American fiction—19th century. 3. American fiction—20th century.
4. Popular literature—United States. I. Cox, J. Randolph.

PS648.D55D37 2007
813'.4—dc22 2006052788

Set in Sabon

Contents

List of Illustrations

Introduction

WHAT IS A DIME NOVEL?

On discovering that someone has stolen his boot, Sir Henry Baskerville tells Sherlock Holmes, in *The Hound of the Baskervilles* (1901), that he feels as if he has "walked right into the thick of a dime novel."

If you ask someone today what dime novels are, you might get a number of different answers. Some people look at a display of modern paperbacks at the supermarket newsstand and call them "dime novels." Some people even call them "dime store novels," although the old-fashioned five-and-dime or dime store has been replaced by the discount store. *Dime novel* seems to be a generic term for a certain kind of fiction.

If you look up the term in *The Oxford Companion to American Literature,* you will find dime novels described as "cheap, thrilling tales of history, romance, warfare, or any violent action, many of which were set in America during the Revolution, Civil War, or frontier period." *The Oxford Companion to Crime and Mystery Writing* calls the dime novel the "generic name for American paper-covered publications of the nineteenth and early twentieth centuries (1860–1915), issued at regular intervals, selling for a fixed amount (usually ten cents), and containing lurid adventures."

The term *dime novel* was originally a brand name. In 1860 publisher Irwin P. Beadle began issuing a series he called *Beadle's Dime Novels.* These were paper-covered booklets, issued at regular intervals (every two weeks or so), and numbered in sequence. There were 321 of these in all, the last one published in 1874. Each was about four by six inches in cover size and one hundred pages in length. The early printings had only the title of the book on the cover, but later printings added lurid illustrations, and eventually this became the prevailing format. New publications were added from time to time, including such titles as *Beadle's Weekly* and *Beadle's Half-Dime Library*. While the early dime novels were intended for an adult readership, after a number of years more and more were aimed at a younger audience. The publisher changed its name to Beadle & Co. and then to Beadle & Adams, the name by which it is known today.

The success of the dime novel was due to several factors. Technological advances in printing methods and papermaking made possible the mass production of reading material, while the development of communication and transportation systems made possible the distribution of cheap publications to newsstands in cities and towns or by subscription through the mail. The passage of compulsory education laws produced a literate public, and the fixed, low price of the dime novel made reading material accessible to even the lowest-paid worker.

WHAT WERE DIME NOVELS ABOUT?

Stories of many genres were published in dime-novel format. There were frontier and western stories, detective and mystery stories, school and sports stories, love stories, and even a primitive form of science fiction. Because so many of the early dime novels were frontier and western stories, some people think that all dime novels were westerns, a myth supported in recent years by the many western movies and novels that include dime-novel writers as characters.

THE DIME-NOVEL WESTERN

The basic theme of the dime-novel western is the conflict between good and evil set in the American West. The story opens with a description of the setting: a forest, the plains, or a town that the frontier hero enters on foot or on horseback. The conflict that follows might include a fight with guns or fists. Before the conclusion of the story there might be more than one subplot alternating with the main plot from chapter to chapter.

There are six basic types of protagonists in the dime-novel frontier and western story: the backwoodsman, the miner, the outlaw, the plainsman, the cowboy, and the rancher. More than one of these types might appear in the same story. There are ranchers and outlaws in the Dick Talbot stories (1880s) by Albert W. Aiken and ranchers, cowboys, and outlaws in the Ted Strong series (1904–07) by Edward Taylor. The outlaw stories about Deadwood Dick are often set in mining camps.

The earliest dime-novel westerns follow the pattern established by James Fenimore Cooper in his Leatherstocking stories. Backwoodsmen guide travelers through the dense forest in story after story. Some backwoodsmen are based on historic figures like Daniel Boone, but the majority of them are fictitious, like Dr. John H. Robinson's Nick Whiffles.

As civilization moved westward, the mining camps of the Dakotas became popular settings for stories, and many heroes and their comrades tried to strike it rich as miners. This provides a plausible reason to place the wandering hero on the scene. It also explains the presence of the gamblers, pioneers, and outlaws who added to the conflict in the story.

The outlaw was driven to a life of crime most often by circumstance. This holds true for the fictional Deadwood Dick and Denver Dan as well as for the historic Jesse James. The gambler or "sport" is usually a peripheral character in the dime-novel western, but occasionally he becomes the central figure in a series of stories. Some examples are Gentleman Joe Gentry and Cool Dan, whose adventures appeared in *The Log Cabin Library*.

The most outstanding example of the plainsman is Buffalo Bill, although at first he was not portrayed as such. In Ned Buntline's original 1869 story in *Street & Smith's New York Weekly,* he is closer to the backwoodsman than to the plainsman of Colonel Prentiss Ingraham and later writers. The fictional Buffalo Bill adheres to a code of chivalric behavior in his quest for justice, while the real Buffalo Bill was often flamboyant and theatrical.

The cowboy, who alternates with the plainsman as the hero in the dime-novel western, is in real life a ranch hand and cowpuncher. In fiction he is a freelance figure moving from place to place in search of adventure. The first dime-novel cowboy appears in Frederick Whittaker's "Parson Jim, King of the Cowboys; or, The Gentle Shepherd's Big 'Clean Out,'" published in *Beadle's New York Dime Library* in 1882. He is followed five years later by Colonel Ingraham's stories of Buck Taylor for *Beadle's Half-Dime Library.*

The dime-novel western continued into the twentieth century with stories about the recent past as well as the contemporary West. Among the most popular publications were *Diamond Dick, Jr., Rough Rider Weekly,* and *Wild West Weekly.*

DETECTIVE AND MYSTERY STORIES

The dime-novel detective and mystery story usually follows a set formula: a mysterious situation is succeeded by startling revelations leading to a resolution. There is little analytical deduction in the Sherlock Holmes tradition. The opening scene is designed to seize the reader's attention. It might be a cry for help, a client calling on the detective with a case to solve, a police inspector or a detective confronted by the most baffling mystery on record, or the plain announcement that a crime has been committed. The story continues with a conversation between the detective and the client in which the mystery or crime is described in greater detail. The detective then questions the suspects to learn more about the background of the case, and often disguises himself to investigate the scene of the crime. He might go to the local saloon to eavesdrop on suspicious characters and gather clues or simply to trail the most likely suspect. In the course of the story he might be kidnapped by the criminals, knocked unconscious, left for dead, or even buried alive. The solution, when it comes, is a surprise to everyone, as one character after another is revealed to have been hiding a secret. Identities are unmasked, long-lost siblings are reunited, parents thought dead are found to be alive, justice is served, and the detective goes home to wait for his next case.

The ability of the detective to track the culprit is evident in the earliest stories from the 1870s and 1880s, and the early detective is often no different from the hero of the frontier and western stories; sometimes he is referred to as a "detective" when he applies the skills of the woodsman to find the guilty person. By the 1880s the detective and mystery story began to replace the frontier and western as the dominant genre in the dime novel. This transition also reflects the shift in America from a frontier to an urban society.

SCHOOL AND SPORTS STORIES

School and sports stories are so closely related that they make up a single category of fiction. The majority of sports stories are set in boarding schools, colleges and universities and describe amateur sports, although there are some stories that deal with characters who try to make a living in the professional sports arena. The students in these stories pay more attention to pursuing after-school recreation or winning the big game than to studying and passing examinations. In the classic plot, the hero wins the game for the home team against the strongest odds. He might be kidnapped or discredited to prevent him from playing until the last possible moment, but escapes his captivity or regains his reputation in time to win the game.

LOVE STORIES

There may have been almost as many love stories published in the dime novels as all other categories combined. Love stories in any era are basically tales of courtship leading to marriage. They may also be stories of a marriage in which difficulties arise between husband and wife and need to be resolved. Dime-novel story conflicts usually involve characters who want to keep the lovers apart, such as family members or romantic rivals. The plot is kept moving by misunderstandings. The stories are frequently told from the point of view of the heroine, who might be an orphan or heiress (though this is not revealed until the final chapter), a working girl trying to make her living in a harsh environment, or the ward of a wealthy businessman. Common plots include the innocent girl enticed into a marriage with a comparative stranger by promises of a bright new world in the city, children of aristocrats kidnapped and raised by gypsies, and changes in financial situations affecting relationships. There are secrets that cannot be divulged, oaths that must not be broken, and resolutions that have to be kept: to do otherwise would destroy the story. These love stories began as story-paper serials and were kept in print for generations in paperback editions.

SCIENCE FICTION

Pure science fiction does not exist in the dime novel, but there are enough stories with plots that contain elements of the fantastic to suggest there was a market for fiction that was not grounded in real-life situations. There are three principal categories: the boy inventor, lost races, and marvel stories; all three overlap to some extent.

The boy inventors use their inventions, especially airships, on voyages to discover lost races and to visit countries filled with marvels of flora and fauna. The inventions are described in just enough detail to make them plausible. The cover and interior illustrations are imaginative in a way that would attract the attention of young readers.

The lost-race stories are usually set in Africa or Central America, where the heroes encounter strange civilizations unknown to the outside world. The writers were no doubt influenced by H. Rider Haggard, whose novels *King Solomon's Mines* (1885) and *She* (1887) were very popular.

The marvel stories are set in strange, unexplored areas on the surface of the earth or beneath it, where the heroes often confront seemingly supernatural elements. Any part of the world that is not well known might be a setting for such a story.

DIME-NOVEL PUBLISHERS:
BEADLE AND ADAMS

In 1860 *Beadle's Dime Novels* was launched with the publication of Mrs. Ann S. Stephens' (1810–86) "Malaeska, the Indian Wife of the White Hunter." Although it wasn't an original story—it had appeared earlier in *The Ladies' Companion* in 1839, and an even earlier version appeared in *Portland Magazine*—Stephens made substantial revisions to it for the *Beadle's* edition. Recognizing that intermarriage was a fact of frontier history, she made it central to her story about a woman who buried both her Indian father and her white husband and was not accepted by either world. "Malaeska" was extremely popular, selling 300,000 copies in 1860 and going into several printings.

Its successors in the *Beadle's* series were also popular, but perhaps the most popular of the early dime novels was the eighth number to appear in the series, "Seth Jones; or, The Captives of the Frontier." Written by Edward S. Ellis, a young schoolteacher, "Seth Jones" is a streamlined version of James Fenimore Cooper's *Leatherstocking Tales,* with incidents of action (primarily captures and escapes) dominating the plot in place of the descriptive passages found in Cooper. Ellis also introduced the theme of identity and disguise (at the end of the novel, Seth Jones turns out to be someone other than the person the reader expects him to be), which became a recurring one in the dime novel.

"Seth Jones" outsold "Malaeska" (nearly half a million copies in six months), which was partly the result of a clever advertising campaign by the publisher. Beadle plastered the countryside with posters designed to interest the public in finding out who Seth Jones was and how they could read all about him.

Until his death in 1916, Edward Ellis continued to write dime novels for Beadle as well as clothbound works of history and juvenile adventure novels for various publishers. Some readers rate his Deerfoot series—frontier novels about a Shawanoe (Shawnee) Indian—to be his best work.

When the Civil War began, the Beadle publications found a new market. Most of the evidence is anecdotal, but apparently thousands of copies were sent by the publishers to soldiers in the Union Army when it was learned that reading material was in great demand. It is said that the little books were shipped out in bales, and that some were buried with their owners.

Beadle & Adams published many other series in addition to *Beadle's Dime Novels* and remained in business until 1898, when the assets were sold to M. J. Ivers, who continued issuing titles until 1905.

It didn't take other publishers long to produce variations on the theme established by Beadle. Besides Beadle & Adams, there were four other major publishers who issued dime novels in the nineteenth century: George Munro, Norman L. Munro, Frank Tousey, and Street & Smith.

DIME-NOVEL PUBLISHERS:
GEORGE MUNRO

Beadle's chief competitor was Canadian-born George Munro, a former employee of Beadle's whose *Munro's Ten Cent Novels* soon rivaled Beadle's series. Besides *Munro's Ten Cent Novels,* Munro's firm published other popular fiction titles. Chief among these were the story paper *The Fireside Companion* and the detective stories in *Old Sleuth Library,* but the most significant may have been *Seaside Library,* which contained reprints of well-known nineteenth-century writers: Charles Dickens, W. S. Gilbert, Sir Walter Scott, Charles Reade, Charlotte M. Brame, Robert Louis Stevenson, Anthony Trollope, and Jules Verne. *Seaside Library* also published novels by once-popular writers who are little remembered today. The firm continued in business until 1906.

DIME-NOVEL PUBLISHERS:
NORMAN L. MUNRO

George Munro in turn found competition from his own brother, Norman L. Munro, who was nineteen years his junior. Norman had worked for George but left his brother's company to form his own publishing firm, which he initially called Ornum & Co. (Ornum is Munro spelled backward). He began by issuing cheap paperback editions of popular Irish novels as well as series in imitation of those published by Beadle & Adams. Among his publications were *The Family Story Paper, The Boys of New York, Golden Hours,* and *Old Cap. Collier Library.* They were more sensational than what his brother published, and there was no brotherly love lost in their efforts to upstage each other in the production of cheap paper-covered fiction. In 1902 the rights to most of Norman Munro's fiction were sold to another publisher, but the firm stayed in business until the 1920s, when only *The Family Story Paper* remained.

The proliferation of cheap fiction in the latter part of the nineteenth century turned the brand name "dime novel" into a generic term for any work of fiction in paper covers. It didn't matter what the cover price was; they were all "dime novels" in the eyes of the public.

DIME-NOVEL PUBLISHERS:
FRANK TOUSEY

The fourth major dime novel publisher was Frank Tousey, who began his apprenticeship in the profession under Norman L. Munro. He soon branched out on his own and purchased the story paper *The Boys of New York,* considered the first of what were known as blood-and-thunder weeklies. Marketed especially for young people, they feature vivid black-and-white front-page illustrations: hooded figures menacing the hero, strange unearthly aircraft being fired upon by native tribesmen, a damsel in distress on the point of rescue, or train robbers in pursuit of a crack steam engine on the prairies. In the first few years Tousey formed a partnership with writer and humorist George G. Small, creating the firm Tousey & Small. The Tousey & Small publications reflected a flair for the dramatic, the lurid, and the sensational. In 1879 the partnership of Tousey & Small was dissolved, but the titles they had started continued under a new imprint called Frank Tousey. Among the titles added to the line after *The Boys of New York* were *Blue and Gray Weekly, Five Cent Weekly Library, Boys' Star Library, Five Cent Wide Awake Library, Frank Reade Library, Happy Days, New York Detective Library, Pluck and Luck,* and *Wild West Weekly.* Tousey died in 1902, but his firm continued under other management until the first quarter of the twentieth century, when yet another publisher purchased its backlist.

DIME-NOVEL PUBLISHERS:
STREET & SMITH

The fifth major publisher of dime novels was Street & Smith, founded in 1855 when Francis Scott Street and Francis Schubael Smith purchased *The New York Weekly Dispatch* from Amor J. Williamson. With Street as business manager and Smith writing much of the copy, they transformed the new weekly into the long-running story paper *Street & Smith's New York Weekly.* While *New York Weekly* was the mainstay of the publishing firm, Street & Smith also experimented with other types of publications, issuing the *Mammoth Monthly Reader* (1873), *Select Series* (1887), *Secret Service Series* (1887), *Sea and Shore Series* (1888), and *Far and Near Series* (1888), and drawing on the resources of the *Weekly* to supply the contents of the new paper-covered novels, or "paperbooks" as the publisher called them. Paperbooks resembled books, but each was assigned an issue number and a publication date to maintain the pretense that they were periodicals, thus guaranteeing lower postal rates. In 1889 the company entered the dime novel market with two titles that combined well-chosen reprints with new material, *The Log Cabin Library* and *Nugget Library*. Many other titles followed. Introduction of a larger, cleaner typeface made Street & Smith publications distinctive in an era of small, dense type. Street & Smith continued as publishers of popular fiction (often buying up the rights to stories issued previously by their competitors) until the 1950s, when the firm merged with Condé Nast Publications.

NEW AND DIFFERENT FORMATS

The four-by-six-inch booklet begun by Beadle & Adams did not remain the standard for long. It was soon supplemented by dime "libraries" and followed by the "half-dimes" or five-cent weeklies. The price varied from five cents to ten cents. The page size was larger (often eight by eleven inches), and the number of pages ranged from sixteen to sixty-four. The audience changed as well. While *Beadle's Dime Novels* were still marketed with the adult reader in mind, *Beadle's Half-Dime Library* was aimed at the juvenile market. The "half-dimes" were intended to be read by boys of eight to sixteen years of age who might not have a dime to spend each week. Besides costing less than dime novels, half-dimes were about half the length.

By the 1890s the term *library* was largely replaced by *weekly,* and the black-and-white cover illustrations were supplanted by color. *Tip Top Library* (later called *Tip Top Weekly*), begun in 1896, has the distinction not only of having published the continuing adventures of one of the most popular characters in the dime-novel era, Frank Merriwell, but also of being the first publication to use color covers on a regular basis.

Whether it was called a library or a weekly, each issue (or number) generally contained a single story. Some publishers might add a second story to fill out the book, but the single story was generally the rule. When the postal authorities expressed objections to the deceptive practice of claiming a series of novels to be a periodical, publishers routinely included additional matter in the form of short stories, installments of serials, and editorials to make each number more closely resemble an issue of a periodical.

The terms *library* and *series* were retained for paperback series that either reprinted from other publishers' novels that had appeared in cloth covers, or collected stories from the five-cent weeklies and serials from the story papers to preserve them for a later generation of readers. Not all of the five major publishers issued paper-covered books, and of those that did, Street & Smith issued the most, continuing until 1933 when that format was largely replaced by the pulp magazine.

A related form of publication was the story paper. While newspapers often printed serialized novels, with new installments every week, alongside the news, the story paper published mainly fiction (serial installments and short stories), together with some poetry and filler information about life in distant parts of the world, in a format resembling a newspaper. There were different categories of story paper: the family papers included something for the entire family—romances, westerns, detective stories, and success stories; boys' papers contained stories designed to appeal to the imaginations of late-nineteenth- and early-twentieth-century American boys—stories of the circus, or travel and exploration, as well as early varieties of science fiction. Between 1830 and 1921 there were more than one hundred story papers published in America. Some of the stories, especially the serials, were collected by the originating publisher and reissued in paperback.

DIME-NOVEL WRITERS

The authors of dime novels came from every walk of life. Doctors, lawyers, teachers, and journalists seem to lead the list, but so little is known about their private lives that generalizations are meaningless. Some authors signed their names to their stories, but many appeared under pseudonyms, and in some cases multiple pseudonyms, obscuring their real identities under layers of fictitious ones. Military titles—legacies of the then-recent Civil War—were attached to some writers' names, although most such titles seem not to have been earned in the military, but were honorary titles meant to lend authority to the storyteller. To attract readers, some stories were signed by well-known personalities like showman Tony Pastor, stage personalities Harrigan and Hart, and scout Buffalo Bill, but were actually written by ghostwriters.

There was little place for nuances of style in a field where what happened next counted more than character development. A writer often did not know how the story would end when he or she began writing and might have to tie up loose ends quickly and sometimes illogically to bring the story to a close within the required number of pages. There is an anecdote, no doubt apocryphal since it is associated with so many writers, about a writer who left the hero in danger at the end of a chapter and then left town. The editor scoured the territory until the writer was found and told to complete his story. The writer glanced quickly over the manuscript, picked up his pen, and scribbled: "With one bound the hero was free!" Too many of these incidents no doubt resulted in changes in editorial policy, requiring that the entire story be in hand before typesetting could begin.

A few writers made a comfortable living from their pens and typewriters, but many seem to have turned to writing only occasionally in order to supplement their regular income. It was the publisher who really made the money. There were no royalties, no subsidiary rights, but there was no income tax either. The prices paid for manuscripts varied according to the popularity of the stories. Works-for-hire, in which the story appeared under a "house name" belonging to the publisher, earned less than stories by "name" writers. A substitute writer filling in for the regular writer on a series might earn $50, while a more famous writer of story-paper serials or five-cent novelettes might command $1,000 an installment. There were far more $50 stories than $1,000 ones.

Several thousand writers wrote dime novels between 1860 and 1915. Some of them displayed high standards of professionalism, while others could be classified as "characters" who might have stepped out of the pages of their own works. It is not possible to catalog them all in this anthology, but a few have been identified as producing work of more than cursory interest or having lived lives that repay close attention. Some of these are discussed below.

Regular readers of the "dimes" looked forward to stories by their favorite authors, not always knowing which were real people and which were pseudonyms: Albert Aiken, Joseph Badger, Bertha Clay, Oll Coomes, Harlan Page Halsey, W. B. Lawson, A New York Detective, Peter Pad, St. George Rathborne, Tom Teaser, and others. One of the most famous pseudonyms was Ned Buntline.

Ned Buntline's real name was Edward Zane Carroll Judson (1821–86). Buntline may be considered the quintessential dime novelist. Journalist, publisher, temperance lecturer, novelist, and entrepreneur, he wrote under his own name and several pseudonyms. There are many conflicting stories about him. He wrote fast in order to make money to support the lifestyle to which he had become accustomed, and it is said that he once stopped off at a saloon to fortify himself on the way to give a temperance lecture, but this may be nothing more than a good story. Certainly, he was not a teetotaler.

While he wrote a great number of sea and pirate stories, and preferred those genres, he is perhaps best known for his frontier and western fiction and his role in promoting the persona of Buffalo Bill in both his serials for *Street & Smith's New York Weekly* and his stage plays. The stage plays not only featured Buffalo Bill as the hero, but for many performances also starred the real William F. Cody portraying Buntline's version of him. One of Buntline's most famous titles was "The Black Avenger of the Spanish Main; or, The Fiend of Blood: A Thrilling Tale of Buccaneer Times," published in 1847. It was given a kind of immortality by Mark Twain who had Tom Sawyer call himself "the Black Avenger of the Spanish Main" in chapter 13 of *The Adventures of Tom Sawyer* (1876).

William Wallace Cook (1867–1933) was born in Michigan. He worked as a stenographer, railroad company ticket agent, paymaster for a firm of contractors, and reporter for the *Chicago Morning News* before becoming a professional writer and contributing serials to a number of story papers as well as novelettes to the five-cent weeklies published by Street & Smith. There was hardly a series for which he did not provide stories. Although he suffered from ill health for long periods of time, he was able to maintain his contacts with publishers and was considered a dependable writer. Among the few dime novel writers who made a smooth transition to writing for the pulp magazines, he wrote an account of his career as a writer in *The Fiction Factory* (1912) under the pseudonym John Milton Edwards, and in 1928 invented an ingenious aid for writers called *Plotto*. There is evidence that mystery writer Erle Stanley Gardner (creator of lawyer-detective Perry Mason) made extensive use of both *The Fiction Factory* and *Plotto*.

Colonel Prentiss Ingraham (1843–1904) wrote an estimated six hundred novels in longhand over a period of thirty-four years. He wrote sea stories and detective stories but was best known for his novelettes about Buffalo Bill published by Beadle & Adams. Street & Smith purchased the rights to the stories and later reprinted them in their five-cent weekly *Buffalo Bill Stories,* then hired Ingraham to supply new stories for the series. When the novelettes were collected as paperbacks in the *Buffalo Bill Border Series* and *Great Western Library* issued by Street & Smith, Ingraham's name was used as the author for all of the titles, including those he did not write.

Gilbert Patten (1866–1945) was born in Maine as William George Patten but took Gilbert Patten as his professional name. He began writing stories for Beadle & Adams, but switched to writing serials for Norman L. Munro's *Golden Hours* before 1896, when he signed a contract to write a weekly Frank Merriwell story for Street & Smith's *Tip Top Library* (later retitled *Tip Top Weekly*). He served as the primary writer for that series for the next seventeen years under the name Burt L. Standish. Patten was one of the few dime novel writers to write autobiographically about the field, first in a series of articles for the *Saturday Evening Post* in 1931, and then in a formal autobiography published posthumously as *Frank Merriwell's "Father"* (1964).

Lurana Sheldon (1862–1945) wrote numerous love, frontier and western, bandit, and detective and mystery stories for Street & Smith and Frank Tousey. She contributed occasional stories to many of the five-cent weeklies, including *Secret Service* and *Jesse James Stories.* Her best-known dime-novel work is the Marion Marlowe series for Street & Smith's *My Queen,* the only five-cent weekly marketed to girls. Besides writing dime novels she wrote stories for the slick magazines and for newspapers and served as editor of her husband's weekly papers published in Maine. Few women writing at this time wrote real dime novels; most of them (like Charlotte Brame, Augusta J. Evans, May Agnes Fleming, Mary J. Holmes, Laura Jean Libbey, Mrs. Alex. McVeigh Miller, and Mrs. E. D. E. N. Southworth) wrote romance serials for the story papers, many of which were kept in print in paperbacks.

Edward Stratemeyer (1862–1930) began his literary career writing story-paper serials and dime novels generally aimed at a juvenile readership. In the early twentieth century he founded the Stratemeyer Syndicate to produce books for boys and girls and as such was responsible for such iconic characters as the Rover Boys, Tom Swift, the Bobbsey Twins, the Hardy Boys, and Nancy Drew. He provided outlines but hired others to do the writing.

Edward L. Wheeler (ca. 1857–ca. 1889) wrote detective and frontier and western stories for Beadle & Adams, but is remembered as the creator of the road agent and sometime detective Deadwood Dick, about whom he wrote thirty-three novels. Little is known about Wheeler, although he seems to have amassed his knowledge of the American West from reading, not from personal observation. After Wheeler's death, Beadle assigned Jesse C. Cowdrick (1859–99) to write a long series of sequels about Deadwood Dick, Jr.

Some of the most distinguished writers in the annals of American literature wrote dime novels or story-paper serials.

Among these were Louisa May Alcott, Theodore Dreiser, and Upton Sinclair.

Louisa May Alcott (1832–88) contributed at least thirty-three sensational thrillers to the publications of Elliott, Thomes & Talbot, and Frank Leslie. They were published anonymously or under the pseudonym A. M. Barnard, and their existence was unknown until 1943, when Leona Rostenberg published an article in *The Papers of the Bibliographical Society of America* identifying the authorship of such titles as "V. V.; or, Plots and Counterplots," "The Mysterious Key and What It Opened," and "The Skeleton in the Closet." The stories were subsequently collected and edited by Madeleine B. Stern in a series of volumes between 1975 and 1993.

Theodore Dreiser (1871–1945) served part of his literary apprenticeship on the staff of Street & Smith, where he contributed to such publications as *The Yellow Kid* and *The Yellow Book* and their successor *Ainslee's Magazine,* as well as *Smith's Magazine,* of which he served as editor. It is thought that he may have edited or even written stories for *Diamond Dick, Jr.* before writing *Sister Carrie* (1900) and the other novels for which he is famous today.

Upton Sinclair (1878–1968) was a well-known novelist, social critic, and politician, best known to the general public as the author of *The Jungle* (1906), which attacked abuses in the meatpacking industry. Less well known is that he wrote dime novels to pay his way through college. His stories about Mark Mallory set in a military academy appeared in *Army & Navy Weekly, True Blue,* and other five-cent weeklies. His publisher was Street & Smith.

DIME-NOVEL HEROES

The heroes in this anthology represent some of the more popular ones: Diamond Dick; Frank Reade, Jr.; Frank Merriwell; Dick Slater and his comrades in arms during the American Revolution; and Nick Carter. Space limitations have ruled out

some significant examples: the Buffalo Bill stories of Ned Buntline, for example, as well as the many love stories, which are
simply too long to fit into a volume of this size without crowding out everything else. For those interested in reading further,
special collections of dime novels can be found in many libraries.

THE DIME NOVEL TODAY

The significance of the dime novel for today's reader is not as
literature but as social history. It is a record of attitudes that
prevailed in the United States from 1860 to 1915. Racial
stereotypes, political opinions, and issues of gender are all
there in these once-popular books. One can trace the development of the myth of the American West as well as the change in
how products were marketed to a mass audience. The cover art
records a period before photographic journalism was common. The topical allusions and contemporary slang that made
the stories resonate with the original readers are keys to understanding a specific era in American history. The heroes are
often patriotic, rugged individuals and represent contemporary
popular concepts of the nation. The books would not have
been bought and read by so many if they had not reflected prevailing beliefs.

J. RANDOLPH COX
NORTHFIELD, MINNESOTA

Suggestions for Further Reading

Bleiler, E. F., ed. *Eight Dime Novels*. New York: Dover Publications, 1974.

———. *The Frank Reade Library*. 10 vols. New York and London: Garland Publishing Co., 1979–85.

———. *Science-Fiction: The Early Years*. Kent, OH: Kent State University Press, 1990.

Brown, Bill, ed. *Reading the West: An Anthology of Dime Westerns*. Boston and New York: St. Martin's Press, 1997.

Cox, J. Randolph. *The Dime Novel Companion: A Source Book*. Westport, CT: Greenwood Press, 2000.

Curti, Merle. "Dime Novels and the American Tradition," *Yale Review* 26 (June 1937).

Denning, Michael. *Mechanic Accents: Dime Novels and Working-Class Culture in America*. New York: Verso, 1987.

Gutjahr, Paul C., ed. *Popular American Literature of the 19th Century*. New York and Oxford: Oxford University Press, 2001.

Hartman, Donald K., ed. *Fairground Fiction: Detective Stories of the World's Columbian Exposition*. New York: Motif Press, 1992.

Harvey, Charles M. "The Dime Novel in American Life," *Atlantic Monthly* 100 (July 1907).

Johannsen, Albert. *The House of Beadle and Adams and Its Dime and Nickel Novels: The Story of a Vanished Literature*. 3 vols. Norman, OK: University of Oklahoma Press, 1950, 1962.

Jones, Daryl E. *The Dime Novel Western*. Bowling Green, OH: Bowling Green University Popular Press, 1978.

Monaghan, Jay. *The Great Rascal: The Life and Adventures of Ned Buntline*. Boston: Little, Brown, 1951.

Noel, Mary. *Villains Galore: The Heyday of the Popular Story Weekly*. New York: Macmillan, 1954.

Patten, Gilbert. *Frank Merriwell's "Father": An Autobiography*. Norman, OK: University of Oklahoma Press, 1964.

Pearson, Edmund. *Dime Novels; or, Following an Old Trail in Popular Literature*. Boston: Little, Brown, 1929.

Reynolds, Quentin. *The Fiction Factory; or, From Pulp Row to Quality Street*. New York: Random House, 1955.

Russell, Don. *The Lives and Legends of Buffalo Bill*. Norman, OK: Oklahoma University Press, 1960.

Schurman, Lydia Cushman, and Deidre Johnson, eds. *Scorned Literature: Essays on the History and Criticism of Popular Mass-Produced Fiction in America*. Westport, CT: Greenwood Press, 2002.

Settle, William A., Jr. *Jesse James Was His Name*. Columbia, MO: University of Missouri Press, 1966.

Shove, Raymond H. *Cheap Book Production in the United States, 1870 to 1891*. Urbana, IL: University of Illinois Library, 1937.

Smith, Henry Nash. *Virgin Land: The American West as Symbol and Myth*. Cambridge, MA: Harvard University Press, 1950.

Springhall, John. *Youth, Popular Culture and Moral Panics: Penny Gaffs to Gangsta-Rap, 1830–1996*. New York: St. Martin's Press, 1998.

Steckmesser, Kent. *The Western Hero in History and Legend*. Norman, OK: University of Oklahoma Press, 1965.

Stern, Madeleine B. *Imprints on History: Book Publishers and American Frontiers*. Bloomington, IN: Indiana University Press, 1956.

————., ed. *Publishers for Mass Entertainment in Nineteenth Century America*. Boston: G. K. Hall & Co., 1980.

Streeby, Shelley. *American Sensations: Class, Empire, and the Production of Popular Culture*. Berkeley: University of California Press, 2002.

Sullivan, Larry E., and Lydia Cushman Schurman, eds. *Pioneers, Passionate Ladies, and Private Eyes: Dime Novels, Series Books, and Paperbacks*. New York: Haworth Press, 1996.

Tebbel, John W. *A History of Book Publishing in the United States*. 4 vols. New York: R. R. Bowker, 1972–81.

A Note on the Text

The text of the dime novels in this collection has been reset from the original five-cent weeklies, *Diamond Dick, Jr.; Frank Reade Library; Tip Top Library; The Liberty Boys of '76*; and *New Nick Carter Weekly*. The text of "Dashing Diamond Dick" was originally published in 1889 in Street & Smith's *Nugget Library* and was reprinted in 1898 in *Diamond Dick, Jr.* The later text has been used here because it was the most readily available. In most cases the original spellings, hyphenations, and punctuation have been retained. Misprints have been silently emended.

Dashing Diamond Dick
and Other Classic
Dime Novels

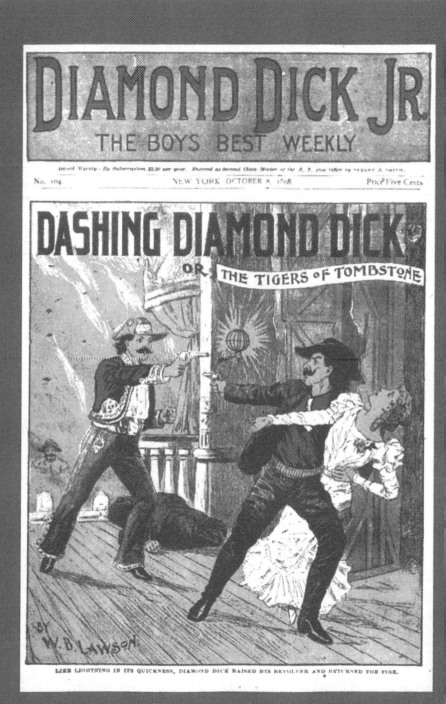

DIAMOND DICK JR.
THE BOYS BEST WEEKLY

Issued Weekly. By Subscription $2.50 per year. Entered as Second Class Matter at the N. Y. post office by STREET & SMITH.

No. 104   NEW YORK, OCTOBER 8, 1898.   Price Five Cents

DASHING DIAMOND DICK
OR THE TIGERS OF TOMBSTONE

BY
W. B. LAWSON.

LIKE LIGHTNING IN ITS QUICKNESS, DIAMOND DICK RAISED HIS REVOLVER AND RETURNED THE FIRE.

The character of Diamond Dick, whose real name was Richard Wade, was created by William B. Schwartz in 1878 for a serial in Street & Smith's New York Weekly. While a second serial appeared in 1880, it wasn't until 1889 that a regular series of stories about the character was initiated with a story for Street & Smith's Nugget Library. The character was undoubtedly inspired by the life and career of herbal-medicine promoter and showman George B. McClellan (ca. 1858–1911), who went by the nickname Diamond Dick and who was the hero of a dime novel by Buckskin Sam Hall, published by Beadle in 1882. The original serials were signed Delta Calaveras, but the five-cent weekly stories were signed with the house name W. B. Lawson. As with many of the Street & Smith dime novels, a dozen or more writers were responsible for the stories in the series. Research suggests that Theodore Dreiser may have written some of the stories and served as editor at one period. The Diamond Dick stories appeared at intervals in the Nugget Library and later in the New York Five Cent Library and Diamond Dick Library before the weekly series called Diamond Dick, Jr., began in 1896. By that time, Diamond Dick's son, Bertie Wade, who was also known as Diamond Dick, Jr., had become the titular hero for the series.

The stories were set in the contemporary West so that as times and modes of transportation changed,

*the stories kept pace. The series that began in 1889
ended in 1911 with automobiles and balloons alongside horses. Besides the two Diamond Dicks (father
and son), the cast of characters includes Billy Doo,
the tough Chicago kid; Belle Bellair, described as Diamond Dick, Jr.'s "girl pard"; and Jack Sinn, gambler,
gunman, and recurring villain. The heroes roam the
Wild West and the frozen North, as well as Central
and South America.*

*The story that follows, with its alliterative title so
characteristic of dime novels, launched the series in
1889 in the* Nugget Library *and is here reprinted from
its later appearance in* Diamond Dick, Jr. *(no. 104, October 8, 1898). The plot is filled with melodrama and
elements that are typical of many dime novels: a hero
with a mysterious background and nearly superhuman powers, the eternal battle of good versus evil, a
tragic love story with the loss of a loved one, and an
ending that promises more to come as the hero sets
out on a trail of vengeance.*

The Leap of the Tigers

Tombstone was booming; the "city," despite its ominous title, had become an established reality as well as a name.

The first vague rumors of the wondrous richness of the region had been discredited, but substantial proofs soon followed, fully confirming the facts, and a mighty rush of gold-seekers had ensued.

In the beginning, the hardy prospector, and then in parties of two, and ten, and twenty, and finally by the hundreds they flocked in.

And lo, behold! as if by magic, a city leaped into being in that rock-bound wilderness of savage cactus and bitter sage.

Tents, shanties, and houses sprang up by the hundreds.

Big hotels with modern conveniences grew, like mushrooms, in a single night; whisky-saloons cropped out by the score.

And as the further explorations proceeded, only the more apparent became the almost incredible richness of the rock-ribbed hills.

Not a week passed but what some wonderful development was made.

The turn of a spade or the prod of a pick might make a man a millionaire.

Everywhere a feverish excitement was visible—one wild, breathless struggle from morning till night, in which the strong predominated and the weak went under, and men went mad in their insane greed for gold.

Money was plentiful—at least its equivalent—gold-dust and silver bullion.

The problem was not how to acquire wealth, but how to spend it.

As a natural sequence gaming-dens and dance-halls were opened, and freely patronized.

Theatres, concert-saloons, and free-and-easies[1]—in short, all the essentials of amusement, so-called, that could minister to the wants, or pamper to the vices of the reckless miners, existed on every hand.

By day the city was comparatively deserted, for as long as a shimmer of daylight remained, by which to see the all-precious metal, the hills reverberated with the click of the drill, and the boom of the blasting cartridge.

But at night the streets presented quite a different spectacle.

Then the various places of amusement were in full blast.

Numerous flaring lights threw their glare down upon a surging, toil-stained, surging mass of reckless humanity, crowding and jostling—all bent upon some errand of idleness or curiosity, or need.

Strains of music floated out upon the air; loud laughter, coarse jests, and quick retort flew about, and inquiries and answers of every description were heard on every hand, as friend met friend, and passed the news of the day.

Nor were these the only sounds, innocent enough in their way.

Sometimes the loud voice of some drunken desperado boomed forth on the night air, proudly proclaiming himself "chief," or the report of the ever-ready revolver and the shriek of its victim.

For men in this mad scramble after fortune forgot the training of the ages, and descended to primeval savagery, stalking about with weapons openly displayed, and ever ready to fight at the slightest provocation—real or fancied.

And in this new El Dorado[2] of the far Southwest, at the close of a long summer day, our story opens.

About midway in the main street, which cut the town in two, was an open space or square called the plaza.

This was the Rialto[3] of Tombstone.

The stage—that connecting link with the outside world— made it a regular stopping-place.

It was the common centre from which all news was disseminated and gossip exchanged.

It was flanked on one side by the low buildings of the Wells, Fargo & Co's Express, and on the other by a large building which bore across its front this legend:

"HERE IT IS
Hotel and Restaurant.
Heinrich Schwauenflegle, Boss"

On the night of which we write a more than usually numerous crowd was collected hereabout.

The stage, due at sundown, was, for some reason, late, and speculation was rife as to the probable cause of its detention.

But another element entered into the motive for this gathering.

From the Here-It-Is Hotel, over which H. Schwauenflegle presides as "boss," there came, ever and anon, the sound of wild laughter, and the miners, ever eager for amusement, pressed in to see the fun.

In the middle of a large room, fitted up with all the accessories of a first-class drinking saloon, stood two men about whom a dense ring of spectators was formed.

One of these men was a perfect mountain, or, rather, let us say, a hill of flesh. He was not tall, but the short-coming in height had been amply compensated for in girth of body. He was a perfect sphere of fat, out of which short arms and legs stuck like cloves in a lemon.

It needed but a look to judge of his nationality. The round, stolid face, the thin, light hair and solemn owl-like eyes could only belong to a child of the Teutonic race.

The other was a finely formed fellow of thirty, richly dressed, and with a face darkly handsome, but sadly marred by the indelible imprints of hot passions and unbridled vices.

He was booted and spurred, as if just from horseback, and was savagely flourishing a heavy riding-whip.

This man's name was Thomas Hart, better known as "Tornado Tom." He was a wealthy gambler and mine-owner, but was known throughout all that region as a "bad man" when in liquor.

And it needed but a glance now into his flushed features to see that he had been drinking deeply.

"Dance, you Dutch dog!" he cried, waving the whip menacingly, "dance, I say, or I'll cut you into sausage meat, ay, and serve you up for free lunch across your own bar. Come, stir her up—there's the music that'll put motion into yer moccasins."

A pistol-crack followed the savage words, as the lash cut into the quivering fat of the German.

A howl of pain followed, almost drowned in a chorus of brutal laughter.

"Say, you! Doan'd you do me dot[4] some more," the German cried, in a voice in which anger, pain and fear were curiously blended. "Himmel! dot purns me mine legs like fire und primstone," rubbing vigorously at the sore spot.

And then he continued, in a tone of resentment:

"Vot haf I done mit you, Tornado Tom, do you cum in mine house und glub me like I vos a no 'count dog or a chackass mule—say?"

"Done?—done nothin'; want ter see yer dance, thet's all."

"Vell, deu, better you chust look mit yourself a little oudt. I vas a man, I vos, from the groundt up, und my name it was Heinrich Schwauenflegle, und I vos de boss in mine own saloon, mineself, und doan'd you forgot me dot, neder."

"You lie like a Greaser,[5] Dutchy—when Tornado Tom turns out fur a little fun, he owns all Tombstone; he's the only baby in the cradle—the one an' only darling of the house; an' when he cries fur a free fight or a frolic, he must have it if it takes the last rock in the reticule.[6] Jess now he's breakin' his little heart to see you step it out on the light fantastic. Come, start her up, or——" and he finished with a significant flourish of the whip.

Poor Schwauenflegle shrank back in fear.

"Bud, look you, Mister Tornado," he expostulated, "I haf not tanse me for finf und drizig year.[7] Und, pesides, I vos too fat—I vos an elephant, and an elephant he cannot tanse, you vos hear me?"

"I know a derned sight better. I've seen 'em dance in a circus up in 'Frisco," Tornado Tom answered, amid general laughter. "It won't do, Dutchy," he continued with all the persistency of a drunken man. "Dance I've said, and dance you must."

"Himmel! bud I vill not! if I vos tanse dere vill pe a pig scare—a panic—de peoples vill dink dere vos an earthquake in the city. Look you! I put me mineself on de schales ofer at de exbress office lasdt veek, und I veigh me chust dree hundert und sefen poundts. Of I vos tanse de house vill fall down all in little bits and kill us all to deadt."

"Let her fall—Tornado Tom'll pay the damages. Now start her up. I'm getting derned dry with all this talking. Away you go."

Again the lash was brought down, but this time the Teuton,[8] clumsy as he looked, adroitly dodged, and its force was expended on the empty air.

And before any further degradation could come upon him, a shout arose at the door.

"Here's the stage coming."

It was followed almost instantly by a cry of wonder.

"Why, what's the matter with it—look at the horses! An' that ain't Sandy driving!"

Attracted by the probabilities of some fresh excitement, the crowd poured out of the saloon, Tornado Tom among the rest, and poor Schwauenflegle was rid, for the time being, of his tormentor.

It was true—something was wrong with the stage.

The familiar form of the driver, genial Sandy Rocks, old "Rocking-horse Sandy," as the boys used to call him, was missing.

The express guard, young Walter James, was in his place on the box, and held the reins.

And the team. One of the leaders was gone, and the "off" wheeler was limping badly.

Besides this, the harness showed here and there some makeshifts of straps and ropes that told a story of disaster.

As the coach drew up to the plaza it was instantly surrounded, and the young express guard was besieged with questions.

"What's kept ye, Walt?"

"Had a breakdown, didn't ye?"

"Where's Sandy?"

And a score of similar questions, all in a breath.

And then a burly miner, keener of vision than his fellows, cried out suddenly:

"Why, Walt, yer hurt! yer hair an' face are all kivered with blood."

The express guard wearily threw down the reins; in the clear moonlight that began to prevail they could see that his face was ghastly pale, and that a blood-stained cloth was bound around his brow.

"I got creased by a bullet," he said, his voice husky with pain, "an' I'm faint an' tired—it's the loss of blood, I reckon," he finished, apologetically.

"Wounded! why, what's bin the row?"

And then from a dozen throats came again the eager questions:

"And whar's Sandy?"

"Whar's the old Rockin' horse?"

The young fellow turned to the seat, and partly removing a blanket that concealed a dark object lying on the top of the coach, said tersely:

"Thar!"

"Dead!" yelled a man, recoiling from the wheel, where curiosity had attracted him.

"Who?"

"What do you mean?"

"Not ole Sandy!"

The express guard nodded briefly.

A little man, with a brisk, determined manner, forced his way to the coach.

"How did this happen, Walter?" he said. It was the agent of Wells, Fargo & Co. in Tombstone—Jack Hamilton by name, and Walter James, recognizing his superior, answered in two significant words:

"Road agents. They struck us just this side of the ford—a dozen of them," he continued, as the crowd became silent, evidently awaiting an explanation of some sort. First we knowed we got a volley that piled the horses all in a heap, an' throwed one of the leaders cold. 'Twas Sandy's pet hoss, Blarney, and I reckon the sight druv him off his base; anyways, he pulled his gun and opened up. But he got salivated[9] the next second. An' I got my medicine, too," he concluded, quietly tapping the bandage about his head.

CHAPTER II
A Beautiful Vision

The young express guard's words were listened to with many expressions of sorrow and regret.

Rough old "Rocking-horse Sandy," as they had named him, with his genial ways, his hearty laugh, and mirth-provoking yarns, had been a prime favorite with all, ever ready to execute a commission, or to do his fellow-man a kind turn, and his sudden, tragic fate was honestly bewailed.

Many a muttered curse came from rough-bearded lips, and threats of vengeance were dire and deep.

And ill, indeed, would it have fared with the miscreants who had ended the driver's career, could the miners have got them into their clutches.

"And do you think you would know any of the fellows, Walt, if you saw them again?" Jack Hamilton continued.

"Nary time; they war all dressed alike—in yaller clothes, with big black splotches all over 'em, an' masks like the face of a cat. But the chief war a little, slim-built cuss, with a soft, cooing voice, almost like a woman's; said they were the Tigers o' Tombstone, an' durn me fur a dummy, if they didn't look it, too, every time."

"The Tigers of Tombstone!" the miners cried in amazement; the strange title was new to them.

"They must be a regularly organized band of robbers. What do you think, Walt?" the agent asked.

"I reckon so; leastwise, the little cuss allowed they war a-goin' to make things hum fur a while around these diggin's."

"We'll see about that later on," Jack Hamilton said, quietly.

He was a nervy man of about forty, this quiet-mannered express agent, and those few words from him meant more than a barrelful of bluster.

"But do you know, cap," Walt James continued, "that war sumthin' as struck me mighty curious in the way that little cuss of a tiger-cat acted."

"Yes? in what way? Give me all the particulars that you can

remember. I must send an account of this to headquarters, and want all the details."

"Wal, cap, it war this: when they had us dead to rights, the little feller he rides up to the stage an' looks in mighty sharp, a revolver in his hand, a self-actin' one—the gun, I mean, 'cause I see the hammer working under the pressure on the trigger. But when he saw what war inside, it seemed to me that he acted kind o' disappointed like; he let rip a cuss, and then growled sumthin' about gittin' him next time, sure."

"That is queer," Jack Hamilton said, a puzzled look upon his face; and the crowd that was listening, with breathless attention, re-echoed the sentiment.

"He must have expected someone by to-day's stage," he concluded, half in inquiry.

"I reckon so; 'tenny rate,[10] that's the way it seemed to me."

"Wal, when he didn't find what he wanted in the hearse, he guv the box an' rack[11] a derned good overhaulin', ripped open the mail-bags, an' looked at every letter, his hands shakin' jest a leetle. When he got through he said a few words to his men, an' they rode off, leavin' me to patch up damages as well as I could."

"All this is curious," the express agent muttered to himself, "and must be investigated. But Walt, you must be in pain," he continued more briskly. "I will ask you no more questions tonight. Get your wound attended to, and see me in the morning. I may want you."

He walked off as he finished speaking, and Walt James was about to follow, when a sudden recollection seemed to overwhelm him with remorse, judging by the crestfallen look upon his features.

"Wal, kick me fur a dummy, anyhow," he muttered, "here I've been preachin' like a phonograph, an' that sweet young lady a-sittin' in thar all alone, an' like's not faintin' fur want o' food an' rest."

And with this, he lowered the window-sash in the coach door, and called out, anxiously:

"I say, miss, are you awake?"

"Oh, yes, sir. I have not been sleeping at all," a low, sweet voice made reply.

And then a sudden, breathless hush fell upon that throng of rough humanity, for out from the semi-darkness in the coach came the bonniest face that mortal eyes had ever gazed upon.

It was like a vision, framed as it was by the door of the coach—a thing of unearthly beauty—such a face as some of the old masters saw in their dreams, and dimly pictured in their waking moments.

Purity sat enthroned on that low, polished brow, where the hair clustered and coiled back and fell in a cascade of reddish gold; and truth looked fearlessly out from the clear depths of the hazel eyes.

A brave face it was too albeit that hardly seventeen summers had blossomed there and left their buds in gleeful dimples on cheeks and chin.

A smile played like a sunbeam about the pretty mouth as the girl surveyed the uncouth beings stricken dumb by her rare loveliness.

"What is it?" she said, her voice sweet as the music of the psalms. "Have we arrived at our destination?"

"Yes, miss, this air the City of Tombstone," Walt answered. "An' now—don't think I want to pry into yer affairs, miss, but you see it's night, an' what I want ter know is hev you got any friends here that you intend stopping with?"

A shadow fell like a cloud over the bonny face, but it brightened again instantly.

"I have no friends," she said, bravely. "But if you will kindly direct me to a hotel that you can recommend, I shall be very grateful."

"Will I! You bet. The Here-it-is Hotel is just what you want, miss. It's kept by a Dutchman, but he's on the square, an' the fixin's is first-class; you'll be comfortable there, I know."

"Then that will do very nicely; please to open the door."

But the young express guard was suddenly thrust aside, and a man took his place at the coach door.

It was Tornado Tom.

"What'r you thinkin' of, Walt James?" he said, contemptuously. "What! trust that parcel of feminine loveliness to the mercies of a Dutchman, whose name would give her a fit the first time she tried to speak it? Nixey!"[12]

A fierce light leaped into Walter James' eyes, and he would have promptly resented the man's interference, but he was worn out by fatigue, and dizzy with pain, and the rough jostle had set his wound to bleeding again.

But Tornado Tom never noticed this.

Turning to the stage, he threw open the door and stretched out his hand.

"You come with me, miss," he said, his eyes devouring the face of the beautiful girl. "I'll show you the prettiest nest you ever laid eyes on—all silk an' down, just fit for a little humming-bird like you."

But the girl shrank from the proffered hand. There was a light in his eye that alarmed her.

"I thank you," she faltered, "but I will not trouble you—the hotel will do very well."

"Nonsense! you'd be dead in a week, eating that Dutchman's messes. Don't you be scart of me, little one, I'm rich, an' I'll see thet you don't want fur nothing. Come, let me help you alight."

And in his eagerness to possess that fair flower, he put his hand upon the arm of the now thoroughly alarmed girl.

At this, something very much like a growl ran over the spectators. There were men among those clustered about the stage—men who, gazing at that beautiful face, suddenly remembered sisters and sweethearts away back in the old life, and who knew what Tornado Tom really was, despite his handsome face and form.

"Look a-here, Tornado, ain't you makin' a mistake?" a tall miner said. "Thet gal ain't one of your kind, I reckon; leastwise we wouldn't like to see——"

"You dry up!" Tornado Tom interrupted, turning fiercely. "I'm running this, an' if any of you fellers interfere, you'll git hurt bad; you hear me?"

Scowling looks was the only answer vouchsafed, and Tornado Tom again turned to the stage.

But like a thunderbolt from a clear sky came an unexpected diversion.

CHAPTER III
A Duel by Moonlight

Soon after the stage-coach had driven into the plaza, and during the excitement that followed, two horsemen had ridden into the square, and quite unobserved, had drawn rein at the outskirts of the crowd.

We say two men, but strictly speaking, one was a boy, a mere child of perhaps ten years.

He was a sturdy little fellow, however, with a fair, fearless face, big brown eyes, and yellow hair floating freely down upon his shoulders.

He sat straight as a clothes-pin in the saddle, albeit he could hardly straddle the horse's back, and curbed the powerful animal with a skill that equalized any apparent want of strength.

The other was a man, tall of stature, but of whose person little could be seen, as his face was shadowed by a slouched hat, and a serape, or Mexican blanket cloak, covered his form almost to his feet.

Attracted by some words he heard, the man had dismounted.

"Take care of the horses, Bertie," he said, throwing the bridle rein to the boy. "Something out of the usual has happened here, and I will find out what it is."

Then, mingling with the crowd, he had been an attentive spectator of all that had passed, gradually worming his way to a position near the coach.

Now, as Tornado Tom, for a second time, stretched out his hand to grasp the form of the shrinking girl, he suddenly felt upon his wrist a grasp that seemed to crush the bones with the power of a closing vise, and with a wrench that almost tore his arm from its socket, he was flung aside.

"Hands off, you hound!" a cold, stern voice said.

Tornado Tom recovered himself by an effort, and with a bitter imprecation, his hand upon a revolver, faced his assailant.

It was the man in the serape, and his eyes were shining with anger and scorn.

"Shame on you!" he said, sternly, "to insult a lady whose isolated position should appeal for protection to any one worthy of the name of man."

The words lashed Tornado Tom into madness. Perhaps for the first time in his arrogant sway had he been thus roughly handled.

"And who in the fiend's name are you?" he hissed, almost frothing at the mouth in his rage.

Hot and quick came the retort:

"Your master!"

And as quick came the retort:

"You lie!"

The stranger started as though stung by a serpent. With a quick, catlike bound he sprang forward; a hand, flashing with jewels, shot from beneath the serape, and fair upon the mouth of the mine-owner fell a terrific blow.

"Take that! Perhaps it will teach you to keep a more civil tongue between your teeth."

Half-stunned and bleeding, Tornado Tom staggered back, and almost fell.

The next instant, with a snarl like that of some wild animal, mad with wounds, he whipped a revolver from his belt.

But before he could level the weapon to fire—even before he could raise the hammer—a voice that almost rose to the screaming pitch in its intensity, cried out:

"Down with that pistol, you dog! Down with it, I say, or I'll perforate your whole hide into porous-plasters!"[13]

Spurring his spirited horse through the dense mass of humanity, and careless alike of the cries and curses of those he overthrew, came the little companion of the man in the serape.

The eyes of the boy were flashing with resolution, his fair, fearless face flushed with a mighty resolve.

One small hand was tight upon the curb, in the other glistened a revolver, the hammer raised, the dark muzzle leveled straight at the heart of Tornado Tom.

It is doubtful if Tornado Tom heard the words that heralded the approach of the boy, so consuming was his rage; nor is it at all certain that he would have heeded their warning had he heard.

But the sight of that small bit of humanity interposing between him and the object of his wrath was a spectacle so unparalleled in his experience, that he could only stop and stare, and gasp in speechless amazement.

"Put that gun back into your belt," the boy commanded, as he reined up his horse in front of the mine-owner. "If there's to be any shooting, it's got to be done on the square, or I'll chip in quick! You hear me?"

The words sounded so curious, coming from the lips of the child, that two or three quick-drawn gasps of stupefaction were painfully audible among the spectators.

Tornado Tom glared at the speaker like one stuck suddenly with paralysis; but the revolver in the hand of the boy never quivered, and mechanically, like one in a dream, he replaced his own weapon in the sheath upon his hip.

Then, before anything further could be said the man in the serape stepped up.

"That will do, Bertie; put up your pistol," he said. "You mean well, I know, but I can fight my own battles. Besides, I am not pleased with your forward conduct. Draw your horse to one side."

The boy shrank back, a mortified look upon his flushed features. The tears sprang into his eyes, but the pride of his stanch heart would not suffer them to overflow.

And then Tornado Tom interposed. He was perfectly cool now, and his hands were empty of weapons.

"Don't lecture the little chief, stranger," he said. "I swear I never got such a turn in my life as he gave me. I almost fainted, I did so. But who is he, anyway?"

"My son."

"You don't say? Stranger, you ought to be proud of him."

The man in the serape made an impatient gesture.

Tornado Tom seemed to comprehend.

"All right, stranger. Don't be in a hurry. You understand of course, after what has passed between us, there can be but one way of settling the matter."

The man in the serape nodded gravely.

"Whenever and wherever it suits you," he said, coldly.

"I reckon now and here will fill the bill," was the grim reply. "You have the choice of weapons, of course."

Again the stranger nodded. And he added, after a slight pause:

"Fifteen paces with pistols."

"Good enough," and the eyes of Tornado Tom gleamed with savage fire.

He was good for the size of a silver dollar every time at that distance.

"Now, stranger," he continued, grimly, "I ginerally have my man planted decently, after an affair of this kind. Will you tell me what name to put on your headstone?"

The man in the serape laughed coolly.

"You are very considerate," he said, mockingly; "however, as I have no intention of putting you to any funeral expenses on my account, my name will not signify. As to the rest, you may call me Diamond Dick."

As he finished he suddenly drew the cloak from his shoulders and tossed it to the care of his boy.

And as he stood thus revealed, there burst simultaneously from the spectators a cry of wonder and surprise.

The stranger was a magnificent specimen of manhood.

He was tall of form and straight as a lance, his every motion being distinguished by a lithe, panther-like grace. His face was very handsome, a strange, white pallor contrasting curiously with the dark, brilliant eyes and hair, and mustache of raven hue.

He was dressed like a Spanish hidalgo,[14] but the fanciful costume was adorned in a manner such as never before was seen.

All about his person a myriad of diamonds flashed and burned, and sparkled, and shot out star-like rays of mystic light. In the snowy frills of the shirt, three stones gleamed like smoldering fire; the short jacket, terminating at the waist, had set in lieu of numerous buttons, on either side of the open front, a mass of sparkling brilliants, the nether garment, slashed open at the side, almost to the hips, was ornamented by a double row of flashing gems, and the soft felt hat upon his head was looped up at the side by a diamond star.

In the silken scarf wound time and again about his waist, the ends trailing gracefully down at the side, were thrust two revolvers with diamond sights.

Many an admiring glance was cast upon this cool, handsome man, who called himself Diamond Dick, and who was so brave in the defense of the weak, and so ready to resent an insult.

Even Tornado Tom, in whose heart burned a fierce hatred of the man who had placed the mark of his hand upon him, could not but admit that he had an adversary every inch his equal.

But meanwhile preparations had been completed for the duel.

A space had been cleared, on either side of which, and out of the line of fire, were grouped the spectators, eager to witness the coming contest.

There remained only to agree upon someone to give the signal to fire.

"Let the little chief give the word," Tornado Tom suggested. "I'll bet a hoss he kin do it."

The boy looked eagerly into his father's face.

"Oh, may I?" he pleaded. "I can do it—you know I can."

Diamond Dick was startled at the proposal, but as he gazed into the fearless eyes of his son, a proud smile lit up his face, and he signified his consent by a rapid gesture.

And do you think, dear reader, that any one tried to dissuade these two men from their reckless course?

Far from it. Instead, bets were freely offered and as readily accepted on the result.

"A hundred to fifty that Tornado throws the stranger cold at the first fire!" cried a man who knew his favorite's skill in the use of the revolver.

"Done—in ounces!" said a brawny miner, producing his bag of "dust."

"Make it wounded,[15] and I'll go my pile on Tornado," said a cautious speculator.

"Well, I've got six bits as says neither o' them'll git touched at the first wang," said a ragged bummer, sticking his head cautiously around the corner of a building, where he was safely ensconced.

"Oh! give us a rest, you old soak."

But we are wrong; someone did try to prevail with one of the principals, at least, to give up this horrible affair.

Diamond Dick had been talking earnestly to his son; he concluded now with these words:

"You have not forgotten the instructions I gave you once before? The same will apply now, in case I go under."

"I remember every word," the boy answered, brightly, "but you do not think he can harm you, do you?"

"I cannot say; I hope not, for your sake." And then, while pretending to be busy with the boy's stirrups, he pulled the young face for a moment down to his own.

Then, with a sigh, he drew a revolver, and stepped over to take his place.

But as he passed by the coach a small white hand was laid upon his arm, and a tremulous voice whispered!

"What are you about to do, sir?"

Diamond Dick saw that it was the beautiful passenger of the stage-coach, who was the indirect cause of all the trouble.

"You here yet?" he said in surprise.

"I could not go until I had spoken with you—had thanked you for your kindness in defending me from that man. But, sir, I see a weapon in your hand. What is it? Ah, I know. You are going to fight a duel, and all on my account. Is it not so?"

"But miss, you should retire to the hotel. This is no place for you."

"You evade my question," the girl cried, passionately.

"Oh, how unfortunate I am!" she continued, clasping her hands together. "I have been the cause of it all. Oh! let me beg of you not to peril your life on my account."

"Nonsense; you overestimate the danger," said Dick, cheerfully. "But come, they are getting impatient over there; I must
ask you not to detain me longer."

The tone of voice in which he finished convinced the girl that
further words would only be thrown away upon this inflexible man.

She made a despairing gesture and turned away.

And Diamond Dick, revolver in hand, took his place.

Tornado Tom was already at his station.

Midway between the two was the boy Bertie, mounted upon
his horse.

And now, everything being in readiness, a silence fell, during
which the boy's clear voice was plainly audible.

"Gentlemen," he said, "these are the conditions that you
will govern yourselves by: I shall ask you if you are ready, and
I will then count slowly, one, two, three. Your shots must not
be delivered before I say one, and not after I have counted
three. Do you understand?"

It was patent to all that the boy was merely repeating words
learned by heart, like a lesson; nevertheless, there was something peculiarly thrilling in his voice.

"Are you ready?"

"Ready!" came simultaneously from the lips of the two men
standing so straight and motionless in the clear light of the
moon; so handsome in form and features both, and, alas, so
soon, perhaps, to become mere clods of senseless clay!

"Fire!"

Two weapons, with death lurking in their depths, fell into
line and remained immovable, each pointing at the heart pul-
sating with intense life.

And at that instant—in that moment between life and
eternity—a strange, mocking voice cried out derisively:

"One, two, three!"

In perfect time with the count came two pistol shots in quick
succession.

Tornado Tom uttered a startled exclamation, and the pistol
in his hand fell to the ground, while Diamond Dick's arm was
whirled half way around.

And then both men gazed at their weapons in stupefied amazement.

From both pistols the hammer had been shot away.

A peal of mocking laughter rang out upon the air.

The sound seemed to break the spell that held all enchained, and they turned to see who the daring marksman could be.

At the head of the plaza stood a something that at first sight looked like an animal perched upon the back of a horse of magnificent mold.

Its body was yellow, and all barred with bands and spots of black; the head was small and round, short ears sticking up on either side; the eyes, fierce and yellow, shone with the phosphorescent glow, and from the red, half-opened mouth, bewhiskered like that of a cat, a double row of cruel-looking fangs gleamed whitely.

This thing, whatever it was, held in one of its paws a revolver, from the muzzle of which the smoke was still slowly oozing.

And then, as all were gazing at this apparition, the young express guard, Walt James, suddenly sprang forward.

"That's him!" he shouted, excitedly, "that's the cuss that held up the stage to-day an' salivated the ole Rockin'-hoss—that's the Thomas K. Cat who bosses the Tigers of Tombstone."

CHAPTER IV
Diamond Dick Receives a Letter

A vengeful yell arose from the miners as the import of Walter James' words became apparent.

Here was the chance they had been wishing for to avenge the death of old Rocking-horse Sandy.

Instantly as if actuated by one common impulse, a half-hundred revolvers gleamed in as many hands.

But, with a bound like that of the wily animal represented upon its back, the big black horse jumped forward, rounded the angle of the corner, and clattered away down the street.

A mocking, taunting laugh came floating back.

With cries of rage the crowd rushed after in pursuit, firing at every jump.

But it was useless.

The sound of the horse's hoofs became less and less, and soon ceased altogether in the distance, and, angry and excited, the miners strolled back to the plaza.

Meanwhile Diamond Dick, Tornado Tom, and the boy had been left alone. The rush of the miners in pursuit of the outlaw had separated them somewhat, but now Tornado Tom came forward.

"Diamond Dick," he said, "I reckon we'll have to cry quits for to-night—this racket has rattled my nerve. Besides, that cuss of a tiger-cat shot too close—see?"

He held up his hand, dripping with blood.

The upper joint of the right-hand thumb had been carried away by the same shot that had ruined his revolver.

"But remember," he continued, and there was the tone of a merciless demon in his voice, "that as soon as I kin hold a weapon again I'll call you out, for no man ever yet struck Tornado Tom and lived. If ye leave town I'll follow, though the trail leads to hell!"

Diamond Dick laughed coolly.

"Have no fears," he said. "I am not going that far. In point of fact, I shall remain right here in Tombstone. You will find me at any time over at the hotel there."

"Good enough!"

And without another word Tornado Tom turned on his heel and walked away.

"Curse him!" he muttered between grating teeth. "If it hadn't been for his infernal meddling, I'd a-had that gal sure. I'll have her, anyway, if all Tombstone has to go down in the struggle! Whew! but warn't she a beauty! Wonder who she is, an' what she's doin' down here? And that bespangled dandy in the Greaser dress—who the devil is he? Diamond Dick, he calls himself—wal, he looks his name, every time. Must have the rocks; he's got the sand in him,[16] too, but may the fiends toast me if I don't get square with him in some way!

I'll wring his heart, if I have to cut the throat of his child to
do it!"

Thus, with black hatred in his heart, Tornado Tom wended
his way.

And return we to the plaza.

The crowd had dispersed—at least it had resolved itself into
smaller groups, but the excitement still ran high.

So many events of a startling nature had been crowded into
the past few hours that ample food was furnished for discussion. The death of Sandy, the fair stranger, and the mysterious
being, disguised as a tiger-cat, who had so curiously interrupted the duel, all came in for their share of debate.

But paramount above all was the interest centred about Diamond Dick.

His handsome face and rich attire had appealed to their admiration, his cool daring and the way he had handled the bully
of the town had won their respect.

"I tell ye what, boys," a burly miner remarked, "he ain't no
slouch, ef ye hear me squeal, but did enny of ye ever see him
afore?"

"I did," a grizzled old prospector answered; "know'd him
over in Greaser Gulch, 'bout 'leven year ago."

"An' what war his record thar?"

"All white; a chief—free with his dust, his dukes, and his
derringers,[17] jess as it'd suit ye; an' clear grit down to hard-
pan."[18]

"I thought so—he looks it. An' that kid o' his'n! I sw'ar he's
a whale! Lord, boys, when the little feller came ridin' in on thet
hoss, an' a-singin' out so like's 'f he meant business, an' I
reckon he did, ye could a-knocked me down with a chaw o' to-
bacco, I war so 'mazed like."

"Same here, pard."

"And here."

But in the meantime Diamond Dick and the "little feller"
had entered the saloon of the Here-it-is Hotel.

Heinrich Schwauenflegle met them on the threshold, his face
radiant.

The German had witnessed all that had happened on the plaza from a window of his saloon.

He advanced now with outstretched arms.

"Velcome to mine house—a hundredt tousand-dimes velcome!" he fairly roared. "Oh, bud dot vos a sight dot make me feel goot all oafer when you knock with your fist in the face of dot schoundrel, Dornado Tom. Himmel donner-vetter! bud I laugh so much dot I putty near schprain me de pack of mine neck!"

Diamond Dick smiled. He was unaware of the cause that the German had for hating Tornado Tom, and these expressions of glee seemed somewhat extravagant to him.

"I want a room and accommodations for myself and this lad," he said, "and send some one to see that our horses are cared for."

"Dot vill I do, you bed; und de best I hef got in de house shall be yours, und by shimmeny cracks, dot vos a fine leedle poy you haf got, Meester Dimundt Tick—he vos a hangel, a cherup, und vill he not cum und gif his oncle a kiss?"

Bertie had been staring with wide-open eyes at the German, for never in all his limited experience had he gazed upon such a mass of fat and flesh.

But now, as Heinrich advanced upon him with open arms, he uttered a yell and dodged behind a table.

"You keep away from me," he shouted, dancing about in what seemed an agony of fear. "I ain't no angel—I'm only just a boy, and I'll butt you in the stumjack if you come any nearer."

The German paused in dismay.

"I say," the boy continued, eyeing him warily, ready to dodge again at the slightest sign of danger, "what do you call yourself, anyway?"

"Heinrich Schwauenflegle."

"Keno! Ten-strike—set 'em up on the other alley."[19]

"Vot's dot?"

"Never mind; did it hurt you much?"

"Dit vot hurt me mootch?" said the perplexed German.

"I mean did it hurt when they gave you that name?"

"Nein."

"Queer! Say, if I was you I'd put a cage around that name!"

"Vot for?"

"Why, it'll get away from you some day and kill somebody."

A roar of laughter ran around the room. And by this time, too, it began to dawn upon the German that he was being made game of.

He shook his fat forefinger disapprovingly at the mite.

"You is too schmardt," he chuckled. "You vill die young—like all goot leetle poys; you will see."

Diamond Dick, laughing heartily, stepped up to the bar to register in a small book kept for that purpose.

A freshly-written name, in neat chirography, caught his eye on the page of the day.

"Alice Marr, San Francisco."

"Alice!" he murmured, and a shadow fell like a pall upon his face.

What bitter-sweet memories that name recalled; how vividly it brought back to his mind the fair, sunny-haired young wife who was sleeping so calmly now where the sweet-odored orange blossoms bloomed in the gleeful sunshine of the Californian land.

But with a sigh he roused himself, and as the German came bustling up to the bar, he inquired:

"Is that the name of the young lady who arrived by the stage to-night?"

"Yaw, dot vos she, und by chimmeny, bud she vos one putty gal, eh?"

"Very; and where is she now?"

"She vos gone mit mine sister Gretchen to her room, bud she vill be town again right away soon to kit her sum toast und some tea. Und you vill want you somedings to eat, too, Meester Diamundt Tick, ain't it?"

"By and by. Give me a glass of wine now."

Heinrich set out a bottle with alacrity.

"Is that fit to drink?" said Dick, doubtfully eyeing the liquid he had poured out.

"Vot, dot vine? You bet you. Vy, dot vos as schweed as baby's milk—chust look at the color!" and Heinrich held up the glass to where the light could shine through it.

As he held it thus, admiring the ruby color, a quick, sudden pistol shot rang through the room, and the glass was shivered to a hundred fragments.

"Murder! bolice! I vos shooted—I vos kilt," Heinrich cried, in his first moments of surprise.

But he soon recovered himself.

"No, I vos not kilt—I vos all ride; bud vare is mine bung-starter? Himmel's dunder-vetter, I vill preak de feller all up in leedle bits who blay me dot trick."

He glared about the room until his gaze rested upon the boy, Bertie, whose eyes were sparkling with mischief, an impish grin upon his face, and who still held in his hand a smoking revolver.

"Vot, you!" the German fairly yelled in his amazement. "Vos it you who shoot me dot glass from mine hand?"

"My gun went off 'fore I could help it," the boy answered, with a look so droll that a snicker of laughter ran around the room.

"You vos one leedle tyful!" the irate man shouted.

"All right, uncle; but I say, don't you want to come and give me a kiss?"

"Nein; bud ven I catch you somedime alone you vill see vat I gif you."

Despite a feeling that he was doing wrong to encourage this mischievous spirit in his son, Diamond Dick could not help laughing.

He knew the skill of the boy in the use of the revolver—a skill that had often looked wonderful to him, for he seemed never to take any aim, and yet the bullets always went true to their mark.

But he came forward now, straightening his face as best he could.

"Bertie," he said, severely, "I have told you time and time again that you are too ready with your revolver; it is not well, and some day it will bring you into trouble; you mark my words."

"Well, a feller couldn't help shoot at a mark like that—it was too temptin'," the boy whined.

But the time was not far distant when he remembered those warning words, and bitterly repented that he had not taken better heed.

And just then a man, of the genus "bum," entered the saloon.

"War's the gay an' festive galoot as goes by the dazzlin' cognomen o' Diming Dick?" he vociferated. "I've got a billy-doo[20] for him."

"You have a letter for me?" Diamond Dick said, slightly surprised.

"I reckon you're the party as fills the bill," the man said, after surveying Dick from head to foot. "Here ye aire; but boss, it's a derned dry walk from the other end of this festive municipality."

Diamond Dick impatiently tossed him a coin.

And then, as his glance fell upon the superscription of the letter, a look came into his face that was not pleasant to see.

"Who gave you this letter?" he asked, in a tone that made the bummer jump.

"It was a woman, cap, an' a derned pooty one, too, if ye hear my gentle racket."

"My God! can that fiend in female form have followed me even here?" muttered Dick.

And then, without further ado, he broke the seal of the letter, and read:

"Diamond Dick—I can imagine the look upon your face as you peruse this handwriting, once so familiar, and which, I have no doubt, you fondly believed you would never see again. Well, such is fate! Do you hope to escape me by fleeing to this wild land? Vain hope; for flee where you will there will I follow until you have either made me reparation or rendered up your life. Have you forgotten that the fury of a woman scorned has no parallel—not even in hell? But we shall meet again—soon, very soon, and until that time allow me to sign myself, your humble servant, Kate."

Diamond Dick groaned as he finished reading.

"Is this fate?" he murmured. "Is there no place in this wide world where I can hide from that wicked woman's importunities?"

And away down in the innermost corner of his heart a voice seemed to answer like the knell of doom:

"None."

CHAPTER V

The California Nightingale

To say that the Tombstone Opera House was crowded, would be describing the fact mildly—it was literally packed.

For the past three days a banner had been swinging across the street, on which was painted in large letters:

"ALICE MARR, THE CALIFORNIA NIGHTINGALE."

The fame of the girl's wonderful beauty had gone forth in Tombstone.

Many had seen her on the night when she first arrived in the city, and the stories they scattered broadcast were largely punctuated with exclamation points, and had aroused the curiosity of all.

Hence it was that the house, on this night of her first appearance, was filled to overflowing, and many had been turned away.

Diamond Dick was there.

So was Tornado Tom, who had sworn to possess the girl; and he was there that night, with a fiendish plot in his heart, to carry out his design.

A roaring prelude had put the audience into a pleasant mood.

And then Alice came forward to the footlights.

She had chosen for her introductory "Coming Thro' the Rye," and as the melody of the old Scottish ballad rang out, men held their breath and clinched their teeth in an agony of pleasure that was almost akin to pain.

Clear and sweet the quaint words thrilled through the hall, now high, now low, like the glad, free cry of some forest bird, or the low sough of the summer wind through whispering reeds.

Not until the chorus was given for the last time and she was making her bow to retire, was a sound heard.

But then there broke forth such a yell of delight, such a prolonged thunder of applause, that the girl was startled.

Cheer after cheer rent the air, and men seemed to go wild in their enthusiasm.

And then Tornado Tom arose, and, as though cramped by long sitting, stretched both hands high over his head.

It was a signal.

There suddenly came a cry so piercing in its intonation, so hideous in its meaning, that a thrill of horror ran like a bolt of lightning through the house.

"Fire—the theatre's on fire!"

And, as if that voice had been a signal to call it into existence, a volume of black smoke rolled into the room.

Instantly there ensued a scene that defies any words of tongue or pen to describe.

With horror and dismay depicted upon their faces, the miners sought to escape from the burning building.

A mad rush was made for the doors and windows and every available avenue of escape.

And then, with a cry of savage exultation, Tornado Tom sprang upon the stage.

Alice had been standing like one turned into stone. The horror of her situation, and the frightful scene enacting before her eyes, had frozen her every faculty.

But now, as she saw Tornado Tom advancing upon her with outstretched arms, she uttered a piercing cry and turned to seek safety in flight. But before she could succeed, Tornado Tom had his arms about her.

"Don't be frightened, little one," he said, "I'll save you from all harm, never you fear."

The words were reassuring, but the look that accompanied them made the girl tremble.

"Take your hands away from me—let me go, I do not want your assistance," she cried, striving to unloose his clasp.

But Tornado Tom only laughed and tightened his grasp.

"No, no, my pretty one," he cried, exultantly. "I've been to too much trouble and expense to let you go so easy now. I've loved you from the time I first set my eyes on your beautiful face, and swore that you should be mine, though all the fiends of hell intervened—see! the firing of this building was done by my orders, it is my gold that has conjured up this scene of destruction and death—and all this have I done for your sake."

"Oh, my God! Help! in the name of Heaven, help!"

Diamond Dick heard that piteous cry.

From the first he had been struggling desperately to reach her side.

But it seemed as though a plot had been preconcerted to hold him back.

A number of ruffianly-looking miners were always around, hampering his every motion.

But now, as he saw Alice struggling in the arms of Tornado Tom, and heard her appeal for help, he uttered a hoarse cry of rage, and with a superhuman effort of strength he burst through all restraint, and sprang upon the stage.

Instantly a revolver was in his hand.

But Tornado Tom had seen him coming, and was prepared.

With a snarl of hate, the villain fired thrice in rapid succession.

But hampered as he was with the girl, who never for a moment ceased struggling to free herself, he could secure no true aim, and his bullets went wide of the mark.

Like lightning in its quickness, Diamond Dick raised his revolver and returned the fire.

But a powerfully-built ruffian struck up his arm at the very moment of firing.

The next instant he received a blow in the face that almost blinded him.

Stunned and bleeding, his brain dizzy with pain, Diamond Dick staggered back, making desperate efforts to keep his feet.

Then a number of villainous-looking men closed upon him.

And then, too, it flashed upon Diamond Dick, as he gazed into their faces and saw how in concert they acted, that they were either friends or tools of Tornado Tom, and a grating curse broke from his lips as he saw the odds arrayed against him.

A quick glance around showed him Tornado Tom disappearing behind the painted scenery that littered the stage, with the form of Alice in his arms.

The sight almost crazed Diamond Dick.

With a bitter imprecation he leveled his revolver.

Men went down before him, dead or dying, cursing and striking at him even as they fell; flashes of fire singed his very face, and bullets hurtled around him like hail.

He was wounded in half a dozen places in as many seconds, but his blood was up now, and he never heeded the hurts.

But this could not last long.

No men, actuated only by the hope of gain, could stand before this living thunderbolt, and with cries of rage and fear, the hired desperadoes of Tornado Tom, now sadly decimated, broke away and fled.

Diamond Dick, his path cleared, now sprang behind the scenery, where he had seen Tornado Tom disappear.

A passage was disclosed, leading to the rear of the building.

To bound down this, dash through an open door and out into the open air, was the work of an instant.

Not many seconds had elapsed since Tornado Tom had preceded him, but when Diamond Dick gazed about, he was nowhere near.

But away off, in the clear moonlight, he saw a horseman galloping toward the distant mountain range that lay dim along the horizon.

He caught the flutter of a white robe, and knew that it was Tornado Tom who was riding away with his fair captive.

Diamond Dick groaned.

"By the memory of my sainted wife, you shall pay for this night's work, Tornado Tom!" he hissed between grating teeth; "and if you do that fair flower the slightest injury, I'll make you wish that you were in the hands of all Hades rather than in mine."

And then a prayer came, like a cry of agony, from his heart:

"God be with her, and shield her from harm!

"But come," he continued, more energetically, "this will not do!—neither curses nor prayers will avail, I fear. I must get my horse and follow. Oh, but can I follow his trail?—the night is young—it will be hours before daylight breaks—can I? I must—I dare not leave that pure girl in his power until morning." And then a sudden fierce look of joy leaped into his eyes. "The dog!" he cried. "Where are my wits?—the bloodhound will scent where I cannot see."

He said no more.

The Opera House was a mass of flames by this time, and burning fiercely as he moved away.

Arriving at the hotel, he ordered his horse saddled, while he made a hasty examination of his wounds.

To his great relief, they were not serious, and by the time he had them dressed his horse was ready.

But Diamond Dick had need of another companion.

Taking a light, he descended into the cellar beneath the hotel.

As he came down the stairs, the rattling of a chain was heard. A low, ominous growl greeted his ears.

But the next instant it changed to a whimper of recognition, and a magnificent bloodhound sprang to the length of his tether to greet him.

He was a large, powerful beast, of nearly pure blood, with yellow, golden eyes, and a front of chest and fangs that boded ill for anything that should awaken his ire.

He was wild with delight when he became unchained and understood that he was to leave the cellar, where he had been cooped up so long; but a few sharp words brought him under control.

Then slinging a Winchester rifle over his shoulder, and assured that his revolvers were in good working condition, Diamond Dick mounted his horse.

"Tell Bertie not to be alarmed if I do not return to-morrow," he said to the German, for his son was sleeping. "And do you look after him a little, and keep him out of mischief if you can."

He had given Heinrich a hasty account of what had happened, and the German was almost heart-broken by the news of Alice's peril.

But he promised to faithfully fulfill Dick's request.

"Good-by then, until I see you again. Come on, El Rey!—click! click!"

Chirping to his dog, Dick put his horse in motion and rode swiftly toward the point where he had caught a glimpse of the fleeing desperado.

Dismounting, he saw that the soil was soft and sandy here, and that a number of hoof-marks were plainly discernible.

By the bright light of the moon the trail could be easily followed, and should the character of the ground change, so that sight could no longer be relied on, he could still follow by the scent of the hound.

Springing upon his horse again he rode swiftly forward, his keen eyes roving over the ground, his face grim and foreboding, in his heart a purpose as set as the fiat of fate.

And alongside ran the hound, with long, bounding leaps that easily kept up with the pace of the horse.

Ah! Thomas Hart—or Tornado Tom, as you are rather proud of being called—it was an ill-starred hour when your planet crossed the orbit of Dashing Diamond Dick!

CHAPTER VI
Tornado Tom's Plight

When Alice Marr awakened from the stupor into which she had fallen, the city was miles behind her.

At first, a sense of rapid motion—a feeling that she was rushing through the air with lightning speed, so bewildered her that she could not realize where she was.

A man's arm held her fast, her head rested upon his shoulder, and she could hear the fierce throbbing of his heart against her ear. But a look into the face so near her own, and she remembered; all the horror of her situation burst upon her.

She gave utterance to a low moan of despair.

Tornado Tom bent his face closer; he saw that the girl had regained consciousness.

"That's music to my ears," he said: "I thought you were never coming out of your faint."

Alice aroused herself by an effort.

"Oh! where are we going—where are you taking me to?" she cried, wildly.

"There, there! calm yourself; no harm will befall you, and where we are going you will be treated well, if you are sensible."

But the reassuring words did not deceive Alice. There was a look of subdued passion in the desperado's eyes that made the girl shudder.

"Oh, take me back!" she pleaded. "What have I done that you should persecute me so?"

A fierce, wild light leaped into the eyes of Tornado Tom.

"Done!" he cried, in a voice intense with passion. "You have bewitched me with your fatal beauty. Your fair face has haunted me ever since I saw you first; I could not rest—neither by night or day could I sleep for thinking of your bonny pure features—aye, I loved you the first night I set eyes upon you. I love you now, a thousand times more."

"Oh, no, no, it is impossible!" cried Alice, in dismay.

"To possess you," Tornado Tom continued, "I would have committed any crime—nay, I have done an act that may outlaw me from civilization if it is brought home, but I hold it cheap when the reward is so sweet."

Alice could only listen with horror depicted upon her face.

And then Tornado Tom continued more mildly:

"I know that I have been a bad man, but I will become your slave in body and soul if you will give me your love. I am rich—more than rich, and your every wish shall be gratified, your every want supplied. See—I love you so passionately—so madly that no sacrifice save that of losing you, will I not make for your sake."

"Oh, stop, stop!" the girl cried, vainly trying to stem this current of words.

But Tornado Tom never heeded.

"You may not love me now—I admit that I have been rather abrupt in my wooing, but love will come when once we are married, and you see how humble and devoted I shall be."

"It can never be!" Alice said coldly. "I do not love you. I never could love you, and I never will!"

"But, by all the fiends of hell, you shall!" Tornado Tom cried, maddened at her cold tone. "You are in my power, and no one shall take you from me while I can pull a trigger."

He had reached the banks of a small stream called the Bronco, and he reined up his horse as he finished speaking.

Then putting a hand to his mouth, he uttered a shrill, peculiar cry.

To the wonder of the girl it was answered like an echo, and a man stepped out on the other side of the stream.

"Is that you, Tornado?" the man inquired.

"Yes, Jack; is everything all right?"

"All fixed; come ahead."

Tornado Tom crossed the ford.

A number of horsemen—ten, all told, gathered around him with rude expressions of greeting.

Three of these men were his brothers, the others were either related to him or were close friends.

They were all finely-formed fellows, but they were all more or less desperate-looking and crime-hardened.

"Did you bring the side-saddle, Jack?" Tornado Tom asked.

But his brother Jack did not answer for a few moments.

His gaze was riveted upon the fair face of the girl in speechless admiration.

"Is that the gal you've been raving about?" he cried, at last. "Wal, I don't blame ye, Tornado, for going to all this trouble—she's worth it."

One of the men led up a fine horse with a lady's saddle upon his back.

"Can you ride?" he asked of Alice.

Alice nodded; she had thought of making an appeal to these men, but the greedy, burning looks of admiration she encountered wherever she looked convinced her of the folly of such a course.

She had almost abandoned hope, and made no resistance when Tornado Tom lifted her into the saddle.

Then the desperado gave a long look backward on the path he had come.

"What's the matter, Tornado?" one of his brothers inquired, noticing the action. "Any one following you?"

"I can't say, Harry. I don't think any one saw me get away with the girl, only——"

"Only what?"

"There was a fellow saw me grab her; but if the boys have done their work he won't trouble us."

"Who was it?"

"Diamond Dick."

Alice raised her head. What power that name had to awaken her emotions.

Was he following after, to tear her from the hands of these ruffians?

The very thought brought the light of hope back to her eyes, and a color into her cheeks that was beautiful to see.

"Wal, spos'n I remain behind here at the ford?" Tornado Tom's brother suggested. "If any one is following I can salivate them here."

"Just as you please, Harry; it might be a good plan; for if any serious pursuit is in progress you could bring me word."

"All right, then; I'll stay."

A few moments after the horses were put into motion, and the cavalcade left the stream behind.

They did not hurry. They had a long journey before them, and the strength of the horses must be husbanded.

Besides, Tornado Tom believed himself safe from pursuit.

But not long had they left the Bronco when a pistol-shot came faintly to their ears.

It was followed, an instant after, by a number of reports in quick succession.

The cavalcade drew rein instantly and listened.

"Harry's fixed 'em, I guess!" a man remarked, as no further noise was apparent.

"I reckon so!" Tornado Tom replied laconically.

But then to their ears came a sound that caused all to start.

The long-drawn, deep-voiced bay of a hound came ringing over the plain.

"Why, it's a dog!" one of the men remarked, in surprise.

"Ay; and yonder he comes!" Jack cried.

"Yes, and there comes Harry, too."

But Tornado Tom cried out suddenly:

"That can't be Harry—that hound would not be trailing for him."

"That's so!" Jack said, struck with the force of this argument. "But who is he?"

Tornado Tom had been gazing intently at the lone horseman. He cried out now, suddenly:

"I know him—it is Diamond Dick, and Harry is dead."

CHAPTER VII[21]
A Wild Ride

From Tombstone to the Mule Pass Mountains is a distance of about twenty-five miles, as the crow flies, and although Diamond Dick may live to a green old age, he will never until his dying day forget that wild ride through the moonlit night.

Every incident is as distinctly impressed upon his memory as though graven there on granite.

It is about eleven o'clock in the night when he takes the trail.

In the clear, dry atmosphere of the Arizona land, the bright-full moon renders objects as plainly visible as though daylight was shining. It is only among the shadows, doubly dark by contrast, that eyesight fails and other senses have to be relied on.

Diamond Dick has settled himself firmly in the saddle.

He knows that he has a long, hard ride before him, and has made sure that girth and stirrups, and bridle and curb are all sound and properly adjusted, each in its place.

His horse he can rely on.

The animal has the blood of a racing sire in his veins, and barring accidents will run as long as he can keep his feet.

He may fail in this wild race where the pace is so killing, but it will only be when his great heart has burst in twain.

And so, sure of his weapons, sure of his steed, and above all, sure of himself, Diamond Dick rides swiftly upon the trail.

He has an idea of where Tornado Tom is going.

He knows that away beyond the pass in the mountain range is a settlement, where the desperado has many friends, and will believe himself safe.

But this fact does not for a moment deter him from his purpose.

He has sworn that he will bring Alice back, or lose his life in the attempt.

There is no middle course.

But, meanwhile, the miles are flying back from his horse's hoofs, and away beyond he sees the fringe of foliage that marks the waters of the Bronco stream.

He has made five miles in eighteen minutes, but the horse never seems to feel the pace.

The dog, too, is doing well.

The brute instinct of his breed has warned him of what is in the wind, and he is running ahead now with long, graceful leaps, carrying the scent high in the air.

Twenty minutes later, Diamond Dick draws rein on the banks of the Bronco.

He has arrived at the ford, and Tombstone lays eleven miles behind.

He pauses in the centre of the stream for a moment to water his steed.

Then calling to the hound, who is eagerly lapping the water with his red tongue, they splash through to the south bank of the stream.

And then, like a bolt of lightning from a dark cloud, a stream of fire shoots out from the black foliage, a stunning report awakes the echoes, and Diamond Dick feels a sting upon his face as though a whip-lash had struck him.

But in a second of time he draws a revolver from his belt, and aiming into the thick underbrush fires three lightning-like shots.

A sudden, quick-drawn gasp of pain follows, and springing from his horse, Diamond Dick rushes into the underbrush.

But the dog has been beforehand.

With a growl of rage as he catches the scent of an enemy in hiding, the hound bounds into the bushes, and when Diamond Dick reaches his side, he finds him standing over the prostrate form of a man, his white teeth gleaming savagely, his nose up sniffing suspiciously at the air.

"Hunt 'em out, El Rey!" Dick cries, thinking there may be more of his enemies in ambush.

But the bloodhound does not move. He gives a final sniff at the atmosphere and commences to wag his tail.

Satisfied by the dog's action that this has been the only one, Diamond Dick seizes the form by the shoulders and drags it into the light.

The man is a stranger to him, and he is quite dead.

Two bullets have entered his body, either of which would have killed.

With a shudder, Diamond Dick rolls the body back into the underbrush, and is about to remount, when his gaze is attracted by a number of fresh signs upon the bank of the stream.

A quick examination soon convinces him that a large body of horsemen had assembled here not very long ago.

Were they friends of Tornado Tom?

Diamond Dick feels satisfied that such is the case, and no doubt the man whom he has slain had been left behind as a scout, to bring intelligence of any possible pursuit.

Then his face grows stern and serious in thought.

He begins to see how thoroughly Tornado Tom has laid his plans to succeed in his design.

This has been a rendezvous where friends have no doubt been in waiting with fresh horses for the fugitive.

Would this make any difference to Diamond Dick?

"No," he says, and he is deadly calm now. "No matter what fate has in store for me this night, I will follow. If the next few hours or minutes are to number the end of my existence, so be it. I could not live and think of the anguish of that innocent girl, whose beauty has strangely stirred my heart. No, though a hundred enemies barred the way, still will I follow. I will either tear her from that villain's power, or meet oblivion in death."

Then giving his steed the rein, he shoots forward once more.

The hound is already upon the trail, his deep-toned bay ringing out impatiently upon the air.

Swiftly the miles fall away; minute after minute passes by, and still the hound runs with his nose in the air, and the horse keeps to the stride that is beginning to make his heart thump with distressful pain.

And still the handsome, dashing young man upon his back seems to feel no fatigue, no emotion, no feeling save that terrible set purpose in his heart to do or die.

And now in his front he can distinguish a number of horsemen standing motionless on the moonlit plain.

A cry of fierce joy rings from his lips.

He imagines for a moment that he has caught up with his quarry.

But the next instant he sees his mistake, for nowhere can he distinguish a sign of the girl.

Nor are these horsemen fleeing—no! they are waiting his coming.

Tornado Tom must have learned or suspected that he is being pursued and has thrown these men out to protect his rear.

Perhaps, after meeting his friends, he has not been so hurried in his flight, and has been within sound of the firing at the ford.

But all conjecture is soon cut short by the action of the men.

Weapons gleam in their hands, quick flashes and sudden re-ports follow, and the bloodhound, who is far in advance, utters a howl of pain.

He comes rushing back, bleeding.

He is wounded, but not disabled, and his growls of rage are blood-curdling to hear.

And then, too, bullets begin to whistle about the pursuer.

But Diamond Dick is yet too far distant to become a sure mark for the revolver, and his enemies seem to be armed with these weapons only.

A light leaps into the eyes of Diamond Dick that is not pleas-ant to behold.

He swings the long Winchester to his shoulder and takes de-liberate aim into the dark mass that is each second becoming more and more distinct.

The next instant the rifle rings out.

A hoarse, agonized cry follows the report, and Diamond Dick knows that the shot has not been wasted.

And then, more rapidly than tongue can count, the deadly repeater vomits out its contents in smoke, and fire, and leaden bullets, winged with sudden death.

And now Diamond Dick is among them.

He hears all around him the shrill, frightened neigh of wounded horses, the cries of men dying or going down to death, and the groans and bitter curses of human beings in the agony of burning gunshot wounds.

He hears all this like one in a dream, for in a few seconds his horse has left the sounds far behind.

Has he killed them all?

He never knows.

A bullet has carried away his hat, and his long dark hair is streaming free in the air.

There is blood upon it, too, where a spiteful bullet has cut the scalp.

Almost mechanically he recharges his rifle, and holds it in readiness across the saddle-bow.

Then on and on in a mad, wild rush that intoxicates the senses and causes the blood to leap in dancing glee.

The mountains are very close now, but the pace is beginning to tell cruelly upon the animals.

The sides of the steed are dripping with sweat, his breath is quick and labored, and big clots of foam fly from his lips and fleck the heaving chest.

He has come twenty miles in a little over an hour, and he is very tired; he would like to stop, at least to moderate his speed, but all the blood of his sire revolts in his veins at the traitorous wish, and he keeps up the fearful pace.

And the hound is in the lead no longer; he is foot-sore and in pain from his wound. His bay is not heard now; he needs all his wind to keep by the side of the animal whose heart is breaking, but who will give no sign.

But Diamond Dick needs the hound no longer. He has sighted his game at last!

Yes, he has just seen a number of dark moving objects leave the plain and file into the pass.

Instinctively Diamond Dick seems to feel that this fearful race is nearing an end.

But the pass is long and winding, and gloomy with shadows dark and deep.

It is just the place for a deadly ambush, and Diamond Dick clinches his teeth as he pictures the peril in his mind.

He knows that Tornado Tom will let slip no such opportunity as this of shooting him down.

And now the pass lies before him, dark, and forbidding, and sullen with silence.

And a great calm comes over his spirit; he knows that the finger of fate is heavy upon him on this night, and that in the dark depths of that tomb-like canyon he may find a sepulchre indeed. And now, too, for the first time in that terrific race, his hand draws in on the curb.

In that rock-strewn path before him he must lessen the speed, or his horse will go down.

Then, with a revolver in his right hand, and bending low down on his horse's neck, he plunges into the rock-walled way.

El Rey is in the van once more.

The diminished speed has given the bloodhound the lead again.

And not five hundred yards have they penetrated into the pass when the hound gives a yell that reverberates through the canyon like a roar of a hungry lion.

At the same instant a flash of light leaps up on either side of the road, and the blended report of two revolvers recoils, repeated in thunderous echoes from the cliffs around.

Diamond Dick laughs.

"A clear miss!" he says, and he gallops on unharmed.

But soon comes the sound of rapid hoof-beats in his rear.

He is being pursued.

This will never do.

Diamond Dick has enemies ahead; he wants none at his back.

He crosses a patch of moonlight and draws up his panting steed in the frowning shadow of a beetling cliff.

Onward come the hoof-strokes, getting near and nearer, and then two horsemen spring into the band of light, lashing their animals into furious speed.

They do not notice that the hoof-beats they are following have ceased—the clattering noise of their own horses fills their ears.

And as Diamond Dick fires, they pitch forward from their steeds and strike the rocky ground with a terrible thud.

They never know what hurt them; at least they never speak of it after, for Diamond Dick is shooting now to kill.

Then onward once more, in that rattling pace that seems to know no end.

Up steep inclines and down precipitous grades, rounding curves and boulders, sharp and jagged, and in and out of light and shade, until the path suddenly widens out and the mountain walls retreat, and Diamond Dick can see the moonlit plain beyond.

And, with a thrill of joy, he marks on one of the horses a form clad in a fluttering robe of white.

He has gained upon his quarry, too, for he can almost see the look upon the face of the girl as she turns her head around.

There are but two of his enemies left, and even as he marks this he sees one of the horses stumble and fall, pitching the rider headlong to the ground.

But the man is on his feet instantly, and faces about, a revolver in his hand.

There is a look of white despair upon his features as he gazes upon that living thunderbolt coming down upon him with such headlong speed.

He seems to know that he is marked for death, but he will have one shot before he dies.

He waits until he thinks his aim is sure, and then fires.

Diamond Dick gives a groan, his bridle falls useless at his side, and dangles there with every motion of his horse.

Then his revolver speaks, and the way is clear once more.

But his arm is giving him a horrible pain, there is a red mist before his eyes, a nausea like death is creeping over him.

Is he to die after all? Is this long, heart-breaking race to fail when he has the object of it all so nearly in his grasp?

No! a thousand times no!

He straightens up in the saddle, dashes the mist from his eyes, and sets his teeth hard to keep down the agony that seems to be rending his very vitals.

And then he utters an involuntary cry of alarm as he sees the steed upon which the girl is mounted stoop and sink down, throwing her heavily to the ground.

And now Tornado Tom faces about.

He stands at bay at last.

A look of terrible joy springs into the eyes of Diamond Dick.

Not fifty yards separates him from his foe.

But then his horse suddenly staggers and stops dead short, and spreads his legs wide apart to keep from falling.

He springs to the ground, and, revolver in hand, advances on foot upon his hated foe.

But he staggers now like a man drunken with wine, his eyesight is blurred, and that sickening nausea is come upon him again.

And calmly, coldly, Tornado Tom waits, his revolver leveled with deadly aim, until his foe shall be near enough to make a certainty doubly sure.

And Tornado Tom waits too long.

Intent only on the man whom he hates, with such bitter feeling, he is oblivious to all else.

But suddenly he hears a long-drawn yell that makes the very marrow in his bones creep.

The next moment, with a bound like that of a tiger, a long, black body shoots from the ground, and fastening its fangs in his throat, pulls him down from the horse.

It is the bloodhound, El Rey!

Tornado Tom utters a gurgling cry of horror and dismay, and tries to shake the dreadful beast from off his throat.

But in vain.

With blood-curdling growls, the hound crushes him down. A horrible sound of crunching bones, a tearing, sickening rending of flesh, a faint, gurgling cry, and then silence.

Tornado Tom's career is ended forever.

Then, too, without a sound, Diamond Dick pitches headlong to the ground, and lies there as motionless as death.

CHAPTER VIII
Bertie in a Bad Fix

On the day after the events narrated in our preceding chapter there appeared, in a prominent place upon the plaza, the following notice:

$1,000 REWARD

Will be paid for the person, dead or alive, of the man who shot and killed a driver in our employ, by the name of Rocks, more commonly known as "Rocking-horse Sandy." The murder is supposed to have been committed by the chief, or leader, of a band of highway robbers known as "The Tigers of Tombstone." A further reward of ONE HUNDRED DOLLARS will be paid for the arrest, or information that will lead to the arrest of each and every one of the band. By order.

WELLS, FARGO & CO.

JOHN HAMILTON, Agent

This notice was posted early one forenoon, and was not known to the majority of the miners until later in the day.

But a crowd of bummers and idlers had been drawn around it, who were passing sage comments and remarks upon it.

Among others was a youth of nineteen or twenty—a gawky, stoop-shouldered fellow, with a freckled face, and a shock of whitey-brown hair, that looked like a dirty mop.

His clothes, ill-made and of rough material, hung loosely about his frame.

He was evidently a stranger to the town, for he carried a bundle, tied up in a handkerchief, under his arm, and his shoes and clothing were travel-stained and dusty.

He had been attracted by the idlers about the board, and was now staring open-mouthed at the notice pasted upon it.

"One thousand dollars!" he ejaculated. "Gosh! but that's a heap o' money!"

And then he continued, smiling slightly.

"I thought the 'Thomas K. Cat who bosses the Tigers of Tombstone' was valued at a higher figure than that."

He shook his head with owl-like gravity.

"It is not enough."

He gave a quick, sharp glance around as he finished speaking, to see that he was not observed.

Then, drawing a pencil from his pocket, he wrote rapidly for a few moments on the margin of the paper.

"There! that will fix things O.K.," he said, surveying his work with a critical eye, "anyway, it'll make it more interesting all around, I guess."

Then hitching his bundle closer up under his arm, he strolled slowly away down the street, and out of town.

But the mysterious action of the youth about the bulletin board had been observed, despite his caution.

At one of the windows of the Here-it-is Hotel, were standing Bertie and the German, who had promised him a hiding for scaring him so badly, a few days before.

But some sort of a truce had evidently been agreed upon between "David and Goliath" as a wag, seeing them together, had named them, for they were conversing together in a friendly manner.

"I say Schwan!" Bertie called out, "look at that tenderfoot out there, will you?"

The German laughed as he looked upon the gawky youth, gazing so intently at the notice.

"Yaw, yaw! he's vos one emegrant van hay-seet."

"But what's he looking at, anyway?"

The German explained. He had read the notice earlier in the morning.

"Why, look ahere, Schwan!" the boy cried a moment later, "he's writing something on that paper."

"Yaw, so he vos. Jek Hamilton vill pull his ears ov he vos see him do dot."

"S'pose I shoot that pencil from his fingers?" Bertie suggested, drawing his revolver.

"I can do it just as easy as a wink," he persisted, as the German demurred.

But by this time the gawky-looking youth had finished, and strolled away.

"I'm going out there and read that notice," Bertie said, a few minutes later.

"All ride; bud donn't you go away; your fadder vos toldt me to look oudt after you."

"Well, I won't hinder you from looking," and the sturdy little fellow marched out, laughing.

He read the notice through, and then came nearer, to decipher the writing on its margin.

This is what he saw:

"And I will pay $5,000 to the man who can take me. Signed: 'The Thomas K. Cat, who bosses the Tigers of Tombstone.'"

The boy's eyes opened wide in surprise.

"Why, that's what Walt James said the other night, when that funny thing broke up the duel," he said, in perplexity. "What'd that tenderfoot want to write that for, anyway?"

Then his brain began to work, and gradually a curious expression came over his face.

He was older, by far, than his years in experience; he had never had any child-life, such as other children have.

The revolver had been his toy from infancy; his horse his only playmate. That he could read and write was due to his father's teaching, for he had never seen the inside of a schoolhouse.

"I wonder who that tenderfoot was?" he muttered. "Maybe he was one of them Tiger fellows in disguise. But he signed himself 'boss'—whew! s'pose'n' he was the cap'n himself! Must have been pleasant, reading this notice. And what a gall he's got to write them words underneath!" he continued, eyeing the writing admiringly.

And then he added, quickly:

"I guess Jack Hamilton would like to talk to that fellow."

Then an idea flashed into his busy little brain, that almost took his breath away.

"S'pose'n' I was to run after that fellow and bring him back!" he whispered.

"Why not?" he continued, as he revolved the idea in all its bearings, "he's a good deal bigger'n I am, but here's the thing that makes big and little equal," and he significantly tapped the revolver in his belt.

Then a look of determination flashed into his face.

"I'll do it!"

He looked toward the hotel, but Schwauenflegle was not observing him.

Then, after having assured himself that his revolver was in good order, Bertie set off down the street at a trot.

Meanwhile the gawky-looking youth had got some distance from town.

But there was nothing gawky about him now.

He was walking with a free, easy stride, his form straight and graceful.

His eyes were bent upon the ground, but his face had upon it a look of intelligence—nay, his face would have been positively handsome had it not been for the dirt and freckles upon it.

He had just reached a point where the road turned and entered a ravine, thickly wooded on either side, when he became aware of pattering footsteps in his rear.

The next instant a shrill voice shouted the command:

"Halt! and throw up your hands!"

The youth turned, an imbecile look of alarm upon his face, and his eyes opened wide at what he saw.

A boy—a mere child, with fair hair, and a face as fearless as a lion's cub, stood before him, a revolver in his hand, the hammer raised, the dark muzzle staring straight into the eyes of the youth.

"You hear what I say?" this apparition remarked. "Up with your hands!"

"Gosh all hemlocks!" was all the youth could gasp, as the bundle slipped from his hand, and fell to the ground.

"What's the matter with you anyway? Are you deaf?" the boy said angrily. "If your hands ain't up in five seconds, off goes the top of your head—one—two—three——"

"Hold on! by ginger! gosh!" the youth spluttered, and his hands were elevated above his head with ludicrous quickness.

"You think you're mighty smart, don't you?" he said, sneeringly. "You're playing it fine, but all the same you about-face and march back to town!"

He had been edging around gradually during this conversation, and now had the youth between himself and the city.

"Why, I jest come from there. What shed I go back fer? I guess you're only foolin', now ain't you?" the youth said, with a sickly attempt at a smile.

"You'll never do no more guessing in your life, if you don't march quick. Come! sharp's the word! Start—one, two——"

"Oh, jumpin' Jews' harps![22] hold on! Don't go off half-cock that way. You take a feller's breath right out of him. But, say, what shed I go back to town agin fur?"

"You're askin' a heap of questions; but I've got the drop on you, and I don't mind answering. I'm going to take you in to Jack Hamilton—he wants to see you."

A troubled look came into the eyes of the youth.

"Jack Hamilton!" he said. "Who's he—an' what does he want with me?"

"Oh, I say! ain't you too amazin' stupid for anything!" the

boy said, in sarcastic admiration. "You thought nobody saw you write them words on that reward paper, didn't you, smarty?"

The youth gave a violent start. Then a dangerous red gleam came into his eyes. It is possible that he had up to this time thought this a comedy, but if such had been the case, these words undeceived him.

A cruel, crafty expression came slowly into his face.

"By gosh!" he cried, suddenly, "look back of you! there's a rattlesnake right at your heels! jump for your life!"

But the boy never budged an inch—not so much as an eye-lash quivered; the revolver in his hand never wavered a hair's breadth.

"Old trick! Diamond Dick taught me that long ago," he said, sententiously. "You want me to turn around, and then you'd grab me. Nixey! no go!"

A spasm seemed to pass over the face of the youth.

"Diamond Dick!" he said, in a voice almost a whisper in its intensity. "What do you know of Diamond Dick?"

"Why, I'm Diamond Dick's boy, and my name's Bertie."

"What? You!"

It was almost a scream, in which hate and savage joy were curiously blended, that the youth gave.

Then a startling change came over him. His form became erect and commanding, his eyes flashed like livid lightning, and in a voice that caused the boy an involuntary thrill of fear, he shouted out:

"Take him!"

The next instant Bertie felt a heavy hand upon his shoulder, and the revolver was wrenched from his grasp.

He looked up, stunned by the sudden turn of affairs.

Two beings, with queer, cat-like faces, and yellow bodies, and barred and spotted with black, stood by his side.

With a thrill of fear the boy realized the situation.

He was in the hands of the Tigers of Tombstone!

CHAPTER IX
Bertie Plays a Trump

The mysterious youth laughed as he saw the look of dismay upon the face of Bertie.

"Well, my little lion cub," he said, mockingly, "which one of us is the smarty now?"

The words recalled the boy to his wits, and instantly his coolness returned.

"Ah, I reckon you take in the pot," he said. "I played my hand for all it was worth, but a fellow can't buck against such a cold deck—nohow."

And then he concluded, coolly:

"It's your deal."

The youth laughed again—a laugh that sounded strangely sweet and silvery to the ears of the boy.

"A chip of the old block," he muttered.[23] "And so you're Diamond Dick's son?" he continued, eyeing Bertie with a strange look. "Curious that I have never seen you until to-day."

"Maybe you was looking the other way," Bertie suggested.

But the strange youth had fallen into a reverie, and seemed not to hear the words.

"I say!" the boy cried, after a moment, "what're you going to do with me?"

"Keep you where the crows won't pick you up," the strange youth answered sternly. "You shall enjoy the hospitality of the Tigers of Tombstone for a while."

"Well, I can't say that I'm hankering after free board now," Bertie muttered. "We generally pay as we go along—Diamond Dick and me."

But the mysterious youth caught the low words.

"Never fear!" he said, with a queer laugh; "both you and Diamond Dick shall pay—ay! and right royally, too."

Bertie stared at these words.

During the conversation he had been eyeing the strange being narrowly, a dim suspicion gradually gaining ground in his mind.

That voice, so musical when he laughed; the slight form, graceful in its every movement, and a soft curve here and there, which the loose clothes, now that the youth stood erect, could not entirely conceal, was making the boy open his eyes.

"I say!" he cried, suddenly, "who are you, anyway?"

The youth smiled.

"I am just what I signed myself to that reward notice—'The Thomas K. Cat who bosses the Tigers of Tombstone.'"

"That ain't what I mean," Bertie persisted. "What I want to know is—who would you be if you was washed?"

"Little children should not ask questions," the youth answered gravely.

"My! how old we are!" the boy sneered.

"Never mind; I'm old enough to be——"

"My mother, eh?" the boy finished, as the youth hesitated. "That's what you was going to say, wasn't it?"

"You're a sharp one."

"Oh, I know'd you was a woman soon's you laughed," Bertie retorted, coolly.

But the strange being took no further heed of his words.

Turning to one of the queerly masked men, she said:

"Are the horses here, Juan?"

"Si, capitano," the man answered, in Spanish.

"Then take and bind that boy upon one. I will be back as soon as I have got rid of this disguise."

Saying which, he parted the bushes, and disappeared in the underbrush.

Then one of the masked men led out a number of horses, and upon the back of one Bertie was soon securely lashed.

"Well, I am in a hole this time, sure," the boy murmured to himself. "Oh, Schwan, won't you catch it when Diamond Dick gets back and finds me gone," and he laughed lowly as he pictured the scene in his mind.

Then he continued, more gravely:

"If only I had half a chance I'd give those fellers the shake. They never searched me, 'cause I'm only a boy, I s'pose, an' I've got a trump yet in my pocket that they know nothin' about. But that's only one, an' then the other feller would knock the top of my head off."

The boy's soliloquy was cut short by a shrill, bird-like whistle.

"Hallo! the captain wants one of us," one of the men said. "You stay by the boy, Juan, and I'll go see what's up."

He dismounted as he finished speaking, and plunged into the woods.

Bertie's eyes began to glow, and his heart thumped with excitement.

They had not secured his arms; only his feet were fast; his hands were free.

The man left on guard was taking no unusual notice of him, no doubt believing that as he was securely lashed he could do no harm.

He was holding the bridle of the boy's horse, and looking off down the road toward the city, to guard against the approach of any danger.

Cautiously the boy's hand was thrust into his pocket, and when he withdrew it he held in his hand a derringer pistol.

Then, silently cocking the weapon, he leveled it at his captor.

At the same time he gave a sudden, quick jerk upon the bridle, and tore it from the man's hand.

"Up with your hands!" the boy shouted, wild with delight at the success of his act.

The masked man started violently at the words, and his hand fell on a revolver in his belt.

"Drop that!" the boy cried; "you attempt to draw, and I'll send an ounce ball through your brains. I mean business, every time!"

The Mexican, for such he evidently was, glared at the boy through the loopholes in his mask.

But the boy never flinched; his eyes were blazing now with resolution, and he meant every word he said.

The masked man saw death in the dark muzzle of that derringer if he hesitated a second longer to obey.

"Mercy! do not shoot!" he said, his voice quavering with fear, and slowly elevating his hands. "I will do what you wish—do not kill me!"

"All right—you mind what I tell you, or off goes the top of your head!—now start!"

With his left hand Bertie struck the Mexican's horse a sharp blow, and the animal, finding the rein loose, bounded forward.

To the horror of the masked man, they were headed toward the town.

"Señor—see! where are you going?" he said, turning half-way round in his saddle, and pointing with one hand toward the city.

At the same time he cunningly attempted to draw a weapon with the other.

But Bertie was watching him like a rattlesnake, and the sudden gleam in his eyes warned the Mexican to desist.

"You try it!" the boy said, in an icy voice, and the masked man groaned and raised his hands again above his head.

And I leave it to your imagination, reader, to picture the scene that followed.

By the time he reached the plaza a regular procession had formed in Bertie's rear, and exclamations and cheers for the brave lad were heard on every side.

But straight up to the express office Bertie marched his prisoner.

He noticed that there seemed to be something going on about here, for armed men were hurrying up every instant.

In fact, the writing on the notice had been observed, and the wildest excitement followed.

From Heinrich Schwauenflegle a description of the gawky-looking youth had been obtained, and Jack Hamilton was hastily gathering together an armed force to follow in pursuit of him when the crowd headed by Bertie's prisoner halted in front of the express office.

"Mr. Hamilton, I reckon I'll relieve the company of a hundred dollars," the boy said, coolly, as he caught sight of the express agent, who was staring in open-mouthed amazement at the scene. "I went gunning after a thousand, but a hundred is all I brought down."

"And, by the bones of Bruce! I'll see that you get it!" Jack Hamilton fairly shouted. "Boy, you're a trump! But how did you get on to this fellow?"

He pointed at the prisoner.

The Mexican had been dragged from his horse, disarmed, and the tiger-mask torn from his face, revealing a villainous-looking, half-breed Greaser of about forty years of age.

In clear, concise words, Bertie narrated all that had happened to him that morning, and when he was finished men crowded about him, and shook his hand, and thumped him on the back, and called him a "trump," and "brick," and "whale,"[24] and various other endearing terms expressive of admiration at his bravery.

And then the noise gradually grew less, and men formed in little groups and began to mutter, and whisper with significant looks, and cast dark, scowling glances upon the prisoner.

The death of old "Rocking-horse Sandy" was not yet avenged.

But meanwhile Jack Hamilton was questioning the Mexican.

"You're in a bad scrape, my man," he said, "but I am authorized to let up on any of the gang who will give away the band."

"Will you let me go free if I will tell you where the band has its hiding place?" the Mexican asked, eagerly.

"I will," Jack Hamilton answered, a look of contempt upon his face.

The Mexican's readiness to betray his comrades disgusted him.

"Then question me, señor; I will answer truly," the Mexican said.

"Who was it among you that killed the stage-driver the other day?"

"It was the capitano, señor—she is a deadly shot and never misses her aim."

"She?" the express agent cried; "do you mean to tell me that your leader is a woman?"

"Yes, señor."

This fact Bertie had not related. A lingering sense of shame at having been outwitted by a being of the "female persuasion" had made the boy shy when speaking of it.

Hence the express agent's surprise.

"And who is this woman?" he inquired.

"I do not know, señor, but she pays us liberally for our services."

And then he added, as he recollected the fact:

"I once heard the man who commands in her absence call her 'Kate.'"

"You say she pays you for your services—what do they consist of?"

"Well, señor, as I understand it, she is trailing after a man who has done her some wrong, and she hires us to help carry out her plans. She had information that this man would arrive by the stage the other night, when the driver was killed, and that's why we attacked it."

"And do you know who the man is that she's after?"

"Yes; he is called Diamond Dick."

"Well, and where does this gang hang out?"

"Over in a place among the spurs of the Dragoon Mountains."

"All right; you can lead us there; and we'll take the trail at once."

But this evidently did not strike the Mexican favorably.

"Señor," he said, "will it be necessary for me to go with you?—I can describe the place, so that you cannot miss it."

"Well, you'll certainly be killed if you remain here—listen! the boys are aching to avenge the death of old Sandy Rocks."

In fact, a sullen murmur was becoming each moment louder.

" 'F I had my say," a red-shirted miner said, "Sandy's score'd soon be wiped out."

And then a snarl was heard, such as dogs give when they fly at each other's throats, and men utter when they fly at a neck— with a rope.

And then the express agent stepped forward.

"I'm going gunning after those Tiger fellows," he cried, "an' this Greaser will show us the place where they make their headquarters. I start in half an hour, and all you who wish can come along."

His words were greeted with a roar of approval, and the crowd scattered, each man who owned a horse, good, bad or indifferent, having determined to make one of the party.

CHAPTER X
Captured by the Tigers

How long he laid in that swoon that was so like death, Diamond Dick never knew. The first sensation he was aware of was the taste of some vile whisky in his mouth.

Then he became conscious that some one was weeping over him, for hot, scalding tears were dropping down upon his face.

And then to his ears came the sounds of heart-breaking sobs, and low moans of pain.

"Oh, my God, have pity on me, and do not let him die!" a voice cried, that even in its pain was sweet to his ears.

He opened his eyes and saw the face of Alice Marr bending over him.

His head was pillowed upon her lap, and she was bathing his face with some of that fiery fluid, whose burning taste was hot in his mouth.

She had her tear-dimmed eyes raised upward at that moment, and did not immediately notice that he had recovered his senses.

"So handsome, so brave," the girl murmured, "and must he die here—here on this lonely plain, and I powerless to help him?"

Diamond Dick placed a hand upon one of hers.

"Be quiet," he said, gently. "I am neither dead nor dying."

Alice uttered a cry of joy as she heard his voice.

"Oh, thank God! thank God!" she said, hysterically.

But the next instant a burning flush suffused her face, and she gently lowered his head, and arose.

Diamond Dick made an effort and sat up, but his left arm gave him such a twinge of pain that he almost fainted away.

"Here, drink this," Alice cried, putting a flask to his lips; "it is whisky. I found it beside the body of Tornado Tom."

"Ha! Tornado Tom!" and the mere mention of that hated name seemed to put life into Diamond Dick; "where is the villain? I remember—"

"Hush! he is dead," Alice interrupted, gently.

"Dead! and did I kill him, too?"

"No;" and the girl shuddered. "He met a more horrible fate than dying by your hand."

As Alice finished, she silently pointed to the bloodhound, whose jaws and neck and chest were smeared with the blood of his victim.

"I understand," Diamond Dick said. "El Rey killed him."

And he, too, shuddered at the horrible fate the outlaw had met.

"How do you feel now?" Alice inquired, anxiously.

"Not very well. It's this arm that's giving me the—such pain. I think it must be broken."

"Oh, I hope not. Let me look at it."

She helped him strip off his jacket, and then bared the arm.

It was much swollen, and the bullet had gone clear through just below the elbow.

But after a moment's examination Diamond Dick felt convinced that neither of the bones were injured.

"I think if you would bathe it with some of that whisky, and then tie it up, it will do very well until we get back to town," he said.

Alice willingly did what he suggested, and when she was through, Diamond Dick gave her a smile of thanks.

"That will do first rate; and now I'll try to get on my feet."

But he was stiff and sore, and every bone and muscle in his body revolted at the exertion.

It was only after two or three trials that he succeeded in gaining his feet.

"It's curious, isn't it?" he said, as he stood, steadied by the arm of the girl. "Here I come out to help you in your distress, and after all is done, it is you who are assisting me."

"Yes, but remember, if it had not been for you, I should not be here by your side even to lend you the support of my poor, weak arm," Alice said, with emotion.

And then she added:

"How brave and noble you are to undertake such a long and dangerous pursuit alone, and all for my poor sake!"

"Hush! You are worthy of all the risks I ran, and I would

have followed, though peril a hundred-fold greater stood in my path. I could not bear to think of you in that villain's power, for your fair, pure face has become very dear to me, Alice."

A beautiful color came into the face of the girl, and a great joy descended upon her heart.

It was as she believed—as she hoped; he loved her.

And Diamond Dick, watching her face, read her secret and asked of himself if it were possible that happiness might yet be in store for him once more.

But he turned away and his gaze fell upon the noble steed who had stood by him so well in his need.

The horse was quietly cropping the scanty grass that grew here and there and gave a whinny of recognition as Diamond Dick came up.

And to his joy he found that the brave animal had recovered in a great measure from his terrible race of the night before.

And Tornado Tom's horse was there, too, and seemed to be on friendly terms with the other animal, for the two were grazing side by side.

The horse that Alice had ridden was dead. He had thrown the girl when he fell, and Alice had fainted, but it was more from fatigue than from any injury sustained in the fall, although she had been severely shaken up.

But meanwhile Diamond Dick had transferred the side-saddle to the horse that Tornado Tom had ridden—that is to say, Alice did under his direction.

Then, mounting the animals, they proceeded to retrace the long, weary way back to the city.

They could hardly go at a pace faster than a walk, for the horses were stiff yet from the work of the night before, and the jolting caused Diamond Dick's arm to ache with a pain that often made him clinch his teeth to keep down the agony.

In the pass they suddenly came upon the bodies of the two men Diamond Dick had shot the night before.

But on the plain beyond the pass Diamond Dick made a detour by the spot where he had made such terrible havoc with his Winchester.

It is a weary ride, and it is long past noon when the Bronco stream is made.

But Diamond Dick has told his love story, and the girl had listened with silent joy, and the answer she gave has made him happy.

"It is not far now to the city," Diamond Dick said, as they dismounted and allowed the horses to cool their noses in the running water, "but, darling, you must be tired from this long ride."

"Yes; but I am very happy, too," the girl answered, with a shy uplifting of the face, as she stands at his side.

And Diamond Dick stooped down and kissed the pure young lips.

And then a sudden, mocking peal of laughter rings out behind them.

Diamond Dick turned like a flash, a revolver in his hand.

But he suddenly starts back as though an adder had coiled in his path, upon which he had almost stepped.

"Kate!" he cried. "You here?"

And then El Rey came rushing in with savage growls.

The bloodhound had been loitering behind, intent on some purpose of his own.

But now he came bounding in, and flew at the bushes with white teeth gleaming savagely.

The next instant a dozen forms sprang from the foliage, surrounded Diamond Dick and tore the revolver from his hand.

Alice uttered a wild scream of terror.

She had seen those beings before—those yellow-clad, black-spotted things with queer, cat-like faces, and curious eyes.

They were in the hands of the Tigers of Tombstone.

But above all she marked with a jealous eye the beautiful woman whom Diamond Dick had called Kate.

What is she to Diamond Dick?

And she noticed with a sinking heart the look of dismay upon Diamond Dick's face as he stands rooted in his tracks gazing at her.

And then, with a blood-curdling yell, El Rey sprang upon one of the men who was holding Diamond Dick fast and bore him to the ground.

But half a dozen of his comrades sprang to his assistance, and stabbed, and kicked, and beat, with clubbed rifles, at the hound.

Diamond Dick spoke sharply to him, but the dog paid no heed.

He had tasted human blood the night before, and the taste was sweet to his lips. He fought now with all the savage instinct of his breed aroused, and tore and bit great mouthfuls of flesh from his assailants, and fought till the cruel bullets cut his heart in two; and then he stretched out his great black body, gave a whine or two, and died.

Brave El Rey, two of your foes will never wear those queer cat-faces again. They are dead, and you have avenged yourself nobly.

CHAPTER XI
A Devilish Shot—Conclusion

We must now go back a few hours in our story to pick up the thread of our narrative.

Not long had Bertie left the ravine with his prisoner, when the masked man returned.

And with him came a woman—a gloriously beautiful woman, with sparkling black eyes and cheeks whereon a delicious tint lay like the bloom of a peach.

She was slight of form, but as graceful as a fawn, and the short-skirted riding-habit she wore fitted her to perfection.

And this being—this woman of a beauty delightful to behold, was the "Thomas K. Cat who bossed the Tigers of Tombstone."

"Why, where's the boy and Juan?" the woman said, as she stepped out on the road. "Is it possible he has escaped me?"

She ran to the turn of the road, and looked toward the city.

Bertie was just entering the town, and at a glance she saw the state of affairs.

A horrible oath hissed from the beautiful mouth as she witnessed the sight, and her cheeks grew pale with anger.

"Why did I not kill that devil's brat when I had the chance— why did I let his fair, fearless face soften my heart into pity?"

and with a gesture of impotent rage, she stamped her foot upon the ground in fury.

"Well, Kate, this will be a serious thing for our plans," her companion said, gravely.

"What do you mean?"

"That Greaser will split."

"Then we must warn the men, and seek a new hiding-place."

"I reckon so, and I know just the place; but it's a good ways from here—down in the Mule Pass Mountains."

"No matter. We can lay low there for a while, until this blows over. Come, let us away."

They mounted their horses, and rode to the eastward, where the Dragoon Mountains rose blue in the sky.

Shortly before noon they arrived at the headquarters of the band, and hastily collecting the Tigers together, they rode away toward the Bronco.

About an hour afterward Jack Hamilton arrived at the rendezvous, and found the birds flown.

But the outlaws had left a plain trail, and the express agent and his men were hot upon the scent when the Tigers stopped to rest and water their horses in the Bronco stream.

But hardly had they been there five minutes when a man and a woman were espied coming toward the water, and the Tiger captain recognized with savage joy that the man was Diamond Dick.

The rest we know.

"May the fiends roast that infernal hound!" the Tiger captain cried, as she gazed upon the deadly work of the dog. "I thought he would never give up the ghost!"

She was holding a smoking revolver in her hand, and it was her bullet that had laid the hound low.

But then she turned to Diamond Dick, and said:

"And so, we meet again, Diamond Dick; and I must say you look considerably the worse for wear. What has been the trouble, Richard?"

"I am wounded in a half-dozen places, and my left arm is powerless, but give me a revolver and half a chance, and I'm

worth all the Tigers that ever walked on two feet," Diamond
Dick answered, defiantly.

The mocking voice of the woman had ruffled his temper.

"Nay, Richard, why should old friends quarrel? Have you
forgotten how sweet we were on one another once, how faithful a knight you were, how loving I was to you; and your
promise, Richard—your promise. We were to have been married; the feast was prepared, but you never came. Richard, why
was it so?"

It is impossible to describe the mocking devil in the woman's
voice, and Diamond Dick was trembling with rage.

But before he could say a word in reply, Alice came to his side.

"Who is that woman, Dick, and what is she to you?"

"Listen, and I will tell you. I met that woman about a year
ago, and was fascinated by her beauty and wealth of intellect. I
soon learned to love her, and found my love returned; we were
to have been married, but, thank God! I learned in time what
she was—as black within as she is fair without—a whitened
sepulchre[25]—a thing so vile that I will give it no name while
you are by—a woman, who, even while yet my kisses were
warm upon her lips, was plotting in the arms of her lover
against my honor, my wealth and my life. Pah! why should I
get angry? It is true she wheedled me out of a sum of money,
but I got off cheap."

Pale as a spirit of the other world the woman listened, her
teeth grating, her eyes blazing with livid light.

"And who is that girl?" she hissed, "that you need give her
an explanation such as this?"

"I hope soon to call her my wife," Diamond Dick answered,
proudly.

"Never!" the woman shrieked, "by the living God, never!"

But Diamond Dick only smiled, and opened his arms, and
Alice nestled down upon his breast with a low cry.

The sight seemed to drive the woman into a frenzy of fury.

With a motion like thought she raised the revolver she still
held in her hand and fired.

Alice uttered a piteous moan of pain, and clutched at Diamond Dick with hands that fluttered and groped, and could

hold nothing, her eyes grew glassy with the agony of pain, and, like the bleat of a poor, stricken lamb, her voice came in gasping breath:

"Dick—darling—kiss me!"

And then a thick stream of blood trickled down from the corners of her mouth, a quick shudder, a final, gasping moan, and the California Nightingale's voice was hushed forever.

Alice Marr was dead.

And oh! the agony that was in Diamond Dick's eyes as he gazed down upon the fair face pillowed on his breast, his arm about her, holding her so tight, so close, as if to keep her from the icy clutch of death.

But she was dead, and he saw it, and tenderly, reverently, he laid her down.

"Great Heaven," he murmured, in an agony of spirit that was worse than dying, "is everything I love fated to die?"

And then his gaze fell upon the human fiend who had wrought this ruthless deed, and he came slowly forward.

"Woman!" he said, and his voice startled all who heard, "for murdering that poor, innocent lamb—that fair, pure flower, may you be accursed! May your life be from this moment one seething, bubbling hell of remorse and unrest, and in every voice, every sound, may you hear the cry of Cain!"[26]

"Stop! for Heaven's sake stop!" the woman cried, her voice quavering with terror at the terrible denunciation. "I was mad—I did not know what I was doing—I swear it!"

"You swear! Now listen to me. I, too, will swear."

Diamond Dick was swaying from side to side now like a drunken man, there was a terrible tightness across his chest, a hideous hammering in his head, and objects wavered and took curious shapes before his eyes. If this did not cease soon he would either go mad or die.

"I swear by the living God above, who hears this oath, and the blood of that sweet-voiced young girl, that I will enact upon you a terrible retribution. I will be a bloodhound upon your trail a thousand times more fierce and relentless than was the brute lying yonder there dead. For what you have done today, I will forget that you are a woman entitled to the respect of men, and think of you only as an adder that must be crushed. For what you have done, I will tear pity and mercy from my heart, and become to you a destroying angel more remorseless than the Danite dogs of the Mormon Church.[27] Hide where you will, flee where you may, I will find you and strike you down, even though it is the sacristy that I defile with your blood. And this I swear I will do as sure as my name is Diamond Dick."

His voice ended in a scream, and, like one stricken with quick, sudden death, he fell forward on his face, and lay there upon the ground without motion.

"My Heaven! this is awful!" the woman cried, her face ghastly with terror and dismay. "Is he dead?"

One of the masked men was bending over Diamond Dick, and it was to him she addressed the question.

"No," the man answered; "he's overworked himself, and has burst some small blood-vessel. He'll be all right in a day or two."

"Well, we must get away from here. Put him on a horse, and that other thing, too," and she pointed with a shudder to the body of the girl.

But while the men were busied about their orders, there suddenly came a ringing cheer and a volley that laid half of their number low, and out upon the bank stepped Jack Hamilton, closely followed by Bertie and half a score of miners.

"We're done for, Kate! Skin out for your life," said the masked man, who was evidently the second in command.

The woman glanced once at her foes, and leveled her pistol at Bertie, but she lowered the pistol again without firing.

"No, I have done mischief enough today," as she lashed her horse into furious flight.

The rest of the Tigers—that is, all who were not killed or disabled—were already fleeing.

And then the miners, still led by the express agent and Bertie, came splashing through the water of the ford and followed after in hot pursuit.

But Bertie suddenly drew up his horse and sprang to the ground.

He had seen the form of his father, where he lay upon the ground, and the body of Alice a little farther away.

"Great Heaven!" the boy cried in dismay, "what's been goin' on here?"

And with trembling hands he lifted the head of Diamond Dick, and then dropped it again and ran to the stream, bringing back water in his hat to bathe his father's face, and chafe his hands.

And under this vigorous treatment Diamond Dick opened his eyes and gazed up into the boy's face, and smiled a slow, sweet smile as he saw the troubled look upon Bertie's face.

"All right, Bertie," he said, cheerfully, "I'll be better in a minute or two."

Then the pursuers came back jubilant. Only two of the Tigers had escaped them, but one was a woman, whose magnificent horse had distanced their animals so easily that it was folly to hope they could overtake her.

But it was a sad cortege that wended its way back to Tombstone, when all was told.

Tenderly they bore the sweet singer of the California land between them, and brought it into the city, and when they laid her away the next day in her last earthly resting-place, men wept and cursed the human fiend who could find it in her heart to crush this beautiful flower, whose life had been so pure, and whose voice had opened up to their eyes a glimpse of the heavenly hereafter.

But I must finish.

It was many days before Diamond Dick was himself again.

The injuries received in that wild race and running fight were slow of healing, and it was nearly two months before he was thoroughly well again.

And one afternoon he came in from a stroll with a stern, set look upon his face, and began to look over his weapons and overhauled his horses' harness, and made preparations of other import that Bertie, who was watching him, knew well.

And when the boy—who, by the way, had received the one hundred dollars reward and the thanks of the express company, for his bravery, asked him where he was going, he answered briefly, "On her trail."

And that night they rode forth, and Tombstone saw them no more.

Reader, my tale is told.

It has been sad in some respects, but I gave it to you as I heard it from the lips of an old gentleman, whom I met one day while rambling around in the Arizona land.

My curiosity had been attracted by a grave in the cemetery, that was very pretty with flowers and blooms, and bending, I deciphered on the white headstone, "Alice Marr, The California Nightingale."

And underneath the name:

"She sang too sweet for the ears of men, and the Lord had need of her in His choir."

As I straightened up again, the old gentleman aforesaid stood by my side, and told me the girl's sad story.

[THE END.]

"Noname's" Latest and Best Stories are Published in This Library.

FRANK READE LIBRARY

Entered as Second Class Matter at the New York, N. Y., Post Office, October 5, 1892.

No. 94. {COMPLETE.} FRANK TOUSEY, PUBLISHER, 34 & 36 North Moore Street, New York. {PRICE 5 CENTS.} Vol. IV.
New York, November 16, 1894. ISSUED WEEKLY.

Entered according to the Act of Congress, in the year 1894, by FRANK TOUSEY, in the office of the Librarian of Congress, at Washington, D. C.

OVER THE ANDES WITH FRANK READE, JR., IN HIS NEW AIR-SHIP; OR, WILD ADVENTURES IN PERU.

By "NONAME."

Frank Reade is the name of a dynasty of inventors in the dime novels. The original Frank Reade stories were written by Harry Enton (1854–1927), whose birth name was Harold Cohen, and who worked his way through college and earned a medical degree by writing dime novels. His Frank Reade stories appeared as serials in Frank Tousey's story paper The Boys of New York, *after which the installments were collected and reprinted in* The Five Cent Wide Awake Library *and* Frank Reade Library. *When the publisher insisted that the stories appear either anonymously or under a house name, Enton broke with Tousey. At that, the publisher hired a young man who had been writing for them for several years, Luis P. Senarens (1863–1939), to continue the series under the house name "Noname." Senarens wrote the new stories about Frank Reade, Jr., the son of the original inventor, and expanded the background of the series to include the settings of Readestown and the workshops in which father and son labored on their inventions. He also added a number of secondary characters as well as a story in which young Frank Reade, Jr., meets a young lady, saves her from danger and marries her, thus producing a son and heir, Frank Reade III, who carries on the family business. Like the original stories, the career of Frank Reade, Jr., was chronicled in serials for* The Boys of New York *and then recycled in* The Five Cent Wide Awake Library *and*

Frank Reade Library. *The stories were popular enough for the publisher to include new stories in the* Frank Reade Library *that had no prior appearances. Some historians have suggested these may not have been the work of Senarens, who was kept busy writing detective stories for Frank Tousey. Senarens eventually became editor in chief and managing editor for the firm, and wrote motion picture scenarios.*

The Frank Reade, Jr., stories have been criticized for their extensive use of racial and ethnic stereotypes (the comic relief characters of Pomp and Barney are a case in point) as well as their excessive violence and sadism. They were perhaps no more guilty of these faults than the majority of popular fiction of the day and thus reflect the myths and attitudes of their time. On the positive side, the stories represent a kind of prototype of science fiction and are filled with descriptions of speculative aircraft and underwater vessels. As such they had an influence on later series for boys, especially the Tom Swift books produced by the Stratemeyer Syndicate. "Over the Andes with Frank Reade, Jr.," was written especially for Frank Reade Library *(no. 94, November 16, 1894) and later appeared with a color cover illustration in* Frank Reade Weekly Magazine, *a short-lived series that reprinted some of the older stories. There was also a British edition.*

The New Air-Ship

What boy has not indulged in dreams of some day being able to master the art of flying in the air? What youth has not felt the fascination of a balloon ascension?

From early years we look upon the blue sky above as a mystic, wonderful and unexplored region. We feel our utter inability to cope with the question of overcoming that specific law of gravitation which prevents our flying in mid-air which is so simple a matter for the birds, and yet there is not one of us but has ever had faith that the problem would some day be solved.

How it has been solved, and the outcome of that wonderful feat we shall endeavor to depict in the incidents of this story.

It had become a famous and well known fact that a certain talented young American had mastered the problem.

Frank Reade, Jr., a native of Readestown, and by nature, tastes and adoption an inventor, had given to the world the Steam Man, the Electric Horses, the Submarine Boat and the Electric Air-Ship. These triumphs placed his name high upon the roll of fame.

But ambition was one of his greatest attributes.

Not content yet, the famous young inventor who had acquired immense wealth with which to ensure success had embarked upon a new project the like of which the world had never before heard of.

"This time," he declared, "I intend to build an air-ship which will be able to carry a dozen or more persons around the world if need be. It shall excel all previous efforts!"

As the report went out to this effect, the whole country became agog with interest.

From near and far letters were showered upon the young inventor, couched in the most varied of terms and containing the most unreasonable of importunities.

Scientists wished the privilege of journeying a few thousand miles toward the moon. Gold-seekers depicted splendid chances for gaining gold from mountain mines inaccessible in any other way.

Thousands of these letters, some couched in threatening terms in case of a refusal, were received.

One implied a threat to destroy the air-ship and the machine works at Readestown, if a committee from the Dynamite Union were not permitted to sail over the big cities and destroy the houses of the millionaires of the country with electric bombs.

Of course Frank consigned all these to the waste basket.

But yet they bothered him not a little, and for fear some insane crank might work harm, a heavy guard was kept over the Readestown works.

The great air-ship was finished.

Frank had christened it the "Era," as it really marked an era in the problem of sky navigation.

It rested upon the stocks in the great yard of the machine works. A description of the aerial wonder might not be out of place, before setting forth further the exciting incidents of our story.

First, Frank Reade, Jr., realized that it was necessary to consider the question of supreme lightness.

He therefore abandoned the idea of suspensory helices or rotascopes,[1] and declared:

"I believe a lighter and swifter ship can be built upon the storage of gas principle. By constructing a reservoir sufficiently strong to resist expansion, I believe that the elevating power can be maintained with lateral wings."

Accordingly, first he constructed the gas reservoir.

This was made a full fifty feet long and cylindrical in shape. Of the best oiled silk six cases each within the other. Frank skillfully arranged a wire frame or belt, which should keep the gas bag always erect.

Then netting was skillfully wove over this; the bottom of the netting and the bag as well was fastened to a long platform of thinly rolled but stiff steel.

Below this was another platform with light standards and partitions which made the cabins and engine room of the air-ship.

This also in weight acted as ballast.

Upon either side of the platform a guard rail extended the whole length.

Four huge wings upon steel frames and made of powerful textured silk were projected from the sides of the air ship to aid in its buoyancy.

These wings were driven by an upright cylinder and a version of walking beam, giving regular action and symmetry of movement.

Forward was a pilot house with windows of heaviest plate glass; also a powerful search-light.

At the bow was the rudder, a huge expanse of silk upon a frame, the turning of which to the right or left deflected the course of the air-ship.

At the stern was the propeller. This, in brief, constitutes a meagre description of the exterior of the air-ship.

It was a marvel of beautiful proportions and effect.

The interior of the cabin was rich and luxurious.

All the necessary appointments were there for a craft of the kind.

There were scientific instruments and books, weapons and ammunition, richly draped furniture and cabinets, soft couches and everything in a palatial sense.

In one compartment was the galley or cook room, where Pomp excelled.

Pomp was a curious little negro, with a vein of darky wit as bright as the scintillations of a star.

He had long been in the employ of Frank Reade, Jr., and was faithful and true to his duties.

There was also Barney O'Shea, a genuine type of Irishman, with a comical mug and a shock of red hair which at once established his identity. Barney was a skilled electrician and a good engineer.

These two employees Frank thought much of and they were his companions in all his travels.

And jolly fellows they were too, though a bit given to playing jokes upon each other, which we shall discover in the course of our story.

The famous air-ship was just finished when Barney came into Frank's private draughting room, and said:

"Shure, sor, an' the Era is all finished, I understand!"

"Yes, Barney," replied Frank. "What do you think of her?"

"Begorra,[2] it's a foine bit av machinery she is."

"I think so!"

"Shure an' yes will be afther taking a thrip in her afore long, sor!"

"Yes," replied Frank. "At a very early day, I hope."

"An' may I ask have yez decided phwere to go, sor?"

"Well, not exactly. There are many parts of the world accessible. Perhaps we will go around the world!"

"Shure, sor, thin cud I make a bit av a sugghestion to yez!"

"Why certainly!" declared Frank. "What may it be, Barney?"

"I'ave a cousin, he's a Frenchman, be the way—yez see it wuz this way! Me mother's sister was afther marrying a frog ater, and shure they had wan boy, an' fer a compromise they called him Pathrick De Frontenac. Arrah, he's a gossoon[3] av a boy, an' there's ivery bit mother in him."

Frank could not help smiling.

"Well, that is truly a wonderful combination!" he declared. "I never before heard of that kind of a marriage!"

Barney scratched his head.

"I niver was in love wid the French meself," he said, "but I'd niver own a sister as wud marry an Eyetalian."

And Barney made a grimace, and executed a quickstep in a manner which boded no good for the sons of sunny Italy.

"All right!" said Frank. "Now let's get down to facts."

"All roight, sor!" agreed Barney. "Me Cousin Pathrick, sor, has been for tin years an explorer in South Ameriky. He has thramped all over the Andes Mountains, sor, an' he is afther askin' me to ask ye if he wudn't think av thryin' a trip over the Andes yesilf, sor!"

"Over the Andes!" exclaimed Frank. "Well, that is not a bad idea. But why is he so interested?"

"Shure, sor, he kin tell yez that betther than I kin. He's this moment outside, sor, an' if yez will do him the favor he'll talk wid yez about it."

"Well," said Frank reflectively. "I'll see him, Barney. Show him in!"

"All roight, sor!"

The Celt disappeared. A moment later a tall, wiry built man, with an olive complexion and shrewd Irish features entered.

He had the unmistakable stamp of a traveler, and was evidently a man of refinement and education.

"Mr. Reade, I am honored to meet you!" he said, politely. "I presume Barney has told you all about me!"

Frank was at once favorably impressed with his visitor.

"Yes," he replied. "You have traveled in the Andes?"

"I have!"

"Barney tells me that you found a great deal of interest there."

Patrick De Frontenac replied earnestly:

"I believe that you, Mr. Reade, with your air-ship, can give to the world one of the greatest benefits to science that the world has ever known!"

Frank was interested.

"Ah!" he exclaimed. "And all this in the Andes?"

"Yes!"

"Pray what may it be?"

Patrick De Frontenac drew from his pocket a number of maps.

These were skillfully drawn, and were evidently of his own construction. He placed his finger upon a certain part of the Andes range.

"There," he said, "is a part of the world which has never been explored. There are hundreds of square miles of wonderful region inhabited by a strange people, who are beyond the reach of the ordinary explorer."

CHAPTER II
The Explorer's Story

De Frontenac's declaration was an earnest one and impressed Frank Reade, Jr., deeply.

Moreover, the young inventor was at once interested.

"An unexplored region!" he declared. "Why, can it not be reached by the ordinary methods?"

"For the reason that the mountain peaks intervene and the cliffs and precipices so completely shut it in, that the place is inaccessible."

"Indeed!"

"It is true."

"And this region is inhabited?"

"By a strange people, perhaps descendants of the Incas. They will not venture out of their fastnesses, and their life and country is one of the hidden mysteries of the world. You, and you alone, can solve it."

"I beg your pardon," said Frank, "but if nobody has ever visited this strange region, how is it known for a fact that this state of affairs exists there?"

"Easy enough," replied De Frontenac. "One of the strange race was captured one day, having found his way down into the valley. He was never able to get back, and affiliating with the native Indians, became one of them. These wonderful stories were told by him."

"Do you consider this authentic?"

"It is the common belief of the country. I see no reason for disbelieving it until the unknown region is explored."

Frank was more interested than he cared to show.

He studied De Frontenac earnestly, and finally made up his mind that the French-Irish adventurer was honest in his statement.

"You are right, De Frontenac, in one thing," he declared. "The solution of the problem can be accomplished by the air-ship."

"Just so!" cried Frontenac, eagerly, "and it will be a great aid to science, and deeply satisfy me as well. I can assure you that I am sincere, and my character is good."

"I believe you," said Frank, now thoroughly convinced. "I will say, De Frontenac, that I am much interested in your story. As my cruise in the air is mainly in quest of adventure, this seems to afford a good incentive."

"Joy!" cried the explorer, wildly, "then you will go, Mr. Reade?"

"I will consider the matter," said Frank; "and let you know tomorrow. Your address——"

"I am stopping at the Palace Hotel, this city."

"Then I will send you a message in the morning!" declared Frank; "you may rest easy till then."

"On the contrary I shall not rest easy!" laughed De Frontenac; "I shall not close my eyes in sleep until I hear your answer. Know that it is the aim of my life to explore that region in the Andes!"

"Indeed!" exclaimed Frank, more than ever interested. "Well, you may expect an answer from me in the morning!"

De Frontenac went away like one in an ecstasy.

Soon after Barney came rushing in. Frank was studying some South American maps.

"Begorra, Misther Frank!" cried the Celt, excitedly. "Will yez be afther sayin' yez will go? Shure ye'll niver be sorry I'm sure."

"I think we shall, Barney!" said Frank.

"Whurroo!"

"Wait!"

"Well, sor?"

"Be sure you have everything shipshape and in readiness aboard the Era. I may decide to take a sudden start."

"I'll do that, sor!"

Barney rushed out into the yard. He was going so rapidly that he did not heed a dark form coming out of a passage between the buildings.

It was Pomp, and in his hands he carried a brush and a pail of whitewash.[4]

The darky was going to whiten the back yard fence.

He had a literal mania for whitening things. This might have arisen from the fact that whitewashing had once been his trade.

He would even have whitewashed the new air-ship if Frank would have allowed him.

"It's mighty quare, naygur, phy it is yez air so fond av a white color when yez air so black yesilf!" said Barney, one day in a facetious manner.

"Jes' bekase I likes de contrast, chile," retorted Pomp with a grin.

Now Barney was crossing the yard so rapidly that he did not see either Pomp or the whitewash pail or the brush.

As a result the first thing he heard was a sharp yell.

"Hi dar, I'ish, don' yo' steer into me! Yo' git de wust ob it! Luk out dar!"

But Barney went biff, bang into the darky.

Pomp tumbled, tried to regain himself, but fell.

And the whitewash pail tilted up, was emptied like a flash, and full into his face.

Barney stood on his head and saw a million bright stars. But he was the first to arise.

The sight he beheld was amusing in the extreme.

There lay the darky spluttering and gasping and white as chalk, for the white liquid had literally changed his sable hue.

"Golly fo' glory! What am dat?" he spluttered, struggling to regain his feet. "Wha' yo' done, yo' fool I'ishman?"

Barney was for a moment aghast, but as he saw the comical aspect of the darky, he could not help a shriek of laughter.

"Ha, ha, ha!" he roared. "On me worrud yez are a beauty, naygur. Shure, yez oughtn't to kick, fer it's a white man I've med av yez!"

"I jes' make a pancake ob yo'!" spluttered the darky, springing to his feet. "Yo' jes' do dat on puppose!"

"Bejabers,[5] don't yez tell me that, naygur!"

"Yo' did, an' I gib yo' a good return fo' it!" yelled Pomp.

Down went the darky's head like a battering ram.

Forward he darted, and before Barney could get out of the way, the darky's head took him full in the abdomen.

It was like being struck by a cannon ball.

The Celt went down as if shot.

He was for an instant winded, but his Irish blood was up, and he quickly gained his feet.

"Whurroo, yez black blaygard!" he yelled, "I'll have the loife av yez fer this! Whurroo!"

But Pomp having had revenge darted back into the passage. He got the start and eluded Barney, who presently gave up the pursuit.

Rubbing his stomach ruefully he returned to the yard, saying:

"On me sowl I have it in fer that naygur now. An' it's a fool I am av I don't have it out wid him."

Then away he went to get the Era in shape for the projected cruise.

Meanwhile, Frank Reade, Jr., had been busily studying the maps.

He was satisfied finally that such a region as De Frontenac described might really exist.

"At least we will make the trip," he finally decided.

He arose to his feet, when there came a tap on the door.

Frank gave a start.

Nobody was ever admitted to the yard without first stating their errand, or being announced by Barney or Pomp.

Yet, here was some visitor who had entered unheralded.

Then Frank remembered that he himself had carelessly left the outer gate open.

Frank opened the door and stood face to face with a man whom he had never seen before.

He was tall and dark, with shrewd piercing eyes, and a peculiar nervous manner. He regarded Frank searchingly and said:

"Is this Mr. Reade?"

"It is!" replied Frank.

The fellow tendered Frank a card. The young inventor glanced at it and gave a little start.

"OSMAN DYKE, Detective,
New York City."

"You will see that I am a detective," said Dyke, politely, "therefore my business with you is important."

"Very good, sir!" agreed Frank. "What can I do for you?"

Frank had motioned his visitor to a chair.

"I think you are the only man in the world who can solve my case for me," said the detective.

"Indeed!"

"That is why I have come to you. But first and before I attempt to enlist your sympathies, let me tell you my story."

"I shall be glad to hear it," said Frank. "Pray go on!"

"The story is a strange one, you will admit," said the detective—"it is a powerful illustration of the power of man's greed.

"Two brothers embarked from New York City for Rio two years ago. Their names were John and Allan Burton.

"They were fortune seekers. Allan was a bluff, large-hearted fellow and John a shrewd, selfish and egotistical chap.

"After reaching Rio they for a time were in business together in fruits, then they quarreled, Allan gave up his share in the firm and went off with an exploring party into the interior.

"The reports say that he reached the Andes and there found a diamond mine. From this he took out some magnificent stones and returned to Rio. Their sale made him a wealthy man.

"He returned to New York. His brother John followed him. Allan married the girl of his youthful love and lived happily with his wife in a fine residence on Fifth Avenue.

"John was insanely jealous of his brother, and angry that he should have acquired such wealth while he yet remained poor.

"This led to recriminations, and he demanded that his brother should help him. Allan being of a generous nature forgave his brother's mistreatment of the past and helped him.

"Gradually the wily John got Allan involved in various speculations. Day by day fresh pledges were obtained to back up a tottering enterprise.

"The end was obvious. One day the crash came. Allan Burton failed and everything was swept away. He was reduced to penury.

"This was all upon his brother's account. The blow was heavy, yet he would have faced it bravely but for a most terrible discovery.

"This was that his brother suddenly blossomed out with money in plenty, which was sheer evidence of terrible duplicity and treachery."

CHAPTER III
Southward Bound

"The truth was, John had been at the bottom of all of Allan's troubles and had profited by them.

"He had, in short, neatly fleeced his brother and turned the tables upon him in the most cowardly manner.

"At first Allan was stunned with this realization. Then he said to his wife:

"'Ellen, we are ruined! John has beaten me!'

"'He is a villain and a thief!' cried the wife, forcibly. 'I demand that you ask satisfaction of him.'

"Allan at once went to John and accused him of treachery. The latter only laughed and sneered bitterly. This stung Allan to the quick.

"'I will have my rights,' he declared, 'in a court of law. I believe you are liable.'

"At this John defied him. But Allan was now in earnest. Able counsel was employed, and the strange suit, brother versus brother, was brought.

"It was bitterly fought out in the courts, but John's dishonesty was shown, and the court promptly ordered that restitution be made to Allan.

"John was under bonds and obliged to comply. But his wrath and hatred of his wronged brother was intense.

"The next time they met was upon the street. A brief altercation ensued. John's black temper got the best of him and he rushed upon Allan, dealing him a blow which crushed his skull.

"The murderer escaped. He managed to get aboard a South American steamer, and was tracked to Rio and thence for some ways into the interior.

"But from that day to this he has not been heard from. The young wife was frantic with grief and horror. Mrs. Burton mourns her murdered husband, but lives with only one end in view and that is revenge.

"She will track the murderer down and bring him to justice if it takes a lifetime. I have her authority to search the world over for him. This is the story."

A moment of silence reigned as the detective concluded this vivid and graphic recital.

Frank Reade, Jr., had been deeply impressed, and now declared:

"Really, sir, that was a very tragic affair. I certainly hope you will succeed, but——"

"Well?"

"In what manner can I hope to give you aid?"

The detective leaned forward.

"You alone can help me," he said, earnestly. "If it is true that you possess an air-ship which can travel the world over——"

"It is."

"Then it is in your power to help this sorrowing woman to gain justice for the loss of her husband."

Frank was deeply impressed.

"How can I track the villain down?"

"The fastnesses of the Andes are mighty, and a man could hide there for a lifetime and never be discovered by ordinary means."

"True."

"But with your air-ship——"

"I understand. You wish me to go there in quest of the murderer?"

"Yes, and bring him back to a just trial in the courts of this country. If you will do this you will be doing an act of justice and philanthropy. The suffering widow has but a fragment of her husband's fortune left, but she will give it to you if you will. I don't know what plans you have made, or whither you intended journeying in your air-ship, but if you will undertake this task you will win everlasting gratitude."

Frank Reade, Jr., was silent and thoughtful a moment.

It could be seen that the detective was extremely nervous and anxious.

Suddenly Frank arose.

"My friend," he said, "I would have a heart of stone if I did not accede to your request——"

"Oh, God bless you!" almost screamed the detective.

"Wait! Let me tell you that it was my intention to go to South America anyway."

"You don't mean it!"

"Yes, I do. I am going to make a sky exploration of the Andes. There are many parts of those mountains as yet unexplored and misunderstood. A scientist will go with me, and we shall explore from the sky all that great region. A thorough map of all will be made."

"Wonderful!"

"Yet it is feasible for me to make a side issue of your case. I will endeavor to find your man."

"A thousand thanks!" cried the detective. "You will be sure to do that! This will be joyful news to the wife!"

Then Osman Dyke paused.

Frank gazed at him keenly, and smiled as he read the impulse of his bosom.

"I understand you," he said.

"Do you?"

"Yes; you are anxious to go aboard the air-ship."

"Will it be too much to ask? I can instantly identify John Burton, you know."

"It is settled," said Frank. "We will have two passengers— you and Mr. De Frontenac. I hope you two will be friends."

"You cannot know my joy!" cried Dyke. "Now I will go at once and wire Mrs. Burton, who is anxiously waiting."

"That would be best."

At the door the detective, whose face was radiant, turned.

"When will the start be made?" he asked.

"At as early a day as possible!" replied Frank. "Give me your address, and I will wire you!"

"Detective Headquarters, New York City."

"Very well! Hold yourself in readiness."

Then Dyke was gone.

Frank took two or three turns up and down the room.

"Well!" he muttered, "we shall have objects enough to attain upon this trip. I hope we will succeed!"

What a thrilling future to look forward to! Surely the voyagers of the Era, the sky explorers, were to be envied.

Preparations were made as speedily as possible for the departure.

When the day came at last the great air-ship rested upon a platform in the yard of the machine works.

De Frontenac and Dyke were on hand.

Barney was in the engine-room, and Pomp at the wheel. Frank Reade, Jr., and the two travelers stood on the deck.

The people of Readestown had turned out en masse to see the wonderful flight of the Era.

Some skeptical ones in the crowd pooh-poohed the invention and predicted that it would never rise.

But at the appointed hour Frank gave final orders to his foreman, and then cutting the anchor rope, shouted.

"Press Lever No. 10, Barney!"

"All roight, sor!"

The next moment the air-ship freed of the detaining ropes rose into the air like a bird.

The huge wings began to act and beat the air strongly.

Up, up went the Era until the city of Readestown looked like a collection of toy houses.

Guns could be heard booming below, and even the faint shouts of the people.

The voyagers clung to the rail and gazed with interest upon the dizzy scene below.

Then the great propeller began to work and like a huge bird the Era sailed away.

Through the air she sped to the southward. The novelty of the experience was most charming to De Frontenac and Dyke.

"Upon my word!" cried the explorer, "nothing can exceed this!"

"Indeed, it is the greatest of all privileges!" declared the detective. "Wonderful beyond all description!"

"That is true!"

Frank had decided to make a straight line across the Gulf of Mexico to Venezuela.

Thence he intended to cross the United States of Colombia and proceed southward along the eastern side of the Andes, into Peru.

The explorer, De Frontenac, had described the direction to take from the head waters of the Amazon.

Across a part of the great United States the air-ship rapidly flew.

At noon the next day, the waters of the Gulf were sighted.

But they were not for long in view. A terrific gale blew from the southeast, and the storm clouds hung in an impenetrable pall below.

The air-ship had safely risen above this warring of the elements.

It was a remarkable spectacle, and being new to the detective and the explorer, they gazed upon it with much interest.

"Indeed it surpasses anything I have ever seen!" declared De Frontenac. "I have heard this spectacle described by balloonists, but never expected to see it."

"If I were only a poet, what inspiration I might get!" declared Dyke. "It is a grand sight!"

And indeed it was.

Below were the angry tossing clouds, and ever and anon the boom of thunder shivered the air.

Above, the sun was shining brightly in a blue sky.

But some hours later the storm passed away to the eastward, and the waters of the gulf once more rolled below.

Frank now shouted to Barney:

"Let the air-ship down a bit!"

Barney at once obeyed.

There was strong need of this, for the air at that tremendous height was so exceedingly rare, that breathing was most uncomfortable.

So the Era descended into a more comfortable stratum.

For hours the air-ship sailed on over the boundless waste.

Land had faded from sight, and vessels were visible only at random intervals.

Thus matters were when the first casualty of the voyage, and which came near nipping it in the bud, occurred.

De Frontenac, Barney, Frank and Dyke, the detective, were upon the lower stage talking when suddenly a startling thing occurred.

A whirring noise came from the engine room.

"What is that?" exclaimed Frank, in alarm.

The young inventor sprang for the pilot-house door. There was need of haste for awful peril threatened.

"My God!" screamed Dyke and De Frontenac in horrified chorus. "We are falling into the sea."

CHAPTER IV
A Close Call

This was true.

The air-ship was descending gradually but certainly toward the tossing waters below.

The great wings had ceased to act and the propeller had come to a stop.

What was the cause was a mystery.

The great wings outspread, however, acted with parachute effect and prevented a violent descent.

Yet to fall into the sea was not a pleasant thing to contemplate.

The powerful waves would no doubt batter the air-ship in pieces.

Destruction would be certain.

Pomp had come out of the galley excitedly. He shouted:

"Golly, Marse Frank, something hab jes' broke in de injine room! I done fink we am done fo' now!"

"Get out the portable boat, Pomp!" shouted Frank. "Lively, you and Barney! We don't want to drown!"

Foreseeing a possible contingency of this kind, Frank had stowed away aboard the air-ship a pontoon rubber boat, made in folding fashion, to occupy as little space as possible.

This Barney and Pomp now rushed to bring out.

"What can we do, Mr. Reade?" cried De Frontenac.

"Yes," chimed in Dyke.

"Keep cool!" returned the young inventor. "When the ship strikes the water will get into the boat."

Then into the engine room Frank quickly dashed.

A glance showed him at once what was the trouble.

The machinery was at a dead stop, but the dynamos were buzzing with awful fury.

He quickly shut off the battery and then quick as a flash set at work to repair the trouble.

Over the main cogs of the propeller shaft was a small iron shelf upon which some wrenches were placed ready for use.

The motion of the ship had jarred one of them off and it had fallen into the cogs.

Of course this obstructed and instantly checked them.

The propeller and the wings ceased to work, and the storage of gas in the reservoir not being sufficient to support the air-ship, it settled.

In a few moments it would be in the water.

Quick as he could Frank turned on the generator cocks, and fresh gas flowed into the reservoir as fast as it could generate.

Then he seized an iron bar and pried the wrench out of the cogs.

But they were a little twisted and yet refused to work. Frank saw that it would require an hour's work to repair them.

Horror seized him.

It seemed as if the air-ship must go into the water. The terrible waves would be apt to beat it to pieces before it could be made to rise again.

The gas, of course, generated slowly, and it would be some time before enough would be provided to make the air-ship go up.

Yet Frank pluckily went to work; he grasped his tools and began to unlock the cogs.

As he did so he felt spray come in through the window. He abandoned his work to rush to the window a moment and shout:

"Get aboard the boat all of you; we must lighten her all we can!"

But Barney already had the pontoon in the water and they all climbed into it.

There was no doubt but that this lightened the air-ship much.

Frank saw that the gas reservoir was swelling and the machine was stationary right on the surface of the water.

The waves rolled over the lower stage or platform, and at times it was entirely submerged.

But no serious damage was being done by this.

Frank realized with a thrill that if the sea did not rise higher the fresh gas in the reservoir would yet lift the air-ship up to a point of safety.

And, in fact, this was the very thing which happened.

The air-ship gradually worked its way upward until it was twenty feet above the surface.

Here it hung suspended until Frank had completed his work on the cogs. This was finished in time.

The four men in the rubber boat were being tossed about on the waves below.

They cheered heartily when Frank appeared on the platform, and shouted:

"All right. Come aboard!"

Then he lowered a long silk ladder until it touched the water. The boat was quickly under it.

The spray-wet quartette came hastily clambering aboard.

The boat was drawn up and folded. Then Frank touched the electric key, the big wings and propellers began to work and up shot the air-ship once more.

There was good reason for mutual congratulations.

"I thought our trip was ended," cried Osman Dyke. "We are indeed in luck!"

"All owing to Mr. Reade's rare presence of mind and action," declared De Frontenac.

"Well, I hope that such a thing will not occur again," said Frank. "Barney, I would not keep tools on that shelf."

"All right, sor," replied the Celt.

Once again to the southward sped the air-ship.

One day Frank came on deck, and said:

"We are upon the Tropic of Cancer now. Within six hours we should sight Cape Catache."

"Cape Catache!" exclaimed De Frontenac, "that is the extreme point of Yucatan."

"Yes!"

"Then we are fully half way to the South American coast!"

"Just about. I shall bear off more to the eastward after leaving the Cape. We will follow the Yucatan Channel into the Gulf of Honduras. From there straight across the Caribbean Sea to the coast of Cartagena, a town at the mouth of the Magdalena River!"

"Thence due south?"

"Yes, passing directly over Bogota, the capital of Colombia. Then we shall be well on our journey."

"I should say so!"

The voyagers kept anxious watch for the first appearance of land, which would be the point of Cape Catache.

Due east was Cape San Antonio, the western point of Cuba.

The body of water between these capes is called the Yucatan Channel.

As Frank had predicted, within six hours land was sighted.

From that height it opened up rapidly on the horizon. As far as the eye could reach to the westward it extended.

Nearer drew the air-ship. Its course was such that a narrow strip of the Cape was passed over.

The tropical vegetation was seen as well as the barren, desolate coast so far below. But there was no sign of habitation.

To the southward along the coast extended highlands thickly grown with tropical growth.

The voyagers studied the scene with their glasses with avidity, for it was an agreeable change from the monotony of the sea.

They were disappointed at not seeing human beings. But now, as they proceeded down the channel, the scene changed somewhat.

Sailing craft became quite common, and were of a type somewhat different from those seen in the Gulf.

"All the natives of this part of the world are mariners," declared Frank Reade, Jr. "They fish, dive for pearls and sponges, and make a living in various ways."

Numerous cays, or small islands, were passed.

Nearly all of these were the rendezvous of fishing, trading, or pirate vessels, for the Caribbean Sea is noted for its pirates.

Frank now bore off a trifle toward Jamaica, and then steered more to the southward.

Night and day the air-ship floated along on her course.

At night the gleam of the electric search-light lit up the sea and heavens for two miles ahead.

It must have been a strange spectacle to the native mariners to see that strange looking ship with its powerful light so high up there in the sky.

No doubt it excited the superstitious fears of more than one and sent him speeding away as if *le diable* was after him.

No incident worthy of note occurred, however, until one day the voyagers turned out of their bunks to behold a magnificent spectacle.

The air-ship was fast approaching a mighty coast, wonderfully green and beautiful in contour.

Wonderful mountain peaks towered up beyond the horizon, and immense cliffs of basalt were in the foreground at the base of which the sea spent its fury upon silver sands.

"Colombia at last!" was the cry.

Beautiful South America was spread before them. Barney and Pomp particularly were interested.

"Begorra, it's almost as purty as the ould sod!" declared Barney. "Shure the green av it luks much the same!"

"Golly! I done fink it knock Norf Kyarline all out!" averred Pomp.

Frank had struck the coast at a point east of Cartagena.

He had no desire to visit that city, or, indeed, to tarry in any of the South American towns.

There were good reasons for this, for the people were of a class hardly to be trusted, and they might do the air-ship some damage.

But at the point where they struck the coast there was a little bay and a small hamlet.

"Let us descend here, and see what the place looks like," said Dyke. "I am dying to stretch my legs on earth once more."

"Ditto!" cried De Frontenac. "With your permission, Frank. Will it not be safe?"

"Why, if you wish!" replied the young inventor. "We will make it safe. Lower the ship, Barney!"

CHAPTER V
News of Burton

The Celt was only too willing to obey.

Down settled the air-ship until it hung not a thousand feet over the little hamlet.

The scene below was an amusing one.

The denizens of the place were out in a body, and were rushing about in the most intense of excitement.

Some were loading rifles, others were arming themselves with clubs and staves, and a score more were pulling an old rusty cannon down the street.

"Look here!" shouted Dyke, in alarm, "I don't know as this is going to be hardly safe, is it?"

"By gracious, it looks to me as if they meant to give us a hot reception," said De Frontenac.

Frank was not a little alarmed.

He studied the scene a moment. Then he drew back with a start.

A rifle ball just clipped the rail, coming within an ace of his face. It was a close call.

"Hold on, Barney!" shouted Frank, "these people mean business. We must first talk with them!"

The air-ship hung suspended about five hundred feet above the town.

Bullets were whistling about the air-ship in showers. Frank stepped into the cabin and rigged up a flag of truce.

With this he stepped to the rail.

It was seen and understood. The firing ceased. The crowd below for a moment became quiet.

Frank saw a tall, powerful-built man mount a stone column and make a number of signals.

Frank answered them.

Then the parley began.

Frank addressed the fellow in English. But he replied in Spanish.

Fortunately this tongue was familiar to the young inventor and he at once answered:

"All right, my friend! Who are you?"

"I am Don Jose de Pasqual, the *alcalde*[6] of San Luis!" was the reply. "Who are you?"

"I am an American, and my name is Frank Reade, Jr."

"An American!" replied the *alcalde*, in alarm, "then you are a filibuster. You come to do us harm!"

"No!" retorted Frank. "I come for nothing of the kind. I am a friend."

But the *alcalde* remonstrated.

"No, no! Señor Americano keep away from San Luis with your floating ship. You are leagued with the devil. Caramba! Be gone or we will fire!"

"Listen to reason!" shouted Frank.

But the *alcalde* had leaped down to signify that the truce was at an end.

Frank was compelled to draw back. He had scarcely done so when the bullets began to fly again.

"No use!" declared the young inventor, "these people are too ignorant to treat with. It would not be safe to land here!"

So the proposed landing was at once abandoned.

The air-ship soared aloft and out of range.

Then Frank Reade, Jr., set the course due south for the northern limit of the Andes.

These were encountered a day later.

Then a course was held for the Ecuador line. A strange and wild country it was which was passed over.

There were many cities and towns all densely populated. Fertile valleys abounded in which long-horned cattle grazed.

In the mountains the scene was of the wildest and grandest.

Many wonderful sights were witnessed, many scenes passed over, but the Era did not descend.

"Wait until you get down into Peru!" declared De Frontenac confidently, "there you will see scenery which will put this to shame!"

But before many days our adventurers thought that the scenery of Ecuador would do.

"Upon my word!" gasped Dyke in sheer amazement. "What awful mountain is that? Why, we are far below its summit!"

"That is Cotopaxi," declared De Frontenac. "Over eighteen thousand feet high. But old Chimborazo, twenty-one thousand, four hundred and twenty-four feet high, is the wonder of Ecuador."

All these were wonderful sights to the voyagers in the air-ship.

These mighty mountain peaks were passed around, not over, for the rarified air at that awful height was painful to the lungs.

De Frontenac was perhaps the one most familiar with all these wonders.

"They are not new to me," he said. "Almost every part of these wonderful mountains, ever visited by man, are quite familiar to me."

"I presume you have thoroughly explored them?" said Frank.

"Ah, no, indeed! There are parts of them which have never been explored by man, and have hitherto been deemed inaccessible."

"And yet," said Dyke, "we are the favored ones to be able to gain that end."

"Would you have thought it easy to track your man Burton in these impenetrable wilds?" asked De Frontenac.

"I should have realized very speedily how utterly impossible it would be to explore this region, to say nothing of finding my man."

"Exactly."

"But——"

"What?"

"On the other hand it would seem to me quite difficult for a man to find a congenial quarter here in which to hide away from justice all his life."

"There are scores of such places," declared De Frontenac. "People inhabit these wilds whose existence is never dreamed of by the passing travelers. There are tribes of natives who have never seen a white man, inaccessible valleys and gulches where the explorer has never penetrated. Moreover, many of these mountaineers, particularly the Peruvians, have comfortable homes among the fastnesses and there they pass their lives. It would not be difficult for a fugitive from justice to find refuge with them."

"Doubtless this is what Burton has done," said Dyke.

"No doubt. I should, however, consider it a Herculean task to find him and very much like looking for a needle in a haystack."

"Indeed, yes," replied the detective, slow, but apparently not yielding hope; "however I shall try."

"Perhaps fortune may favor you."

"I pray that it may."

The air-ship had for some while kept far above the country spread below.

As there was a general desire to get a better look at the region, Frank now allowed the Era to descend.

They hung over a mighty gorge thousands of feet in descent. This was spanned by a curious rope bridge.

A path led in winding form along the verge of awful precipices. Over this path, nearly naked natives toiled with great bundles upon their heads and backs, bound on by straps.

They walked with ease and surety, where the slightest misstep would have meant sure death.

Quite a number of these mountain carriers were thus climbing the peaks when the air-ship appeared above them.

The effect was peculiar.

Astounded by such a strange and inexplicable spectacle, all of the natives paused in superstitious terror.

The hideous vultures peculiar to the Andes soared around the air-ship, but were not lighter on the wing than it.

What the natives took the air-ship for it would be hard to say. One thing was certain, they were terrified.

And yet they could not retreat in haste. To descend the narrow path rapidly was dangerous indeed.

So they cowered upon the narrow path, muttering superstitious prayers. Frank allowed the Era to settle in the gorge, and then appeared on the deck.

He addressed the mountain carriers in Spanish.

This was the necessary open sesame.

They responded at once.

"For the love of our Holy Mother, señor!" cried one of the Indians, "how can you float in the air that way? Does Satan support you?"

"Not a bit!" replied Frank. "This is an air-ship!"

"Jesu pity! We have never seen one before!"

"Well, you see it now. I am Frank Reade, Jr., an American. Do you know of a white man sojourning in this part of the world?"

There was a moment's consultation, and then one of them replied:

"Si, señor. We know him well. He has gone into the Isabella diamond mine."

"Ah!" cried Frank, eagerly. "Can you tell me what was his name?"

"Si, señor!" cried one of the carriers. "He was Señor Burton, a rich American. Ah, but he scattered silver in the streets of Bonita!"

"He is wild and reckless!" cried another. "He will risk his life to find the Light of the Mountains, which is said to be the largest diamond in the world. You Americans are brave and skillful."

Dyke, the detective, gripped the rail of the air-ship and gasped:

"Great heavens, Frank, I am on the right track at last! What a stroke of luck!"

"You are indeed lucky to get news of Burton so quickly!"

"But—in what direction has he gone? How shall we find him?"

"I will learn at once."

Frank leaned over the rail and questioned the carriers again.

"Where do you carry your packs?" he asked.

"To Bonita," was the reply. "It is a city in the hills. We came from Iquique, which is by the sea."

"When do you expect to reach Bonita?"

"Before another evening, señor!"

"And then——"

"We will reload our packs and return to Iquique."

"Very good!" said Frank. "Now can you tell me where I can fine the American, Burton?"

There was a moment of silence.

Then one replied:

"We can do that, señor. He is in the Isabella mine."

"Ah, but where is that?"

One of the carriers arose and pointed to the southward.

"A hundred leagues thither!" he exclaimed, "the mountain is one of stone. You will know it when you see it. There is the Isabella mine! It will be easy to find Burton there!"

A few more questions in regard to Burton and the diamond mine, and Frank turned, saying:

"I am going to the Isabella mine at once! Dyke, you may be quite sure of caging your man!"

CHAPTER VI
At Isabella

Osman Dyke, detective, was delighted with Frank's proposition.

"Good!" he cried. "That is the sort of talk I like. I hope we shall win success as you say."

"If he is in the mine you may be sure of it."

Over the mighty gorges and peaks sailed the air-ship.

To attempt to describe the wonderful scenery which was witnessed would be quite impossible.

So, with the reader's permission, we will pass it over and continue with thrilling incidents which were close at hand.

After some hours of random sailing over the wild region Barney cried:

"Bejabers, Misther Frank, I think I can see the Isabella Mountain!"

At once all were interested.

"Where, Barney?" asked Frank eagerly.

"Shure, sor, jist atween thim two tall peaks."

Everybody looked in the direction indicated and not one in the party but gave an exclamation.

Sure enough there was the mountain of stone as described by the Andean native.

At once the air ship was headed for it. Soon it towered before them almost a perfect cone of solid rock.

At the base of this mountain there was a level plain with much green verdure.

Here there was a pleasant little town surrounded by vineyards and gardens replete with rich fruits.

They knew that this was Isabella, the beautiful little town at the entrance to the diamond mines.

Here a tributary to the Amazon ran leaping and foaming over hundreds of miles of rapids and cataracts to the mighty selvas below.

Upon the west was the great Peruvian seaboard, and from Calloa and Lima merchants sent great pack trains over these mighty heights to barter for gold and diamonds and rich wines.

The Isabella diamond diggings were an alluvial tract of country, just halfway up the slopes of the great mountain.

Here there were table-lands and basins covering thousands of acres, and in the red earth the precious gems were found.

That Burton should have sought this region was quite natural.

Back of it was a region full of hiding-places, and inhabited by an extremely treacherous type of Indians.

Among the Chilkat people the fugitive would be certain to find a covert safe enough from ordinary pursuit.

Indeed Burton had made friends with the chief of the Chilkats, and it would therefore be an easy matter for him to set all pursuit at naught.

Before the air-ship descended into the Isabella valley a consultation was held.

"There is a question," said Frank, "whether it is wiser to go openly down into the town with the air-ship or not."

"Why not?" asked De Frontenac.

"For the reason that Burton seeing us coming would get the alarm and skip out," said Dyke.

"That is true!" agreed Frank. "It is quite impossible to approach the town in the Era without being seen!"

For a moment all were thoughtful.

"Don't you suppose they have seen us already?" asked De Frontenac.

"Begorra, I don't see how they cud iver help it," cried Barney. "Shure we've been in soight av the town fer a long while!"

"Which is very true!" agreed Dyke. "I don't know as we would gain anything, Frank, by any other course than by going boldly down into the place."

"Perhaps so!"

"If there is any law in the place I think I can get the authorities on my side."

"There ought to be plenty of law!" declared Frank. "Peru is an independent nation and on the best of terms with the United States!"

"Oh, I have provided for that!" said Dyke; "before I left home I secured through the foreign consuls extradition papers in all of the South American States."

"Then you are all right!" cried Frank. "Of course Isabella is a sufficiently important place to have an alcalde and a tribunal."

"I should think so!"

"Of course it is!"

"Then our best move is to descend and attempt to enlist the officers of the law in our behalf."

"Exactly!"

"All right. I am agreeable."

So Barney allowed the air-ship to float down into the valley.

They were now a thousand feet over the wonderful vineyards and the town, and a startling scene was revealed.

The appearance of the air-ship in the sky above their heads, was no doubt a bit of a surprise to the Peruvians.

They had never seen anything of the sort, and in many cases superstitious fear prevailed.

Great trains of heavily burdened llamas were trailing into the town. In many cases the native drivers fled incontinently at the sight of the mysterious wonder.

In other cases merchants and vineyard-keepers stood staring at the ship in stupid wonder.

The native soldiers of the little fort recognized the apparition as a certain scheme of their foes and Chilean neighbors to destroy the country, and at once beat to arms.

Great excitement reigned generally in the little hamlet.

Those on board the air-ship viewed the scene with deepest interest.

It was a serious question in the minds of all as to whether they were to be received in a friendly fashion or not.

The incident with the Colombian alcalde was fresh in their minds. Much depended upon their reception in Isabella.

Suddenly as the air-ship was hovering over the town a startling thing happened.

It came near proving a catastrophe also.

Some of the defenders of the little fort had elevated the muzzle of a cannon to the right degree and sent a ball hurtling upward.

It narrowly missed striking the hull of the air-ship.

"Whew!" exclaimed De Frontenac, in consternation, "that was a close call."

"Right!" cried Dyke. "They evidently mean business. Eh, Frank?"

"You are right!" agreed the young inventor. "We are to be treated as a foe!"

"I return the compliments, Señor Americano. I am Joaquin Murillo, the governor of the Providence of Isabella."

"I am honored, most noble Governor!"

"The honor is mine most gifted Señor," replied the governor urbanely. "Will you not descend and try of the vintage of Isabella?"

"A thousand thanks."

Frank turned to Barney:

"Let the air-ship go down!" he said. "She may rest in the yard of the fort."

Barney obeyed orders.

The Era descended into the fort yard. Frank stepped down from the platform and saluted Joaquin Murillo.

A few moments' conversation made them fast friends.

Other Spanish or Peruvian notables came forward and were introduced. Frank brought his companions forward also.

Then wine was imbibed, and Frank next invited the governor and his friends to go aboard the air-ship.

They were delighted and wonderstruck with its fine appointments. After all this was over Murillo said:

"Pardon, Señor Reade, but will it be an impertinence to ask what has brought you to Isabella?"

"By no means," replied the young inventor. "It is a matter of very serious moment, I can assure you."

"Indeed!"

"We are here with extradition papers for the proper arrest of a fellow countryman guilty of murder."

"What, a murderer!" exclaimed Murillo. "An American here in Isabella?"

"That is what we believe, your excellency."

"Pray let me see your papers."

Frank motioned to Dyke.

The detective came forward.

He produced his papers at once, and the Spanish governor glanced over them.

"These are true," he said. "They bear the correct seal of our court. We cannot deny the right."

"Do you know of this man Burton?" asked Frank.

The governor drew a deep breath.

"Indeed, I know him well," he said. "He has been here in our midst somewhile. But I never deemed him a murderer. However, you shall have the aid of our law to capture him."

CHAPTER VII
The Capture of Burton

The delight of Osman Dyke, the detective, can hardly be expressed in words.

"Good!" he cried. "I shall succeed in bringing John Burton to justice!"

"Then Burton is at present in Isabella?" asked Frank in Spanish.

"Yes," replied the governor, "or at least he goes every day to the diamond field, where he owns a claim."

"How shall we catch him?"

"If you wish I will take some officers and go thither with you now."

"That will be a great favor to us."

The governor gave a few sharp orders to an aid.

In a few moments four uniformed men appeared.

They were Peruvian police and were ready for duty.

The start was made at once.

The governor and the four officers got aboard the air-ship. Frank motioned to Barney.

The Celt pressed the key and the air-ship shot upward. The people below cheered wildly.

It was a new and wonderful sight to them as well as a novel experience to the new passengers.

At first they all turned pale and were not a little alarmed at leaving the earth so rapidly.

But Frank quieted their fears by saying repeatedly in Spanish:

"Have no fear, gentlemen. If harm comes to you it befalls us also."

The air-ship struck out direct for the Isabella mines.

Soon the immense diamond fields came into view.

A strange sight it was.

There were mighty excavations, immense heaps of thoroughly sifted soil and everywhere throngs of natives were working in the boiling sun.

Here some of the most valuable of stones were recovered.

As the air-ship sailed on the governor, who was at the rail, pointed to an adobe building at the base of a rocky cliff.

"There is the claim of Burton the American," he said. "You will find him there I think!"

A number of natives were digging near the hut. By them was a tall man in white duck and a Panama hat.

The appearance of the air-ship over the plain had of course attracted much attention.

Astonished, the diamond diggers quit work and craned their necks to look at the wonder.

At this the Spanish governor smiled.

"I was like them!" he said, "truly, I do not wonder!"

But the moment Burton looked up, he gave a tremendous backward leap.

His sunburned face clearly revealed in the sunlight, seemed to turn aghast with horror and fear.

"That is him!" cried Dyke; "that is my man! Don't let him escape!"

The air-ship was soaring down to the spot like a mighty vulture. Frank leaned over the rail, and shouted:

"John Burton, we want you. Stand where you are or be shot!"

The murderer made no reply, nor did he heed the warning.

Swift as a flash he sprang into a copse and then was seen running along a path which led around the mountain.

"Stop him!" screamed Dyke. "Don't let him escape!"

Frank raised his pistol.

"Shall I stop him?" he asked.

"No, no! Don't shoot him!" cried Dyke. "He must be captured alive!"

Frank then cried to Barney:

"Follow him close around the mountain, Barney!"

"All roight, sor!"

Around the mountain wall the path ran, and here was an awful gorge more than a thousand feet deep.

Its walls were a sheer descent, and below was a torrent.

Along this path the fugitive was running. Into the gorge the air-ship at once sailed.

Here it seemed was a chance both for the fugitive and for the pursuers.

If Burton could reach a cavern far above, he might seek a hiding place in it.

On the other hand, the air-ship could be sailed up to the wall and he could be headed off on the path. For a time it was hard to tell which plan would succeed.

But as it happened neither did.

Suddenly, and without warning, Burton slipped over the edge of the path. Down he went into space.

"My God! that is the end of him!" cried all in chorus.

They rushed to the rail to see his body dashed to pulp so far below. But this did not happen.

Down the sheer wall he slid like a rocket. But not two hundred feet below was a jutting shelf.

Here, from a crevice, several mountain pines grew, and projected far out over the chasm.

Into the branches of these the fugitive slid with great force.

For a moment it seemed as if he must go down through them. But he did not.

To everybody's surprise he clung there. He was saved from an awful death.

But it was only rescue from one fate to meet another. He was now at the mercy of his pursuers.

"Now we have him!" yelled Dyke. "Luck is ours! The game is bagged at last!"

So indeed it seemed.

The air-ship sailed down to a level with the shelf of rock.

There in the branches crouched the desperate-looking man. His face was copper-colored and his eyes blood-shot.

Foam was upon his lips, and in one hand he clutched a revolver. But Frank Reade, Jr., had covered him.

"None of that!" he cried, sternly; "drop that weapon or it
will be the worst for you!"

Burton muttered a savage oath.

"Curse you!" he gritted. "You want my life!"

"Not without a fair trial, John Burton," cried Dyke; "it is
better for you to surrender and meet it."

"You will hang me?"

"Not unless you deserve it."

"You have no proof that I killed my brother," sneered the
villain.

"Then you have less to fear. Better take your chances in a
United States Court. Come aboard and give yourself up!"

There was a snaky gleam in the villain's eyes.

The hand which held the revolver twitched nervously for a
moment, as if he longed to use it.

Then he flung it from him.

"I yield!" he cried, "on the condition of fair play."

"You shall have it!" declared Dyke.

"Who are you!"

"I am a U.S. detective!"

"From New York?"

"Yes!"

"All right! I'll surrender to you. I'm not guilty, and have
nothing to fear!"

Dyke smiled contemptuously.

He read the villain's soul through and through. He saw the
cunning purpose lurking in his evil eyes!

"Once he is in the Tombs," he muttered, "he'll never come
out till he stretches hemp!"[8]

The bow of the air-ship was now run close to the ledge of
rock. A rope ladder was thrown out.

Burton came across it quickly.

The moment he stepped on deck the detective slipped manacles upon his wrists.

The villain growled.

"What's that for?" he demanded. "Are you afraid of me? That's not fair play. There are six of you to one!"

"All right!" said Dyke, coolly. "We'll let you wear them a little while. Now, Frank, where will we put him?"

"In stateroom No. 5," replied the young inventor, "he will be safe there, for the door is of steel and the window heavily guarded."

Accordingly Burton, despite his protests was locked in stateroom 5.

When Dyke came on deck, Frank had turned the prow of the air-ship back towards Isabella.

Governor Murillo had been more than delighted with the trip.

"It is a wonderful experience!" he said. "Only to think that you Americans have at last solved the problem of flying in the air!"

"But we have not forgotten that it was a Spaniard who discovered our wonderful country," said Frank.

This pleased the Peruvian governor immensely, and he demonstrated it with a smile.

When Isabella was reached again, the place was up in arms to welcome the air-ship.

A band was playing and a salute was fired from the fort.

Darkness was coming on and it was proposed that they spend the night in the town.

So the air-ship was landed near the fort upon a broad patch of green.

Murillo detailed a guard of soldiers to guard against harm being done the air-ship.

Then as darkness came down Frank turned on the electric lights and dazzled the Andean people.

The search-light made the green as bright as day. A little evening fete had been arranged.

The governor caused a string band to play and a bevy of pretty Spanish girls went through a mazy dance upon the green.

It was a picturesque and beautiful sight, and the aerial travelers gazed upon it spell-bound.

Until long past midnight this sort of thing continued.

Then finally all retired to wait the coming of day. During all this Burton, the murderer, was sullen and silent in his stateroom.

Barney and Pomp took turns as sentry, though Murillo had furnished a military guard.

Nothing worthy of record occurred during the dark hours of the morning. But when the Andean sun peeped over the high peaks all were quickly astir.

"Now," said Frank to the detective Dyke, "what shall we do? I can take you over to Callao and you can get a steamer home. Or you can remain aboard the air-ship."

"Why not do the latter?" replied the detective.

"Certainly, unless you are in haste to have your man tried."

"Where are you going from here?"

"With De Frontenac to explore an inaccessible valley inhabited by an unknown race!"

The detective was interested.

"With your permission," he said, "I will stay with you. I can afford to wait, for you would beat any steamer back to New York."

CHAPTER VIII

The Valley Above the Clouds

"Don't be so sure of that!" said Frank. "We may be delayed a long while in the unexplored Andes."

"I don't care. I am sure of my man, and he cannot escape!"

"Very true. So let it be!"

Governor Murillo made overtures to Frank to remain longer at Isabella.

But Frank replied:

"I have another project on hand which will take much of my time and energy during the rest of my stay in South America."

So he shook hands with the Spanish governor, and the Era sailed away over the mountains amid the plaudits of the Isabella people.

Frank now gave his whole attention to the problem of find-ing the mysterious valley above the clouds described by De Frontenac.

The French-Irish explorer recognized many localities as they sailed on, as placed he had visited.

Once he said:

"It is here that I first learned of the Cordillera Los Angeles, or the Mountain of the Angels, as the natives call it. They imagine that the people who live up there are a race superior to man and endowed with supernatural traits."

"Indeed!" exclaimed Frank. "Then we cannot be far from the Cordillera?"

"Yonder it is."

De Frontenac pointed to the southward.

There against the horizon was a long, ragged array of peaks with a serrated effect.

They extended in what seemed a long oval far to the south-ward.

At once all began to study the distant peaks with their glasses.

It could be readily seen that there was doubtless an inclosure or valley within those mountain walls.

That a race of native Incas might there yet find a secluded home was not altogether improbable.

"It will be interesting to visit that unknown and hitherto un-seen nation above the clouds," cried Frank. "Set a straight course for the Cordillera, Barney!"

The cool, refreshing breezes of the morning were blowing up from the depths below.

The voyagers were all in the best of spirits.

The only human being on board at all out of sorts was the prisoner, Burton, in stateroom 5.

Thus far the murderer had given no trouble.

He had been extremely taciturn, even sullen, yet he ate his meals heartily, and seemed to be in good spirits bodily.

The Era now swiftly bore down for the Los Angeles valley. As it drew nearer the peaks Frank sought an opening between them.

Through this the ship sailed.

A wonderful scene was spread to the view of the voyagers.

At last they really gazed upon the nation above the clouds. The scene was a marvelous one.

An immense flat plain, covering hundreds of square miles, was inclosed by the precipitous mountain walls and inaccessible peaks.

As green and bright as could be imagined was the verdure of this lovely valley.

And there, down in its midst and by a sparkling lake, was a city of marvelous beauty.

Its walls and towers and domes were of whitest stone and glistened in the sun amid groves of green trees like a scene in fairyland.

Upon the plain were productive farms which men, strangely clad, were working. The llama seemed the beast of burden.

The city of the elevated nation was thronged with people. At that distance their personal appearance could not be judged.

But it all looked like a high grade of civilization.

The voyagers gazed spellbound.

"Upon my word!" cried Frank Reade, Jr., excitedly, "this is a discovery of benefit to science! Did ever anybody dream of such a thing?"

"Wonderful!" cried Detective Dyke. "And to think that we are the first privileged in many centuries to visit them and perhaps talk with them."

"That is indeed a wonderful thing to contemplate," declared De Frontenac. "I only hope they will receive us in a friendly way."

"I have no doubt they will!" said Frank, "they are evidently a pastoral people."

"Yes, for they have never had anybody to make war with."

"That is true!"

The air-ship sailed over a vast tract of land where natives were at work gathering what looked like maize.

At that height they were seen to be of a similar type to the average South American native or Indian.

But they were dressed in a more comely fashion with blankets made of gayly colored material.

As the air-ship appeared above them it made a sensation.

The working natives in some instances flung themselves upon their faces in superstitious terror.

In others, they fled incontinently as if pursued by a demon.

This made the voyagers laugh, for it indeed looked comical. Into their adobe houses the natives fled.

"They no doubt think we are some strange supernatural visitation," said Frank. "I don't much blame them for being terrified."

"Begorra, it's the naygur they saw hanging over the rail!" cried Barney, willing to make a shot at Pomp.

"Golly dey jes' needn't take no mo' dan one look at yo', chile!" cried Pomp, in retaliation. "Dat mug ob yours done scare de wits out av anyfing!"

Everybody laughed, and the air-ship now boomed on toward the city.

Everywhere the natives fled in terror before the advance of the Era.

But Frank kept on, the air-ship sailing a couple of hundred feet above the plains. Now elegant paved roads were reached.

These led into the city.

This was a marvel in its way.

The style of architecture was something indeed unique. The buildings were not of great height, but much of the stone was delicately sculptured.

That the strange people were lovers of art was evident, for every portico, and even roof, was adorned with not altogether crude statuary.

The streets of the city were broad, and neatly paved.

There were no vehicles of any kind, that is, none with wheels, consequently sidewalks were not needed.

Palanquins[9] carried by gigantic men were quite common.

There were shops and bazaars, temples and public edifices the same as in eastern cities.

And in the huge central square of the city was a mammoth basin and acqueduct which brought the purest of water from the mountains.

The windows, housetops and balconies all held people, men, women and children.

The streets were densely thronged.

A particularly large crowd were gathered in a square where there was an immense idol. Before this there was a mighty altar and here a fire was burning.

At once De Frontenac cried:

"Ah, like the old Incas, they are idolaters and given to human sacrifice. Look!"

"Horrors!" exclaimed Dyke; "they are cutting that poor wretch to pieces!"

Instinctively everyone was obliged to turn their eyes away from what was really a horrible sight.

The high priests, four in number, were deliberately hacking a poor victim to pieces with their sharp cleavers, and throwing the pieces into the eternal fire as it was probably designated.

Off came an arm and then the head. When entirely dismembered, the trunk was also thrown in.

It was a horrible spectacle and sickened the voyagers.

"Ugh!" exclaimed Dyke. "If that is the sort of people they are, I don't want anything to do with them!"

"It is terrible!"

"But see!"

"We have created a sensation."

This was true. The people had now caught sight of the strange air-monster hovering over them.

The result was thrilling.

In an instant all was in a turmoil. There came up from the streets an awful din.

The priests rushed hither and thither, shouting incantations. The people were in a panic.

"What will they do!" cried Frank, "have they no king or recognized ruler?"

"Hold on!" cried De Frontenac. "Here he comes!"

Out of a massive and richly sculptured building came a richly draped open palanquin.

It was in fact really a kind of portable throne, carried by twenty stout men, five at each bar.

Upon this throne sat a man dressed in what seemed to be cloth of gold. Barbaric splendor attended him.

Precious stones fairly studded his garments. The throne was golden, and all of the attendants were dressed in the same cloth of gold.

It was afterwards learned that this cloth was indeed far superior to the cloth of gold known in the civilized world.

Its texture was really partly of spun gold. The weaving, however, was a secret of the natives, which it was death to part with.

"Upon my word!" cried Dyke, "his Royal Highness is a fine-looking man!"

This was true.

The king was a powerful-built man, with aquiline features and pure white beard and hair.

This gave him a patrician appearance and was very grand indeed.

The king and all his retainers gazed at the air-ship in amazement. Many of the people fell on their faces.

But the old king appeared to be undaunted.

He sprang up swinging his mace defiantly, and hurled anathemas at the strange visitor.

Evidently they regarded the air-ship as a foe, perhaps a minion of the Evil Spirit, and they hoped to drive it away.

One of the high priests even began shooting sacred arrows with a sacred bow at the Era.

But these, of course, could do no harm. One of them, however, was captured by De Frontenac.

The tip or head was of solid gold.

"Well!" cried the explorer, "they can shoot those arrows at us a month if they wish; they will be very welcome."

"How are we going to make friends with them?" asked Dyke.

CHAPTER IX
The Hidden Race

Indeed this was a question well worth considering.

It was necessary to make friends with the strange people. This it did not seem would be easy to do.

They were influenced no doubt by an intense superstitious fear.

This must first be overruled. Frank leaned over the rail and tried to make pacific gestures.

For a time this was of no avail.

The natives made all manner of fierce gestures for a time. Then the king evidently saw that this was not going to frighten the air-ship away.

Also it had given him time to collect his senses a bit.

He saw that the air-ship was a tangible article and no doubt concluded very sensibly to first investigate its character.

So he suddenly changed his tactics.

His orders went forth that there be silence. As this command was seen to travel through the crowd silence instantly became the order.

Then the king arose in his palanquin.

He had caught sight of Frank leaning over the rail. It did not require a second glance for him to see that it was a man of flesh and blood like himself.

There was a plain look of astonishment on the king's face which amused Frank not a little.

The young inventor could not understand a word he uttered, but he replied with many smirks and smiles.

"We are your friends. Yes! Why don't you receive us socially?"

Of course the native ruler did not understand Frank, but he seemed to comprehend that he was of a different race of people come to pay him a visit.

This changed the complexion of everything.

The native king was all right now. He addressed the people

in apparently explanative terms and returned Frank's smirks and smiles with interest.

A space was cleared in the crowd, and the native king made motions for the air-ship to descend.

Frank hesitated.

"I don't know whether to trust those heathens or not!" he said.

"I think it will do if we arm ourselves!" declared De Frontenac.

"Very well."

Accordingly rifles were brought out of the cabin, and all was made ready for the repelling of an assault.

Then Frank allowed the air-ship slowly to descend. It rested upon ground where the space had been cleared.

The throng kept a respectable distance, evidently by the king's orders, for which Frank was very grateful.

Frank stepped forward, and greeted the native ruler. Of course it was very difficult to exchange any comprehensive words.

But Frank speedily found that the other was quick-witted and would easily embrace any sign talk.

After some persistent work this attempt at crude intercourse became quite successful.

Frank managed to convey the fact that they belonged to a people far to the north, and that they were simply exploring the mountains for a pastime.

This seemed to please the native king, who had evidently feared that they had come for conquest.

He conveyed the information that his people were not war-like and shunned open battle.

For this reason, hundreds of years previous, his ancestors had sought this secluded valley.

An earthquake had blocked the exit and also made it inaccessible, but none of the tribe ever ventured to leave the valley.

Thus they had dwelt for centuries in this retreat.

A nation above the clouds, they had been oblivious of all the world's great doings outside.

It was a strange story, and Frank gathered it with interest. He speedily found that the Hualpamas, which was their tribe name, were an exceedingly docile and peaceable people.

Now that their superstitious fears had vanished, they made great manifestations of friendliness.

This was most agreeable, and Frank lost no opportunity to cultivate the feeling.

De Frontenac had already entered into sign talk with a number of them. They were exceedingly bright.

But the air-ship was a source of much wonderment.

Frank tried to explain the mechanism of the air-ship to King Orullo, which was the monarch's name.

But it was impossible for him to understand the theory and application of electricity.

He nodded his head in a good-natured way, and Frank abandoned the attempt.

King Orullo proved himself a hospitable monarch, for the carcass of a mountain deer was brought and roasted upon the spot.

Also some peculiar wine, which was possessed of a musty flavor, was furnished.

Our adventurers partook of the repast so as not to offend the native monarch.

After this the voyagers were the best of friends with the Hualpamas.

They had nothing to fear from these simple children of the wilderness. They were honest and peaceable.

So De Frontenac was able to conduct his researches most successfully.

One thing was most remarkable.

The ancient Incas had been noted for the amount of pure gold they mined and used.

But almost the only metal known to the Hualpamas was gold.

It furnished material for nearly all their tools and weapons.

Indeed, many of the idols in their temples were of pure gold.

Various dishes, and even the commonest of domestic ware was of the precious metal.

To them steel was much more precious.

Our adventurers acquired great quantities of gold by simple exchange.

De Frontenac learned the valley was rich in gold and diamonds.

Indeed, the king gave Frank a jacket fairly studded with beautiful and rare diamonds.

In return the young inventor gave him steel knives and a sword. This delighted Orullo.

A more hospitable people than the Hualpamas could not be imagined. Anything and everything was at the disposal of their wonderful visitors.

King Orullo was never tired of making sign talk with Frank.

He listened for hours to conversation made by the young inventor upon wonderful far away America.

The king made signs that he would like to have more of Frank's countrymen visit him.

Frank replied that he ought to visit America, but he shook his head violently, replying:

"It is against the will of our sacred gods that any of us should leave this valley ever."

"Then the world will have to take our word for these strange people," thought Frank, "for no ordinary method of travel will enable anybody to reach them."

Several days were spent in the city of the Hualpamas.

Then one day Frank said to De Frontenac:

"Well, have you had enough?"

"Yes," replied the explorer. "I am satisfied; let us go."

"We have visited the most wonderful people in the world!"

"Very true. It will be many years perhaps before they are visited by white men again."

King Orullo was much disturbed when he heard that his interesting visitors were about to leave him.

He held out many inducements, but Frank was resolute.

"We must go!" he said. "There are other parts of the Andes to explore. Then we must get Burton home."

Thus far the murderer had seemed to accept his imprisonment philosophically.

He seemed to have no plan for escape. Indeed if he had, it

would not be easy to execute it with the manacles yet on his wrists.

Frank conferred with Dyke and it was decided to remove them.

The prisoner had seemed docile enough, and it seemed harsh indeed to take such extreme measures.

"At any rate!" said Frank, "he cannot get away from us, for the stateroom is strongly fortified."

Burton made no comment when the manacles were removed, but his eyes gleamed dangerously.

The air-ship left the city of Hualpamas finally, and a northward course was taken.

Frank had heard of a volcanic lake at the summit of a high mountain near, and was anxious to visit it.

So the air-ship's course was set for the volcano of Tambobambo. Before the next nightfall it was in sight.

De Frontenac stood by the rail, and all were studying the country, as he said:

"Down there is the great mountain trail from Central Brazil to the western coast."

"Indeed!" exclaimed Dyke, in surprise. "I don't see anything but a footpath."

"Perhaps not, but thousands of heavy-burdened men and beasts go over that route every year!"

"An immense carrying trade!"

"I should say so! They carry minerals, dye-stuffs, certain kinds of fruits, and bring back cloth and knick-knacks from Yankeedom, which are bartered with the natives for their products."

"And everything must be carried by pack train?"

"Certainly!"

"Will they never have railroads?"

"Not through these inaccessible mountain fastnesses," declared De Frontenac. "They could never climb the grades."

"I presume not; but what an immense forest down there. See the beautiful plumage birds. See—there is a tiger!"

"A jaguar. Yes, in these woods you will find chattering monkeys, screeching parrots, little wood deer, and—the deadly python."

"The python!" exclaimed the detective. "Ah, I would like to see one!"

"You may have a chance if Frank makes a landing anywhere in the lowland wilds."

A sudden cry came from forward.

Pomp had been on guard there, and his startled words came aft with thrilling force:

"Golly, Marse Frank, come quick! Dere am de debbil to pay jes' below us!"

CHAPTER X
Burton's Escape

Of course such an exclamation could not help creating general excitement and interest.

Everybody rushed to the rail and looked over.

And there down below in the mountain path, was a thrilling scene.

A pack train of llamas, with native attendants, had been climbing the mountain side. In the party were three Europeans.

At least such their dress betokened them. English tourists evidently, two men and one woman.

Part of the way up the mountain, the path led under copiously leaved beech trees.

Passing under one of these the lady had received an awful shock. When a huge python slid its folds down and about her and her donkey.

Scream after scream pealed from her lips.

The great rearing head of jaws of the python were above her. They seemed certain to strike her.

Her two escorts seemed to have become stupefied and unable to act. The native mountaineers were too far in the rear to give immediate help.

As luck had it Frank had been aft with a rifle striving to get a shot at a huge condor.

The moment he heard the woman's screams he leaned over the rail and took in the situation.

"A horrible python!" yelled Dyke. "My God! he will strike her!"

One blow of those awful jaws would have struck the fainting woman dead.

But quick as a flash and wholly on the impulse of the moment Frank flung his rifle to his shoulder, took aim and fired.

Crack!

The aim had been swift, true and deadly. The rifle ball flattened the snake's head like a pancake.

The reptile relaxed its folds and rolled back upon the ground, a wriggling, dying mass.

Then those below ran to catch the fainting woman and looked up with amazement to see the air-ship above them.

Frank shouted to Barney:

"Lower the ship!"

Down settled the Era rapidly.

Dyke and De Frontenac were now by Frank's side much excited.

"Upon my word, Frank, you deserve commendation. You made a wonderful shot!"

"That is so!" cried Dyke. "It was just in the nick of time!"

"Thank Heaven, I was able to save her," said Frank.

Down settled the air-ship and touched the ground.

The rescued woman had recovered, and one of her escorts came forward to the rail of the Era.

"We owe you more than we can ever repay for that timely shot!" he cried. "It was a magnificent bit of marksmanship."

"That is all right," said Frank. "Is the lady recovered?"

"Oh, yes, thank you."

The speaker was a short, thick-set Englishman, with a genial cast of features.

He introduced himself.

"I am Lord Harry Cheswick of Cornwall, England!" he declared. "May I ask whom I have the honor of meeting?'"

"Frank Reade, Jr., of Readestown, U.S.A.," replied Frank.

"An American!" cried Lord Cheswick. "Well, I might have known that nobody but an American would solve the problem of aerial navigation. Your air-ship is a perfect wonder!"

"I am satisfied with it," replied Frank.

"You are traveling over this region for pleasure?"

"And exploration!"

"Good! We, my partner, Earl Warlock and Lady Warlock, his wife, with myself, are doing South America. We hope to reach Callao some time, from which place we shall go to Chile."

"That is pleasant," agreed Frank. "Can I be of further assistance to you?"

"I think not, sir. But pardon, please. Give the lady the chance; she desires to thank you in person."

Lady Warlock, a beautiful and intellectual woman, now came forward on her husband's arm. She greeted Frank warmly and thanked him earnestly.

"It is nothing!" replied the young inventor with a happy smile. "I am always honored to serve!"

"I shall never forget you, Mr. Reade," replied the English lady warmly.

After some further pleasant talk the episode ended.

The air-ship went on its way and the pack train likewise.

The python had been examined and found to measure forty-five feet in length.

"That's the biggest snake I ever saw!" declared Dyke. "I don't think I fancy this country."

"Or rather the snakes," laughed De Frontenac.

"Yes."

Tambobambo Mountain was now rapidly approached.

It was in appearance very much like Catopaxi. The same funnel-like column of smoke arose from it.

The air-ship floated up the sides until the great crater was reached and here was revealed the volcanic lake.

Here right in the top of the mighty mountain was a hissing, boiling lake of water.

It occupied the whole of what had been a vortex of burning lava.

But the smoke of the once active volcano had been changed to steam. Water in gushing torrents took the place of lava.

At times mighty geysers shot up to a height of fully a hundred feet. Surely this was very odd.

Frank at once figured out the cause to the satisfaction of his listeners.

"Under the mountain," he declared, "there were great springs of water. These doubtless found a vent through the crater shaft, and coming up with greater strength killed out the volcanic fires!"

"I hardly know which I would rather be immersed in," declared Detective Dyke, "boiling water or lava!"

"I think I would take the water," declared De Frontenac.

"There is really little to choose," said Frank, "it is death in either case."

As there was imminent danger of the air-ship being drawn into the gases of the crater by reason of the powerful draughts or currents of air, Frank caused the ship to descend upon a flat surface of rock some distance from the crater.

And here it was securely anchored while the voyagers all took a trip across to the verge of the crater lake.

Only Barney was left aboard the air-ship. The others, led by Frank, proceeded to explore the mountain top.

No thought had been given to Burton who was deemed secure in the cabin.

And right here was where a fearful mistake was made.

The villain during his confinement had not been idle.

If his captors fancied that he did not meditate escape they were exceedingly in error, as events proved.

It had been an unwise thing to remove his manacles. To Burton it was a godsend.

The villain had not been idle a moment.

In the stateroom he extracted a steel spike from a portion of the woodwork. With this he had contrived to wear away one of the bars of the grating in his stateroom door.

These were of iron and easily yielded to the steel. So cleverly was the gap in the iron covered up with a bit of clay which the villain had in some way secured that it was not noticed.

So now, when all the explorers left the air-ship and it was

resting upon the earth, the villain believed that his chance had come.

From his window he saw them leave the air-ship.

He chuckled well at this.

"I'll learn them that John Burton is no fool!" he hissed. "I'll cheat them of their game yet."

With vengeful declaration, the villain deftly removed the sawed bar, and putting his arm out through the aperture shot back the outer bolts.

The door easily swung open and the escaped murderer crept into the cabin.

As he passed through the gun-room he took down a brace of pistols and thrust them in his pockets.

Then he crept out upon the deck.

Barney was standing forward and wistfully watching the explorers.

He had been greatly disappointed at his inability to accompany them.

"Begorra, it's a shame!' he muttered. "That naygur jest gits iverything he wants. Ah, well, me turn will come next!"

And as Barney stood there he suddenly heard a slight noise in his rear.

Like a flash he turned.

He was aghast to be confronted by the villain Burton, who, with a revolver pointed full at him, cried:

"Stand where you are! You are in my power!"

For a moment the Celt was in a quandary. His lion courage would have prompted him to spring full at his foe.

But as he looked into the deadly tube he knew that it held death.

This man was a murderer, and would as soon take his life as not. It would be folly to court that fate.

A thousand terrible reflections passed through Barney's mind.

He realized at once what it meant to have the air-ship fall into the power of this fiend.

The Celt was quite desperate, but what could he do? The native cunning of his shrewd nature asserted itself, and he instantly resolved to resort to stratagem.

"Begorra, I'll fool him!" he muttered to himself. "I'll wait me toime!"

But aloud he said:

"All roight, me frind. Don't shoot, fer I'm yure prisoner!"

"That's common sense," said Burton vindictively. "Now, my fine pup, I want you to do just what I tell you and no fooling about it, or by the justice I'll kill you!"

"Ye've said that wanst," retorted Barney. "Phwat the divil do yez want av me?"

"You know how to run this air-ship—send her up!"

Barney's face paled.

"Shure an' lave all the rist av thim?" he asked in consternation.

"Yes, of course."

"Och! begorra, I'll niver do that!"

"You won't, eh?" gritted the villain, savagely. "I will give you one minute to make up your mind! If you don't do it you shall die!"

CHAPTER XI
Barney's Brave Work

Barney was in a terrible predicament.

He did not wish to go off in this manner and lose his companions. Yet ought he to sacrifice his life?

One moment he hesitated; then the reflection came to him that he could return for them. There was no alternative in any event, so he cried:

"All roight, me friend, I'll do jist what yez tell me."

"See that you do."

Barney started along the platform to the pilot-house.

He kept an eye covertly on Burton, hoping to see a chance to down him; but the villain followed him close, holding the revolver at his head.

There was no opportunity and Barney was reluctantly obliged to press the key and set the wings in motion.

Up sprang the air-ship like a bird. Up, up over the crater, leaving the others below.

And they upon the verge of the crater heard the movement of the air-ship and looked up to see it sailing away to the southward.

Their astonishment and dismay can hardly be imagined.

"By the powers!" gasped Osman Dyke, "there goes the ship!"

"What is Barney up to?"

"Does he mean to leave us?"

Then one common thought came to all. Had Burton got free and overcome Barney? Was this his work?

"Golly fo' glory!" gasped Pomp. "De I'ishman am killed fo' suah! Dis chile ought to hab stayed dar wid him!"

"It never occurred to me that there was risk!" exclaimed Frank. "But we have done wrong in leaving Barney alone!"

"True, but it is too late now!" groaned Dyke. "Our man is lost and the air-ship too!"

"We will not admit that yet," said Frank. "Barney would not give up without a struggle."

"Yet the air-ship is leaving us!"

"It must be in Burton's hands."

"What are we to do?"

Indeed this was a problem of no light sort. Dismayed and indeed overwhelmed by their hard luck, the party remained gazing vacantly after the disappearing air-ship.

And aboard the Era Barney was yet under the deadly muzzle of Burton's revolver.

The villain sat close by the Celt in the pilot-house and directed him how to make the course of the air-ship.

Barney was in agony of doubt and apprehension.

In vain he groped about for a way out of the dilemma.

In some way he must outwit his captor.

But as matters stood now, it was very plain that Burton held the upper hand, and seemed likely to hold it for an indefinite length of time.

The volcanic mountain of Tambobambo was now hidden behind other peaks.

Still Burton compelled Barney to sail the air-ship on.

"You're an Irishman?" he said to Barney. "You have wit."

"I'm not ashamed av the green, sor," retorted the Celt.

"Ha, ha! that is good! You have good sense. Now, you'll do what I tell you, and I'll spare your life. I ought to kill you for my own safety!"

"Bejabers, so far as that goes, yez had better do it!" returned Barney, fearlessly.

"Then you won't make friends with me?"

"Divil a bit! I niver loiked the company av a snake!"

An oath quivered upon Burton's lips, and he seemed for a moment likely to pull the trigger.

But he did not do so.

"I ain't through with you yet," he said, "but you must not give me too much impudence."

"If I cud give phwat yez deserve, it would be a bit av rope," returned the Celt, coolly.

Burton was angry, but he only said in a steely way:

"We've gone far enough."

"Oh! it's to descind, is it?"

"Yes!"

Somewhat surprised, Barney at once complied. The air-ship settled down rapidly.

The spot was a lonely plain, yet a path could be seen which seemed to lead into the mountains.

The Celt half divined the villain's purpose.

"He means to take leave av me here!" he muttered. "Bejabers, I'll niver object to that."

But Burton had a deeper and darker purpose in view.

The air-ship settled down rapidly until it rested upon the plain.

Then Burton arose, saying:

"Put out your anchors!"

They went out on deck, Burton yet holding the pistol close to Barney's head. The Celt proceeded to moor the air-ship.

Then Burton said:

"Look here, you impudent rascal, there is dynamite aboard this ship!"

With an awful wave of horror Barney realized the villain's purpose.

For a moment his face was ghostly, but he quickly replied:

"Divil a bit, sor!"

"Don't you lie to me! Bring it out here at once!"

"But, sor——"

"You can't deceive me. The dynamite is here and you know it. I know where it is. Come with me!"

For a moment Barney's form quivered. A terrible deadly resolution had half come over him.

But yet again he looked into the deadly muzzle of that death-dealing revolver and knew that he must obey.

Would no opportunity occur for him to turn the tables upon the wretch? He was in despair.

"Shure it's sthuck I am!" he reflected, "the black-hearted divil means to blow up the air-ship!"

This was Burton's plan.

By destroying the Era he could end the pursuit of his foes. This would enable him to make good his escape.

What to do with Barney was yet a question to the villain. He had half decided to kill him.

Had the Celt known this he would perhaps have taken a desperate chance long ere this.

But he obeyed his captor, and proceeding to the ammunition locker took out one of the fearful dynamite bombs which were an invention of Frank Reade, Jr.'s.

This Burton carried, and then said:

"Now I want connections made with the dynamos. Lay a wire for me!"

Barney could not evade the command.

A cold sweat broke out over the Celt. He mentally resolved to die before he would see the air-ship blown up.

But the time had not yet come for him to act.

So he followed Burton's directions and laid the wire from the dynamos to a safe distance from the air-ship.

A key was provided which could open or close the current, and the connection were made with the bomb which was placed under the air-ship.

But Barney deftly fixed the connections in the key so that it would not work. With a fiendish light in his eyes Burton took the key from Barney's hand.

He pressed it in one hand, but it did not work.

His face turned black.

"What's this?" he hissed. "Have you made the connections right?"

"Yis, sor," replied Barney, coolly, "but yez don't press hard enough on the keys, sor."

"Oh, that's it, eh?"

For one supreme instant, in his intentness to accomplish his fiendish purpose, the villain forgot himself.

He applied both hands to the key.

It was Barney's moment.

The aim of the deadly revolver was diverted for an instant. But that was time enough.

With a howl Barney launched himself upon the murderer.

One quick blow of his hand sent the revolver flying from Burton's grasp.

Then the two men were locked in a deadly embrace.

"Yez dhirty, lyin' thavin' ould vaggybond!" yelled the Celt. "Now I've got the best av yez, an' be me sowl I'll kape it!"

"Curse you!" gritted Burton. "I ought to have killed you!"

Burton was a powerful man, but Barney was a tough little Irishman, and could stand a heap of punishment.

The fight was a most terrific one. Burton tried in every way to down his man.

But Barney hung on to him desperately, and it soon became evident that Burton was tiring.

The Celt seized a good opportunity, and tripping his man, threw him heavily. Over they rolled.

But Barney came out on top.

He was a hustler in a tussle of this kind, and soon he held his man down exhausted and a prisoner.

"Now be me sowl!" cried Barney, greatly elated, "if yez thry to git away again, I'll kill yez!"

"I yield!" gasped Burton.

Barney swiftly pulled off his coat, and bound the villain's hands behind him.

Then he led him aboard the air-ship.

Burton's face was ashen white.

"For God's sake take that bomb out from under the ship!" he cried.

But Barney laughed.

"Shure, if it explodes it'll only take the both av us out av the worruld, an' that wud be a small loss!" he cried. "Go in there wid yez!"

And the Celt forced his man into the stateroom and locked the door. Then he made sure that Burton could not again escape in the interim and went out to remove the bomb.

He broke the connection and relegated the bomb again to the locker.

"Upon me sowl!" he muttered, "it was a close call that divil gave me an' the air-ship! But divil a bit will he iver play it on me agin!"

It was rapidly growing dark, but nothing daunted the Celt started upon the return to Tambobambo.

He well knew that Frank and the others would be in a fever of excitement and unrest.

"Shure I'm afther thinkin' they'll be glad to see the air-ship again!" he muttered.

He turned on the search-light and sent its rays quivering across the mountain peaks.

He was not quite sure of his course to Tambobambo, but nevertheless kept on at a good pace, looking the while for his friends.

CHAPTER XII
A Timely Rescue

The horror and mystification of the party left by the volcano's crater can hardly be described.

"Great Jericho!" gasped Dyke in dismay. "Now we're in a scrape!"

"It is Burton's work!"

"Certainly!" agreed Frank Reade, Jr. "Barney would not go off and leave us for any slight reason!"

"What shall we do?"

The explorers stood looking blankly at each other.

Truly they were in a fix.

To leave the spot was hardly advisable for the air-ship might return. To remain there did not seem very feasible with the lack of provisions.

But fortunately they had their rifles with them.

This would enable them to do such hunting as was necessary to obtain game for food.

A consultation was held and it was decided to remain on the spot.

All interest now was lost in the volcanic lake.

All spent their time studying the horizon, vainly waiting the return of the air-ship.

But it did not reappear, and as time passed darkness most intense came on.

The explorers made a rude camp among the rocks, and prepared to thus spend the night.

Sleep was almost out of the question, for the nerves of all were extremely taut.

But after a while some of the weary ones lapsed into gentle sleep.

Pomp, however, sat up, studying the blackness of the southern sky.

The darky was secretly mourning what he believed was the sure loss of his confrere, Barney.

"Golly, but dis chile am gwine to be drefful lonesome wifout dat I'ishman," he declared. "He jes' had his faults, but all said and done, he amn't sich a bad fellow as he looked to be."

Thus communing with himself, the darky passed the time away.

But suddenly as he was studying the dark sky he gave a violent start.

"Golly!" he gasped. "Wha' am dat? Dat am berry queer!"

To the darky it looked like an enormous star in the horizon. What was more it was wavering greatly.

"It looks somefing like a star," he muttered, "but I disremember eber seeing a star act dat a'-way afore!"

Then a sudden idea flashed across him and he gasped:

"Fo' de Lor', I done believe it am a fac'. Marse Frank! quick sah, I done beliebe it am de air-ship!"

The startled cry aroused every one in the camp.

In a moment they had sprung up.

"What's the matter with you, Pomp?" asked Frank sharply.

"Jes' yo' look yender, sah," cried the darky, "fo' de lan's sake, I done beliebe it am dat I'ishman coming back a'right, sah!"

Frank now saw the distant star as did the others. They gazed at it hard for some moments.

Then Dyke cried:

"Upon my word, Frank, I believe it really is the air-ship!"

"That is good news!"

"Yes, that is the search-light of the Era as I live!"

"It seems to be coming this way."

"Yes."

"Barney is looking for us."

"But he'll never find us."

"How can we signal him?"

Instantly De Frontenac cried:

"Build a huge fire!"

This idea was embraced instantly. At once all set to work to pile up a great heap of wood.

There was plenty of this a short distance down the mountain side, stumps and fagots and fallen logs.

These were heaped up and fired.

The blaze shot upward, a literal tower of fire. It could not help but be seen many miles distant.

Meanwhile, the star of light was rapidly drawing nearer. That is was the search-light of the air-ship was certain.

Whether Barney saw their signal fire or not the explorers were not certain, but still the air-ship came on.

And now, back of the glimmering light, a dark body was seen. It was the air-ship.

All doubt was settled.

"Hurrah!" shouted Dyke, excitedly, "it is the air-ship coming back for us!"

The mystery of its leave-taking of course yet remained a mystery.

Every moment now the search-light became brighter. Soon its pathway of light struck the mountain top.

It was true that Barney had seen the beacon fire.

At first he had thought it flame from an active volcano, but on second thought he recognized its character.

He now bore down with all speed upon Tambobambo, and when at length he was able to focus the search-light upon the mountain top, he saw some tiny dark forms there.

"Begorra, there they are!" he cried, joyfully. "Shure, it's luck for me an' fer thim, too!"

Down settled the air-ship quickly. Soon it rested upon the mountain side, and with cheers the explorers quickly rushed aboard.

It did not take Barney long to give a faithful account of himself. As he portrayed his experiences, the explorers listened with wonder.

"Mercy on us!" cried Dyke. "You are a hero, Barney. What a big thing for you to outwit the villain that way. Is he safe aboard?"

"Shure, he's locked up all safe!" cried Barney, "but I'd advise ye to git him back to Ameriky, an' hang him as quick as iver ye kin, or the divil will help him to escape again!"

Everybody laughed at this, and Frank said:

"We shall all return home at once."

"After a most successful voyage," declared De Frontenac.

"Right there!" cried Dyke.

"I hope you gentlemen are satisfied!" said Frank.

"Why shouldn't we be!" cried De Frontenac. "I visited the hidden nation above the clouds. The greatest object of my life was attained."

"And I bagged my man!" cried Dyke. "Which was my great object."

All were in the happiest of spirits. Daylight was at hand, so nobody went back to sleep.

Good care was taken now that Burton's stateroom was well guarded. Another escape would not be possible.

With the first break of day the air-ship shot up into the sky and took a northward course.

The sky explorers were northward bound.

But they had not yet escaped all perilous adventure. An incident transpired that very day which was of thrilling sort.

John Burton had by no means given up his plans of escape.

Now that he knew that they were homeward bound and he was every moment drawing nearer to a court of justice he became doubly desperate.

"They will never hang me!" he gritted. "Curse them! I will cheat the gallows!"

He spent all his time in carefully studying his chances.

Before he had escaped by the door. This was, however, now doubly barred and locked.

He therefore turned his attention to the window.

This he found was a thin frame set in steel. By dint of much exertion and patient labor he managed to bend the frame and slide the window down.

It left an aperture just large enough for his body to pass through.

He crawled through one dark evening, and swinging downward grasped the rail. Along this like a monkey he made his way.

But the air-ship was full a thousand feet above the earth. How could he hope to escape!

He could not lower the ship himself, for there in the pilot-house was Barney.

The alarm would be given and he would be recaptured. The murderer was in a desperate frame of mind.

While cowering in the shadows by the rail he was apt to be discovered. But a sudden thrilling idea came to him.

He acted upon it.

His plan was to throw over one of the anchor cables and descend by it to the end.

Somewhere the end of the cable would be apt to touch the earth when he could disengage himself and be free.

Forward crept the prisoner until he was in the bow.

All of the voyagers were in the main cabin talking merrily except Barney who was at the wheel.

Some motive prompted Detective Dyke to go forward. He advanced with quick, firm steps, but suddenly halted.

A dark, crouching form was by the rail.

It was Burton, and he had just fastened the rope about his waist. It was a thrilling moment.

The detective started forward in surprise, exclaiming:

"Who is that?"

Then another cry pealed from his lips.

"John Burton!"

"Curse ye!" gritted the villain, as he tried to slide off the deck, "don't ye put a hand on me!"

But the detective had already gripped him by the throat. In an instant a terrible struggle was in progress.

Dyke had but one thought.

He would never let his man get away. Barney sprang down out of the pilot-house.

He saw the two men struggling and would have taken a hand in the contest.

But before he could do so an awful cry of horror escaped his lips. He saw both men slide, and slip and vanish over the edge of the air-ship's deck.

CHAPTER XIII
The End

Down into space slid the struggling men. But they did not fall to meet the awful death Barney had thought of.

They did not reach the earth. The cable fastened to Burton brought them to a halt.

But there they swung in mid-air and fighting madly.

In the darkness Barney did not see this, of course. He could realize but one thing, and this was that they had gone down to certain death.

His cries brought all from the cabin in a hurry.

The air-ship was instantly stopped. It was the horrified belief of all that both Dyke and Burton lay mangled and dead a thousand feet below.

"Quick, Barney!" shouted Frank, "focus the search-light downward and see if you can locate them!"

The Celt required no second bidding.

He hastened to obey.

The search-light swept the ground below. But the bodies were not seen.

However, De Frontenac leaning far over the rail, saw the two men dangling in mid-air, and cried:

"There they are alive, and hanging onto the anchor rope!"

A glance was enough for Frank.

"Down with the ship, Barney!" he cried.

The Celt rushed into the pilot-house. The air-ship began to descend.

It touched the earth, and there Dyke, the plucky detective, was found hanging onto his man.

The voyagers could not help a cheer. Burton was quickly secured and taken aboard again.

This was the murderer's last attempt at escape.

His courage seemed crushed, and he sullenly resigned himself to his fate.

The air-ship once more sped on its way.

Over Ecuador once more and Colombia, and then came the Caribbean Sea.

The Gulf of Mexico was crossed, and the shores of America once more burst into view.

The famous voyage of the sky explorers over the Andes of South America was at an end.

Back to Readestown went the air-ship. Here Frank Reade found that the frame had become badly twisted, and that it would not be able to stand another long voyage.

"Never mind," he said, philosophically; "I'll build another to beat her. I can do it."

And he at once began work upon some new plans.

Barney and Pomp had enjoyed the South American trip, but, on the whole, were not sorry to get home again.

They resumed their duties about the yard and quickly fell into the old routine.

Osman Dyke, the detective, was a hero when he brought the murderer Burton back safely to New York.

It was an achievement of which he had reason to be proud and won him promotion.

Burton died on the scaffold.

De Frontenac proceeded to write his book upon the hidden nation of the Andes, and at some future day the world will see it.

And thus having reached the end of our narrative, we will beg leave to bid the reader a fond adieu.

[THE END.]

TIP TOP LIBRARY.

Issued Weekly—By Subscription $2.50 per year.   Entered as Second Class Matter at the N. Y. Post Office by STREET & SMITH.

February 6, 1897.   Vol. 1.   No. 43.   Price Five Cents.

FRANK MERRIWELL'S FINISH
OR
BLUE AGAINST CRIMSON

By the Author of "FRANK MERRIWELL"

CRACK!—BAT AND BALL MET FAIRLY, AND AWAY SAILED THE SPHERE OVER THE SHORTSTOP'S HEAD.

Frank Merriwell, one of the most popular characters in the dime-novel era, is the creation of Gilbert Patten (1866–1945), who went on to write most but not all of the contents of the 986 issues of the combined Tip Top Library *(later to be called* Tip Top Weekly*) and* New Tip Top Weekly *published from 1896 to 1915. Merriwell's career is solidly grounded in sports, but he takes time out from winning the big game in order to tour the world, and has many adventures doing so. He was the ideal and idol of American youth. Readers wrote letters to the publishers (subsequently published in the "Applause" column of each issue) to suggest new storylines and to choose sides in debates about which direction the saga should take. The most famous of these debates concerned whether Frank should marry brunette Inza Burrage or blonde Elsie Bellwood. When Inza (whom Frank had saved from a runaway horse in the very first story) won out, the adherents of Elsie swore to stop reading* Tip Top, *but it's unlikely that many of them carried through with their threats.*

After nearly a year of adventures at Fardale Academy, Frank enters Yale University and finds new challenges to keep him occupied. Some of these challenges are on the athletic field, while others are presented by students jealous of his ability to come out on top against all adversaries. "Frank Merriwell's Finish" (Tip Top Library, *no. 43, February 6, 1897) is from* *his first year at Yale and establishes the pattern that was to follow for decades in what has been called the longest serial in fiction. As the story opens, the Yale freshman baseball team is in a hotly contested game against the freshmen of its traditional rival, Harvard. Among Frank's classmates is Harry Rattleton, who uses spoonerisms—inversions of words—when he is excited. Patten uses Rattleton's speech for comic effect, but some of the author's other characters have a way with words as well. Dismal Jones suggests he and Lewis Little get "tootsy-frooskied" at the "nearest lemonade shop" when it appears that Yale may lose the game. Patten's distinctive use of the language of sport was acknowledged by his editors at Street & Smith, who referred to it as "Patten patter" and encouraged other writers who worked on the series to match his example. This may account for his use of "coacher" instead of "coach." "Frank Merriwell's Finish" can also be found in a book called* Frank Merriwell at Yale *(1903).*

CHAPTER I
A Change of Pitchers

"The game is lost!"

"Sure."

"Yale has not scored since the second inning."

"That's right. She made one in the first and three in the second, and then comes four beautiful whitewashes.[1] Harvard hasn't missed a trick, and the score is 11 to 4 in her favor."

"Lewis, this is awful!"

"Right you are, Jones. Hear those Harvard rooters whoop up! It gives me nervous prostration."

"And it drives me to drink! Think of coming all the way from New Haven to Boston to see those fresh Harvard Willies[2] do up our boys! How have the mighty fallen! I long for a lodge in some vast wilderness! Little, let's not remain to see the crowning calamity; let's amble forth to the nearest lemonade shop and get tootsy-frooskied.[3] It is the only way to drown our grief."

"Wait a minute, old man. What is Putnam up to now?"

"It is too late for him to be up to anything. No matter what he tries, it will simply prolong the agony. He'd better let her rip and get it over as soon as possible."

Dismal Jones started to slip down from the bleachers and make his way toward the gate, but Lewis Little caught him by the arm and held on, urging him to wait a minute and see what Old Put, the manager of the Yale freshman baseball team, was about to do.

The Yale freshmen were playing the Harvard freshmen on the grounds of the latter team, and quite a large delegation had come on from New Haven to witness the game, which was the second of the series of three arranged between the freshman teams of the two colleges. The first had been played at New Haven, and the third was to be played on neutral ground.

Yale had won the first game by heavy batting, the final score being 12 to 11. As the regular 'varsity nine had likewise won the first of their series with Harvard, the "Sons of Eli"[4] began to think they had a sure thing, and those who came on from New Haven were dead sure in their minds that they would bring back the scalps of the Harvard freshmen. They said over and over that there would be no need of a third game to settle the matter; Yale would settle it in the second.

Walter Gordon had pitched the whole of the first Harvard game. He had been hammered for thirteen singles, two two-baggers, and a three-bagger, and still Yale had pulled out, which was rather remarkable. But Walter had managed to keep Harvard's hits scattered, while Yale bunched their hits in two innings, which was just enough to give them the winning score.

It was said that Frank Merriwell was to be given a show in the second game, and a large number of Yale men who were not freshmen had come on to see what he would do. Pierson, the manager of the 'varsity nine, had been particularly anxious to see Merriwell work, and he had taken a great deal of trouble to come on. The "great and only" Bob Collingwood, of the 'varsity crew, had accompanied Pierson, and both were much disappointed, not to say disgusted, when Old Put, the manager of the freshmen, put in Gordon and kept him in the box, despite the fact that he was being freely batted.

"What's the matter with Putnam?" growled Pierson. "Has he got a grudge against Merriwell, or does he intend to lose this game anyway?"

"He's asleep," said Collingwood, wearily. "He's stuck on Gordon."

"He must be thick if he can't see Gordon is rapidly losing his nerve. Why, the fellow is liable to go to pieces at any minute and let those Willies run in a score that will be an absolute disgrace."

"Go down and talk to him, Pierson."

"Not much! I am too well known to the Harvard gang. They wouldn't do a thing to me—not a thing!"

"Then let's get out of here. It makes me sick to hear that Harvard yell. I can't stand it, Pierson."

"Wait. I want to see Merriwell go into the box, if they will let him at all. That's what I came for."

"But he can't save the game now. The Yale crowd is not doing any batting. All Harvard has to do is hold them down, and they scarcely have touched Coulter since the second inning."

"That's right, but the fellow is easy, Coll. If they ever should get onto him——"

"How can they? They are not batters."

Pierson nodded.

"That is true," he admitted. "They are weak with the stick. Diamond is the only man who seems to know how to go after a ball properly. He is raw, but there is mighty good stuff in that fellow. If he sticks to baseball he will be on the regular team before he finishes his course."

"I believe Merriwell has shown up well as a batter in practice."

"He certainly has."

"Well, I should think Old Put would use him for his hitting, if for nothing else. He is needed."

"It seems to me that there is a nigger in the woodpile."[5]

"You think Merriwell is held back for reasons not known?"

"I do."

"Say, by jingoes! I am going down and talk to Putnam. If he doesn't give Merriwell a trial he's a chump."

"Hold on."

"What for? If I wait, it will be too late for Merriwell to go in on the first of the seventh."

"Perhaps Merriwell may stand on his dignity and refuse to go in at all at this late stage of the game." ·

"He wouldn't be to blame if he did, for he can't win it out."

"Something is up. Hello! Merriwell is getting out of his sweater! I believe Putnam is going to send him out!"

There was great satisfaction in Pierson's voice. At last it seemed that he would get a chance to see Merriwell work.

"Somebody ought to go down and rap Putnam on the coco[6] with a big heavy club!" growled Collingwood. "He should have made the change long ago. The Harvard Willies have been piling up something every inning."

Down on the visitors' bench Merriwell was seen to peel off, while Gordon was talking rather excitedly to Burnham Putnam. It seemed evident by his manner that he was speaking of something that did not please him very much.

Merriwell was pulled out of his sweater, and then somebody tossed him a practice ball. Little Danny Griswold, the Yale shortstop, put on a catcher's mitt and prepared to catch Frank.

Yale was making a last desperate struggle for a score in the sixth inning. With one man out and a man on first, a weak batter came up. If the batter tried to get a hit, it looked like a great opportunity for a double play by Harvard.

Old Put, who was in uniform, ran down to first, and sent in the coacher, whose place he took on the line. Then he signaled the batter to take one, his signal being obeyed, and it proved to be a ball.

Put was a great coacher, and now he opened up in a lively way, with Robinson rattling away over by third. Put was not talking simply to rattle the pitcher; he was giving signals at the same time, and he signed for the man on first to go down on the next pitch, at the same time giving the batter the tip to make a fake swing at the ball to bother the catcher.

This programme was carried out, and it worked, for the runner got second on a slide and a close decision.

Then the Yale rooters opened their throats, and blue banners fluttered in a bunch over on the bleachers where the New Haven gang was packed together.

"Yell, you suckers, yell!" cried Dickson, Harvard's first baseman. "It's the only chance you'll get."

His words were drowned in the tumult of noise.

Up in the grand stand there was a waving of blue flags and white handkerchiefs, telling that there were not a few of the fair spectators who sympathized with the boys from New Haven.

Then the man at the bat reached first on a scratch hit and a fumble, and there seemed to be a small rift in the clouds which had lowered over the heads of the Yale freshmen so long.

But the next man up promptly fouled out, and the clouds seemed to close in again as dark as ever.

In the mean time Frank Merriwell was warming up with the aid of Danny Griswold, and Walter Gordon sat on the bench, looking sulky and downcast.

"Gordon is a regular pig," said one of the freshmen players to a companion. "He doesn't know when he has had enough."

"Well, we know we have had enough of him this game" said the other, sourly. "If we had played a rotten fielding game Harvard would have a hundred now."

"Well, nearly that," grinned the first speaker. "Gordon hasn't struck out a man."

"And still he is sore because Putnam is going to put Merriwell in! I suppose that is natural, but—— Hi there! look a' that! Great Scott! what sloppy work! Did you see Newton get caught playing off second? Well, that gives me cramps! Come on; he's the last man and we'll have to go out."

So, to the delight of the Harvard crowd, Yale was white-washed again, and there seemed no show for the New Haven boys to win.

Walter Gordon remained on the bench, and Frank Merriwell walked down into the box. Then came positive proof of Merriwell's popularity, for the New Haven spectators rose as one man, wildly waving hats and flags, and gave three cheers and a tiger for Frank.[7]

CHAPTER II
Merriwell Shows His Mettle

"That's what kills him!" exclaimed Pierson in disgust. "It is sure to rattle any green man."

"That's right," yawned Collingwood. "It's plain we have wasted our time in coming here to-day."

"It looks that way from the road. Why couldn't the blamed chumps keep still, so he could show what he is made of?"

"It's ten to one he won't be able to find the plate for five minutes. I believe I can see him shaking from here."

The Harvard crowd had never heard of Merriwell, and they regarded him with no little interest as he walked into the box. When the Yale spectators were through cheering Harvard took it up in a derisive way, and it certainly was enough to rattle any fellow with ordinary nerves.

But Frank did not seem to hear all the howling. He paid no attention to the cheers of his friends or the jeers of the other party. Even when a rude Harvardite proposed three cheers for him, but purposely made the mistake of pronouncing his name as if it were spelled with an "h" in the place of the "w," he did not seem aware that anything unusual was taking place.

"That's what he will give you!" cried one of Frank's admirers at the fellow who had made the jocular call for cheers.

"It would be rather pleasant if he might, but I don't see much show for him," said Collingwood to Pierson.

"Not unless he has nerves of iron," returned the disgusted manager of the 'varsity nine. "Freshmen are always fools!"

"Well, you will make an occasional exception."

"It will be mighty occasional, and that's right."

Merriwell seemed in no great hurry. He made sure that every man was in position, felt of the pitcher's plate with his foot, kicked aside a small pebble, and then took any amount of time in preparing to deliver.

Collingwood began to show some interest. He punched Pierson in the ribs with his elbow and observed:

"Hanged if he acts as if he is badly rattled!"

"That's so. He doesn't seem to be in a hurry," admitted Paul. "He is using his head at the very start, for he is giving himself time to become cool and steady."

"He has Gibson, the best batter on the Harvard team, facing him. Gibson is bound to get a safe hit."

"He is pretty sure to, and that is right."

Merriwell knew that Nort Gibson was the heaviest and surest batter on the Harvard team, but he had been watching the fellow all through the game, trying to "get his alley."[8] He had seen Gibson light on a drop and smash it fiercely, and then he had seen him get a safe hit off a rise, while an outcurve did not fool him at all, as he would bang it if it came over the plate or let it alone when it went outside.

Frank's mind was made up, and he had resolved to give Gibson everything in close to his fingers. Then, if he did hit it, he was not liable to knock it very far.

The first ball Merriwell delivered looked like a pretty one, and Gibson went after it. It was an inshoot, and the batter afterward declared it grazed his knuckles as it passed.

"One strike!" called the umpire.

"What's this! what's this!" exclaimed Collingwood, sitting up and rubbing his eyes. "What did he do anyway?"

"Fooled the batter with a high inshoot," replied Pierson.

"Well, he doesn't seem to be so very rattled, after all."

"Can't tell yet. He did all right that time, but Gibson has two more chances. If he gets a drop or an outcurve that is within his reach, he will kill it."

Ben Halliday was catching for Yale. Rattleton, the change catcher and first baseman, was laid off with a bad finger. He was rooting with the New Haven gang.

Halliday returned the ball and signaled for a rise, but Merriwell shook his head and took a position that meant that he wished to try the same thing over again. Halliday accepted, and then Frank sent in the ball like a shot.

This time it seemed a certain thing that Frank had depended on a high straight ball, and Gibson could not let it pass. He came near breaking his back trying to start the cover on the ball, but once more he fanned the air.

"Great Jupiter!" gasped Collingwood, who was now aroused. "What did he do then, Pierson?"

"Fooled the fellow on the same thing exactly!" chuckled Paul. "Gibson wasn't looking for two in the same place."

Now the freshmen spectators from Yale let themselves out. They couldn't wait for the third strike, but they cheered, blew horns and whistles, and waved flags and hats.

Merriwell had a trick of taking up lots of time in a busy way without pitching the ball while the excitement was too high, and his appearance seemed to indicate that he was totally deaf to all the tumult.

"That's right, Merry, old boy!" yelled an enthusiastic New Haven lad. "Trim his whiskers with them."

"Wind them around his neck, Frank!" cried Harry Rattleton, Merriwell's chum and roommate. "You can do it!"

Harry had been trying to get Putnam to give Frank a chance, but Old Put had held off for reasons that were not apparent at the time. Rattleton had the utmost confidence in his chum, and he had offered to bet that not one of the first three men up would get a safe hit off him. Sport Harris, who was always looking for a chance to risk something, promptly took Harry up, and each placed a "sawbuck"[9] in the hands of Deacon Dunning.

"I am sorry for you, Harris," laughed Rattleton after Gibson had missed the second time, "but he's going to use them all that way."

"Wait, my boy," returned Sport, coolly. "I am inclined to think this man will get a hit yet."

"I'll go you ten to five he doesn't."

"Done!"

They had no time to put up the money, for Merriwell was at work again, and they were eager to watch him.

The very next ball was an outcurve, but it was beyond Gibson's reach and he calmly let it pass. Then followed a straight one that was on the level with the top of the batter's head, and Gibson afterward expressed regret that he did not try it. The third was low and close to Gibson's knees.

Three balls had been called in succession, and the next one settled the matter, for it stood three and two.

"Has he gone to pieces?" anxiously asked Collingwood.

"I don't think so," answered Pierson, "but he has wasted good opportunities trying to pull Gibson. He is in a bad place now."

"You have him in a hole, Gibson," cried a voice. "The next one must be right over, and he can't put it there."

"It looks as if you would win, Rattleton," said Harris in mild disgust. "Merriwell is going to give the batter his base, and so, of course, he will not get a hit."

Harry was nettled, and quick as a flash returned:

"Four balls hits for a go—I mean goes for a hit in this case."

Harris laughed.

"Now I have you, sure," he chuckled.

"In your mind, Sport, old boy."

Merriwell seemed to be examining the pitcher's plate, then he looked up like a flash, his eyes seeming to sparkle, and with wonderful quickness delivered the ball.

"It's an outcurve," was the thought which flashed through Gibson's mind as he saw the sphere had been started almost directly at him.

If it was an outcurve it seemed certain to pass over the centre of the plate, and it would not do to let it pass. It was speedy, and the batter was forced to make up his mind in a fraction of a second.

He struck at it—and missed!

"Three strikes—batter out!" called the umpire, sharply.

Gibson dropped his stick in a dazed way, muttering:

"Great Scott! it was a straight ball and close to my fingers!"

He might have shouted the words and not been heard, for the Yale rooters were getting in their work for fair. They gave one great roar of delight, and then came the college yell, followed by the freshman cheer. At last they were given an opportunity to use their lungs, after having been comparatively silent for several innings.

"Whoop 'er up for 'Umpty-eight!"[10] howled a fellow with a heavy voice. "What's the matter with 'Umpty-eight?"

"She's all right!" went up the hoarse roar.

"What's the matter with Merriwell?"

"He's all right!" again came that roar.

When the shouting had subsided, Rattleton touched Harris on the shoulder and laughingly asked:

"Do I win?"

"Not yet. There are two more coming."

"But I win just as hard, my boy."

"Hope you do."

The next Harvard batter came up, determined to do something, although he was just a trifle uncertain. He let the first one pass and heard a strike called, which did not please him much. The second one was a coaxer, and he let that go by. The umpire called a ball. The third was a high one, but it looked good, and he tried for it. It proved to be a rise, and he struck under it at least a foot.

Bob Collingwood was growing enthusiastic.

"That Merriwell is full of tricks," he declared. "Think how he secretly coached the freshman crew up on the Oxford stroke last fall and won the race at Saltonstall. If it hadn't been for a traitor nobody would have known what he was doing with the crew, for he wouldn't let them practice at the machines."

"I have had my eye on him ever since he entered Yale," confessed Pierson. "I have seen that he is destined to come to the front."

The batter seemed angry because he had been deceived so easily, and this gave Frank satisfaction, for an angry man can be deceived much easier than one who keeps cool.

Merriwell held them in close on the batter, who made four fouls in succession, getting angrier each moment. By this time an outdrop was the thing to fool him, and it worked nicely.

"Three strikes and out!" called the umpire.

Frank had struck out two men, and the Yale crowd could not cheer loud enough to express their delight.

Old Put was delighted beyond measure, but he was keeping pretty still, for he knew what he was sure to hear if Yale did not pull the game out some way. He knew everybody would be asking him why he did not put Merriwell in the box before.

Lewis Little was hugging himself with satisfaction, while Dismal Jones' long face actually wore something suggestive of a grim smile.

Rattleton felt like standing on his head and kicking up his heels with the delight he could not express.

"Oh, perhaps they will give Frank a show after this!" he

thought. "Didn't I tell Put, the blooming idiot? It took him a long time to get out of his trance."

Sport Harris coolly puffed away at a black cigar, seeming perfectly unconcerned, like a born gambler. He had black hair and a faint line of a mustache. He was rather handsome in a way, but he had a pronounced taste for loud neckties.

The next batter to come up was nervous, as could be seen at a glance. He did not wish to strike out, but he was far too eager to hit the ball, and he went after a bad one at the very start, which led him to get a mild call down from the bench.

Then the fellow let a good one pass, which rattled him worse than ever. The next looked good and he swung at it.

He hit it, and it went up into the air, dropping into Merriwell's hands, who did not have to step out of his tracks to get it.

Yale had whitewashed Harvard for the first time in that game.

CHAPTER III
The Game Grows Hotter

By the noise the Yale crowd made one might have fancied the game was theirs beyond a doubt.

"Poor fellows!" said one languid Harvardite to an equally languid companion. "It's the only chawnce they have had to cheer. Do let them make a little noise."

"Yas," said his companion, "do. It isn't at all likely they will get another opportunity during this game."

There were cheers for Merriwell, but Frank walked to the bench and put on his sweater as if utterly unconscious of the excitement he had created. His unconcerned manner won fresh admiration for him.

Old Put congratulated Frank as soon as the bench was reached.

"That was great work, Merriwell. Keep it up! keep it up!"

"That kind of work will not win the game as the score stands," returned Frank. "Some batting must be done, and there must be some score getting."

"You are right, and you are the second man up this inning. See what you can do."

"If I had known I came so soon I wouldn't have put on my sweater."

"Keep it on. You must not get chilly. We can't tell what may happen. Harder games than this have been pulled out. They lead us but five scores."

"Blossom bats ahead of me, does he? Well, he never got a hit when one was wanted in all his life; but he's got a trick that is just as good, if he will try to work it."

"Getting hit by the ball? He is clever at that. Tell him to work the dodge this time if he can. Get him onto first some way. We must have some scores, if we steal them.

"I wish we might steal a few."

"If I get first and Blossom is ahead of me on second, let us try the double steal. I may be caught at second or he may be caught at third, and there is a bare possibility that we'll both make our bags. At any rate, but one of us is liable to be caught, and if it is Blossom it will leave us scarcely any worse off than before. If it is myself, why, Blossom will be on third, we'll have one man out, and stand a good show of scoring once at least."

Merriwell said this in a quiet manner, not at all as if he were trying to dictate, and Putnam made no reply. However, he spoke to Blossom, who was picking out his bat.

"Look here, Uncle," he said, "I want you to get first base in some way. Do you understand?—in some way. If you can't make a hit or get it on balls, get hit."

Blossom made a wry face.

"Coulter's got speed to burn," he said, "but I'll try to get hit if he gives me an in, even though it kills me."

"That's what I want," returned Old Put, grimly. "Never mind if it does kill you. We are after scores, and a life or two is of small consequence."

"That's a pleasant way of looking at it," muttered Blossom as he advanced to the plate. "Here goes nothing!"

The very first ball was an inshoot, and Blossom pretended to dodge and slip. The ball took him in the side and keeled him over instantly. He was given a little water, whereupon he got up and trotted down to first, his hand clinging to his side, but grinning a bit in a sly way.

There was a brief discussion about giving Blossom a runner, but when one was chosen who could not run as well as he could himself, he suddenly found himself in condition to get along all right.

Merriwell took his place at the plate, having selected a bat that was a trifle over regulation length, if anything. His favorite ball was an outcurve that he could reach, and he needed a long bat.

Frank saw a hole in right field, and he hoped to be able to place a hit right there. If he could do it, there was a chance for Blossom to get around to third on a single.

Coulter knew nothing of Merriwell's batting, and so he was forced to experiment on the man. He tried a drop that almost hit the plate, but Frank did not bite. Then Coulter sent over a high one, and still Merriwell refused to swing, and two balls had been called.

Coulter had a trick of holding a man close on first, and so Blossom had not obtained lead enough to attempt to steal second.

Frank felt that Coulter would make an attempt to get the next one over the outside or inside corner of the plate, as it would not do to have three balls in succession called without a single strike.

Merriwell was right. Coulter sent one over the inside corner, using a straight ball. Still Merriwell did not offer at it, for he could not have placed it in the right field if he had tried.

"One strike!" called the umpire.

Although he seemed quite unconcerned, Sport Harris had been nettled when Rattleton won the ten-dollar bet, and he now said:

"I will go you even money, Rattleton, that Merriwell does not get a hit. If he goes down on four balls the bet is off."

"I'll stand you," nodded Harry, laughingly. "Why, Harris, I

When the shouting had subsided in a measure, Rattleton was heard to shout from his perch on the shoulders of a comrade, to which position he had shinned in his excitement:

"Right here is where we trick our little do, gentlemen—er—I mean we do our little trick. Ready to the air of 'Oh, Give Us a Drink, Bartender.'[12] Let her go!"

Then the Yale crowd broke into an original song, the words of which were:

> "Oh, hammer it out, Old Eli, Old Eli,
>   As you always have, you know;
>   For it's sure that we're all behind you, behind you,
>   And we will cheer you as you go.
> We're in the game to stay, my lads, my lads,
>   We will win it easily, too;
> So give three cheers for old 'Umpty-eight—
> Three cheers for the boys in blue!

> "Breka Co ax, Co ax, Co ax!
> Breka Co ax, Co ax, Co ax!
>   O—up! O—up!
>   Parabaloo—
>   Yale! Yale! Yale!
>   "Rah! 'rah! 'rah!
>   Yale!"

The enthusiasm which this created was immense, and the next man walked up to the plate filled with determination. However, Old Put was shrewd enough to know the man might be too eager, and so he gave the signal for him to take one anyway.

Coulter was decidedly nervous, as was apparent to everybody, and it seemed that there was a chance of getting him badly rattled. That was exactly what the Yale crowd was doing its best to accomplish.

Merriwell crept away from first for a long lead, but it was not easy to get, as Coulter drove him back with sharp throws each time. Then Blossom came near being caught napping off second, but was given "safe" on a close decision.

Suddenly Coulter delivered, and the batter obeyed Old Put and did not offer, although it was right over the heart of the plate.

"One strike!" was called.

Now came the time for the attempted double steal that Frank had suggested. Putnam decided to try it on, and he signaled for it. At the same time he signaled the batter to make a swing to bother the catcher, but not to touch the ball.

Frank pretended to cling close to first, but he was watching for Coulter's slightest preliminary motion in the way of delivery. It came, and old Put yelled from the coach line, where he had replaced Griswold:

"Gear!"

Frank got a beautiful start, and Blossom made a break for third. If Blossom had secured a lead equal to Merriwell's he would have made third easily. As it was, the catcher snapped the ball down with a short-arm throw, and Blossom was caught by a foot.

Then it was Harvard's turn, and the Cambridge lads made the most of it. A great roar went up, and the crimson seemed to be fluttering everywhere.

"Har-vard! Har-vard! Har-vard! 'Rah! 'rah! 'rah! 'Rah! 'rah! 'rah! 'Rah! 'rah! 'rah! Har-vard!"

One strike and one ball had been called on the batter, and Merriwell was on second, with one man out. Yale was still longing vainly for scores. It began to look as if they would still be held down, and Coulter was regaining his confidence.

Frank was aware that something sensational must be done to keep Coulter on the string. He longed for an opportunity to steal third, but knew he would receive a severe call down from Old Put if he failed. Still he was ready to try if he found the opportunity.

Frank took all the lead he could secure, going up with the shortstop every time the second baseman played off to fill the right-field gap. He was so lively on his feet that he could go back ahead of the baseman every time, and Coulter gave up trying to catch him after two attempts.

Frank took all the ground he could, and seeing the next ball was an outdrop, he legged it for third.

"Slide! slide! slide!" howled the astonished Halliday, who was still on the coach line at third.

Frank obeyed, and he went over the ground as if he had been greased for the occasion. He made the steal with safety, having a second to spare.

Rattleton lost his breath yelling, and the entire Yale crowd howled as one man. The excitement was at fever pitch.

Bob Collingwood was gasping for breath, and he caught hold of Paul Pierson, shouting in his ear:

"What do you think of that?"

"Think of it?" returned Pierson. "It was a reckless piece of work, and Merriwell would have got fits if he'd failed."

"But he didn't fail."

"No; that lets him out. He is working to rattle Coulter, but he took desperate chances. I don't know but it's the only way to win this game."

"Of course it is."

"Merriwell is a wonderful runner. I found that out last fall, when I made up as Professor Grant and attempted to relieve him of a turkey he had captured somewhere out in the country. I blocked his road at the start, but he slugged me with the turk and then skipped. I got after him, and you know I can run some. Thought I was going to run him down easily or make him drop the bird; but I didn't do either and he got away. Oh, he is a sprinter, and it is plain he knows how to steal bases. I believe he is the best base runner on the freshman team, if he is not too reckless."

"He is a dandy!" exclaimed Collingwood. "I have thought the fellow was given too much credit, but I've changed my mind. Pierson, I believe he is swift enough for the regular team. What do you think about it?"

"I want to see more of his work before I express myself."

Merriwell's steal had indeed rattled Coulter, who became so nervous that he sent the batter down to first on four balls.

Then, with the first ball delivered to the next man up, the fellow on first struck out for second.

Merriwell was playing off third, and pretended to make a break for home as the catcher made a short throw to the short-stop, who ran in behind Coulter, took the ball and lined it back to the plate.

But Frank had whirled about and returned to third, so the play was wasted, and the runner reached second safely.

Then there was more Yale enthusiasm, and Coulter was so broken up that he gave little Danny Griswold a shoulder ball right over the heart of the plate.

Griswold "ate" high balls, as the Harvard pitcher very well knew. He did not fail to make connection with this one, and drove it to deep left for two bags, bringing in two scores.

CHAPTER IV

The End of the Game

Now the New Haven crowd took their turn, and took it in earnest. Rattleton stood upon the shoulders of a friend, and fell off upon the heads of the crowd as he was cheering. He didn't mind that, for he kept right on cheering.

"Merriwell, I believe you have broken the streak!" cried Old Put, with inexpressible satisfaction.

"Well, I sincerely hope so," returned Frank. "I rather think we are all right now, but we've got a hard pull ahead of us. Harvard is still five in the lead, you know."

"If you can hold them down——"

"I am going to do my best."

"If you save this game the boys won't do a thing when we get back to New Haven—not a thing!"

The next batter flied out to shortstop, and Griswold remained on second.

Now there was suspense, for Yale had two men out. A sudden hush fell on the field, broken only by the voices of the two coachers.

Coulter had not recovered his nerve, and the next batter got a safe hit into right field, while Danny Griswold's short legs fairly twinkled as he scudded down to third and then tore up the dust in a mighty effort to get home on a single.

Every Yale man was on his feet cheering again, and Danny certainly covered ground in a remarkable manner. Head first he went for the plate.

The right fielder secured the ball and tried to stop Danny at the plate by a long throw. The throw was all right, but Griswold was making too much speed to be caught.

The instant Old Put, who had returned to the coach line, saw that the fielder meant to throw home, he howled for the batter to keep right on for second.

Griswold scored safely, and the catcher lost little time in throwing to second.

"Slide!" howled a hundred voices.

The runner obeyed, and he got in under the baseman, who had been forced to take a high throw.

It is impossible to describe what followed. The most of the Yale spectators acted as if they had gone crazy, and those in sympathy with Harvard showed positive alarm.

Two or three men got around the captain of the Harvard team and asked him to take out Coulter.

"Put in Peck!" they urged. "They've got Coulter going, and he will lose the game right here if you do not change."

At this the captain got angry and told them to get out. When he got ready to change, he would do so without anybody's advice.

Coulter continued to pitch, and the next batter got first on an error by the shortstop.

"The whole team is going to pieces!" laughed Paul Pierson. "I wouldn't be surprised to see Old Put's boys pull the game out in this inning, for all that two men are out."

"If they do so, Merriwell is the man who will deserve the credit," said Collingwood. "That is dead right."

"Yes, it is right, for he restored confidence and started the work of rattling Coulter."

"Paul," said the great man of the 'varsity crew, "that fellow is fast enough for the regular team."

"You said so before."

"And I say so again."

Now it became evident to everybody that Coulter was in a pitiful state, for he could not find the plate at all, and the next man went down on four balls, filling the bases.

But that was not the end of it. The next batter got four balls, and a score was forced in.

Then it was seen that Peck, Harvard's change pitcher, was warming up, and it became evident that the captain had decided to put him into the box.

If the next Yale man had not been altogether too eager to get a hit, there is no telling when the inning would have stopped. He sent a high-fly foul straight up into the air, and the catcher succeeded in gathering it in.

The inning closed with quite a change in the score, Harvard having a lead of but three, where it had been seven in the lead at the end of the sixth.

"I am afraid they will get on to Merriwell this time," said Sport Harris, with a shake of his head.

"Hey!" squealed Rattleton, who was quivering all over. "I'll give you a chance to even up with me. I'll bet you twenty that Harvard doesn't score."

"Oh, well, I'll have to stand you, just for fun," murmured Harris as he extracted a twenty-dollar bill from the roll it was said he always carried and handed it to Deacon Dunning. "Shove up your dough, Rattle."

Harry covered the money promptly, and then he laughed.

"This cakes the take—I mean takes the cake! I never struck such an easy way of making money! I say, fellows, we'll open something after the game, and I'll pay for it with what I win off Harris."

"That will be nice," smiled Harris; "but you may not be loaded with my money after the game."

The very first batter up got first on an error by the second baseman, who let an easy one go through him.

"The money is beginning to look my way as soon as this," said Harris.

"It is looking your way to bid you good-by," chuckled Harry, not in the least disturbed or anxious.

Merriwell had a way of snapping his left foot out of the box for a throw to first, and it kept the runner hugging the bag all the time.

Frank also had another trick of holding the ball in his hand and appearing to give his trousers a hitch, upon which he would deliver the ball when neither runner nor batter was expecting him to do so, and yet his delivery was perfectly proper.

He struck the next man out, and the batter to follow hit a weak one to third, who stopped the runner at second.

Two men were out, and still there was a man on first. Now it looked dark for Harvard that inning, and not a safe hit had been made off Merriwell thus far.

The Harvard crowd was getting anxious. Was it possible that Merriwell would hold them down so they could not score, and Yale would yet pull out by good work at the bat?

The captain said a few words to the next batter before the man went up to the plate, and Frank felt sure the fellow had been advised to take his time.

Having made up his mind to this, Frank sent a swift straight one directly over, and, as he had expected, the batter let it pass, which caused the umpire to call a strike.

Still keeping the runner hugging first, Frank seemed to start another ball in exactly the same manner. It was not a straight one, but it was a very slow drop, as the batter discovered after he had commenced to swing. Finding he could not recover, the fellow went after the ball with a scooping movement, and then did not come within several inches of it, greatly to the delight of the Yale crowd.

"Oh, Merry has every blooming one of them on a string!" cried Rattleton. "He thon't do a wing to 'em—I mean he won't do a thing to 'em."

The Yale men were singing songs of victory already, and the Harvard crowd was doing its best to keep up the courage of its team by rooting hard.

It was a most exciting game.

"The hottest game I ever saw played by freshmen," commented Collingwood.

"It is a corker," confessed Pierson. "We weren't looking for anything of the sort a short time ago."

"I should say not. Up to the time Merriwell went in it looked as if Harvard had a walkover."

"Gordon feels bad enough about it, that is plain. He is trying to appear cheerful on the bench, but——"

"He can't stand it any longer; he's leaving."

That was right. Gordon had left the players' bench and was walking away. He tried to look pleased at the way things were going, but the attempt was a failure.

"Merriwell is the luckiest fellow alive," he thought. "If I had stayed in another inning the game might have turned. He is pitching good ball, but I'm hanged if I can understand why they do not hit him. It looks easy."

Neither could the Harvard lads thoroughly understand it, although there were some who realized that Merriwell was using his head, as well as speed and curves. And he did not use speed all the time. He had a fine change of pace, sandwiching in his slow balls at irregular intervals, but delivering them with what seemed to be exactly the same motion that he used on the speedy ones.

The fourth batter up struck out, and again Harvard was retired without a score, which caused the Yale crowd to cheer so that some of the lads got almost black in the face.

"Well! well! well!" laughed Rattleton as Deacon Dunning passed over the money he had been holding. "This is like chicking perries—I mean picking cherries. All I have to do is to reach out and take what I want."

"If the boys will capture the game I'll be perfectly satisfied to lose," declared Harris, who did not tell the truth, however, for he was chagrined, although he showed not a sign of it.

"How can we lose? how can we lose?" chuckled Harry. "Things are coming our way, as the country editor said when he was rotten-egged by the mob."

It really seemed that Yale was out for the game at last, for they kept up their work at the bat, although Peck replaced Coulter in the box for Harvard.

Merriwell had his turn with the first batter up. One man was out, and there was a man on second. Coulter had warned Peck against giving Merriwell an outcurve. At the same time, knowing Frank had batted to right field before, the fielders played over toward right.

"So you are on to that, are you?" thought Frank. "Well, it comes full easier for me to crack 'em into left field if I am given an inshoot."

Two strikes were called on him before he found anything that suited him. Harris was on the point of betting Rattleton odds that Merriwell did not get a hit, when Frank found what he was looking for and sent it sailing into left. It was not a rainbow,[13] so it did not give the fielder time to get under it, although he made a sharp run for it.

Then it was that Merriwell seemed to fly around the bases, while the man ahead of him came in and scored. At first the hit looked like a two-bagger, but there seemed to be a chance of making three out of it as Frank reached second, and the coachers sent him along. He reached third ahead of the ball, and then the Yale crowd on the bleachers did their duty.

"How do you Harvard chaps like Merriwell's style?" yelled a Yale enthusiast as the cheering subsided.

Then there was more cheering, and the freshmen of 'Umpty-eight were entirely happy.

The man who followed Frank promptly flied out to first, which quenched the enthusiasm of the Yale gang somewhat and gave Harvard's admirers an opportunity to make a noise.

Frank longed to get in his score, which would leave Harvard with a lead of but one. He felt that he must get home some way.

Danny Griswold came to the bat.

"Get me home some way, Danny," urged Frank.

The little shortstop said not a word, but there was determination in his eyes. He grasped his stick firmly and prayed for one of his favorite high balls.

But Peck kept them low on Danny, who took a strike, and then was pulled on a bad one.

With two strikes on him and only one ball, the case looked desperate for Danny. Still he did not lose his nerve. He did not think he could not hit the ball, but he made himself believe that he was bound to hit it. To himself he kept saying:

"I'll meet it next time—I'll meet it sure."

He knew the folly of trying to kill the ball in such a case, and so when he did swing, his only attempt was to meet it squarely. In this he succeeded, and he sent it over the second baseman's head, but it fell short of the fielder.

Merriwell came home while Griswold was going down to first.

And now it needed but one score for Yale to tie Harvard.

The man who followed Griswold dashed all their hopes by hitting a weak one to short and forcing Danny out at second.

Harvard cheered their men as they came in from the field.

"We must make some scores this time, boys," said the Harvard captain. "A margin of one will never do, with those fellows hitting anything and everything."

"That's exactly what they are doing," said Peck. "They are getting hits off balls they have no business to strike at."

"Oh, you are having your troubles," grinned a friend.

"Anyone is bound to have when batters are picking them off the clouds or out of the dirt. It doesn't make much difference where they are."

"This man Merriwell can't hold us down as he has done," asserted Dickson, Harvard's first baseman.

"I don't know; he is pretty cagey," admitted Nort Gibson.

"I believe he is the best pitcher we'll strike this season," said another.

"Here, here, you fellows!" broke in the captain. "You are getting downhearted, and that won't do. We've got this game and we are going to hold it; but we want to go in to clinch it right here."

They didn't do much clinching, for although the first man up hit the ball, he got to first on an error by the third baseman, who fumbled in trying to pick it up.

Blossom was the third baseman, and he was confused by his awkwardness, expecting to get a call down.

"Steady, Blos, old boy!" said Frank, gently. "You are all right. The best of us do those things occasionally. It is nothing at all."

These words relieved Blossom's feelings and made him vow that he would not let another ball play chase around his feet.

Frank struck the next man out, and held the runner on first while he was doing it. The third man sent an easy pop-fly to Blossom, who got hold of it and clung to it for dear life.

Then the runner got second on a passed ball, but he advanced no further, for the following batter rolled a weak one down to Frank, who gathered it in and threw the man out at first.

In three innings not a safe hit had been made off Merriwell, and he had struck out five men. No wonder his admirers cheered him wildly as he went to the bench.

Yale started in to make some scores. The very first man up got a hit and stole second. The next man went to the bat with the determination to slug the ball, but Old Put signaled for a sacrifice, as the man was a good bunt hitter.

The sacrifice was tried, and it worked, for the man on second got third, although the batter was thrown out at first.

"Now we need a hit!" cried Put. "It takes one to tie and two to win. A hit ties the game."

Rattleton offered to bet Harris two to one that Yale would win, but Sport declined the offer.

"It's our game fast enough," he said. "You are welcome to what you won off me. I am satisfied."

But the game was not won. Amid the most intense excitement the next man fouled out.

Then Peck seemed to gather himself to save the game for Harvard. He got some queer quirks into his delivery, and, almost before the Yale crowd could realize it, two strikes were called on the batter.

The Yale rooters tried to rattle Peck, but they succeeded in rattling the batter instead, and, to their unutterable dismay and horror, he fanned at a third one, missed it, and—

"Batter is out!" cried the umpire.

Then a great roar for Harvard went up, and the dazed freshmen from New Haven realized they were defeated after all.

CHAPTER V
Rattleton Is Excited

"It wasn't Merriwell's fault that the freshies didn't win," said Bob Collingwood to Paul Pierson as they were riding back to New Haven on the train that night.

"Not a bit of it," agreed Pierson. "I was expecting a great deal of Merriwell, but I believe he is a better man than I thought he could be."

"Then you have arrived at the conclusion that he is fast enough for the regular team?"

"I rather think he is."

"Will you give him a trial?"

"We may. It is a bad thing for any freshman to get an exalted opinion of himself and his abilities, for it is likely to spoil him. I don't want to spoil Merriwell——"

"Look here," interrupted Collingwood, impulsively. "I am inclined to doubt if it is an easy thing to spoil that fellow. He hasn't put on airs since coming to Yale, has he?"

"No."

"Instead of that, he has lived rather simply—far more so than most fellows would if they could afford anything better. He has made friends with everybody who appeared to be white,[14] no matter whether their parents possessed boodle[15] or were poor."

"That is one secret of Merriwell's popularity. He hasn't shown signs of thinking himself too good to be living."

"Yet I have it straight that he has a fortune in his own right, and he may live as swell as he likes while he is here. What do you think of that?"

"It may be true," admitted Pierson. "He is an original sort of chap——"

"But they say there isn't anything small or mean about him," put in Collingwood, swiftly. "He isn't living cheap for economy's sake. You know he doesn't drink."

"Yes. I have made many inquiries about his habits."

"Still they say he opens wine for his friends now and then, drinking ginger ale, or something of that sort, while they are surrounding fizz, for which he settles. And he is liberal in other ways."

"He is an enigma in some ways."

"I have heard a wild sort of story about him, but I don't take much stock in it. It is the invention of some fertile brain."

"What is it?"

"Oh, a lot of trash about his having traveled all over the world, been captured by pirates and cannibals, fought gorillas and tigers, shot elephants and so forth. Of course that's all rot."

"Of course. What does he say about it?"

"Oh, he simply laughs at the stories. If a fellow asks him point blank if they are true he tells him not to let anybody string him. He seems to regard the whole business as a weak sort of joke that some fellow is trying to work."

"Without doubt that's what it is, for he's too young to have had such adventures. Besides that, there's no fellow modest enough to deny it if he had."

"Of course there isn't."

In this way that point was settled in their minds, for the time, at least.

There was no band to welcome 'Umpty-eight back to New Haven. No crowd of cheering freshmen was at the station, and those who had gone on to Cambridge to play and to see the game got off quietly—very quietly—and hurried to their rooms.

Merriwell was in his room ahead of Rattleton. Harry finally appeared, wearing a sad and doleful countenance.

"What's the matter, old man?" asked Frank as Harry came in and flung his hat on the floor, after which he dropped upon a chair. "You do not seem to feel well."

"I should think you would eel felegant—I mean feel elegant!" snapped Harry, glaring at Frank.

"Oh, what's the use to be all broken up over a little thing?"

"Wow! Little thing!" whooped Harry. "I'd like to know what you call a little thing—I would, by jee!"

"You are excited, my boy. Calm down somewhat."

"Oh, I am calm!" shouted Harry as he jumped up and kicked the chair flying into a corner. "I am perfectly calm!" he roared, tearing up and down the room. "I never was calmer in all my life!"

"You look it!" came in an amused manner from Frank's lips. "You are so very calm that it is absolutely soothing and restful to the nerves to observe you!"

Harry stopped short before Frank, thrust his hands deep into his pockets, hunched his shoulders, thrust his head forward, and glared fiercely into Merriwell's face.

"There are times when it positively is a crime not to swear," he hoarsely said. "It seems to me that this is one of the times. If you will cuss a little it will relieve my feelings immensely."

"Why don't you swear?" laughed Frank.

"Why don't I? Poly hoker—no, holy poker! I have been swearing all the way from Cambridge to New Haven, and I have completely run out of profanity."

"Well, I think you have done enough for both of us."

"Oh, indeed! Well, that is hard on me! I came in here expecting to find you breaking the furniture, and you are as calm and serene as a summer's morning. I tell you, Frank, it is an awful shock! And you are the one who should do the most swearing. I can't understand you, hanged if I can!"

"Well, you know there is an old saw[16] that says it is useless to cry over spilled milk——"

"Confound your old saws! Crying and swearing are two different things. Don't you ever cuss, Frank?"

"Never."

"Well, I'd like to know how you can help it on an occasion like this! That is what gets me."

"Never having acquired the habit, it is very easy to get along without swearing, which is, beyond a doubt, the most foolish habit a man can get into."

Rattleton held up both hands, with a look of absolute horror on his face.

"Don't—don't preach, now!" he protested. "I think the habit of swearing is a blessing sometimes—an absolute blessing. A man can relieve his feelings that way when he can't any other."

"You don't seem to have succeeded in relieving your feelings much."

"I don't? Well, you should have seen me when I got aboard the train! I was at high pressure, and there was absolute danger of an explosion. I just had to open the safety valve and blow off. And I find you as calm as a clock! Oh, Frank, it is too much—too much!"

Harry pretended to weep.

CHAPTER VI
Harry Explains Matters

Frank sat down.

"Go it, old man," he smiled. "You will feel better pretty soon."

"I don't know whether I will or not!" snapped Harry. "It was a sheastly bame—I mean a beastly shame! That game was ours!"

"Not quite. It came very near being ours."

"It was! Why, you actually had it pulled out! You held those fellows down and never gave them a single safe hit! That was wonderful work!"

"Oh, I don't know. They are not such great batters."

"Gordon found them pretty fast. I tell you some of those fellows are batters—good ones, too."

"Well, they didn't happen to get onto my delivery."

"Happen! happen! happen! There was no happen about it! They couldn't get onto you. You had them at your mercy. It was wonderful pitching, and I can lick the gun of a son—er—son of a gun that says it wasn't!"

"I had a chance to size every man up while Gordon was pitching, and that gave me the advantage."

"That makes me tired! Of course you had time to size them up; but you couldn't have kept them without a hit if you hadn't been a dandy pitcher. Your modesty is simply sickening sometimes!"

Then Harry pranced up and down the room like an infuriated tiger, almost gnashing his teeth and foaming at the mouth.

"If I didn't think I could pitch some I wouldn't try it," said Frank, quietly. "But I am not fool enough to think I am the only one. There are others."

"Well, they are not freshmen, and I'll tell you that."

"I don't know about that."

"I do."

"All right. Have it as you like it."

"And you batted like a fiend. Twice at bat and two hits—a two-bagger and a three-bagger."

"A single and a three-bagger, if you please."

"Well, what's the matter with that? Whee jiz—I mean jee whiz! Could anybody ask for anything more? You got the three-bagger just when it was needed most, and you would have saved the game if you had come to the bat in the last inning."

"You think so, but it is all guesswork. I might have struck out."

"You might, but you wouldn't. Oh, merry thunder! To think that a little single would have tied that game, and we couldn't get it! It actually makes me ill at the pit of my stomach!"

The expression on Harry's face seemed to indicate that he told the truth, for he certainly looked ill.

"Don't take it to heart so, my boy," said Frank. "The poor devils earned that game, and they ought to have it. We'll win the last one of the series, and that's all we want. Do you want to bury poor old Harvard?"

"You can't bury Harvard so deep that it won't crawl out, and you know that. Those fellows are decidedly soon up at Cambridge, and Yale does well to get all she can from them. You can't tell what will happen next game. They have seen you, and they may have a surprise to spring on us. If we had pulled this game off, the whole thing would be settled now."

"Don't think for a moment that I underestimate Harvard. She is Yale's greatest rival and is bound to do us when she can."

"We made a good bid for the game today, but it wasn't our luck to win, and so we may as well swallow our medicine and keep still."

"It wasn't a case of luck at all," spluttered Harry. "It was sheer bull headedness, that's what it was! If Put had put you in long before he did the game might have been saved."

"He didn't like to pull Gordon out, you see."

"Well, if he's running this team on sentiment, the sooner he quits the better it will be for the team."

Frank said nothing, but he could not help feeling that Harry was right. Managing a ball team is purely a matter of business, and if a manager is afraid to hurt anybody's feelings he is a poor man for the position.

"Why didn't he put you in in the first place?" asked Harry.

"I don't know. I suppose he had reasons."

"Oh, yes, he had reasons! And I rather think I know what they were. I am sure I do."

"You are?"

"You bet!"

"What were they?"

"Didn't you expect to pitch the game from the start to-day?"

"Yes I did."

"I thought so."

Harry nodded, as if fully satisfied that he understood the whole matter.

"Well," said Frank, a bit sharply, "you have not explained yourself. I am curious to know why I was not put into the box at the start."

"Well, I am glad to see you show some emotion, if it is nothing more than curiosity. I had begun to think you would not show as much as that."

"Naturally I am curious."

"Do you know that Paul Pierson, manager of the 'varsity team, went on to see this game?"

"Yes."

"Why do you suppose he did so?"

"Oh, he is acquainted with several Harvard fellows, and I presume he went to see them as much to see the game."

"He wasn't with any Harvard fellows at the game."

"I didn't observe."

"I did."

"Well, what are you trying to get at?"

"Don't be in a hurry," said Harry, who was now speaking with unusual calmness. "You regard Old Put as your friend?"

"I always have."

"But you think he didn't use you just right to-day?"

"I will confess that I don't like to be used to fall back on with the hope that I may pull out a game somebody else has lost."

Harry nodded his satisfaction.

"I knew you would feel that way, unless you had suddenly grown foolish. It's natural and it's right. There is no reason why you shouldn't be the regular pitcher for our team, as you have shown yourself our best man, but still Gordon is regarded as the pitcher, while you are the change pitcher. Frank, there is a nigger in the woodpile."

"You will have to make yourself clearer than that."

"Putnam knew that Pierson was going to be present at the game."

"Well?"

"Pierson didn't go on to see any Harvard friends. He couldn't afford the time just at this season with all he has on his hands."

"Go on."

"Putnam knew Pierson was not there to see any Harvard men."

"Oh, take your time!"

Harry grinned. He was speaking with such deliberation that he did not once twist his words and expressions about, as he often did when excited and in a hurry.

"That's why you wasn't put in at the start-off," he declared.

"What is why? You will have to make the whole matter plainer than you have so far. It is hazy."

"Putnam did not want Pierson to see you pitch."

"He didn't? Why not?"

"Because Pierson was there for that very purpose."

"Get out!"

"I know what I am talking about. You have kept still about it, but Pierson himself has let the cat out of the bag."

"What cat?"

"He has told—confidentially, you know—that he has thoughts of giving you a trial on the regular team. The parties he told repeated it—confidentially, you know—to others. It finally came to my ears. Old Put heard of it. Now, while Old Put seems to be your friend, he doesn't want to lose you, and he had taken every precaution to keep you in the background. He has made Gordon more prominent, and he has not let you do much pitching for Pierson to see. He permitted you to go in to-day because he was afraid Gordon would go all to pieces, and he knew what a howl would go up if he didn't do something."

Frank walked up and down the room. He did not permit himself to show any great amount of excitement, but there was a dark look on his handsome face that told he was aroused. Harry saw that his roommate was stirred up at last.

"As I have said," observed Frank, halting and speaking grimly, "I have regarded Burnham Putnam as my friend; but if he has done as you claim for the reasons you give he has not shown himself to be very friendly. There is likely to be an understanding between us."

Rattleton nodded.

"That's right," he said. "He may deny it, but I know I am not off my trolley. He didn't want Pierson to see you work because he was afraid you would show up so well that Pierson would nail you for the regular team."

"And you think that is why I have been kept in the background so much since the season opened?"

"I am dead sure of it."

"Putnam must have a grudge against me."

"No, Frank; but he has displayed selfishness in the matter. I believe he has considered you a better man than Gordon all along, and he wanted you on the team to use in case he got into a tight corner. That's why he didn't want Pierson to see you work. He didn't want to lose you. But he was forced to use you to-day, and you must have satisfied Pierson that you know your business."

"Well, Harry, you have thrown light on dark places. To-morrow I will have a little talk with Put about this matter."

"That's right," grinned Harry; "and Pierson is liable to have a little talk with you. You'll be on the regular team inside of a week."

CHAPTER VII
What Ditson Wanted

On the following day the great topic of conversation for the class of 'Umpty-eight was the recent ball game. Wherever the freshmen gathered they discussed the game and the work of Gordon and Merriwell.

Gordon was a free-and-easy sort of fellow, and he had his friends and admirers, some of whom were set in their belief that he was far superior to Merriwell as a pitcher.

Roland Ditson attempted to argue on two or three occasions in favor of Gordon, but nobody paid attention to what he said, for it was known that he had tried by every possible means to injure Merriwell and had been exposed in a contemptible piece of treachery, so that no one cared to be known as his friend and associate.

Whenever Ditson would approach a group of lads and try to get in a few words he would be listened to in stony silence for some moments, and then the entire crowd would turn and walk away, without replying to his remarks or speaking to him at all.

This would have driven a fellow less sensitive than Ditson to abandon all hope of going through Yale. Of course it cut Ditson, but he would grind his teeth and mutter:

"Merriwell is to blame for it all, curse him! I won't let him triumph! The time will come when I'll get square with him! I'll have to stay here in order to get square, and stay here I will, no matter how I am treated."

Since his duplicity had been made known and his classmates had turned against him Ditson had taken to grinding in a fierce manner, and as a result he had made good progress in his studies. He was determined to stand ahead of Merriwell in that line, at least, and it really seemed that he might succeed, unless Frank gave more time to his studies and less to athletics.

This was not easy for a fellow in Merriwell's position and with his ardent love for all sorts of manly sports to do. He gave all the time he could to studies without becoming a greasy grind, but that was not as much as he would have liked.

To Ditson's disappointment and chagrin Merriwell seemed quite unaware that his enemy stood ahead of him in his classes. Frank seemed to have quite forgotten that such a person as Roll Ditson existed.

Ditson was an outcast. The fellow with whom he had roomed had left him shortly after his treachery was made public, and he was forced to room alone, as he could get no one to come in with him.

Roll did not mind this so much, however. He pretended that he was far more exclusive than the average freshman, and he tried to imitate the ways of the juniors and seniors, some of whom had swell apartments.

Ditson's parents were wealthy, and they furnished him with plenty of loose change, so that he could cut quite a dash. He had fancied that his money would buy plenty of friends for him. At first, before his real character was known, he had picked up quite a following, but he posed as a superior, which made him disliked by the very ones who helped him spend his money.

He had hoped to be a leader at Yale, but, to his dismay, he found that he did not cut much of a figure after all, and Frank

Merriwell, a fellow who never drank or smoked, was far more popular. Then it was that Ditson conceived a plot to bring Merriwell into ridicule and at the same time to get in with the enemies of the freshmen—the sophomores—himself.

At last he had learned that at Yale a man is not judged so much by the money he spends and the wealth of his parents as by his own manly qualities.

But Ditson was a sneak by nature, and he could not get over it. If he started out to accomplish anything in a square way, he was likely to fancy that it could be done with less trouble in a crooked manner, and his natural instinct would switch him off from the course he should have followed.

He was not at all fond of Walter Gordon, but he liked him better than he did Merriwell, and it was gall and wormwood for him when he heard how Merriwell had replaced Gordon in the box at Cambridge and had pitched a marvelous game for three innings.

"Oh, it's just that fellow's luck!" Roll muttered to himself. "He seems to be lucky in everything he does. The next thing I'll hear is that he is going to pitch on the 'varsity team."

He little thought that this was true, but it proved to be. That very day he heard some sophomores talking on the campus, and he lingered near enough to catch their words.

"Is it actually true, Parker, that Pierson has publicly stated that Merriwell is fast enough for the 'varsity nine?" asked Tad Horner.

"That's what it is," nodded Puss Parker, "and I don't know but Pierson is right. I am inclined to think so."

"Rot!" exclaimed Evan Hartwick, sharply. "I don't take stock in anything of the sort. Merriwell may make a pitcher some day, but he is raw. Why, he would get his eye batted out if he were to go up against Harvard on the regular team."

"Oh, I don't know about that," said Andy Emery. "He is pretty smooth people. Is there anybody knows Pierson made such an observation concerning him?"

"Yes, there is," answered Parker.

"Who knows it?"

"I do."

"Did you hear him?"

"I did."

"That settles it."

"Yes, that settles it!" grated Roland Ditson as he walked away. "Parker didn't lie, and Pierson has intimated that Merriwell may be given a trial on the 'varsity nine. If he is given a trial it will be his luck to succeed. He must not be given a trial. How can that be prevented?"

Then Ditson set himself to devise some scheme to prevent Frank from obtaining a trial on the regular nine. It was not an easy thing to think of a plan that would not involve himself in some way, and he felt that it must never be known that he had anything to do with such a plot.

That night Ditson might have been seen entering a certain saloon in New Haven, calling one of the barkeepers aside, and holding a brief whispered conversation with him.

"Is Professor Kelley in?" asked Roll.

"He is, sir," replied the barkeeper. "Do you wish to see him?"

"Well—ahem!—yes, if he is alone."

"I think he is alone. I do not think any of his pupils are with him at present, sir."

"Will you be kind enough to see?" asked Ditson. "This is a personal matter—something I want kept quiet."

The barkeeper disappeared into a back room, was gone a few minutes, and then returned and said:

"The professor is quite alone. Will you go up, sir?"

"Ye-e-s," said Roll, glancing around, and then motioning for the barkeeper to lead the way.

He was taken into the back room and shown a flight of stairs.

"Knock at the door at the head of the flight," instructed the barkeeper, and after giving the man some money Ditson went up the stairs.

"Come in!" called a harsh voice when he knocked at the door.

He entered a wretched and poorly-furnished room. A big man with a thick neck and bull-dog face was sitting with his feet on a table, while he smoked a strong-smelling cigar. There were illustrated sporting papers on the table, crumpled and ragged, and pictures of prize fighters on the walls.

"Well, young feller, watcher want?" demanded the man, without removing his feet from the table or his hat from his head.

Ditson closed the door. He was very pale and somewhat agitated.

"Are we all alone?" he asked, choking a bit over the question.

"Dat's wot we are," nodded the professor, who was known far and wide as Buster Kelley.

"Is it a sure thing that our conversation cannot be overheard?"

"Dead sure."

Ditson hesitated. He seemed to find it difficult to express himself just as he desired.

"Speak right out, chummy," said Kelley in a manner intended to be reassuring. "I rudder t'inks yer wants ter lick some cove, an' yer've come ter me ter put yer in shape ter do der job. Well, you bet yer dough I'm der man ter do dat. How many lessons will yer have?"

"It is not that at all," declared Roll.

"Not dat?" cried Kelley in surprise. "Den wot do youse want?"

"Well, you see, it is like this—er, like this," faltered Roland. "I—I've got an enemy."

"Well, ain't dat wot I said?"

"But I don't want to fight him."

"Oh, I sees! Yer wants some odder chap ter do der trick?"

"Yes, that is it. But I want them to more than lick him."

"More dan lick him? W'y, yer don't want him killed, does yer?"

"No," answered Ditson, hoarsely; "but I want his right arm broken!"

CHAPTER VIII
Frank's Foe

"Hey?"

Down came Buster Kelley's feet from the table, upon which his knuckles fell, and then he arose from the chair, standing in a crouching position, with his hands resting on the table, across which he glared at Roland Ditson.

"Hey?" he squawked. "Just say dat agin, cully."

Roll was startled, and looked as if he longed to take to his heels and get away as quickly as possible; but he did not run, and he forced himself to say:

"This is a case of business, professor. I will pay liberally to have the job done as I want it."

"An' youse wants a bloke's arm bruck?"

"Yes."

"Well, dis is a quare deal! If yer wanted his head bruck it wouldn't s'prise me; but ter want his arm bruck—jee!"

"I don't care if he gets a rap on the head at the same time, but I don't want him killed. I want his right arm broken, and that is the job I am ready to pay for."

Kelley straightened up somewhat, placed one hand on his hip, while the other still rested on the table, crossed his legs, and regarded Ditson steadily with a stare that made Roll very nervous.

"I might 'a' knowed yer didn't want ter fight him yerself," the professor finally said, and Ditson did not fail to detect the contempt in his face and voice.

"No, I do not," declared Ditson, an angry flush coming to his face. "He is a scrapper, and I do not think I am his match in a brutal fight."

"Brutal is good! An' yer wants his arm bruck? Don't propose to give him no show at all, eh?"

"I don't care a continental[17] what is done so long as he is fixed as I ask."

"I s'pose ye're one of them stujent fellers?"

"Yes, I am a student."

"An' t'other feller is a stujent?"

"Yes."

"Dem fellers is easy."

"Then you will do the job for me, will you?"

"Naw!" snorted Kelley. "Not on yer nacheral! Wot d'yer take me fer? I don't do notting of dat kind. I've got a reperta-tion to sustain, I has."

Ditson looked disappointed.

"I am willing to pay well to have the job done," he said.

"Well, yer can find somebody ter do it fer yer."

"But I don't know where to find anybody, professor."

Kelley sat down, relighted his cigar, restored his feet to the table, picked up a paper, seemed about to resume reading, and then observed:

"Dis is no information bureau, but I s'pose I might put yer onter a cove dat'd do der trick fer yer if youse come down heavy wid der stuff."

"If you will I shall be ever so much obliged."

"Much erbliged don't buy no whisky. Money talks, me boy."

Ditson reached into his pocket and produced some money.

"I will give you five dollars to tell me of a man who will do the job for me," he said, pulling a five-dollar bill from the roll.

"Make it ten an' I goes yer," said Kelley, promptly.

"Done. Here is your money."

Ditson handed it over.

"I'd oughter made it twenty," grumbled the pugilist. "Dis business is outer my line entirely, an' I don't want ter be mixed up in it at all—see? I has a repertation ter sustain, an' it wouldn't do fer nobody ter know I ever hed anyt'ing ter do wid such a job as dis."

"There is no danger that anybody will ever know it," de-clared Ditson, impatiently. "I will not say anything about it."

"Well, yer wants ter see dat yer don't. If yer do, I'll hunt yer up meself, an' I won't do a t'ing ter youse—not a t'ing!"

"Save your threats and come to business. I am impatient to get away, as I do not care to be seen here by anybody who may drop in."

"Don't care ter be seen here! I like dat—nit! Better men dan youse has been here, an' don't yer fergit dat!"

"Oh, I don't care who has been here! You have the money. Now tell me where I can find the man I want."

"D'yer know Plug Kirby?"

"No."

"Well, he is der feller yer wants."

"Where can I find him?"

"I'll give yer his address."

Kelley took a stub of a pencil out of his vest pocket and wrote with great labor on the margin of one of the papers. This writing he tore off and handed to Ditson. Then, without another word, he once more restored his feet to the top of the table and resumed reading as if there was no one in the room.

Ditson went out without a word. When he was gone Kelley looked over the top of the paper toward the door and growled:

"Dat feller's no good! If he'd wanted ter fit der odder feller hisself I'd tole him how ter bruck der odder chap's wrist, but he ain't got der sand ter fight a baby. His kind makes me sad! I'd like ter t'ump him a soaker on de jaw meself."

That evening Merriwell went out to call on some friends. He was returning to his rooms between ten and eleven, when, as he came to a dark corner, a man suddenly stepped out and said:

"Give us a light, young feller."

"I have none," said Frank, attempting to pass.

"Den give us a match," demanded the man, blocking the road.

"As I do not smoke I never carry matches."

"Well, den, I s'pose I'll have ter go wit'out er light, but—you'll take dat!"

Like a flash the man struck straight and hard at the youth's face. It was a wicked blow, delivered with marvelous swiftness, and must have knocked Frank down if it had landed.

But Merriwell had suspected all along that it was not a light the man was after, and he had been on the watch for just such a move as was made. For all of the man's swiftness Frank dodged, and the blow passed over his shoulder.

Now, Frank Merriwell was a trained athlete, and he had made the art of self-defense with his fists a special study. For his age he was a wonderful boxer. He was not a fellow who went around looking for trouble, but once his blood was aroused he did not seem to fear anybody or anything.

When Frank ducked he also struck out with his left, which he planted in the pit of the assailant's stomach.

It was a heavy blow, and for a moment it rounded the man up. Before the ruffian could recover he received a thump under the ear that made him see stars and sent him sprawling.

But the man had a hard head, and he hastily got upon his feet, uttering fierce words. He expected to see the young in full flight, and was astonished to perceive that Frank had not taken to his heels.

With a snarl of fury the wretch rushed at Merriwell.

Frank dodged again and came up under the man's arm, giving him another heavy blow. Then the man turned, and they sparred for a moment.

"Durned if youse ain't der liveliest kid I ever seen!" muttered the astonished ruffian. "Youse kin fight!"

"Well, I can fight enough to take care of myself," returned the lad, with something like a laugh.

Smack! smack! smash! Three blows in rapid succession caused the ruffian to reel and gasp. Then for a few moments the fight was savage and swift.

It did not last long. The ruffian had been drinking, and Frank soon had the best of it. He ended the encounter by striking the man a regular knock-out blow, and the fellow went down in a heap.

When the ruffian recovered he was astonished to find Frank Merriwell had not departed, but was bending over him.

"How do you feel?" the boy calmly inquired.

"Say, I'm all broke up!" was the feeble reply. "Are youse der feller wot done me?"

"I presume I am."

"Well, wot yer waitin' fer?"

"To see how badly you are hurt. Your head struck the stones with frightful force when you fell."

"Did it? Well, it feels dat way! Here's a lump on it as big as yer fist. But wot d'youse care?"

"I didn't know but your skull was fractured."

"Wot difference did dat make?"

"I didn't want you to remain here and suffer with a broken head."

"Didn't, eh? An' I tried ter do ye up widout givin' yer any warnin'! Dis is der quarest deal I ever struck! I was tryin' ter knock yer stiff an' den break yer arm."

"Break my arm?"

"Dat's wot I was here fer."

Frank was interested.

"Then you were here on purpose to meet me?"

"Sure, Mike."[18]

"But why were you going to break my arm?"

" 'Cause dat's wot I was paid fer, me boy."

Frank caught hold of the ruffian, who had risen to a sitting posture and was holding onto his head.

"Paid for?" cried the boy, excitedly. "Do you mean to tell me that you were paid to waylay me and break my arm?"

"I didn't mean ter tell yer anyt'ing, but a feller wot kin fight like you kin an den stay ter see if a chap wot tried ter do him was hurt—dat kind of a feller oughter be told."

"Then tell me—tell me all about it," urged Merriwell.

"Dere ain't much ter tell. Some sneak wanted yer arm broke an' he come ter me ter do der job. He paid me twenty ter lay fer youse an' fix yer. I was hard up an' I took der job, dough I didn't like it much. Den he put me onter yer, an' I follered yer ter der house where youse went dis evenin'. I watched till yer comes out, and den I skips roun' ter head yer off yere. I heads yer an' asks fer a light. Youse knows der rest better dan wot I does."

"Well, I swear this is decidedly interesting! So I have an enemy who wants my arm broken?"

"Yes, yer right arm."

"That would fix me so I'd never pitch any more."

"Dat's wot's likely, if ye're a pitcher."

"Would you know the person who hired you if you were to see him again?"

"Sure."

"Did he give you his name?"

"Dat's wot he did."

"Ha! That's what I want! See here! Tell me his name, or by the gods of war I will see that you are arrested and shoved in jail for this night's work!"

"An' you will let me off if I tells?"

"Yes."

"Swear it."

"I swear it!"

"You won't make a complaint agin' me?"

"I will not."

"Well, den, yere's his card wot he give me."

The ruffian fumbled in his pocket and took out a card, which he passed to Frank who eagerly grasped it.

"Here's a match, me boy," said the man. "I had a pocketful w'en I braced yer for one."

He passed a match to Frank, who hastily struck it on a stone and then held it so that he could read the name that was engraved on the card in his fingers.

A cry of astonishment broke from Merriwell's lips, and both card and match fell from his fingers to the ground.

This is the name he had read upon the card:

"Mr. Burnham Putnam."

CHAPTER IX
Ditson Is Trapped

"It don't make a dit of bifference, Frank!" spluttered Harry Rattleton. "I don't care if you have got his card! That thug lied like blazes! Putnam may be selfish—he may have other faults, but he never hired anybody to break your arm."

"I cannot think he would do such a thing myself," said Frank; "but this Plug Kirby, as he is called, seemed honest and in earnest. He stands ready to identify the fellow any time."

"Then why not settle it by bringing him before Putnam this very afternoon? That's the way to mix the fatter—I mean fix the matter."

"It is a good idea, Harry, and we will have to carry it out. I'll need your assistance."

"You shall have it, old man."

So Frank and Harry arranged to bring Putnam and his accuser together that afternoon, it being the day after the assault on Merriwell. Frank was to look out for Kirby while Harry brought Putnam along to the saloon over which Buster Kelley had rooms.

Frank and Kirby were there in advance, and they sat down in a corner, where they were not likely to be observed by anybody who entered.

Kirby's face was cut and scarred where he had felt Frank's hard fists, and the tough looked on the cool lad with genuine respect and admiration.

"I wants yer ter understan' dat I'd never gone inter dat game if I hadn't been hard up an' in a bad way," he said, trying to apologize for himself. "T'ings have been runnin' agin' me, an' I've been on de rocks fer a long time, an' I didn't know how I was ter make a haul any easier dan by breakin' a kid's arm. It warn't no killin' matter nohow, an' so I took der job. I never s'pected I was ter run up agin' anyt'ing like wot you are. If I had, why, wild hosses wouldn't got me ter tried it."

"My enemy knew enough not to meet me himself."

"Dat's right, an' now I want ter git square wid him fer steerin' me up agin' anyt'ing of der sort. Wot yer goin' ter do wid him—break his neck?"

"I have not decided what I shall do, but I shall not lay a hand on him."

"Yer won't?"

"No."

"Well, I would if I was in your place. I'd t'ump der everlastin' stuffin' outer der bloke—dat's wot!"

"If it is the man whose name is on the card that was given you I shall be sorry for him, for I have always believed him to be a white man."

"An' yer'll be sorry?"

"I will."

"Well, ye're der funniest cove wot I ever saw. After ye hed knocked der wind outer me, ye stayed eround ter see dat I wasn't hurt too bad, w'en anybody else would 'a' kicked me inter der gutter an' left me. An' now youse say dat you'll be sorry fer der feller wot hired me ter do yer! I'd like ter know jes' how ye're put up."

"I can't help being sorry to know that a fellow I have considered white and a friend is crooked and an enemy, if it is to prove that way."

"Say, young feller, I likes you, durn me ef I don't! If you ever has anyt'ing ye wants done, jes' come ter me, an' I'll do it if I kin, an' I won't charge yer nottin'."

"Thank you," smiled Frank; "but I do not fancy I shall have anything in your line. While we are talking, though, let me give you some advice. Turn over a new leaf and try to be on the level. You will find it the best policy in the long run."

"I t'ink ye're right, an' I'm goin' ter try ter do it. I allus did hate ter work, but if I kin git any kind of a job I'm goin' ter try it once more. I don't know w'y it is, but jes' bein' wid youse makes me want ter do der square t'ing."

Frank might well have felt pleased that he exercised such an influence over a man like Plug Kirby.

The door opened and Rattleton came into the saloon, followed by Old Put and Dismal Jones.

"Come on, Kirby," said Frank quietly. "Here is the man we are waiting for."

Putnam had halted near the bar, a puzzled look on his face, and Frank heard him say to Harry:

"What in the world did you drag me in here for, old man? You know I am not drinking anything now, and——"

"As I told you," interrupted Harry, grimly, "I brought you in to see a man. Here he is."

Frank and the rough had come up behind Putnam, who now turned, and with still greater astonishment, cried:

"What—Merriwell? What in the world are you doing in this place?"

"Permit me to introduce to you Mr. Plug Kirby—Mr. Burnham Putnam. Have you ever met the man before?"

Old Put drew back, staring at the ruffian in astonishment.

"What in blazes is this?" he gasped. "Is it a joke?"

"No joke," returned Frank, sternly. "It is a matter of business. Mr. Kirby, have you ever met Mr. Putnam before?"

"Naw!" cried the man. "Dis ain't der cove wot come ter me ter do der job. Dis is anodder feller."

"You are sure?" demanded Frank, with an expression of positive relief. "His name was on the card you gave me."

"I don't care if it was, dis ain't der feller wot give der card ter me, not by a great big lot."

"Well, I am glad of that!" cried Frank, and he grasped Putnam's hand. "It is a great relief."

"Didn't I tell you!" almost shouted Harry.

"Well, now, I want to know what all this is about," said Old Put, who was greatly puzzled. "I am all at sea."

Without hesitation Frank explained how a person had hired Plug Kirby to break his arm and what the result had been; how the person who made the bargain had given a card on which Putnam's name was engraved. Frank took the card from his pocket and Putnam said it was one of his regular visiting cards.

"Some fellow has been working on my name in order to hide his own identity!" cried Put, who was greatly angered. "Oh, I'd like to get hold of the skunk!"

At this moment the door which led to the back room opened and Roland Ditson, who had again visited Buster Kelley, came into the saloon. He started back when he saw the little group of students, but Plug Kirby saw his face and hoarsely exclaimed:

"Dere's der mug now! Dat's der feller wot hired me an' give me der card! I'll swear ter dat!"

Seeing there was no way out of it, Roll came forward. He was rather pale, but he succeeded in putting on a front.

"Hello, fellows!" he cried. "What are you doing in here?"

Merriwell had him by the collar in a twinkling.

"Looking for you," he said, "and we have found you! So you are the chap who hired this man to break my arm in order to fix me so I couldn't pitch any more! Well, I declare I didn't think anything quite as low as that even of you!"

Ditson protested his innocence. He even called Kirby a liar, and Frank was forced to keep the ruffian from hammering him. He swore it was some kind of a plot to injure him, and he called on the boys to know if they would take the word of a wretch like Kirby in preference to his.

"Oh, get out!" exclaimed Putnam in disgust. "Take my advice and leave Yale at once. If you do not I'll publish the whole story, and you will find yourself run out. Go!"

Ditson sneaked away.

CHAPTER X
"Play Ball!"

Before night Merriwell received an appealing letter from Ditson, in which the young scapegrace protested his sorrow and entreated Frank to do what he could to keep the matter quiet, so he would not be forced to leave Yale.

Ditson declared it would break his mother's heart if he failed to complete the course at Yale. Over and over he entreated forgiveness, telling how sorry he was that he had ever tried to injure Merriwell in any way, and declaring that if Frank would forgive and forget he would never cause him any further trouble.

Frank pondered over the letter so long and with such a serious look on his face that Harry asked him what he had struck. Then Merriwell read it to his roommate.

"Oh, what a snizerable meak—I mean miserable sneak that fellow is!" exclaimed Harry. "He goes into a dirty piece of business like this and then he gets down and crawls—actually crawls!"

"I have no doubt but his mother is proud of him," said Frank. "He says he is an only son. It is his mother, not Ditson, I am thinking about. I do not wish to cause her so much pain."

"Oh, come off! If a fellow is such a snake as Ditson he must get it from his parents on one side or the other. Perhaps his mother is not so good."

"I do not wish to think that of any fellow's mother. I much prefer to think that he takes all his bad qualities from the other side of the house. I remember my own mother—the dearest, gentlest, sweetest woman in all the world! How she loved me! How proud she was of me! All the better part of my nature I owe to her, God bless her!"

Frank spoke with deep feeling, and Rattleton was touched and silenced. Merriwell arose and walked the floor, and there was an expression of the utmost tenderness and adoration on his face—a look that brought something like a mist to Harry's eyes. Frank seemed to have forgotten his companion, and he gently murmured:

"My angel mother!"

That was too much for Harry, and he coughed huskily in an attempt to break the spell without being rude. Frank immediately turned and said:

"I beg your pardon, old man. I forgot myself for a moment."

"Oh, don't pard my begoner—that is, begon my pard—no, I mean peg my bardon! Hang it all! I'm all twisted! I don't know what I am trying to say!"

In confusion Harry got up and went to look out of the window.

"Jeewhittaker! I'm glad Merry don't get this way often!" he thought. "Never knew him to do it before."

After some moments Frank declared:

"I am going to try to hush this Ditson matter up, Harry."

"You are?"

"Yes, for the sake of Ditson's mother. I want you to help me. We'll go see Putnam and Jones. If they have told anybody we'll see the others. I am the one who has the greatest cause for complaint, and if I am willing to drop it I am sure Putnam should be. Come on, old man. Let's not lose any time."

"Well, I suppose you are right," admitted Harry as he reached for his cap. "But there's not another person on top of the earth who could induce me to keep still in such a case. It is a second offense, too."

So they went out together and searched for Putnam and Jones.

At first Putnam was obstinate and utterly refused to let Ditson off; but Frank took him aside and talked earnestly to him for fifteen minutes, finally securing his promise to keep silent. It was not difficult to silence Jones, and so the matter was hushed up for the time. Nothing was said to Ditson, who was left in suspense as to what course would be pursued.

A day or two later came the very thing that had been anticipated and discussed since the freshman game at Cambridge. Merriwell was selected as one of the pitchers on the 'varsity nine, and the freshmen lost him from their team.

Putnam came out frankly and confessed that he had feared something of the kind all along, and Frank was in no mood to kick over his past treatment, so nothing was said on that point.

In the first game against a weaker team than Harvard Merriwell was tried in the box and pitched a superb game, which Yale won in a walk.

Big Hugh Heffiner, the regular pitcher, whose arm was in a bad way, complimented Merriwell on his work, which he said was "simply great."

Of course Frank felt well, as for him there was no sport he admired so much as baseball; but he remained the same old Merriwell, and his freshman comrades could not see the least change in his manner.

The second game of the series with Harvard came off within a week, but Frank got cold in his arm, and he was not in the best possible condition to go into the box. This he told Pierson, and as Heffiner had almost entirely recovered Frank was left on the bench.

The 'varsity team had another pitcher, who was known as Dad Hicks. He was a man about twenty-eight years old, and looked even older, hence the nickname of Dad.

This man was most erratic and could not be relied upon. Sometimes he would do brilliant work, and at other times children could have batted him all over the lot. He was used only in desperate emergencies, and could not be counted on in a pinch.

During the whole of the second game with Harvard Frank sat on the bench, ready to go into the box if called on. At first it looked as if he would have to go in, for the Harvard boys fell upon Heffiner and pounded him severely for two innings. Then Hugh braced up and pitched the game through to the end in brilliant style, Yale winning by a score of 10 to 7.

Heffiner, however, was forced to bathe his arm in witch hazel frequently, and as he went toward the box for the last time he said to Frank with a rueful smile:

"You'll have to get into shape to pitch the last game of the series with these chaps. My arm is the same as gone now, and I'll finish it this inning. We must win this game anyway, regardless of arms, so here goes."

He could barely get the balls over the plate, but he used his head in a wonderful manner, and the slow ball proved a complete puzzle for Harvard after they had been batting speed all through the game, so they got but one safe hit off Heffiner that inning and no scores.

There was a wild jubilee at Yale that night. A bonfire was built on the campus and the students blew horns, sang songs, cheered for "good old Yale," and had a real lively time.

One or two of the envious ones asked about Merriwell— why he was not allowed to pitch. Even Hartwick, a sophomore who had disliked Frank from the first, more than hinted that the freshman pitcher was being made sport of, and that he would not be allowed to go into the box when Yale was playing a team of any consequence.

Jack Diamond overheard the remark, and he promptly offered to bet Hartwick any sum that Merriwell would pitch the next game against Harvard.

Diamond was a freshman, and so he received a calling down from Hartwick, who told him he was altogether too new. But as Hartwick strolled away Diamond quietly said:

"I may be new, sir, but I back up any talk I make. There are others who do not, sir."

Hartwick made no reply.

As the third and final game of the series was to be played on neutral ground, there had been some disagreement about the location, but Springfield had finally been decided upon and accepted by Yale and Harvard.

Frank did his best to keep his arm in good condition for that game, something which Pierson approved. Hicks was used as much as possible in all other games, but Frank found it necessary to pull one or two off the coals for him.

Heffiner had indeed used his arm up in the grand struggle to win the second game from Harvard—the game that it was absolutely necessary for Yale to secure. He tended that arm as if it were a baby, but it had been strained severely and it came into shape very slowly. As soon as possible he tried to do a little throwing every day, but it was some time before he could get a ball more than ten or fifteen feet.

It became generally known that Merriwell would have to pitch at Springfield beyond a doubt, and the greatest anxiety was felt at Yale. Every man had confidence in Heffiner, but it was believed by the majority that the freshman was still raw, and therefore was liable to make a wretched fizzle of it.

Heffiner did not think so. He coached Merriwell almost every day, and his confidence in Frank increased.

"The boy is all right," was all he would say about it, but that did not satisfy the anxious ones.

During the week before the deciding game was to come off Heffiner's arm improved more rapidly than it had at any time before, and scores of men urged Pierson to put Old Reliable, as Hugh was sometimes called, into the box.

A big crowd went up to Springfield on the day of the great game, but the "Sons of Old Eli" were far from confident, although they were determined to root for their team to the last gasp.

The most disquieting rumors had been afloat concerning Harvard. It was said her team was in a third better condition than at the opening of the season when she took the first game from Yale; and it could not be claimed with honesty that the Yale team was apparently in any better shape. Although she had won the second game of the series with Harvard, her progress had not been satisfactory.

A monster crowd had gathered to witness the deciding game. Blue and crimson were the prevailing colors. On the bleachers at one side of the grandstand sat hundreds upon hundreds of Harvard men, cheering all together and being answered by the hundreds of Yale men on the other side of the grandstand. There were plenty of ladies and citizens present and the scene was inspiring. A band of music served to quicken the blood in the veins which were already throbbing.

There was a short preliminary practice, and then at exactly three o'clock the umpire walked down behind the home plate and called: "Play ball!"

CHAPTER XI
A Hot Finish

Yale took the field, and as the boys in blue trotted out the familiar Yale yell broke from hundreds of throats. Blue pennants were wildly fluttering, the band was playing a lively air, and for the moment it seemed as if the sympathy of the majority of the spectators was with Yale.

But when Hinkley, Harvard's great single hitter, who always headed the batting list, walked out with his pet "wagon tongue," a different sound swept over the multitude and the air seemed filled with crimson pennants.

Merriwell went into the box, and the umpire broke open a pasteboard box, brought out a ball that was wrapped in tin foil, removed the covering and tossed the snowy sphere to the freshman pitcher Yale had so audaciously stacked up against Harvard.

Frank looked the box over, examined the rubber plate, and seemed to make himself familiar with every inch of the ground in his vicinity. Then he faced Hinkley, and a moment later delivered the first ball.

Hinkley smashed it on the nose, and it was past Merriwell in a second, skipping along the ground and passing over second base just beyond the baseman's reach, although he made a good run for it.

The centre fielder secured the ball and returned it to second, but Hinkley had made a safe single off the very first ball delivered.

Harvard roared, while the Yale crowd was silent.

A great mob of freshmen was up from New Haven to see the game and watch Merriwell's work, and some of them immediately expressed disappointment and dismay.

"Here is where Merriwell meets his Waterloo," said Sport Harris. "He'll be batted out before the game is fairly begun."

That was quite enough to arouse Rattleton, who heard the remark.

"I'll bet you ten dollars he isn't batted out at all," spluttered Harry, fiercely. "Here's my money, too!"

"Make it twenty-five and I will go you," drawled Harris.

"All right, I'll make it twenty-five."

The money was staked.

Derry, also a heavy hitter, was second on Harvard's list. Derry had a bat that was as long and large as the regulations would permit and as heavy as lead; yet, despite the weight of the stick, the strapping Vermonter handled it as if it were a feather.

Frank sent up a coaxer, but Derry refused to be coaxed. The second ball was high, but Derry cracked it for two bags, and Hinkley got round to third.

It began to seem as if Merriwell would be batted out in the first inning, and the Yale crowd looked weary and disgusted at the start.

The next batter fouled out, however, and the next one sent a red-hot liner directly at Merriwell. There was no time to get out of the way, so Frank caught it, snapped the ball to third, found Hinkley off the bag, and retired the side without a score.

This termination of the first half of the inning was so swift and unexpected that it took some seconds for the spectators to realize what had happened. When they did, however, Yale was wildly cheered.

"What do you think about it now, Harris?" demanded Harry, exultantly.

"I think Merriwell saved his neck by a dead-lucky catch," was the answer. "If he had missed that ball he would have been removed within five minutes."

Pierson, who was sitting on the bench, was looking doubtful, and he held a consultation with Costigan, captain of the team, as soon as the latter came in from third base.

Costigan asked Frank how he felt, and Merriwell replied that he had never felt better in his life, so it was decided to let him see what he could do in the box the next inning.

Yedding, who was in the box for Harvard, could not have been in better condition, and the first three Yale men to face him went out in one-two-three order, making the first inning a whitewash for both sides.

As Merriwell went into the box the second time there were cries for Heffiner, who was on the bench, ready to pitch if forced to do so, for all of the fact that it might ruin his arm forever so far as ball playing was concerned.

In trying to deceive the first man up Merriwell gave him three balls in succession. Then he was forced to put them over. He knew the batter would take one or two, and so he sent two straight, swift ones directly over, and two strikes were called.

Then came the critical moment, for the next ball pitched would settle the matter. Frank sent in a rise and the batter struck at it, missed it, was declared out, the ball having landed with a "plunk" in the hands of the catcher.

The next batter got first on a single, but the third man sent an easy one to Frank, who gathered it in, threw the runner out at second and the second baseman sent the ball to first in time to retire the side on a double play.

"You are all right, Merriwell, old man," enthusiastically declared Heffiner as Frank came in to the bench. "They haven't been able to score off you yet, and they won't be able to touch you at all after you get into gear."

Pierson was relieved, and Costigan looked well satisfied.

"Now we must have some scores, boys," said the captain.

But Yedding showed that he was out for blood, for he allowed but one safe hit, and again retired Yale without a score.

Surely it was a hot game, and excitement was running high. Would Harvard be able to score the next time? That was the question everybody was asking.

Yedding came to the bat in this inning, and Merriwell struck him out with ease, while not another man got a safe hit, although one got first on the shortstop's error.

The Yale crowd cheered like Indians when Harvard was shut out for the third time, the freshmen seeming to yell louder than all the others. They originated a cry which was like this:

"He is doing very well! Who? Why, Merriwell!"

Merriwell was the first man up, and Yedding did his best to get square by striking the freshman out. In this he was successful, much to his satisfaction.

But no man got a hit, and the third inning ended as had the others, neither side having made a run.

The fourth opened in breathless suspense, but it was quickly over, neither side getting a man beyond second.

It did not seem possible that this thing could continue much longer, but the fifth inning brought the same result, although Yale succeeded in getting a man to third with only one out. An attempt to sacrifice him home failed, and a double play was made, retiring the side.

Harvard opened the sixth by batting a ball straight at Yale's shortstop, who played tag with it, chasing it around his feet long enough to allow the batter to reach first. It was not a hit, but an error for short.

This seemed to break the Yale team up somewhat. The runner tried for second on the first ball pitched, and Yale's catcher overthrew, although he had plenty of time to catch the man. The runner kept on to third and got it on a slide.

Now Harvard rejoiced. Although he had not obtained a hit, the man had reached third on two errors, and there was every prospect of scoring.

Merriwell did not seem to lose his temper or his coolness. He took plenty of time to let everybody get quieted down, and then he quickly struck out the next man. The third man, however, managed to hit the ball fairly and knocked a fly into left field. It was gathered in easily, but the man on third held the bag till the fly was caught and made a desperate dash for home.

The left fielder threw well, and the ball struck in the catcher's mitt. It did not stick, however, and the catcher lost the only opportunity to stop the score.

Harvard had scored at last!

The Harvard cheer rent the air, and crimson fluttered on all sides.

Frank struck out the next man, and then Yale came to bat, resolved to do or die. But they did not do much. Yedding was as good as ever, and the fielders gathered in anything that came their way.

At the end of the eighth inning the score remained 1 to 0 in Harvard's favor. It looked as if Yale would receive a shutout, and that was something awful to contemplate. The "Sons of Old Eli" were ready to do anything to win a score or two.

In the first half of the ninth Harvard went at it to make some more runs. One man got a hit, stole second, and went to third on an error that allowed the batter to reach first.

Sport Harris had been disappointed when Merriwell continued to remain in the box, but now he said:

"He's rattled. Here's where they kill him."

But Frank proved that he was not rattled. He tricked the man on third into getting off the bag and then threw him out in a way that brought a yell of delight from Yale men. That fixed it so the next batter could not sacrifice with the object of letting the man on third home. Then he got down to business, and Harvard was whitewashed for the last time.

"Oh, if Yale can score now!" muttered hundreds.

The first man up flied out to centre, and the next man was thrown out at first. That seemed to settle it. The spectators were making preparations to leave. The Yale bat tender, with his face long and doleful, was gathering up the sticks.

What's that? The next man got a safe hit, a single that placed him on first. Then Frank Merriwell was seen carefully selecting a bat.

"Oh, if he were a heavy hitter!" groaned many voices.

Yedding was confident—much too confident. He laughed in Frank's face. He did not think it necessary to watch the man on first closely, and so that man found an opportunity to steal second.

Two strikes and two balls had been called. Then Yedding sent in a swift one to cut the inside corner. Merriwell swung at it.

Crack! Bat and ball met fairly, and away sailed the sphere over the head of the shortstop.

"Run!"

That word was a roar. No need to tell Frank to run. In a moment he was scudding down to first, while the left fielder was going back for the ball, which had passed beyond his reach. Frank kept on for second. There was so much noise he could not hear the coachers, but he saw the fielder had not secured the ball. He made third, and the excited coacher sent him home with a furious gesture.

Every man, woman and child was standing. It seemed as if every one was shouting and waving flags, hats, or handkerchiefs. It was a moment of such thrilling, nerve-tingling excitement as is seldom experienced. If Merriwell reached home Yale won; if he failed the score was tied, for the man in advance had scored.

The fielder had secured the ball, he drove it to the shortstop, and the shortstop whirled and sent it whistling home. The catcher was ready to stop Merriwell.

"Slide!"

That word Frank heard above all the commotion. He did slide. Forward he scooted in a cloud of dust. The catcher got the ball and put it onto Frank—an instant too late!

A sudden silence.

"Safe home!" rang the voice of the umpire.

Then another roar, louder, wilder, full of unbounded joy. The Yale cheer! The band drowned by all the uproar! The sight of sturdy lads in blue, delirious with delight, hugging a dust-covered youth, lifting him to their shoulders, and bearing him away in triumph.

Merriwell had won his own game, and his record was made. It was a glorious finish!

[THE END.]

THE LIBERTY BOYS OF "76"

A Weekly Magazine containing Stories of the American Revolution.

Issued Weekly—By Subscription $2.50 per year.

No. 1.　　　NEW YORK, JANUARY 4, 1901.　　　Price 5 Cents.

THE LIBERTY BOYS OF "76"

OR

FIGHTING FOR FREEDOM

BY HARRY MOORE.

CAPT. DICK SLATER

Leaving their quarters, the boys marched up the street, past the commander-in-chief's head-quarters. General Washington was out on the stoop, and as Dick and his company of "Liberty Boys of '76" marched past, he waved his hand in a salute and smiled.

Among the earliest dime novels are historical novels set during the period of the American Revolutionary War. Principally, these are stories in which historical or fictional characters reenact the battles, skirmishes, and espionage activities of the thirteen colonies in their war for independence from Great Britain. Individual novels as well as popular biographies of such figures as George Washington and Ethan Allen found a ready market. The contrast between the condescending Tory and the self-reliant patriot forms a subplot in many stories. While the five-cent weeklies experimented in the 1890s with entire series set during the Civil War, there was no corresponding series about the American Revolution until the early twentieth century, when Frank Tousey's Liberty Boys of '76 *and Street & Smith's* Paul Jones Weekly *and* Boys of Liberty Library *were published. By far the most popular and long-lasting of the three was the Tousey series.*

The name Harry Moore used on the stories is a pseudonym that masks the identities of Cecil Burleigh (1850–1921) and Stephen Angus Douglas Cox (1865–1944). Cox, who often signed his stories with his initials S. A. D. Cox, was the creator of the series about Dick Slater and his comrades in arms. He had previously written all the stories for Tousey's Three Chums, *about the adventures in school and abroad of two boys and a girl at the turn of the century. He wrote the first 125 stories in the* Liberty Boys *series before turn-*

ing over the work to Burleigh, who penned an additional 487 stories for a total of 612 in all. While the stories are definitely set between 1776 and 1783, and actual historical figures and events are described, they are not told in chronological order, and each story can stand by itself. The end of the war, for example, is mentioned in two separate stories that were published eight years apart. Besides working undercover, the boys are involved in nearly all the famous battles of the war and frequently fight American Indians and infamous renegades along the frontier.

The story reprinted here was written by S. A. D. Cox and is the first story in the series (Liberty Boys of '76, no. 1, January 4, 1901). It tells of the founding of the Liberty Boys group and their first assignment for General Washington. It was reprinted in facsimile for dime novel collectors in 1946 but otherwise has not seen print since its original publication in 1901.

CHAPTER I
A "Liberty Boy of '76"

On the morning of July 6th, 1776, a family of four sat at a table in a farmhouse a few miles from Tarrytown, N.Y.

The family consisted of Mr. and Mrs. Slater; their son, a bright-faced, handsome youth of eighteen years; and a daughter, bright and beautiful, aged fifteen. The boy's name was Richard, and the girl's, Edith.

The family was at breakfast, and a pleasant sight the members presented, for they seemed happy and contented.

"What is the latest news of the war, husband?" asked Mrs. Slater, as she poured the coffee.

"Well, the situation remains about the same, wife," replied Mr. Slater, who had been to New York the day before, but had been delayed and had not reached home until such a late hour that his wife and children were in bed asleep.

"General Howe[1] has not made any attack on General Washington's army yet, then?" asked Dick, his eyes glowing with the fire of the soldier.

"No; you know it is stated that he has orders to await the coming of his brother, Admiral Howe, who is to try to conciliate the patriots, and get them to lay down their arms and renew allegiance to the king."

"I hope the Admiral won't succeed!" said Dick, his eyes shining.

"And so do I!" declared Edith. "I think we ought to be free!"

"Right, my children," said Mr. Slater. "I stand on exactly the platform adopted by Patrick Henry[2]—'Give me liberty or give me death!' The people of the colonies must be free! They must not go back to the slavery of allegiance to the king!"

Mr. Slater and his two children, as will be seen, were true and earnest patriots. Mrs. Slater was patriotic, also, but she loved her husband, and saw in his attitude great danger to himself, for she was aware that they lived in the midst of a

Tory community, the majority of their nearest neighbors being loyal to King George.[3]

They were very bitter toward Mr. Slater, for the reason that he was a very plain, outspoken man, and spoke his sentiments freely, no matter where he was or to whom he might be talking. He was a man utterly fearless, and the threats made against him by his Tory neighbors, which found their way to his ears occasionally, were laughed at. He was not worried a particle, and often when meeting one or more of those same neighbors on the road or elsewhere, he would refer to the matter, tell them he had heard that they had threatened him, and coolly tell them that if they wanted to do anything to him, to do it then and there. His very boldness, however, had saved him, for there was something about him that inspired respect for his prowess. It was not so much what he had done, though he had been a brave soldier of the French and Indian War,[4] as it was the fear of what he might do. The majority of his neighbors had seen Hiram Slater when angry, and they knew he was a dangerous man. So, although living in a Tory neighborhood, and being as plain and outspoken as it was possible for one to be, Mr. Slater had so far escaped being harmed.

The bitter hatred which his Tory neighbors felt toward him was to bear fruit soon, however.

"I wish you would be a little more careful what you say to our Tory neighbors, Hiram," said Mrs. Slater. "I am afraid they will do you an injury one of these days. They murder people in these cruel times, and call it some other name."

"Oh, there is no danger, Lizzie," said Mr. Slater. "My neighbors know me too well to do me any hurt. They would get the worst of it."

"But they might not give you any chance to defend yourself, Hiram."

"I don't think there is any danger of anything like that."

"Oh, I don't know about that," said Dick. "There is Hank Scroggs, who is mean enough, I am sure, to do anything. His cowardice is all that holds him back. Then there are Joe Bilkins and Carl Shinker; they are the same kind of men."

"And Samuel Estabrook, Dick?" remarked Edith, demurely.
Dick flushed and looked slightly confused.

"No, Edith," he replied; "Mr. Estabrook is a different sort of
man. He is a strong Tory, but I don't think he would do a mean
thing, or take advantage of a neighbor because the neighbor
differed with him in his views regarding the war."

"Alice is not a Tory," said Edith, with a smiling glance at her
brother; "I guess you have converted her, Dick."

Dick flushed, and then laughed.

"That is all right, Sis," he said; "neither is Bob Estabrook a
Tory. I wonder if you couldn't explain why? He's been over
here considerable, and may have told you his reasons for taking the side of the patriots."

It was Edith's turn to blush now, and Mr. Slater laughed.

"That is all right, Edie," he said; "Bob is almost old and big
enough to go into the army, and I would rather he would fight,
if he fights at all, on the side of Right and Justice than on the
side of a tyrannical king!"

"Bob is a fine boy," said Mrs. Slater.

"Of course Bob's a fine boy," said Dick. "I haven't a friend I
think more of than Bob, and I'm sure that if he fought at all, it
would be for the cause of freedom, and not to help perpetuate
the slavery of the colonists."

"And so would Alice!" smiled Edith.

"Yes; I think she would," agreed Dick, smiling and blushing.

Dick had finished his breakfast by this time, and rising
from the table, he walked to the door, which was open, and
glanced out.

"Yonder comes a horseman, riding at a gallop, as if in a
hurry," said Dick. "I am going to hail him. Perhaps he may
have heard what was done in Philadelphia the Fourth. I am
anxious to know whether Congress declared for liberty."

"That's right; ask him, Dick," replied the youth's father.

Dick hastened out to the road, and called to the man as he
came up:

"Have you heard what was done at Philadelphia the
Fourth, sir?"

The man reined up his horse, and looking at the bright, handsome-faced youth with interest, replied:

"Yes, my boy, I have just come from New York, and they had just received the news there that the Declaration of Independence was adopted and signed, and that now it is to be war to the death. The people of the Colonies will be free from the yoke of British oppression, or they will die fighting for liberty!"

"Hurrah!" cried Dick, his face shining with delight. "Father! Father!" he called; "the Declaration of Independence has been adopted and signed, and we are free!—or will soon be free, which amounts to the same thing!"

"Say you so, my son?" cried Hiram Slater, and he came running out to the road to question the stranger.

When the man repeated his statement, Mr. Slater, like Dick, became excited, and cried:

"Thank God for that! I am glad; and I have high hopes, now, of living to see our beautiful country freed from the rule of the king!"

At this instant a body of horsemen, consisting of about a dozen men, rode up.

They were the Tory neighbors of Mr. Slater, and were armed with muskets and pistols. As they came even with the horseman, and with Mr. Slater and Dick, they drew up, and stopping, glared at Mr. Slater threateningly.

"What is all this noise about?" snarled Hank Scroggs, who was the leader of the horsemen.

"Why, haven't you heard, Hank?" asked Mr. Slater, promptly, and meeting the fierce gaze of the man unflinchingly, even smilingly; "the Declaration of Independence was adopted and signed at Philadelphia the Fourth, and the Colonies are going to be free and independent!"

"You are a cursed traitor, and orter be shot!" snarled Scroggs.

"And you are a fool for not wanting to be free and independent of King George, who robs us at every opportunity, and——"

"Treason! Treason!" the Tories cried.

"There is no treason about it!" replied Hiram Slater, scorn-fully; "Congress has adopted and signed the Declaration of Independence, and I am not now a subject of King George, or any other king!"

"It's a lie!" cried Scroggs, fiercely; "you are just as much a subject of the king as you were before, and the doings of your Congress, as you call it, amount to nothing! In three months' time the king's soldiers will have whipped George Washington's army of traitors, and things will be as they were before this rebellion started."

"Never!" cried Mr. Slater. "Never again will King George, or any king, rule over the American Colonies! We will win in this fight just as sure as that sun rises in the east and sets in the west! We will win, and I thank God for it!"

The stranger who had brought the news of the Declaration of Independence had withdrawn a few yards, and sat on his horse watching the horsemen closely, and the same time flashing an occasional admiring glance upon the bold man who was thus bearding the Tories.

"There is a brave and noble man!" he said to himself; "but he is taking his life in his hands, I should say, in talking thus to these men, who look mean enough, and desperate enough, to commit murder."

Mrs. Slater, having come to the door when her husband went out to speak to the horseman, was still standing there when the band of Tories rode up, and her heart sank with a terrible feeling of fear and misgiving.

"They are in a body, and armed," she said to herself; "and I fear they have come here to do my husband injury. What shall I do? He will speak up boldly, as he always does, and they may murder him!"

She listened to the conversation which ensued with fear and trembling, and unable to control herself longer, she now called out:

"Hiram! Hiram! please come in! Don't talk to them!"

"That's right; call your old man in, Mrs. Slater!" cried Scroggs, sneeringly; "call him in before we do our duty, and fill his traitorous carcass full of bullets!"

"Shoot, if you dare, Hank Scroggs!" cried Hiram Slater, his voice ringing with defiance, his eyes flashing with the scorn he felt for the Tories. "Shoot, if you like, you coward, but little good it will do you if you should kill me, for the people of the Colonies will be free in spite of the snakes in the grass, such as you are, who would murder your neighbors to perpetuate your own slavery! You are miserable cowards and curs! and you yourselves know it! Now, shoot, if you dare!" and the bold man folded his arms and gazed unflinchingly into the faces of the Tories.

Mrs. Slater's fears were well founded. These men, who had many a time been forced to listen to the scathing language of the fearless and outspoken patriot, and who had come to hate him as only men possessed of such miserable natures can hate, had got together on this morning, and had come to Mr. Slater's home for the express purpose of killing him. They had already heard of the signing and adoption of the Declaration of Independence, and this had made them very angry, so they had mounted and, as we have seen, appeared before the Slater home just at an opportune (for their purpose) time, inasmuch as Mr. Slater's words gave them an excuse for doing the dastardly deed they contemplated.

"What is that?" almost howled Scroggs, when the brave patriot had spoken; "do you dare call us cowards and curs? By the heavens above us, you shall die for that! You deserve death, anyway, for being a traitor, and you have sealed your doom! Fire, men! Shoot the traitor!" and with the words, Scroggs raised his rifle, and fired point blank at the breast of his neighbor!

"My God! I am shot!" cried the patriot, staggering backward; "wife!—Dick!—Edie!—I am wounded unto death!" and he would have fallen, had not Dick leaped forward and caught his father, and eased him to the ground. At the same instant three or four more of the Tories fired at the wounded man, another of the bullets striking him, and one or two just missing Dick.

"Lizzie!—Dick!—Edie!—good-by!" gasped the dying man, and then, as his eyes were closing in death, he, by a superhuman effort, lifted his head, and raising one trembling hand toward heaven, said: "God, I thank thee!—I die a free man!"

Then his head dropped, a tremulous sigh escaped his lips, and the dauntless spirit took its flight.

Dick realized the fact in an instant, and with a wild, incoherent cry, he leaped to his feet and ran to the house, followed by the jeers of the Tories, who thought he was running because he feared they might shoot him.

But they were soon to discover their mistake. In the body of that handsome, eighteen-year-old youth was all the spirit and indomitable courage of the father, and leaping past his mother, who stood in the doorway paralyzed with horror at the terrible spectacle she had witnessed, Dick seized a rifle, which rested on a couple of wooden forks nailed to the wall, rushed back out of the house to the road, and before the startled Tories realized what was happening, the boy raised the rifle, taking quick aim, and as the sharp ping! of the weapon sounded, Hank Scroggs threw up his arms, dropped his rifle, and fell forward upon the neck of his horse, mortally wounded. The horse became frightened, and bounded away down the road, and Scroggs, though fatally hurt, managed to hold onto the animal's mane, and keep from falling off.

Then, with a wild, inarticulate cry of rage and terrible sorrow combined, Dick clubbed his rifle and attacked the other Tories, striking swiftly and surely with the ironbound butt of the gun. Such was the fierce energy of the onslaught, so swiftly and bewilderingly did he rain the blows upon the horsemen, that they were rendered unable to fire upon him, and after three of their number had received broken heads, and one or two broken arms, they hastened to spur their frightened horses away from the vicinity, nor did they stop while within sight of the youth.

He had put the entire band of Tories to flight!

But the husband and father was dead! and the grief of the wife, son and daughter was terrible to witness, and the stranger, who had dismounted, and stood uncovered, was very much affected.

Mrs. Slater was seated on the ground, her dead husband's head in her lap, while on one side was Dick, on the other, Edith.

The three wept for several minutes, during which time the man was silent, and then, as the sobs of the sorrowing ones became more subdued, the stranger spoke comforting words to them, and did all he could to lessen their grief.

Presently, Dick, who was kneeling beside his father's form, lifted his tear-stained face toward the sky, and lifting his right hand, said, in a firm, determined voice:

"My father is a martyr to the cause of Liberty, and I, his son, do solemnly swear that I will devote all my energies to the Cause for which my father died, the Cause he loved so well— the Cause of Liberty! I shall become a patriot soldier, and fight for the freedom of our people. I shall devote my whole energies, give up my life, if need be, to the great and glorious Cause! My father would wish it, and I swear to do it, and ask you, mother, and Edie, and this kind gentleman here, to bear me witness in it!"

"Oh, my son! am I to lose you, too!" moaned his mother.

"No; not lose me, mother. I am simply going to do what father would have wished me to do, and when we have whipped the British and Tories and gained our freedom, I will return to you and Edie."

"You are a brave and noble youth!" said the stranger, earnestly; "you are a true type of the 'Liberty Boys of '76.'"

CHAPTER II
An Interesting Chapter of History

And now, kind reader, in order that you may better understand this story—which is to be a story of the War of the Revolution— I am going to interpolate a synopsis of the war to date. While not strictly necessary to the story, it is so thrilling, so full of interest, that it will well repay the reading:

At the time of which we write—July, 1776—a state of war had existed between the American Colonies and Great Britain for a period of a little more than fourteen months, the first battle of the Revolution—the battle of Lexington—having taken place April 19, 1775.

The British, angered by the resistance of the American Colonies to the attempt to tax them in order to raise the money necessary to pay off the debts incurred in the French and Indian War, had appointed General Gage[5] governor of Massachusetts, and he had taken up his quarters in Boston, and carried things with a high hand.

The colonists had become greatly worked up over this, and on every side could be heard the thrilling words of Patrick Henry: "Give me liberty or give me death!"

Not all the people took this view, however. There were men who were in favor of remaining loyal to King George, and these people were called Tories, the people in favor of establishing a Continental Union and pulling entirely away from British rule being called Whigs.

Companies of soldiers from among the Whigs were formed, and these companies of soldiers were called "Minute Men." They made no secret of the fact that they were ready to fight for freedom at any minute, and General Gage became frightened, fortified Boston Neck, and seized powder wherever he could find it, as he reasoned that if the Minute Men could get no powder they could not do much shooting.

General Gage heard that the people were gathering military stores at Concord, and sent out Colonel Smith[6] and Major Pitcairn[7] with eight hundred men to seize and destroy the stores.

The patriots of Boston were not caught napping, however. They were watching Gage, and knew of his intentions in time. Messengers were sent out to rouse the people. Paul Revere was one of these messengers, and it was then that he made his wonderful ride, made famous by Longfellow.

When the British soldiers reached Lexington they found a company of Minute Men gathered there. Major Pitcairn, who was something of a fire-eater, and hot-headed, rode up to the Minute Men, and cried: "Disperse, you rebels; lay down your arms!"

But the Minute Men did not disperse worth a cent. They stood their ground, like the brave men they were.

Their commander was John Parker,[8] a veteran of the French and Indian War, and when Pitcairn ordered them to disperse, he said to his brave Minute Men: "Stand your ground! Don't fire unless fired upon; but if they mean to have war, let it begin here!"

"Disperse, ye villains!" again roared Pitcairn; "d——n you, why don't you disperse!" and then being angered by their refusal, he roared out the order to his soldiers:

"Fire!"

The soldiers hesitated. They had more sense than their commander, and had no stomach for firing into the ranks of a band of men who were not interfering with them in any way, but Major Pitcairn drew a pistol and fired, repeating his order to fire in a roar like that of a lion, and his soldiers, not daring to disobey a second time, raised their guns to their shoulders and fired a murderous volley, which killed eight of the Minute Men outright, and wounded ten.

The Minute Men at once returned the fire, and for a few minutes a lively scrimmage raged; but Colonel Smith and his company of British soldiers coming in sight at this time made it unwise to keep up the conflict longer at that time, and Parker, the commander of the Minute Men, ordered them to retire, which they did.

The encounter at Lexington had delayed the British, however, and the messengers had had time to reach Concord ahead of them, with the result that when Smith and Pitcairn reached Concord, the patriots had hidden the stores and ammunition, and Minute Men were gathering from all directions.

The British set fire to the court house, chopped down the liberty pole, spiked a few cannon, destroyed a few barrels of flour, and hunted for the ammunition, but failed to find it.

At about this time, the Minute Men, having increased in numbers to more than four hundred, they attacked the British guarding North Bridge, and after receiving and returning their fire, charged across the bridge and put the British, numbering about two hundred, to flight, they retreating into the village. This incident, and the fact that the Minute Men were constantly being augmented by new arrivals from the surrounding villages, alarmed Colonel Smith, and although he had practically accomplished nothing, he ordered a retreat, and the British soldiers started back toward Boston.

And then began a running fight that was particularly galling to the British. The Minute Men followed them, and kept along at the sides, taking refuge behind hills, and in clumps of trees, and they kept up a constant fire upon the fleeing British.

Major Pitcairn, who had fired the first shot of the Revolution, lost his horse, and with it the gold-mounted pistols, from one of which the first shot had been fired, and those pistols may be seen to-day in the town library at Lexington.

The British threw away their muskets, which impeded them in running, and the retreat became a rout. They finally reached Boston, under full run, and were so exhausted they could only fall down and pant and gasp for breath.

The British lost on this day two hundred and seventy-three, while the American loss was ninety-three.

And thus ended the first battle of the Revolution. The British had failed to accomplish what they had set out to do, and had been unmercifully whipped in the bargain, and the patriots were jubilant.

Not so with King George and the British, when they heard the news in England, five weeks later. There was general consternation, and they did not know what to think. That their trained regulars, soldiers who had fought in many a battle, should be defeated by a band of "peasants," as the patriots were termed, was past all understanding.

But the effect of the battle was electrical. From all over New England came the companies of Minute Men, gathering near Boston, until very shortly General Gage found himself and his army besieged by an army of "peasants" to the number of sixteen thousand.

The next encounter with the British was when Ethan Allen and Benedict Arnold,[9] with a small company of volunteers, captured Fort Ticonderoga. They secured, here, large stores of cannon and ammunition, which were badly needed by the troops at Boston. Soon afterward Crown Point was captured.

On June 17 occurred the memorable battle of Bunker Hill. All know the history of this battle. The patriot army had to retreat, after having used up all its ammunition, but although forced to retreat, the effect upon the soldiers and upon the patriots generally was the same as that of a victory. All were greatly encouraged, and the determination to fight for liberty was strengthened and intensified.

Late that summer an expedition was organized to go into Canada. The army was in two divisions, one under General Montgomery going by way of Lake Champlain, and capturing St. Johns and Montreal, and then appearing before Quebec, where it was joined by another small army under Colonel Arnold. They attacked Quebec in a blinding snowstorm, but the attack failed, and although they remained during the winter blockading the city, in the spring they had to retreat and return, the British receiving reinforcements.

On May 10, 1775, the Second Continental Congress met in Philadelphia, and George Washington was appointed commander-in-chief of the Continental Army. He proceeded to Boston, and on the third day of July, 1775, took charge of the army, then numbering fourteen thousand men.

Washington remained there with his army, keeping the British penned up in Boston, and about the middle of March, 1776, he decided to make the British fight or run, and to that end he fortified Dorchester Heights, overlooking Boston, doing the work in a night, and the sight of the cannon frowning down upon them next morning so frightened the British that their commander, General Howe, hurriedly got his army aboard the British fleet, and sailed away to Halifax. A great many Tory families accompanied him.

Next morning Washington entered Boston, and there were great demonstrations of rejoicing. For eleven months the

people of Boston had been compelled to have the British soldiers among them, and to put up with their insolence and arro-
gance, as well as submit to having their houses pillaged and
stores rifled of their contents, and it was like getting out of jail
to be rid of the enemy.

The following little story we find in the history of the Revolutionary War, and give it:

"The boys in Boston were wont to amuse themselves in winter by building snow-houses and by skating on a pond in the
Common. The soldiers having disturbed them in their sports,
complaints were made to the officers, who only ridiculed their
petition. At last a number of large boys waited on General
Gage. 'What!' said Gage, 'have your fathers sent you here to
exhibit the rebellion they have been teaching you?' 'Nobody
sent us,' answered the leader, with flashing eyes; 'we have never
injured your troops, but they have trampled down our snow-
hills and broken the ice on our skating-pond. We complained,
and they called us young rebels, and told us to help ourselves,
if we could. We told the captain, and he laughed at us. Yesterday our works were destroyed for the third time, and we will
bear it no longer.' The British commander could not restrain
his admiration. 'The very children,' said he, 'draw in a love of
liberty with the air they breathe. Go, my brave boys, and be assured if my troops trouble you again they shall be punished.'"

Such is the story, and we suppose it is true; at any rate, we
know the spirit shown by the boys was in them then, and that
the boys of this period are possessed of the same spirit.

It shall be my pleasure to, in the story which follows, detail
the doings of some such boys as were those who waited upon
General Gage—the "Liberty Boys of '76."

General Howe and his army, after evacuating Boston, and
going to Halifax, soon afterward sailed to New York, and
were joined there by Admiral Howe's fleet, and by General
Clinton.[10] General Washington came to New York with his
army, to keep the British from capturing the city, if he could.

And this was the situation on the Fourth day of July 1776,
when Philadelphia, throbbing with excitement, the people

thronging the streets, awaited the decision of the Colonial delegations regarding the disposition that was to be made of the Declaration of Independence, which was to be presented by the committee appointed to draft it.

With the adoption of this report would come the severance, at once and forever, from Great Britain—from allegiance to King George III.

With the adoption of this report would come Freedom, the most blessed boon enjoyed by man. Why, then, should not the people throng the streets, crowd around Independence Hall, and wait in impatient eagerness to learn whether or not the Declaration of Independence would be adopted and signed?

In the steeple of the old State House was a bell on which, by a strange and happy coincidence, was the inscription: "Proclaim liberty throughout all the land unto all the inhabitants thereof." In the morning, when the delegations assembled, the old bell-ringer had gone to his post, leaving his boy below to announce to him when the Declaration was adopted, so that he might ring the bell and announce the glad fact. The old man waited all day long, hardly taking time for his dinner, and as the hours rolled away and the tidings did not come, he shook his head, and said: "They will never do it! They will never do it!"

But they did. Along toward evening he heard his boy clap his hands, and then a voice came up to him: "Ring, father, ring!"

The old man seized the iron tongue and swung it to and fro, and thus were the glad tidings promulgated to the waiting thousands on the streets.

The excitement was intense; people acted as though they were crazy. All night long cannon boomed, the people shouted for joy and the illumination from bonfires made the city as light, almost, as day.

And now, reader, after having given you this synopsis of the situation, I will proceed, in chapter three, to detail the wonderful, thrilling adventures during the Revolutionary War—which really dates from this time—of the "Liberty Boys of '76."

CHAPTER III
Dick and Alice

"And are you going into the patriot army and fight for freedom, Dick?"

"I am, Alice. My poor father died for the cause he loved so well, and I am going to place my life at the service of Washington, and will fight till we are free, or until I am killed in battle!"

Dick Slater and Alice Estabrook sat on a rustic bench under the shade of an apple tree in the orchard belonging to Alice's father, Samuel Estabrook.

Three days have passed since the terrible morning on which Dick's father was shot down by the Tories, and when Dick had made such a fierce attack on the murderers of his father, and after mortally wounding Hank Scroggs, who had shot Mr. Slater, had put the rest to flight by attacking them with a clubbed rifle.

Scroggs had died the next day from his wound, and that was about all Dick had heard, save that he had been warned by Alice and her brother, Bob, to be on his guard, as it was possible the Tories would try to get revenge on him for the death of Scroggs.

"Let them try it!" Dick had said, his eyes dashing; "several of those fellows fired upon father, after Scroggs had mortally wounded him; I did not see which one fired, as I was assisting father, and my attention was on him, but some of them did it, and if they attack me I will kill a few more of them on suspicion!"

There was a fierceness in Dick's tones that reminded Alice and Bob of Dick's father; but they did not blame him for feeling as he did.

"I wish papa was a patriot!" said Alice, wistfully. "I cannot understand how he can be in favor of remaining a subject of the king."

"I can't understand it, either, Alice; but, of course, he is honest in his views. He thinks it would be best for the people."

"How could it be best, Dick? Just think how glorious it would be to be able to stand erect, throw your head back, and say, 'I am a free man! I am not the subject of a king, but am the equal of any king!'"

"That would be splendid, Alice! And it will be that way, sooner or later, too! This war has but practically begun. The patriots will never give up and become subjects of the king, now that the Declaration of Independence has been adopted and signed. Nothing short of absolute liberty and freedom; nothing short of absolute severance from British rule will satisfy our people now. I am sure of it!"

"I am sure of it, too, Dick, and I am glad! I hope to one day see my father a free man, even though it is against his wishes at the present time."

"He would like it after he had had a taste of it, Alice, I am confident."

"I am sure of it, too, Dick."

"Well, there is one thing about your father, Alice: He is an honest and honorable man, even though he is a Tory. He is not the kind of man to go out and shoot a neighbor because the neighbor differs with him in his views, as is the case with men of the Scroggs, Bilkins, Shinker stripe."

"No, indeed! My father is just the best man in the world, and honestly thinks it would be best for our people to remain loyal to the king. He would not do a mean thing for the world."

"How comes it that you are a little patriot girl, Alice?" asked Dick, regarding his fair companion with a look of admiring interest.

Well might he look admiringly at Alice Estabrook, for she was as beautiful a sixteen-year-old girl as ever the sun shone on. The luxuriant, wavy hair, the rosy cheeks, the dimpled chin, pearly teeth, perfect nose, roguish blue eyes and tempting red lips, all went to make up a picture such as would delight the soul of any man or boy to look upon.

When Dick asked Alice how it happened that she was a patriot, the beautiful girl looked up into his face shyly, and smiling, said:

"You are responsible for that, Dick."

"I?" he exclaimed. There was a pleased tone to his voice.

"Yes; I have heard you talk a great deal, Dick, when you did not know it—last winter at school, for instance, when you had so many arguments with Joe Scroggs and the other Tory boys, and at other times."

"I remember," said Dick; "I did have a good many arguments with the boys last winter at school."

Dick was like his father in the respect that he said openly and frankly just what he thought, on any and all occasions, and under any circumstances. He was absolutely fearless, and this had caused him to have numberless encounters with the Tory boys at school, and elsewhere, but they always got the worst of it, for although only eighteen years old, Dick was a natural athlete, and was very strong and active. These natural physical qualities, together with his indomitable courage and iron will, made him simply unconquerable, and he had, on one occasion the winter before, thrashed four boys who had waylaid him in the woods as he was on his way home from school. They had at first got the better of the combat, owing to force of numbers, but the youth just simply fought on with terrible persistence and fierceness, and his opponents became frightened at last, and the result was that they finally took to their heels and ran, as if for their lives, with Dick in full chase. The spectacle, had anyone seen it, of one boy chasing four must have been ludicrous, to say the least; and each and every one of the four was fully as large and heavy as Dick. One of the four had been Joe Scroggs, the son of the Tory who had shot Mr. Slater, and Joe had cherished a terrible hatred for Dick ever since the time when he and his three cronies were whipped and put to flight in the woods.

"Then I have heard Bob talk a good deal, you know. He was converted by hearing you, and being with you, and he has talked to me a good deal, as he did not dare to talk to papa, and he seemed to want to talk to someone."

"Bob is all right!" said Dick, earnestly.

"Yes; and he thinks that whatever you say is absolutely right, Dick!"

"And how about his sister?" asked Dick, his voice almost trembling, and his handsome eyes shining as they gazed into the roguish blue eyes of his companion.

The girl blushed, looked down in some confusion, and then lifting her eyes to meet his gaze again, said, in a low voice:

"I think about as Bob does, Dick!"

Dick gave a quick glance around, saw no one near, and slipping his arm around the waist of the unresisting girl, he gave her a hug and a kiss.

"Alice," he said, his voice vibrating with feeling, "you are the best, the prettiest, the sweetest little girl in the world, and I am going to go into the patriot army and fight for freedom with a vigor and energy thrice what it would otherwise be, on account of the fact that your sweet face will be ever before me, urging me on!"

"Oh, Dick!" That was all the girl said, but the tone in which she said it was sufficient for Dick, and he kissed the beautiful girl again.

"Here! Here! What is going on here?" cried a voice, and leaping to their feet, the two found themselves confronted by a stern-looking but rather handsome man of about forty-five years.

"Papa!" exclaimed Alice, her face flushed and confused-looking.

"Mr. Estabrook!" said Dick, his face flushing also, but he met the stern gaze of the man unflinchingly. The youth was a splendid reader of faces, and instinctively he seemed to feel that back in the stern eyes of Alice's father was a faint expression of amusement.

"I repeat, what is going on here?" remarked Mr. Estabrook, for he it was, and he looked from one to the other inquiringly, and with an apparently stern expression of countenance.

"Did you not see what was going on, sir?" asked Dick, boldly.

"I saw you kissing my daughter, young man!" in a stern voice; "and I ask by what right you take such liberties?"

Dick was an impulsive youth, with the feelings of a grown man, and squaring his shoulders, and taking a step nearer Alice, who stood looking at her father half-fearfully, he looked Mr. Estabrook straight in the eyes, and said:

"You ask by what right I kissed your daughter, Mr. Estabrook? Well, I will tell you: By the right which my love for her gives me!"

Alice gave a quick start; she flashed one happy glance into Dick's eyes; her face took on added color, and her breast heaved with emotion.

"What's that, young man! You, a mere youth, talking of love! You do not know the meaning of the word 'love,' nor can she—a sixteen-year-old child."

"I am no child, papa!" said Alice, so promptly that Dick saw something like the ghost of a smile curl the corners of her father's lips.

"I know I am only a youth in years, sir," said Dick, manfully and earnestly; "but I am a man in feelings, and I think I know the meaning of the word 'love.' I know that I love Alice, Mr. Estabrook. I love her dearly, and I am going into the patriot army to fight for freedom and liberty!—and then, if I come forth from the conflict alive, I am going to come to you and ask you to let me have Alice for my wife! I love her dearly, and—she loves me, I think! Do you not, Alice?" and Dick slipped his arm around the girl's waist, and she looked shyly up into his face, and said: "I do love you, Dick!" A great look of happiness appeared in the youth's eyes, and he drew her closer, and met Mr. Estabrook's stern look unflinchingly and bravely, but without any show of bravado.

"Well, well! of all the impudence!" that gentleman exclaimed. "To talk that way to me, a loyal king's man! To tell me that you are going into the patriot army, and that when you return, after fighting against the king whom I honor, and to whom I am loyal, you are going to ask me to let you have my daughter for a wife! If that isn't the coolest proposition I ever was confronted with, then I don't know what I am talking about!"

"I don't mean to be impudent, sir," said Dick, earnestly; "I am no sneak, to try and hide my views or intentions from the father of the girl I love, and I ask you, would you not rather have me as I am, than to not know where I stand, or what my intentions are?"

"I will admit, Dick," said Mr. Estabrook, in a voice from which much of the sternness was gone, "that I would rather have you as you are than to have you any other way. I have known your parents many years, and I know that two more honest and honorable people never lived. Your father's word was as good as his bond, and he was as true-hearted as mortal man could be! He would stand by a friend to the death. I fought by his side in the French and Indian War, and although we differed in our views regarding the present war, we were the best of friends, and no one regrets the manner of his death more than I—you know that, Dick."

"Yes; I know it," Dick nodded.

"And, as I was saying, my boy, I honor you, and feel that my little girl could not have the love of a more worthy young man. I am, as you know, a Tory; but I am honest in my views, and think it would be better to remain loyal to the king. I may be wrong, and I don't quarrel with anyone for being a patriot. Go into the patriot army if you like, Dick—I know that you will make as brave a soldier as ever shouldered a musket—and when the war is over, no matter which side triumphs, if you return alive, and you and Alice still love each other, I shall offer no objections to your becoming man and wife, after you have reached the proper age, of course. You are too young to think of marrying as yet, and if the war should end in a few months, I shall ask that neither of you speak a word to me on the subject until you, Dick, are twenty-one years old."

"That is all right, Mr. Estabrook," said Dick; "we love each other, but we are willing to wait, and something tells me that the war will not end soon—that it will last several years, and if that is the case, I will be needed in the patriot army, to fight for the glorious cause of freedom!"

Alice now gently disengaged herself from Dick's encircling arm, and stepping forward, she threw her arms about her father's neck.

"Oh, papa! you have made me so happy!" she breathed. "You are the best papa any girl ever had! and I hope you are not angry because I am a patriot. I cannot help feeling that the people should be free, papa! Dick says they ought to be free, and——"

"Dick has converted my little girl, I see!" half-sadly, but with a smile on his face as he stroked his daughter's hair, and then bent down and kissed the red lips. "Well, I don't know that I blame you for thinking as he does."

"I never tried to talk her into thinking as I do, Mr. Estabrook," said Dick; "she just——"

"I got to thinking for myself, papa," said the girl, "and I made up my mind that the people ought to be free!"

"You are your mother's girl, when it comes to that," said Mr. Estabrook. "She leans that way."

"And I wish you did, papa."

The father sighed.

"I really feel that it would be best to remain loyal to the king," he said; "still, I shall not take it to heart, should the people of the American Colonies prove successful, and gain their independence."

"That's the way to look at it, father!" said Bob Estabrook, who had approached unobserved, and who had heard the most of the conversation. "That's the way to look at it! You'll come around all right yet."

Bob was a jolly, lively youth, good-natured, and thoroughly imbued with the belief that the people ought to be free. He was filled with enthusiasm, and burned with the fire of patriotism.

He took after his mother, who was a patriot, and then he was a great friend of Dick Slater, and had heard that youth talk patriotism so much that he was the strongest kind of a patriot.

"Ah! here is Bob," said Mr. Estabrook, with a smile; "I guess I will have to retire! The enemy has received reinforcements," and giving Bob a shake as he passed him, Mr. Estabrook turned and walked in the direction of the house.

"Oh, ho! What fun!" grinned Bob. "I was watching you two billing and cooing, and hugging and kissing, so as to get a line on that kind of business for my own benefit in the future, and I saw the governor coming. He caught you at it! He, he, he!"

Dick and Alice blushed, and looked at each other sheepishly, and then laughed.

"Yes, I suppose you wanted to see how it was done, and then go over and teach Edith, you mean, wicked boy!" said Alice.

Whereat Bob flushed up; and then he grinned, good-naturedly.

"I wouldn't mind it, now that you speak of it!" he said, coolly. "It must be pretty good, the way you two seemed to enjoy it!"

"Thrash him, Dick!" said Alice.

"I have a good mind to!" said Dick. "I would, only I know I would have Edith in my wool[11] when she found it out!"

CHAPTER IV
The "Liberty Boys of '76"

"Say, Dick, are you really going to join the patriot army, and fight for freedom?" asked Bob, eagerly.

"I certainly am, Bob!" was the decided reply.

"I heard you say so a while ago. Well, one thing you can count on, and that is that you are not going without me! If you go, I'm going, and that's all there is about it!"

"But your father will object, Bob."

"No, he won't; and if he does it won't matter. I'll run away and join the army!"

"Would that be right, Bob?" Dick asked, doubtfully.

"Of course it would. All is fair in love or war!" with a significant wink and a grin.

"I don't think papa would object," said Alice. "He knows how mamma feels about the war, and would be willing for Bob to fight on whichever side he wished."

"I'm going if you go, Dick, and that's all there is about it!" the youth declared, and Dick and Alice felt that he meant it.

"I shall be glad to have you along, Bob," said Dick.

"So will Sis be glad to have me go with you, Dick. I can see that very plainly. She wants me to take care of you, and keep you from being too reckless; isn't that right, Sis?"

"Well, you are pretty reckless yourself," she said; "but perhaps both of you would be less reckless if you went to war together."

"We're certainly going to war together!" declared Bob. Then to Dick:

"When are you going?"

"The first of next week."

"Good enough! I'll be ready to start then."

"Are you going so soon as that, Dick?" from Alice.

"Yes; I will have things so arranged that I can leave mother and Edith by that time. You must come over to the house and see them often when we are gone, Alice."

"You may be sure I will, Dick!"

"Are you going to New York to enter the army, Dick?" asked Bob.

"Yes; straight to General Washington!"

"Hurrah!" cried Bob. "Say, I'm tickled to think we are to go into the army and help fight for freedom! I hope we will be able to do good work for the glorious cause of liberty, Dick!"

"And so do I, Bob."

The three talked for some time, and then, bidding the two good-by, Dick parted from them and made his way back to his own home, which was about a quarter of a mile distant.

The youth's face saddened as he entered the yard and approached the house, the sight of which brought back memories of what had happened there a few days before.

"Poor father!" Dick said to himself; "he died a martyr to his patriotism. Well, I will enter the patriot army and try to do credit to him, and help make the great cause which he loved so well successful!"

Dick's mother and sister were seated in the front room of the house. They were sad-faced, for they had loved the husband and father devotedly; but their faces brightened as Dick entered.

"Where have you been, Dick?" asked Edith.

"Over to Mr. Estabrook's, Edith."

"Did you see Bob?" eagerly.

"Yes, Sis. He is going to go to war with me."

"What! Bob is going to go with you?"

"Yes."

"Going to join the patriot army, and fight against the king!"

"Yes, Edith."

"And his father a king's man! I should not think Mr. Estabrook would let him do so." This from Mrs. Slater.

"But his mother is a patriot, mother," said Edith; "and Mr. Estabrook is not the man to try to force Bob to do anything against his wishes. Bob will be left to do as he likes in this matter, I am confident."

"I think you are right about that, Edie," said Dick. "Mr. Estabrook is a sensible man, and will not try to turn Bob from his purpose, I am confident."

The three conversed together for some time, and then Dick left the mother and sister, and went to his room. He was busy all the rest of the day, getting ready to go to New York the first of the week to join the patriot army.

That evening, at about nine o'clock, as they were seated in the sitting room talking, there came the sound of hurried footsteps outside, and then the door opened, and Bob Estabrook entered.

"Excuse me for entering so unceremoniously," he said, bowing to Mrs. Slater, and smiling at Edith; "but I have important news for Dick, and did not want to waste any time in stopping to knock."

"That is all right, Bob; sit down," said Dick. "What is the news you speak of?"

"I'll tell you: The Tories, under the leadership of Joe Bilkins and Carl Shinker, are going to attack you, here in the house, to-night, Dick!"

An exclamation of terror escaped Mrs. Slater.

"Oh, what shall we do!" she cried; "they will murder Dick, as they did my poor husband!"

"No, they won't, mother!" said Dick, his eyes flashing, "forewarned is forearmed, you know, and they will get the worst of it, if they try it on! But how do you know they are going to do this, Bob?"

"You will never tell, I know," said Bob; "so I don't mind telling you that father told me. The neighbors know that he is loyal to the king, and one of them let the cat out of the bag to him. Of course, he is your friend, and he told me, so that I could come to warn you."

"I am much obliged to you and your father, Bob; but do you suppose they will really dare to try to do anything?"

"Of course they will! They want revenge on you for shooting Scroggs, and they will be expecting to take you by surprise, you know."

"Well, they'll miss it there."

"You must not remain here to-night, my son!" cried Mrs. Slater. "You must leave, and at once."

"What, leave home? Run away from a gang of cowards such as are those fellows? Never! Mother, I will stay here and fight them to the death! I have father's rifle and pistols, and plenty of ammunition, and I shall stay and fight them!"

"Good for you!" cried Bob, admiringly; "and, Dick, I've got a surprise for you!"

"A surprise for me?"

"Yes."

"What is it?"

"I'll show you—see here," and going to the door, he gave a shrill whistle, and a few moments later a dozen youths of about Dick's and Bob's age filed into the house and bowed to Mrs. Slater and Edith.

Dick recognized the boys at once. They were the sons of the patriot neighbors, and were all schoolmates of himself and Bob.

"Well, well! this is a surprise, sure enough!" he exclaimed, and then he shook hands with the boys.

Each of the newcomers carried a rifle, and in a belt at their waists were pistols, while hanging at their sides were the powder-horns and bullet-pouches.

"You boys look as if you were going to war!" said Dick, when the greetings were over. "What means this warlike demonstration?"

"We have come to help you fight the Tories to-night, Dick!" said Bob.

"I suspected as much!" said Dick.

"We will make them wish they had stayed away and attended to their own business," said Bob.

"That's right," said Mark Morrison, a handsome youth of eighteen years.

"We will give them a lesson that they won't forget soon!" from another of the boys.

Dick's face glowed with pleasure.

"You are friends worth having," he said. "I am glad you have come; and now, when those cowardly Tories come here to-night, thinking to surprise me, they will themselves be surprised!"

"So they will!" grinned Bob.

"What time will they be here, do you think, Bob?"

"About midnight, I think was what the Tory said that told father about it."

"Very well; we will be ready for them!"

The boys talked the matter over, and arranged their plans. The house was a story-and-a-half structure, and Dick told his mother and sister to go to bed at the usual hour in one of the upstairs rooms, while he and his companions would remain downstairs in readiness to greet the Tories when they put in an appearance.

This was done, and the boys extinguished the candles, and sat in the darkness, talking in whispers. They did not know but the Tories might come earlier than was expected, and did not wish to betray their presence in the house.

The door was bolted, so that they could not be taken by surprise.

It was about half-past eleven when the boys heard the sound of footsteps outside.

"They are coming!" whispered Dick.

The boys grasped their rifles with nervous energy, and listened intently.

The footsteps approached the house, and it was easy to know from the sound that there were a number of men outside.

The footsteps ceased presently, and the boys heard a fumbling noise at the door.

"Who is there?" called out Dick, in a stern voice.

There was no reply, but utter silence for a few moments, and then Dick called out once more:

"Who is there?"

"A friend; open the door," was the reply, in what was evidently a disguised voice.

"You are a liar, you Tory soundrel!" cried Dick, defiantly; "go away, now, at once, if you know when you are well off!"

An exclamation, sounding like a curse, was heard, and then a gruff voice called out:

"Open the door, Dick Slater, or we will smash it in!"

"If you smash that door, you will sign your own death warrant!" retorted Dick. "There are a number of us in here, and we are armed. Go about your business, and thank your lucky stars that we were willing to let you escape!"

"Bah! you can't frighten us away with such words, Dick Slater!" came back the reply. "We are going to drag you out of the house and hang you to one of the trees in your own door yard! That is the way we intend serving all traitors!"

"Go ahead and do it, then, if you think you can!" replied Dick, defiantly.

"That's just what we will do!"

There was the sound of shuffling feet outside, and Dick took advantage of the opportunity, and told his companions to be ready to fire at the word.

"They will batter the door down," he said; "and as soon as the door gives way, I will give the order, and we will fire a volley into the midst of the scoundrels! If a second volley is necessary, draw your pistols and fire."

A few moments later the sound of rushing footsteps was heard, and crash! something heavy came against the door, which shook and creaked under the impact.

"They have found a heavy sill, or something of the kind, and are using it for a battering-ram," said Dick. "The door will go down next time; and be ready to fire if it does!"

The boys replied in low tones that they would be ready, and then, crash! came the battering-ram against the door a second time—this time with success, for the door burst from its hinges, and fell inward to the floor.

A wild yell of triumph escaped the lips of the Tories, and they started to leap through the open doorway into the house. At this instant, however, the word "Fire!" in a clear, ringing voice was heard, and the crash of a dozen or more rifles as they were discharged almost raised the roof!

Immediately following the volley from the rifles, came a chorus of yells of pain, rage and astonishment, and these were followed by groans and curses.

Dick had all the qualities of a good general. He seemed to realize, intuitively, that it would be an easy matter to put the enemy to complete rout by charging out upon them, and he gave the order to do this.

He leaped through the open doorway the first one, and after him came the other boys, pell mell, anxious, now that their blood was up, to get at the enemy. In a moment they were upon the astonished Tories, who, although numbering fifteen at least, immediately took to their heels and ran for their lives. The shock of the volley from the rifles had shattered their nerves, and the fierce charge of the youths had been too much for them; they could not stand their ground. Doubtless they thought they were being attacked by a regiment of soldiers.

"Go it, you cowards and murderers!" cried Dick, scornfully; "run, like the cowards that you are—and if you know when you are well off, you will stay away from here in the future!"

The boys were jubilant over their quick and decisive victory. They had put the Tories to flight much quicker than they had anticipated being able to do.

Dick stationed a couple of the youths for guard duty, while he and the others went to work to mend the broken door.

Mrs. Slater and Edith were delighted when they learned that not one of the boys had been injured in the least, and they were glad when Dick told them that he did not know whether or not they had killed any of the Tories.

"They deserved killing, whether we killed any of them or not!" said Bob. "They would have hung Dick, had they got hold of him."

"True," acknowledged Mrs. Slater; "but it is a terrible thing to have to shed human blood in this manner!"

"All is fair and right in war times, mother," said Dick. "We are fighting for our rights, for liberty, and I do not think it is wrong to shoot our enemies. If we don't shoot them, they will shoot us."

After the door had been repaired, Mrs. Slater and Edith returned to bed, and the boys sat up the rest of the night, talking of the war.

And there in the house that night, the boys, after due consideration and discussion of the subject, decided to get up a company from among the boys and young men of the neighborhood, elect Dick captain, and go down to New York and offer their services to General Washington.

This would take a couple of weeks, as they would have to hunt around a good deal to find a sufficient number to make out the company, but it was decided to do it.

"And what will we call ourselves, when we have organized our company?" asked Bob. "We must have a name."

"We will call ourselves the 'Liberty Boys of '76!'" said Dick.

CHAPTER V
Dick and the Commander in Chief

The great General George Washington sat in a room at his headquarters in the city of New York.

He was in a deep study.

The British were threatening to attack the American Army on Brooklyn Heights, and as General Howe had fully twenty-five thousand troops, while Washington had only eighteen thousand, the problem of how to hold the Heights was a serious one.

And hold it he must to retain control of New York, for Brooklyn Heights commanded New York, the same as Bunker Hill commanded Boston.

While the General sat buried in thought an orderly entered, and bowing, said:

"A young gentleman to see your excellency."

"Ah!" abstractedly; "who is the young gentleman, orderly?"

"I don't know, sir. He did not give his name, but said, 'Please tell General Washington that a Liberty Boy of '76 wants to see him.'"

"A 'Liberty Boy of '76,' eh? A good title!—yes, a very good title, indeed! Show him in, orderly."

The orderly retired, but returned soon, and ushered a handsome youth of about eighteen years into the room.

"How do you do, young man?" remarked General Washington, pleasantly: "To whom am I indebted for this call?"

"My name is Dick Slater, your excellency. I am a patriot, and the son of a patriot who was killed a short time since by Tories. I wish to offer my services, and I have out here a company of youths like myself, all of whom wish to join your army and help fight for liberty. We call ourselves the 'Liberty Boys of '76.'"

The eyes of the commander in chief shone with pleasure.

He stepped forward and extended his hand.

"Master Slater—Dick," he said, feelingly, "I accept the offer of yourself and company of Liberty Boys with pleasure; and I will say, while I am on the subject, that the Cause of Liberty cannot fail when such brave boys as yourself will get up companies and come and offer yourselves to be used for the purpose of fighting for freedom! We cannot lose; we must not lose; we will not lose!"

There was a determined ring to the voice of the great man, and Dick felt that he stood in the presence of a wonderful man, a genius for generalship such as the world has never seen—and probably never will see—excelled.

"Will your excellency review my company of Liberty Boys?" asked Dick. "They would like to see you and have you see them."

"Yes, indeed, Dick," was the prompt reply, for, like the majority of great men, he was courteous and kindly; "march them past and I will review them."

"Very well, your excellency; and thank you, sir."

Dick saluted, and started to withdraw, but Washington said, "Wait a moment," and Dick paused.

The commander in chief looked at Dick long and searchingly. He seemed to be sizing the youth up, and undoubtedly the verdict as a result of the scrutiny was satisfactory, for he said:

"After I have reviewed the company of Liberty Boys, and they have returned to their quarters, you will please report to me as soon as possible, Dick."

"Here, sir?" asked Dick.

"Here."

"Very well; I will lose no time in reporting to your excellency," and with a bow, Dick left the room and the house.

"A likely-looking youth!" murmured Washington, when Dick was gone; "I believe he might succeed where men have failed. I will give him the opportunity, at any rate."

"I wonder what the general wants to see me about!" thought Dick. "Well, it doesn't matter; whatever he says for me to do, that will I do, or die trying!"

Dick returned to the company of Liberty Boys, his face glowing.

"The commander in chief will review our company, boys!" he cried; "get ready at once. And we must do our best and make as good a showing as possible!"

The boys were eager and excited, but fifteen minutes later they were ready, and leaving their quarters they marched up the street past the commander in chief's headquarters. General Washington was out on the stoop, and as Dick and his company of "Liberty Boys of '76" marched past, the great man waved his hand in a graceful salute and smiled. Dick returned the salute, and then the Liberty Boys returned to their quarters, and Dick hastened to return to the commander in chief's headquarters.

He was shown into Washington's presence as soon as he gave his name, the orderly having been instructed to admit him at once.

Washington nodded and smiled.

"You have a splendid company, my boy!" he said. "It is my prophecy that your 'Liberty Boys of '76' will make a name for themselves before this war ends. If I had ten thousand such troops, I could bid defiance to Generals Howe and Clinton."

"I am glad you liked their looks," said Dick, simply; "they are each and every one ready to lay down their lives for the great cause of freedom."

"I believe you," the general said; and then he looked searchingly at Dick, and asked:

"If I were to say to you, Dick, that I would like to have you enter upon a dangerous undertaking, an undertaking in which your life would be threatened at every turn, would be in danger every minute, what would be your reply?"

"That you have only to command, your excellency," was the prompt response. "I am here at your service, and if I go where my life pays the forfeit, it will be lost in a noble cause. I am ready to go anywhere, undertake anything, risk everything. You have only to tell me what it is that you wish me to do."

"Nobly spoken!" exclaimed Washington, in admiration. "Dick, you are a true Liberty Boy, and I am going to honor you by sending you upon a difficult and dangerous, nay, desperate undertaking. If you should succeed in doing what I wish done, you will have rendered me an inestimable service, and perhaps saved the lives of thousands of patriot soldiers."

"I will do my best to succeed, sir," said Dick, his handsome face lighting up with enthusiasm.

"I know you will, my boy; and I hope and trust you will succeed."

Then the commander in chief looked down at the floor for a few moments, as if in deep study.

"Dick," he said, slowly and deliberately, "just outside the Narrows lies the British fleet, under Admiral Howe, and on the southwest shore of Long Island, just off which lie the ships, is General Howe's army. The British outnumber us considerably—just how much I do not know, but wish to—and I wish you to go over to Long Island, and make your way, if possible, into the enemy's lines, and find out not only how many troops they have, but what their intentions are. I fear an attack on Brooklyn Heights, and I would give much to find out when the attack is to be made. Do you think you could do this for me?"

"I am willing to try, your excellency!" said Dick, promptly.

"You are a brave and noble youth," said Washington; "and I dislike to send one so young on such a perilous undertaking. I have already sent two of the best spies in the Continental Army, and they have not returned. They were captured, undoubtedly, and were likely shot or hanged. And such would be your fate, my boy, if you were captured and thought to be a spy."

"I am ready to go, sir," said Dick, firmly; "I am willing to risk my life for the good of the great Cause; am willing to, if need be, lose it. I think, though, your excellency, that a boy like myself would be less liable to be suspected of being a spy than a man, and I have hopes that I may be able to penetrate into the enemy's lines and escape death as a spy."

"I had thought of that, my boy; in fact, that was the reason I decided to send you. Two of my best spies, both men grown, have failed, and I thought that a boy might be able to do what those men have failed to accomplish. Then you are willing to undertake this dangerous work?"

"Not only willing but eager to undertake it, your excellency! I wish to do something that will be of moment; something that will be of value to the patriots' cause."

"Good! and thank you, my boy. I shall let you go upon this dangerous errand, but it would be well to wait till evening. Come to me at four o'clock, and I will give you a letter of introduction to General Putnam,[12] who has charge of the forces on Brooklyn Heights. He will give you further aid and instructions."

"Very well, your excellency; I will return at four."

Then Dick took his leave, and returned to his company of Liberty Boys, and told them of his good fortune—as he considered it—in being chosen by the commander in chief to go over onto Long Island to act as a spy among the British.

They were excited, and each and every one thought exactly as Dick did regarding the matter. They were proud that their captain should be chosen by the commander in chief to go on such a dangerous and important errand.

"The general couldn't have done better than to pick on you, Dick," said Bob, earnestly; "you will succeed, and find out all about the British, if anybody can do so!"

Bob thought there was nobody quite the equal of Dick Slater.

"I hope to be successful," said Dick, modestly.

"You will be; I am sure of it!" said Bob. "How I wish I could go with you," he added, wistfully.

"Do you think you would like to be a spy, Bob?" asked Dick.

"I know I should like it!"

"Well, if I am successful the commander in chief will probably keep me at the same kind of work, and he would no doubt then be willing to give you work in the same line, Bob."

"I hope you will be successful, then."

At a quarter to four that afternoon, Dick bade good-by to his Liberty Boy friends, and went to General Washington's headquarters. The general gave him the letter to General Putnam, with instructions regarding the best route to take to reach Brooklyn Heights, and then Dick took his departure, the cheery words of encouragement from the commander in chief ringing in his ears for a long time.

It was almost dark when Dick finally reached the headquarters of General Putnam, and when "Old Put," as he was familiarly called, read the letter, he looked at the youth before him in astonishment.

"And you, a mere boy, are going to try to penetrate the British lines and spy on them!" he exclaimed. "My boy, you are going on a dangerous errand."

"I know that, sir," was the quiet reply.

"And yet you are not afraid?"

"I go where duty calls me, sir. If I were very, very much afraid, I would go just the same. I have but one life, but I am

willing to risk, and if need be lose, it in fighting for the great
Cause of Liberty."

"Bravely and nobly spoken!" said Putnam, admiringly,
and he gazed into the frank, bright face of the youth with interest. "I will give you all the aid in my power—which in this
instance is confined to directions as to the best course for
you to take in trying to reach the British Army, down on the
south shore."

"Give me such information as you can," said Dick, simply,
"and I will start at once."

"But you must have something to eat and drink first. You
can eat while I give you your instructions."

"A piece of bread and a cup of water is all I care for, sir."

Food was brought, and Dick ate heartily, for he was a boy,
and a healthy one with a good appetite, and by the time he had
finished he knew all that General Putnam knew regarding the
location of the British Army, and regarding the best way in
which to go in order to reach the army.

It was now quite dark, and he left Putnam's headquarters,
and with a good-by to the orderly who had accompanied him
through the American lines, he plunged into the darkness and
set out afoot in the direction in which he knew was the British
Army.

"Let's see; General Putnam said it was about five miles, as
near as he could judge, to the British lines. Well, I ought to
reach there in a couple of hours, anyway."

Thus thought Dick, as he made his way along. He was
headed for Flatbush, and thought that he might learn something there regarding the British.

Dick reached Flatbush, but decided not to tarry there long,
as he saw a couple of companies of redcoats walking about.
He was questioned by the captain of one company, who asked
him where he lived, and Dick said, "Out in the country."

"Well, it is time you were getting home," said the officer;
"you are liable to be gobbled up by the rebels."

"I am not afraid," said Dick, quietly; and then he drew back
the skirts of his coat, and said:

"See; I have my father's pistols, and if the rebels try to catch me, I will shoot them!"

The officer gave a start, and looked at Dick suspiciously.

"See here, my young friend, you are pretty young to be sporting pistols!" he exclaimed; "that savors more of the style of the sons of the cursed rebels than of the son of a king's man. Who are you, and where are you going?"

The British soldiers now came crowding around, and they all regarded the youth suspiciously.

"He's a young rebel spy and you may be sure of it, captain!" said one. "He looks it; see what a wicked eye he has!"

"It isn't any more wicked than yours!" retorted Dick, who was a youth not to be awed.

"Better take him prisoner, captain!" advised another. "He is too saucy, altogether!"

"I am going to do so," said the officer; "disarm him, men!"

But Dick was not disposed to submit to capture this early in his career as a spy. Simulating a fear which, strange to say, he did not feel, although surrounded by British soldiers, Dick drew his pistols from his belt, and said:

"Here are my pistols; take—their contents!" and as he spoke thus he quickly fired the weapons point blank in the faces of the officer and his men; then striking right and left with the weapons, the bold youth broke from among the soldiers, who were surprised and thrown into disorder by being fired upon by the boy, and before they realized it, he was clear of them, and running down the street like the wind.

"Don't let him escape!" howled the officer, who had been wounded in the cheek by one of the bullets, and was in a rage as a result; "don't let the cursed rebel spy escape! Shoot him dead!—fire, men, fire!"

The soldiers had recovered from their amazement and disorder, now, and raising their muskets, they fired a volley. At the same instant the fleeing youth fell forward upon his face, and a wild shout of joy went up from the British soldiers.

They thought they had killed the youth, but they were mistaken. By a fortunate accident, Dick stumbled and fell just as the British were pulling the triggers, and the result was that he went down just in time to escape the hail of leaden pellets, they going above him. Then he leaped to his feet, with a shout of defiance, and springing around the corner of a house, disappeared from the sight of the amazed and discomfited British.

CHAPTER VI
Within the British Lines

"That was a close call," said Dick to himself, as he ran rapidly out of the village and into the country and darkness; "it was a close call, but a miss is as good as a mile. I rather think I astonished those fellows a bit, anyhow!" and the youth smiled grimly.

"Gracious, though," he murmured; "the British are crowding up close to the American positions! I hope I will be able to discover something of importance, and get back to General Washington with the news."

The youth struck into the country road which ran almost due south, and followed it for about a mile, when hearing the sound of horses' feet behind him, he stepped aside and took refuge in the edge of a field.

"I'll reload my pistols while waiting for those people to pass by," Dick thought, and he proceeded to do so.

As the horsemen drew near, Dick listened intently, and soon decided that it was a company of British soldiers.

"They are not the fellows I had my encounter with back at Flatbush, however," he decided; "they are laughing and joking at a great rate, while the fellows I met would be talking in a different strain.

"They have been on a foraging expedition," he said to himself, as he heard their remarks; "and are on their way back to the main army."

A bright idea struck Dick.

"I'll follow them," he decided; "and in that manner I will be led direct to the British Army."

The horsemen were riding at a leisurely gait, so it was not a difficult matter to keep up with them, and Dick was glad they had come along.

A mile further, and the horsemen reached the main encampment of the British, and Dick had been forced to stop a quarter of a mile back, as he was aware of the fact that he could not enter the lines by way of the road without being challenged, as there would be pickets out.

"I'll take a circuit out and around, and see if I can slip in unobserved," thought Dick, and he proceeded to put this move into practice.

"I am in a dangerous neighborhood," he said to himself; "but no matter; I will find out how many men the British have, and what they intend doing, or die trying!"

The youth made his way through the underbrush, which was quite thick here, and by listening intently at intervals he was enabled to locate the sentinel, and by the exercise of considerable woodcraft he succeeded in slipping through between two of the pickets, although they were within a few yards of each other—were so close that they were talking to each other, in fact.

The youth had just managed to get across the line, and was congratulating himself, when he stepped on a dry twig, and it broke with a loud snap, sounding trebly sharp in the stillness.

"Halt! Who comes there?" cried both sentinels.

Dick paused, but made no reply.

"Who comes there?—quick! or we fire!" cried the sentinels, and knowing they would keep their word, Dick leaped away through the underbrush as rapidly as he could go in the darkness. He made considerable noise, and the sentinels, locating him as well as they could by this, fired, the reports of the weapons arousing the encampment almost in an instant.

The bullets came so close to Dick that he heard their whir, but he did not care for that. They had not found lodgment in his body, and he was satisfied.

He was confronted with a difficult problem now, however: He was within the British lines, and the entire encampment was in an uproar. It would be a difficult matter to escape detection and capture; in fact, it would be almost an impossibility, and the youth thinking quickly and to the point, decided upon a bold stroke: He would walk boldly into camp, and pretend that he wished to join the British Army!

"I don't know whether I can make it win or not," the youth murmured; "but I'll try it. A bold game is often successful where any other kind would fail."

Then he advanced rapidly and walked right up to the main body of the British.

"Hello! who are you?" exclaimed an officer, staring at Dick.

"I'm a boy," replied Dick, coolly.

"So I perceive; but who are you and where did you come from?"

"Me? Oh, my name is Sam Sly, and I live up the other side of Bedford."

"Ah, you do? Well, how in blazes did you get through our lines?"

The British soldiers had gathered around, and were listening to the youth, and watching him with interest, the camp fires throwing out sufficient light so that it was possible to see very well.

"Why, I walked through."

"Ah, you did? Didn't you see any sentinels?"

"No; but I heard some!" and Dick grinned.

"Was it you who caused the disturbance out there just now?"

"I guess it was, sir. At any rate, a couple of your sentinels fired at me, and I heard the sing of the bullets as they went past."

"You did? Were you not scared?"

"No."

"You weren't?"

"No; there was no use to get scared after the sentinels had fired and missed."

The officer gave Dick a shrewd look.

"Well, you are right about that," he said; "but it is seldom that such a philosophical head is found on such young shoulders. What did you want here, anyway, that you should be slipping into our lines in this manner?"

Dick saw that the officer's suspicions were aroused, and he made up his mind that he would have to be very circumspect if he succeeded in disarming suspicion.

"I wasn't slipping into your lines," the youth said, quietly.

"You were not?"

"No."

"What were you doing, then?"

"I was walking into your camp, with no attempt at secrecy, when the sentinels heard me and fired upon me."

"Indeed? What were you coming into camp for?"

"I wanted to offer my services as a soldier in your army."

The officer studied the face of the youth closely.

"You did, eh?" he remarked.

"Yes, sir."

"You are loyal to the king, then?"

"Oh, yes, sir!"

Dick's nature was so open and frank; he had such a native dislike for falsehood that even though he felt that he was justified in telling an untruth to deceive the British, yet the falsehood came so stumblingly from his lips that the keen-minded officer became suspicious.

"You are sure of that?" he asked.

"Yes, I am sure of it," the youth declared. Then, feeling that some decided statements were needed, he added:

"Just give me a chance to prove it, is all I ask! If I don't do as good fighting as any of your men, then you can shoot me!"

"You look to me somewhat like a rebel!" the officer remarked, coldly, and Dick began to see that he was in for trouble. This was made more of a certainty a few moments later, when the company of soldiers with whom Dick had had his encounter at Flatbush an hour or so before, rode into camp.

The captain had his face tied up in a silk handkerchief, and the instant his eyes fell on Dick, he pointed at him, and cried:

"Tie that young scoundrel up! He is a rebel, and, I am confident, a spy! He shot me back at Flatbush an hour ago, and wounded one of my men so badly we had to leave him behind! Tie the young scoundrel up!"

The officer who had been questioning Dick looked at him and smiled coldly.

"What have you to say to that, my loyal young friend?"

He accented the "loyal."

"What have I to say to that?" coolly.

"Yes."

"Simply that the gentleman lies!"

Dick spoke so calmly, and in such a matter-of-fact way, that the British officer gave a gasp of astonishment.

"Do you mean to say you did not shoot the captain, back at Flatbush, as he says?" he asked.

"Oh, no; I don't mean to say that. I mean that he lies when he says I am a rebel."

"Oh; you still claim to be loyal to the king?"

"Yes; and wish to join the army, and fight for him."

The captain had dismounted by this time, and now advanced and confronted the youth threateningly.

"Have the young traitor tied up at once, Captain Park," he said; "he is a rebel spy, and I am sure of it! Put him in the prison-pen along with the other two spies who were recently captured, and see how he will like that!"

Dick almost gave a start. He remembered that General Washington had said he had sent two men to spy on the British, and they had not returned. The words of the wounded captain would indicate that the two men in question were held prisoners, and the youth's heart leaped when he thought that perhaps he might succeed in rescuing them, and aiding them to escape and return to New York.

"They will have some valuable information, and if I can free them, and we can get away, I think I will have done more than the commander in chief expected I would be able to do."

"The captain is mistaken," he said aloud; "I am not a spy, but a loyal subject of the king. However, I suppose you will do as you like with me. I cannot prevent you."

"Why did you shoot me, then?" asked the wounded captain.

"Because I thought you were going to hang me for a spy at once, without giving me a chance to prove my loyalty, and I decided to escape if I could, and join the army."

"I believe it will be best to give him a chance to prove his loyalty to the king," said the other captain.

The fact of the matter was that there was bad blood between these two officers on account of a love affair with one of the pretty, buxom Dutch girls of the vicinity, and Captain Park was secretly glad Dick had shot the captain in the cheek, and he hoped the wound would spoil the gallant captain's beauty.

"Oh, all right; do as you like!" half-snarled Captain Frink. "I hope he will turn out to be the rankest kind of a rebel, and shoot you full of holes!"

With this amiable remark, Captain Frink stalked away, followed by an amused laugh from Captain Park.

"I am going to give you a chance to prove your loyalty, young man!" he said.

"That is what I want," replied Dick.

CHAPTER VII
Gathering Information

Dick was allowed his freedom, and he wandered about, seemingly merely interested by the novelty of the sight of so many soldiers, but the shrewd boy spy was listening to the conversation about him, and treasuring up every word.

The soldiers of the king were not believers in the "early to bed, early to rise" philosophy, evidently, for they did not turn in until after eleven—that is, the majority of them did not.

This gave Dick some little time in which to circulate around and hear what was being said.

"When are we to move on the rebels?" he heard one soldier ask another.

"I don't know," was the reply; "before very long, though, I think."

"We'll eat them up, when we do go after them!"

"Yes; I understand that General Howe says the capture of the Heights now occupied by the rebels will practically end the war, as it will win New York for us at once, and force Washington to retreat out of the city."

"That's right; I wish we could capture Washington himself; that would put an end to the whole business."

"So it would; I wish it, too, as I am anxious to get back home. I don't like this business of being over here and having to fight these bushwhacking rebels."

"Neither do I; but I think that the capture of the Heights of Brooklyn will end the matter, practically."

"You will find that you are mistaken about that!" thought Dick, and then as the two began conversing about home affairs in England, he moved on.

"Who in blazes are you, and what are you wandering around here for, like a restless spirit?" asked a sergeant of Dick, a few minutes later.

"I'm just looking at the soldiers," replied Dick, quietly. "No harm in that, is there?"

"That depends. Who and what are you?"

"My name is Sam Sly."

"Sam Sly, eh?"

"Yes."

"Well Sam Sly, how sly are you?"

The officer chuckled; he thought he was saying something smart.

"Slyer than you think, perhaps!" thought Dick; but aloud he said:

"I am not very sly. I am a country boy from up Bedford way, and I have come down here to join the army, and fight for the king."

"You are loyal to the king, then, are you?"

"Oh, yes, sir."

"Well, that's the way to be. And you want to fight for him, eh?"

"Yes."

"Jove! I wish you could take my place and fight, and let me go back to England!" with a dry laugh. "After you have been in one battle, you won't be so eager to fight for the king, or anyone else!"

"Maybe not," simply. "I want to try it, anyway, and see."

"Bah! you couldn't fight anything!" sneered a soldier, who had been drinking a bit more than was good for him, and who had listened to the talk of the youth with a scornful expression of countenance. "You would run at the first fire."

"Judging me by yourself, I suppose?" remarked Dick, coolly.

A number of the soldiers who sat near and heard the remark laughed loudly at this, and began chaffing the soldier.

"Ha-ha! he was too much for you, Moggsley!"

"The kid is lively with his tongue!"

"He's all right!"

"You had better keep still, Moggsley!"

But the British soldier was of a mean, quarrelsome disposition, especially when he was in his cups, and he became very angry.

"Why, you cursed little whelp!" he cried, leaping to his feet and glaring at Dick in a manner intended to frighten him half to death, but which failed of doing so, as the youth met the look unflinchingly; "I have half a mind to wring your neck! You are altogether too free with that tongue of yours, and for two shillings I would cut it off!"

"Would you?" remarked Dick, coldly; "I don't think you would!"

"Oh, you don't, eh?"

"I do not!"

"The boy is spunky!" exclaimed a soldier, admiringly.

"He is gritty!"

"He has enough spirit for a rebel!"

The angry soldier advanced threateningly, and drawing a knife from his pocket, and opening the blade, which converted the knife into a dirk with a blade six inches long, he held it up and smiled in a fiendish manner.

"D'ye see that knife?" he asked.

"I see it!"

Dick was perfectly cool. He felt that he was more than a match, physically, for any king's soldier, on account of the fact that he was a trained athlete, and he did not exhibit the least nervousness.

"Well," said the soldier, fiercely, "I am going to use that knife on you!"

"I'd advise you not to attempt it!" said Dick, promptly.

"What?"

The soldier was astonished at the youth's coolness, as were the onlookers also.

"You heard what I said."

Dick was as calm as ever.

"You say you'd advise me not to attempt it, eh?"

"Yes."

"Why, what would the young high-cock-a-lorum do?"

"He would knock you down!" was the prompt reply.

The soldier laughed hoarsely.

He considered it a rare, good joke that a boy should talk of knocking him down.

"Why, ye little whelp!" he said, scornfully; "ye couldn't knock me down in a week!"

"You try using that knife on me, and see!" said Dick quietly.

"Well, that's just what I am going to do! I said I thought of cutting your tongue off, but that would be too bad, I guess; so I will content myself with cutting a piece off the top of each of your ears! That is the private mark which Hank Moggsley puts on people he doesn't like!"

"Have you ever put the mark on anybody?"

"Yes, sirree; on lots of people."

"Defenseless old men, and boys ten or twelve years old, I suppose!"

Dick's tone was scathing, and the laughter which greeted this remark of Dick's made the soldier very angry.

"You insolent young hound!" he hissed; "you do not know what you are doing! Anger me too much, and I will kill you!"

"Try it, you coward, and see what you will get!" said Dick, who had made up his mind to give this arrogant, boastful fellow a lesson.

"Jove! but the boy is gritty!"

"He is a good one!"

"That's right!"

The remarks of the soldiers made the fellow more angry than ever, and when he found his speech—Dick's last remark had almost paralyzed him—he hissed:

"So! you will have it, eh? Well, your blood be on your own head, then! You should have kept a civil tongue, and not been so saucy!"

Then he crouched for a spring at the daring youth.

The soldiers sitting around cried to Dick in warning, but it was not necessary. The youth was watching the angry man, and was ready for him.

As the soldier leaped forward, knife in hand, with a snarling cry of rage and menace, Dick's right arm shot out, and the king's soldier was knocked down with a neatness and dispatch that was remarkable, and the force with which he struck the ground caused him to give utterance to a grunt.

And now the soldiers who were witnesses to the remarkable affair were astonished as they had never been before.

Exclamations of wonderment escaped them.

Moggsley was a bad man, and was feared and disliked by his comrades on account of the fact that he was of such a vicious nature. He would as lief kill a man as not, and had done so on several occasions. It was war time, however, and he had been let go. After the war was over, he would probably be hanged.

Moggsley lay there on the ground, blinking up at the sky, for nearly half a minute.

Then Dick stepped forward and gave him a poke with the toe of his boot.

"Get up, you coward!" he said, sharply. "Get up, and finish killing me, if you are going to do so; I am in a hurry to have the affair over with."

This aroused the fallen man, and caused murmurs of astonishment at the youth's temerity from the spectators.

"You'd better run, young fellow, instead of staying and making him madder than ever."

"He'll kill you!"

"That's right; you'd better get out while you have a chance."

"What! run from a coward such as he is?" exclaimed Dick, with scorn; "not much! I am not through with him yet! He shall not escape me so easy as all that! The scoundrel has, I have no doubt, murdered defenseless people, and I am going to give him such a thorough thrashing that he will be in no condition to do any more such work for a long time to come!"

The soldier had now scrambled to his feet, and he stood and stared about him for a few moments, as if still somewhat dazed. Then he caught sight of Dick, and it all came back to him.

He gave vent to a snarl of rage.

It wounded like the snarl of a wounded panther.

He leaped toward Dick, knife in hand, his face convulsed with rage and the light of murder.

He would have no mercy on the youth, if he could once get him in his power.

But Dick was not disposed to let this happen.

He disliked all king's soldiers.

He disliked this one more than any one he had yet seen.

To his mind, Moggsley was worse than a ravening wolf.

So he made up his mind to treat the scoundrel roughly.

As the man leaped forward, Dick jumped to one side.

The stroke of the knife, which the fellow made as he came forward, missed Dick by a foot at least.

Then, crack! the youth's wonderful fist took Moggsley on the jaw, and down he went again, with a thud.

A long drawn out "Ah-h-h-h!" escaped the spectators.

They were never so surprised in their lives.

That a youth such as was this should floor a grown man like Moggsley was almost unbelievable.

But the evidence was before their eyes.

Moggsley lay there on the ground, looking up at the stars in a dazed way, helpless for the time being.

Doubtless he saw a great many stars not down on any astronomer's chart.

Dick stood there, his arms folded, looking down at his fallen foe.

"Come, come!" he said, sarcastically; "you will never finish me if you don't do better than you have been doing! Get up and try it again!"

"Young fellow, you are a good one!"

"Yes; but Moggsley'll kill you yet! You'd better get away while there is yet time."

"That's what he will do; and it would be a pity, too, to see such a brave fellow die! Get out, and stay away from Moggsley in the future."

"I'm not through with Moggsley yet!" said Dick, in the grim, determined tone which was his birthright. "I am not going to let him escape so easily."

"Listen to that!"

"You are a bold one!"

"He has made his words good, though, so far!"

Moggsley was stirring now, and the attention of all was turned to him.

He raised himself to a sitting posture and looked around him in a bewildered manner.

"What has happened?" he asked; and then he felt of his jaw, and made a grimace.

"My jaw hurts," he said; "what is the matter with it?"

"That is where I hit you just now," said Dick, calmly. "Get up, quick, and I will give you another in the same place!"

This brought the soldier back to a realization of all, and he scrambled to his feet.

He had dropped the knife when he went down the last time. He made no effort to regain it.

Doubtless the two attempts he had made to reach the youth, failing each time, had taught him the uselessness of trying to prosecute the attack further at short range.

At any rate, he decided on another course of procedure.

He reached his hand to his belt, quickly, and drew his pistol.

He leveled it at the youth.

There was a fiendish look, a look of fierce joy and triumph, on his face.

"I am going to shoot you down like a dog! you cursed young whelp!" he cried; "die!"

But the wonderful quickness of the youth foiled him again.

Dick leaped aside with the quickness of thought, and as he swayed his body downward, and to one side, he struck upward with his arm, striking the pistol arm of the soldier, and knocking the arm upward, so that when the pistol was discharged, the bullet went whistling up in the air.

Then, crack! the youth's terrible fist took the would-be murderer on the jaw, and down he went for the third time.

The spectators stared in open-mouthed amazement.

They had expected nothing else than that the youth would be shot down, but again he had outgeneraled his opponent.

The noise of the pistol-shot alarmed the camp, and officers of the guard came running up to see what was the trouble.

When they learned what it was, they turned on Dick.

"What do you mean by coming into the camp and raising such a disturbance?" an officer asked.

"I didn't raise any disturbance, sir."

Dick was cool and composed.

"You did not?"

"No, sir; that fellow started it himself."

"I don't believe it!"

The officers feared the fellow, as he was an inveterate gambler, and it happened that they owed him considerable in the way of gambling debts, and they did not wish to have to say anything to Moggsley.

"It is the truth, just the same," said Dick; "and I can prove it by the soldiers who saw the affair from the start."

"Who are you?" abruptly.

"Sam Sly."

"What are you doing here?"

"I am a king's man, and I came here to join the army, and fight for King George."

"Oh, that's it. Well, you have made a very poor start, as you have been fighting against the king's soldiers, from the looks of things."

"No; only against one, and he is not a soldier, but a scoundrel!"

"That will do! Go to the supply tent and get you a blanket, and turn in for the night. You have done enough deviltry for the once."

"I don't want to go till I have given this coward the lesson he needs."

"He will be in no condition to fight you; see, he is dazed."

This was really the case, and feeling that he had punished the fellow pretty thoroughly, Dick walked away without another word.

He made a few inquiries, here and there, and presently found the supply tent, and securing a blanket, he lay down, and wrapping himself in the blanket, was soon fast asleep.

CHAPTER VIII
The Prison-Pens

One would have thought that the young patriot spy would not have slept much.

There are not many who, placed in his position, would have done so.

The majority in his situation—a patriot spy in the midst of the British Army—would have been so nervous and frightened that they would not have been able to close their eyes in sleep at all.

But not so Dick.

He was a peculiar youth.

He had nerves of steel, had perfect control of himself, and no feeling of uneasiness came to disturb his mind and keep him from sleeping.

He went to sleep and slept as soundly as he would have slept had he been at home in bed.

Imagination he had none.

No fear of what might happen ever bothered Dick Slater's mind.

He was intensely practical.

It was his way to wait till danger actually threatened, and then meet it as best he might be able at the time.

These peculiar qualifications would make him a splendid spy.

Dick awoke much refreshed next morning, and after having eaten a good solid breakfast, he felt that he would be in good condition to prosecute his investigations during the day.

Captain Park ran across him at an early hour, and after questioning him further, found him a place in a company of his regiment.

The soldiers did pretty much as they liked, excepting during drill hours.

They wandered here and there, and squads were constantly going and coming from the beach, where they bathed.

Dick went along with one of those squads.

When they came to the beach, Dick noticed several old hulks lying near the shore in a little cove, sheltered from the rougher waters of York Bay, where the British fleet lay at anchor.

"What are those old hulks there for?" he asked of a fellow with whom he had struck up a sort of friendship.

"Those are intended for the reception of such prisoners as we capture when we storm Brooklyn Heights," was the reply.

"Ah! I see; prison-pens, eh?"

"Yes."

"They have no occupants as yet, have they?"

"A dozen or two. You see, we pick up a few stragglers occasionally, and there are a couple of spies in there, too."

"A couple of spies, you say?"

"Yes. They are to be shot in a few days."

"And serve them right!" declared Dick, with assumed fierceness. "The idea of their turning traitor, and working against the king! They ought to be hung!"

"You're right about that!"

"Are they all in the same hulk?" asked Dick, looking at the prison-pens with disguised interest.

"Yes; they're in this one, nearest the shore."

Dick had learned what he wished to know, so said no more just at that time.

When they came in sight of the British fleet in York Bay, Dick asked how dangerous the vessels were.

"Are they all in good fighting trim, and well-manned?" he asked.

"Oh, yes; the ships are all right, and there are plenty of men aboard them," was the reply.

"That is good; there is no danger that Washington and his army of traitors will come down and capture them, then."

The soldier laughed.

"Well, I guess not!" he said.

"There must be an awful lot of soldiers here!" said Dick, presently. "I never saw so many men together before in all my life."

"There are at least twenty-five thousand men in the army that has been landed since the ships reached here from Halifax and England."

"Phew!" whistled Dick; "why don't they attack the American Army at once, and wipe it out of existence?"

"We are going to do so in a few days, now—so I heard the captain say yesterday."

"What day, do you know?" asked Dick, so eagerly that his companion looked at him somewhat suspiciously.

"What makes you seem so excited?" he asked, cautiously.

"Why, I want to be in the fight!" the youth cried. "How I wish we were going to attack them to-day!"

"You're all right, I guess!" with a smile. "Well, I don't know the exact day we will move on Brooklyn Heights, but it will be within four days, at any rate."

Four days!

Dick made a mental note of this.

This was important news, indeed!

It was something that General Washington ought to know at once.

Dick made up his mind that the commander in chief of the Continental Army should know it very soon.

The youth was determined not to leave, however, until after he had at least made a desperate effort to set the spies and other patriot prisoners free, and aid them to escape.

He was not the kind of a youth to go off and leave the poor men to their fate.

That fate would be death by hanging, or by bullet, and as he had four days in which to return to the commander in chief with the information which he had gained, he was determined to take the prisoners with him when he went.

Dick went in bathing with the others, and spent a couple of hours there. He was careful to count the British warships and take particular note of them.

He saw that carpenters were at work on three or four and he jumped to the conclusion that the vessels were not as seaworthy as they might be—at least some of them were not.

"I wish I could sink the whole fleet!" he thought, and he got to pondering, in the hope that he might think up some scheme whereby this might be accomplished.

It was a difficult problem, however, and he dismissed it, finally, as impracticable.

Dick spent the day much after the same fashion as the rest of the soldiers. He saw the soldier Moggsley once during the day, but the fellow for some reason pretended not to see the youth.

The fact was, he was afraid of Dick, and although burning with hatred for the youth, he did not dare show it, but hid it, and awaited an opportunity to strike Dick when he was not looking.

Dick read the fellow correctly, however, and smiled to himself.

"He would murder me if he got the chance," he thought; "well, I won't give him the chance."

When evening came, and it grew dark, Dick began to grow restless.

He could not content himself to sit by the camp fire and listen to stories.

He was anxious to be away to the old prison-pens made from the hulks of dismantled vessels.

He was eager to rescue the spies and the other patriots imprisoned there.

Dick got up and sauntered slowly away, looking here and there in the most natural and careless manner imaginable.

No one to have seen him would have thought that he was burning with the desire to leap away at a run, and race down toward the waterfront to where the old hulks lay.

The youth had splendid control of himself.

This was what was going to make him such a wonderful success as a spy.

"Where are you going, Sly?" asked Captain Parks, as he passed where that officer sat engaged in gazing up at the stars in meditation.

"I feel restless, captain," replied Dick; "I will take a little walk before turning in for the night."

"Very well; but don't go far."

"I will be back in a few minutes."

Dick passed on, and as he left the light thrown out by the dozens of camp fires, and entered the darkness, a dark form went stealing along in his wake.

He was followed; and the man following him was bent on murdering the youth.

Moggsley had been sitting near the camp fire reading, when he happened to look up and saw Dick leaving camp, and he at once leaped up, and assuming a carelessness he was far from feeling, he followed the youth.

Dick kept on down the road toward the beach, walking quite rapidly now, for he was where he would be unobserved, he was sure, and he wished to get to the old hulk which was the prison-pen of the patriots as quickly as possible.

The fact that he walked quite fast saved him from being assaulted a much longer time than would otherwise have elapsed. Moggsley was surprised at the speed at which the youth was going.

"What in blazes is he up to?" he asked himself. "Why is he walking so fast? I wonder if he has discovered that he is followed?"

This thought gave the scoundrel some uneasiness.

He was a coward at heart, and the thrashing Dick had given him the night before had inspired him with a wholesome respect for the youth's prowess.

If the youth suspected that he was being followed, and was

on his guard, it would be a difficult and dangerous undertaking to attack him.

Moggsley was desperate, however, and gritting his teeth, he hastened after the youth, and gradually drew nearer to his intended victim.

Dick really had no thought that he was followed, but he had a splendid hearing, and as he was walking rapidly along, he heard a noise behind him.

He whirled quickly.

He was only just in time.

As he whirled, he saw a dark form coming toward him.

The form was that of a man, and was only a few feet distant.

Instinctively the youth knew someone had followed him from the camp, and he felt that it would be a fight to the death.

He had splendid eyes, and possessed the cat-like faculty of seeing after night—not to the degree possessed by the members of the feline tribe, of course, but to a degree more than the average human being—and he detected the flash of steel.

He reached up and grasped the wrist of the arm, in the hand of which was, he was confident, a knife, or weapon of some kind.

Having got hold of the wrist, the youth held on firmly, for he knew that his safety lay in doing so.

His assailant speedily proved himself to be no mean opponent, and the struggle which was waged there in the darkness was a terrible one.

Not a word was spoken.

Breath was too precious to be wasted in that manner.

Backward and forward, around and around the two moved, each striving to get the advantage of the other.

Dick was a skilled wrestler, and was as hard to get off his feet as a cat. Moreover, he was more powerful than most men, and his assailant had his work cut out for him.

Suddenly, in moving about, Dick's foot caught in a vine or something, and although he made an almost superhuman effort to keep from falling, he could not save himself.

Exercising his cat-like faculties, however, Dick, in falling, managed to make a quick twist and reverse movement, at the same time turning his assailant's body halfway around, and the result was that when they struck the ground Dick was on top.

A peculiar, gasping groan escaped the fellow, and Dick wondered at it.

"Is it a trick to get me to let go of him?" the youth asked himself.

He held onto the fellow's wrists with a grip of iron for a few moments, and then as the fellow made no movement, nor tried to wrench his wrists loose, Dick became convinced that his assailant had been badly hurt in the fall.

One of the fellow's arms—the one in the hand of which was the knife—was doubled under his body, and Dick, possessed of a strange suspicion, made an examination by feeling about.

Suddenly he made a discovery:

The knife which the fellow had in his hand had got turned with the point upward as they fell, and he had fallen on it, and had been killed by his own weapon almost instantly!

A feeling of horror came over Dick, but he dismissed it as quickly as it came, almost.

"It is war times, and he would have killed me," he said to himself. "Self-defense is the first law of nature, and I but defended myself—as I intend to do under any and all circumstances, if I have to kill redcoats by the score! My services are needed by my country, and I am going to live to be of service to the great Cause of Freedom just as long as I can!"

Dick wondered who his assailant was, and taking out a flint and steel, and gathering some twigs and dried grass, he struck a light and as his eyes fell upon the face of the dead man, he exclaimed:

"Moggsley!"

CHAPTER IX
Dick to the Rescue

Yes, the dead man was Moggsley, the soldier who had picked the quarrel with Dick the night before, and whom Dick had given a thrashing.

The youth understood the situation perfectly.

Moggsley, burning with a desire for revenge, had followed him, with the intention of murdering him.

He had failed, and had accomplished his own destruction.

"Well, served him right!" thought Dick, and extinguishing the light, he went his way, having first taken the pistols and cartridges off the dead man.

"He won't need them any more," the youth said to himself; "and I will put them to better use. I will use them in the service of my country."

One thing Dick was glad of, and that was that he could now be reasonably sure that he was not suspected of being a spy, and had not been followed for that reason.

Moggsley's incentive was hatred and revenge.

He doubtless had had no thought that the youth was a patriot spy.

Dick hastened on his way.

Every few minutes he paused and listened intently.

He feared he might have been followed by others besides Moggsley.

Such was not the case, however, and of course he did not hear anything more of an alarming nature from the rear.

Dick reached the beach presently, and paused.

"Now, how am I to reach the prison ship?" he asked himself.

He pondered a few moments.

"I can and will swim, if I have to do so," he said to himself; "but," he added; "I should think there would be a boat near here somewhere."

This was reasonable to suppose.

The prisoners would have to have food every day.

The food would have to be taken to them from the shore.

Therefore, it followed that there must be a boat not far away.

"I'll find it," the youth thought. "It is close by, and I would be willing to wager that such is the case."

Dick hunted around, and was fortunate enough to find a stick, with a crook at one end of it in the shape of a hook.

Holding to the straight end of the stick, Dick walked slowly along the shore of the cove, dragging the stick along in such a manner that the hook would catch the rope or chain holding the boat.

He had not gone far before he was stopped by feeling the stick held back, it having caught something pretty solid.

"That's the rope, I'll bet!" the youth thought, and feeling, he found that this was the case.

"Good!" he murmured; "now to get aboard the prison ship!"

The youth climbed into the boat, untied the rope, and taking the oars, rowed slowly and carefully out into the cove.

He was careful not to make any more noise than was possible.

There would be a guard on the prison ship, and if he was heard he might get shot.

"I will have to be careful," he thought. "I don't want to fail now that I have gone this far and met with success. I must free those prisoners!"

Ahead of him he saw a light flash up and then go out again, and the youth slowed up, and moved very cautiously.

"That was the guard lighting his pipe," he thought; "I am close to the prison ship now."

And such was the case, for presently one of the oars struck against the hull of the old hulk.

It made a rasping noise that was heard on deck, for Dick heard a stir, and a voice exclaimed:

"What was that!"

Footsteps approached the side at a point almost directly above where Dick sat in the boat, and a voice cried out:

"Who comes there?"

Of course, Dick made no answer.

He sat there as motionless as a statue.

He scarcely breathed.

It would not do to be discovered now.

It would spoil all his plans.

He was determined to free the prisoners.

So he sat there as silent as the Sphinx.

"Hello! hello! I say! Who comes there?"

The guard's voice had an impatient ring.

Of course, Dick did not respond, and presently, after a silence of half a minute, the guard gave utterance to an exclamation of vexation, and walked away from the rail, as Dick could tell by the sound of his footsteps.

"A narrow escape!" thought Dick. "Well, I must get aboard."

He tied the rope to the rail, so the boat would not drift away, and then he listened, so as to locate the guard.

"I must overcome him first of all," the youth said to himself.

Then he thought that perhaps there might be more than one.

It would be best to investigate before making an attack on the guard.

It would never do to attack one guard, and have three or four more leap upon him and make him prisoner.

Dick was brave, but he was cautious.

So he stole along the deck of the prison ship, and paused every three or four steps to listen.

He became convinced at last that there was but one man on guard.

There might be three or four on board, but the rest, if this was the case, were probably asleep.

Only one man was on guard at a time.

Dick located the guard, and stole toward the fellow.

The youth was glad the guard had lighted his pipe.

The faint glow of the fire in the bowl could be seen, and served as an excellent guide for Dick.

He stole forward, and being enabled to determine in which direction the guard was facing, the youth slipped around so as to approach the fellow from behind.

Closer and closer crept Dick.

He was almost within reach of the fellow.

"Blame such business as this!" the guard suddenly exclaimed, pettishly; "this is the dullest business I ever got into! Here I have to sit, with nothing to amuse me, while the boys over at the camp are playing cards, and telling stories, and singing songs, and having a good time. I like it where things are lively."

"All right; I'll make it lively for you, then!" said Dick, aloud, and then he leaped upon the startled British soldier, and bore him to the deck.

The fellow struggled fiercely, but it was no use.

He was a strong man, but Dick was stronger.

Then, too, he had taken the guard by surprise, and had succeeded in getting him by the throat.

This was a big advantage, for Dick squeezed the fellow's windpipe so tight that his wind was entirely shut off, and struggle as he might, the fellow could do nothing.

He speedily collapsed, and became unconscious.

"I am glad I didn't have to kill the fellow," thought Dick. "Now to tie and gag him."

Dick soon found a piece of rope, and bound the man's hands together behind his back.

Then the youth gagged the Briton, and rose to his feet with a sigh of satisfaction.

"Good!" he thought; "so far I have done very well. Now to see if the prisoners are aboard—but I know they are."

Dick made his way down the companionway, and went down the short stairway.

At the bottom was a door which led into a cabin.

Dick tried the door.

The knob turned, and he was enabled to push the door open.

The youth entered softly, and pausing, listened.

The sound of snoring came to his ears.

"Another guard, likely," the youth thought. "He must be a musician—he plays a horn while asleep."

Dick stole across the floor in the direction of the snoring.

Soon he came to a door, and he knew that the sleeper was in a room adjoining the one in which he stood.

"I must have a light," the youth thought.

He began feeling about and presently found a table.

On the table he found a candle and tinder, and flint and steel.

In a few moments he had a light.

He looked around the cabin.

It was a room perhaps twelve feet square, but contained nothing of interest.

Dick's attention was attracted toward the door opening into the room whence came the sound of snoring.

"There's another guard in there, and I must make him a prisoner," he thought, and he stole across the room and tried the door.

It opened to his touch.

In a bunk at the side of the little room revealed to view lay a British soldier.

Dick did not hesitate.

He had no time to waste.

He leaped forward and throttled the fellow, quickly choking him into insensibility, and then tied him up as he had the other guard.

"I wonder if there are any more?" Dick asked himself. "I'll see," and he quickly made a search.

There were several staterooms, but none of them were occupied.

"I guess there are no more guards than two," the youth thought. "Now to find the prisoners."

The youth looked around him undecidedly.

"I wonder where they would be?" he asked himself; and then he gave a start.

"Of course!" he exclaimed; "the hold! That's where I will find them!"

He took up the candle and began searching for the entrance to the hold.

He soon found it, and making his way down the ladder leading to the dark depths of the hold of the old, waterlogged hulk, he held the candle above his head and looked about him.

The candle was insufficient to dispel the darkness of the hold, and seeing nobody, the youth called out:

"Hello! Is anybody here?"

"Who are you?" came back in weak tones from toward the end of the hold, where the darkness was most dense.

Dick made no answer at once, but hastened forward.

He was soon among the prisoners, and found that there were twelve of them.

They lay on their backs on the damp, slimy bottom of the hold, and their hands were tied behind their backs. Their ankles were bound also.

"Who are you?" asked one of the men, a man of perhaps forty years.

"I am Dick Slater, a patriot spy," replied Dick, quietly; "and I have come to set you free!"

"Thank God!" went up from the lips of the suffering men.

Dick drew a knife from his pocket, and quickly cut the ropes binding the men's arms and ankles, and they sat up.

They could not get up, however, as they had lain there so long trussed up that the blood had stopped circulating in the arms and legs, and it was nearly half an hour before the blood could be gotten into circulation again.

At last they were enabled to stand up, however, and walk about, and during the time they were doing this, Dick explained the situation.

The men were the two spies—one was named Robert Bird, the other Thomas Harper—and ten soldiers who had been captured by the British.

They were surprised to think that a youth like Dick had accomplished so much, and shown so much daring.

"You took your life in your hands when you ventured within the British lines, my boy!" said Bird.

"I suppose so," replied Dick, simply. "I am ready to risk my life at any time for the sake of accomplishing something toward bringing about the freedom of the Colonies."

"That is the way to talk!" said Harper, approvingly.

"Had you learned much that will be of benefit to our commander in chief before you were captured?" asked Dick.

"Yes; we had come in possession of considerable information of importance," replied Bird.

"If we can only escape now, and get back to New York to General Washington, we will be all right," said Harper.

"Have you learned anything of importance?" asked Bird.

"Yes; an attack is to be made on Brooklyn Heights within four days."

"Phew! say you so?"

"Yes."

"Then we must hasten back to New York and inform the commander in chief of this fact."

"So we must. Well, let us be going at once."

"We are only too glad to get a chance to get out of this horrible place!" said Harper, with a shudder.

They left the hold, and entered the cabin.

The guard whom Dick had surprised asleep still lay where he had left him.

He glared at the youth and his companions with a look of murder in his eyes, but could not say anything, the gag preventing utterance.

"Good-by!" said Bird, with a triumphant look. "We will leave you here, in your present condition, all night, and see how you like it!"

Dick now extinguished the candle and placed it in his pocket, and then led the way up on deck.

All was quiet there.

His presence had not attracted the attention of anyone save the two guards, and they were prisoners.

"Come," said Dick, and he led the way to the boat.

"The boat is small; we will have to make two trips," he said.

This was done, and half an hour later the entire party of patriots stood on the shore of the little cove.

"Hark!" said Dick, suddenly, in a low, cautious tone; "do you hear that?"

"It is the tramp of a body of men!" said Bird.

"It is a company of British soldiers!" said Harper.

"We must get away from here in a hurry," said Dick, and he told them to follow him, which they did, and he led them away at right angles, and as they got out of the line of march of the company of men, they paused and listened.

It was a body of British soldiers.

And what was more, they were in search of Dick.

He had left the camp two hours before, and not having returned, Captain Parks had become suspicious, and had sent out this body of men to look for him.

Parks had at last become suspicious that Dick was, after all, what Captain Frink had accused him of being—a patriot spy.

"The captain said that if the boy was a spy, he might try to set the prisoners free from the prison ship," Dick and his friends heard one of the British soldiers say; "so we had better go aboard and see if everything is all right there."

Then the party of British passed on, and Dick said:

"They will go aboard the prison ship and learn all within twenty minutes! If we escape, we will have to hurry, for they will arouse the entire army, and men will swarm about us like hornets!"

CHAPTER X
The Liberty Boys in Battle

"That is as true as anything you ever said," said Bird.

"We must hurry!" said Harper.

"What direction shall we take?" asked Dick. "Shall we go around to the eastward, or in the other direction?"

"It is not so far to Stirling's outpost as it is to Sullivan's,"[13] replied Bird, "so I am in favor of going around to the westward, and trying to reach Stirling's division."

"Very well; we will go that way, then," said Dick; "you lead the way, as you are more familiar with the lay of the land hereabouts than I am."

Bird took the lead, and they set out.

They had not been moving along more than twenty minutes when there was an outcry in the direction from which they had just come.

"They have discovered the escape of their prisoners!" said Harper, grimly.

THE LIBERTY BOYS OF '76

"Yes; and we will have to look out now!" said Bird.

It was evident that a general alarm had been sounded, for the little party of patriots soon found themselves in the midst of the British, and it was only by the exercise of great caution that they kept from being captured.

Once they ran almost into the arms, figuratively speaking, of a company of British, but the ready wit of Dick saved them.

"Have they found the escaped prisoners yet?" he asked, in well-simulated eagerness.

It will be remembered that it was quite dark, and it so happened that they were so far from the nearest camp fire that it was impossible for the British to see that they were not what they pretended to be—British soldiers like themselves. It was possible, only, to see the outlines of each other, and know that they were men, and that was all.

Dick's question threw the British off their guard and disarmed suspicion.

"No; they haven't found them yet," was the reply to Dick's question; "but we'll get them very soon. They can't get away."

"Oh, no; they can't get away!" said Dick, and the British captain failed to distinguish the sarcasm of the tone.

"You go that way, and we will go this," said Dick, in an authoritative tone; "there is no use of our going in the same direction."

"True; all right," and the company of British went on its way in blissful unconsciousness of the fact that its captain had talked with the escaping prisoners.

"Well, you have nerve, young man!" said Bird, admiringly; "I take off my hat to you!"

"That was a bold stroke!" said Harper.

"And like most bold strokes, it won," said Bird.

The little party hastened onward, and on a dozen occasions they were on the verge of discovery by the British, but they managed to escape detection till they were within half a mile of the American outpost, when they were confronted by a company of British, the commander of which ordered them to halt.

"Fire a volley into their ranks, and then run!" said Dick, in a low tone, and at the word he fired, the others doing likewise—

they had found and repossessed themselves of their pistols before leaving the prison ship—and as exclamations of amazement and consternation escaped the British, Dick and his companions darted away.

They were quick, but so were the British, and they fired a volley after the fleeing patriots.

One of the patriot soldiers was wounded, but only slightly, and he kept on running.

They got away out of range before the British could fire a second volley, and kept running at as rapid a pace as possible, as they would not have allowed themselves to be recaptured now, when so close to the outpost of the Continental Army, for the world.

They were soon within the lines of Stirling's division, and as he was up, having been aroused by an orderly as soon as the fact was ascertained that something unusual was transpiring over within the British lines, Dick and his companions were taken before him at once.

Stirling was delighted when he learned of the escape of this little party from the prison-pen of the British, and he complimented Dick highly on the wonderful work which he had performed.

"It was not much to do," said Dick, modestly.

"It was a great deal to do!" was the reply; "and you have gained some important information, which will be of great value to the commander in chief."

"Yes, indeed!" said Bird.

"We wish to go right on," said Dick. "We must be at the headquarters before morning."

"I will furnish you three horses," said Stirling. "Then it will take you but a short time to reach your destination. The other men can stay here."

"We are from Sullivan's division," one said; "why not let us go on up there and rejoin our company?"

"That will be all right," Stirling said; "only you must be careful, and not allow yourselves to be recaptured."

"Trust us for that!" with a grim laugh. "They won't catch us again! We will fight to the death first! We have had one taste of British prison-pen, and we don't want another!"

Dick, Bird and Harper, mounted on good horses, were soon riding northward, along the old Narrows road, and two hours later—they had to ride slowly on account of the darkness— they arrived at Brooklyn Heights.

They paused there long enough to put General Putnam on his guard, as they feared the British, now that the spies had escaped, might move on the Continental forces at once, and attack the Heights before morning, if they were successful in driving back Sullivan's and Stirling's divisions.

"Let them come, if they want to," said Putnam, with flashing eyes; "we will make it so hot for them, they will wish to go up into the Arctic regions to cool off!"

The spies left the horses here, and crossed over to New York, reaching the headquarters at about three o'clock.

It was thought best to report to the commander in chief at once, as in case the British decided to move on the American lines immediately, General Washington would wish to have information regarding the matter.

The great general was very glad they did report, and he greeted the three with delight.

"So you are back again, Bird and Harper!" he exclaimed, "and you, Master Dick! I am glad to see you!"

"We are glad to get back, your excellency!" said Bird; "and Harper and I owe our presence here to this brave youth, who penetrated into the British lines, and finally found and rescued us."

"Indeed! Well, well! I thought that perhaps the boy might succeed where men had failed, and that was the reason I sent him; but I did not expect that he would do so well as he has done."

Dick blushed at this praise, and tried to make out that he had not done much of anything, but the commander in chief hushed him up.

"That will do, my boy," he said, kindly; "you have done a wonderful thing, and your work in this matter has been greatly to your credit. I will say that no spy of the Continental Army has ever done better work than that you have performed."

"That is absolutely true," said Bird.

Then Dick and the other two spies quickly put the commander in chief in possession of all the facts in the case, and he decided to send reinforcements to General Putnam at once.

"Please send my company of 'Liberty Boys' among the others, your excellency," said Dick, and the commander in chief smilingly said the company of "Liberty Boys" should go, if Dick desired it.

Soon all was hustle in and around headquarters, and in the encampment of the Continental Army.

Three thousand troops were quickly on the move, Dick's company among them, and they crossed the river and reached Brooklyn Heights before the sun had risen.

The British did not move on the Americans that night.

Only General Howe could have told why they had not done so.

Doubtless his experience at Bunker Hill had imbued him with such a wholesome respect for the prowess of the patriots that he wanted more time in which to make up his mind.

Nor did the British move to the attack within four days, as Dick had heard several say they intended doing, when he was in the lines, and their reason for this was obvious: The British Army knew the spies reached General Washington with the information, and it was decided to delay attacking.

Dick and Bob and the other members of the company fretted at the inactivity.

They had come over from New York to the Heights in the expectation of becoming engaged in battle with the British within a few hours, and as day after day passed and still the British held off, the boys became very restless.

"I want to fight!" said Bob Estabrook. "I want to get a chance to show the British what the 'Liberty Boys of '76' can do!"

All were eager for the conflict, and in their eagerness they got Dick to ask that their company be transferred to Stirling's division, it being a self-evident fact that the outposts should be the first to be attacked when the attack was made.

Putnam, willing to please the youths, he having taken a great liking to Dick, the boy spy, gave orders to have the boys uniformed and equipped, and allowed them to go down and join Stirling's division, and the youths were better satisfied, as they knew that they would be in the fight among the very first, when the battle should begin.

But the British delayed attacking for days and weeks, and it was not until the twenty-seventh day of August that they finally made the attack.

The British fleet, under Admiral Howe, advanced and made a feint upon New York, while General Howe's troops advanced on the American outposts on shore.

The main portion of the British Army, under Generals Howe, Clinton, Percy and Cornwallis,[14] made a night march, away around to the right, until they struck the Jamaica road, and when the other portion of the army attacked Stirling's and Sullivan's divisions, this large force was moving to attack the rear of Sullivan's position.

The force that was advancing on Stirling's division, and which came in sight just as the sun came up, was made up of the highland regiments of Scotland, and Stirling himself was a Scotchman.

"We are going to have a hard fight, my boys!" he said; "we will hold out as long as possible, however. Stand ready, and fight as men fighting for liberty should fight!"

A ringing cheer greeted his words, and it was evident that the patriots would fight like demons, before falling back toward the main body of troops at Brooklyn Heights.

Soon the attack began, and the "Liberty Boys of '76" were getting their first taste of war—cruel war.

They went into the battle with the enthusiasm of youth, however, and loaded and fired as rapidly as possible, standing their ground like veterans.

Dick was at their front and stood there like a statue, excepting when he was firing, when he became all life and action.

He fired rapidly, and cheered the boys with lively words of encouragement. He seemed not to realize that he was in danger.

And this was characteristic of all the members of the company of Liberty Boys, and they fought with the coolness and precision of veterans.

Stirling was here, there and everywhere, encouraging his men, and he noted with wondering admiration the brave manner in which the boys were fighting.

He spoke to them in complimentary terms, and was answered with a cheer.

The fire of the British was galling, and as they outnumbered the American Army greatly, they kept on advancing, even in the face of the terrible hail of bullets, and it became evident that the Americans would have to fall back, and retreat to Brooklyn Heights.

Stirling had just given the order to retreat in good order, when the British Army, under Howe and the other three generals above named, attacked the patriot army from the rear. The British had surprised Sullivan's division from the rear in the same manner, and had then advanced and fallen upon the rear of Stirling's division.

It was evident, now, that it was going to be simply a question of reaching the Heights as quickly as possible, and Stirling told his men to fight their way through, if possible, and escape.

More desperate fighting between the Americans and the British never took place anywhere than now. The Americans fought like fiends, and in the front ranks of the fighters, doing the work of double their number, were the "Liberty Boys of '76."

They did wonderful service, and earned a reputation then and there for personal bravery, for intrepid daring in the face of superior numbers, that remained with them throughout the entire war.

The majority of the patriot soldiers succeeded in reaching the Brooklyn Heights, among them the "Liberty Boys of '76," but the brave Stirling himself was captured, though Dick, at the head of his company, made desperate efforts to prevent the capture.

The division under Sullivan—those who had escaped being killed—had already reached the Heights, and that same afternoon General Washington brought over several thousand troops to reinforce the Heights.

"If they try to take the Heights by force, they will be repulsed with great slaughter," said the commander in chief; but the British general had not forgotten Bunker Hill, and he was afraid to try to storm the works.

He settled down, instead, to make a siege, and General Washington, seeing that it would be impossible to withstand a siege, and realizing, too, that if the British should come around to the rear and cut them off from retreat, they would eventually have to surrender, quietly made arrangements with the owners of all the river craft available, and that night, under cover of darkness, the entire patriot army was transferred across the river to New York.

Next day the British were thunderstruck to find that their prey had escaped them. This feat, in which ten thousand troops, with cannon, stores, etc., got away from a virtual death-trap in a night, and without the knowledge of the enemy, is considered as being one of the most wonderful and brilliant strokes of generalship the world has ever seen, and it placed Washington at once at the top, ranking with the great generals of the world.

The commander in chief learned of the gallant conduct of the "Liberty Boys of '76," and complimented them highly.

"Ah!" he said to Dick, "if I had ten thousand additional troops made up of 'Liberty Boys' such as are the members of your company, I would cross back over the East River and drive the British into the ocean!"

Dick repeated the commander in chief's words to Bob and the other members of the company, and they were as proud a lot of boys as ever the sun shone on.

The "Liberty Boys of '76" were destined to do wonderful work for the great Cause of Liberty during the remaining years of the war.

[THE END.]

NEW NICK CARTER WEEKLY

Issued Weekly. By Subscription $2.50 per year. Entered as Second Class Matter at New York Post Office by STREET & SMITH, 238 William St., N. Y.

No. 414.   Price, Five Cents.

DR. QUARTZ II. AT BAY
OR A MAN OF IRON NERVE
By The Author of "Nick Carter"

The instant that Nick Carter leaped upon him, Dr. Quartz seemed to come to himself again, but already the blow from the butt of the revolver had fallen.

Nick Carter, the New York detective, is the creation of John R. Coryell (1851–1924). Coryell's first Nick Carter story was published in 1887 in Street & Smith's New York Weekly, *but Coryell abandoned the character after three novels. The series resumed in 1891 in the pages of the weekly* Nick Carter Library, *which was later retitled* Nick Carter Weekly *and finally just* Nick Carter Stories. *There are 1,261 issues in the three series, but some of the stories were reprinted at least once, so the total number of original stories about Nick Carter is less than that.*

Nick Carter was very popular, especially with the young boys who were his largest audience, but grown men read the stories as well. The character appeared on the stage, in the movies (both silent and sound), in comic books, and in a long-running radio drama that began in 1943. His most recent appearance was as an espionage agent, much like James Bond, in a series of modern paperback novels.

While approximately twenty-five writers contributed to the dime novel series, the most prolific writer was Frederic Merrill Van Rensselaer Dey (1861–1922). Each story can be read independently of the others, but Dey created a number of recurring characters to populate the world in which Nick Carter's adventures took place. These included Nick Carter's assistants Chick and Patsy as well as the many colorful villains Carter brought to justice. The most mem-

orable of these is his archenemy, Dr. Jack Quartz, who first appears in 1891 and 1893 in four stories in the Nick Carter Library. *Nick has great respect for the wily doctor and does not underestimate his ability. Quartz was so popular that the author brought him back in a total of nineteen stories. The second group of stories was published in 1904 and 1905, and the final encounter between the two characters took place in 1910. (The first thirteen stories were reissued in sequence in 1911 and 1912.) The original Dr. Quartz dies at the end of the first sequence of stories, but he returns in spirit, in the characters of his younger brother, or his nephew, or his son, to battle Nick Carter. Each is named John (or James or Jack) Quartz, and each is identical in appearance to his predecessor; the only difference seems to be that each has a different middle initial. The author appears not to have noticed this and had Nick claim that they all bore the same middle name.*

The story reprinted here is the second installment from the second sequence of cases, published in New Nick Carter Weekly *(no. 414, December 3, 1904). Even after this story, Nick Carter is fated to meet Dr. Quartz again in the very next issue.*

CHAPTER I
A Criminal for Crime's Sake

Nick Carter and the chief of police of Kansas City were facing each other across the big table desk in the private office at headquarters.

"Mr. Carter," said the chief, lighting a cigar and leaning back in his chair while he slowly elevated his feet to the edge of a couch near him, "the mayor has given me directions to engage your services in this matter of the freight car murders. I don't suppose you will hesitate to undertake the case, will you?"

"Not at all, sir. To tell you the truth, I want the case."

"Oho! You do, eh? Well that is pleasant news. It is also unusual."

"Well, it is true at least. The fact is, this chap who calls himself Dr. Quartz the second, interests me more than I can say. I will give you my word, chief, that the fellow even looks the part he is playing."

"Really?"

"Yes. In appearance, he is precisely what the original Dr. Quartz was, ten years ago."

"Perhaps he is a son of Dr. Quartz."

"No; he is not young enough for that."

"He might be a younger brother."

"I have thought of that; but——"

"You don't think so, eh?"

"No; and yet, after all it is more than likely that he is. However I cannot imagine one brother so closely resembling another unless they happen to be twins."

"Then why not twins? They may have been that."

"No. This fellow is not old enough. If Dr. Quartz were alive, he would be fifty years old now. This man is not yet forty, if I am any judge of the matter."

"Then how do you account for the resemblance?"

"I don't account for it at all—yet; but I will do so later on."

"The resemblance is not the only point of similarity between them, is it?"

"It is the least of all."

"Tell me something about the original Dr. Quartz," said the chief.

"Tell you something about him? My dear chief, a book as big as Blane's 'Twenty Years In Congress'[1] would not be half big enough to tell you about that man."

"He must have been a Jim Dandy, eh?"[2]

"He was the handsomest man I ever saw—and the wickedest. He was at once the gentlest mannered, and the most cruel; he had the softest and most musical voice you ever heard, and it could be the harshest and coldest you could imagine. His smile was the smile of a saint, but it emanated from the soul of a devil incarnate. His hands were as soft as velvet, but they were as inflexible as bands of steel when he chose to make them so. His motions were slow and methodical, but he could move as quick as a tiger cat, and as fiercely. His muscular strength was as great as mine; indeed, I have sometimes thought it was greater. He was the most profoundly learned man I ever knew in any walk of life, for he seemed to speak every language with equal fluency, to be a past master of every science, and to have acquired with thoroughness every branch of human knowledge. He was the most skillful surgeon of his time, and the most learned physician. I never knew from whence he came. He was a mystery when he appeared on the scenes in which I took a prominent part, and he was just as great a mystery when he died.

"He laughed at prison walls, and at prison officials; he even laughed at me, although I succeeded in laughing last."

"You have a habit of doing that, Carter."

"Ay; but have I succeeded in doing it, in his case? I thought so until now; but now——"

"Well, what now?"

"Here is this new character which crops up when it is least expected."

"What has that got to do with the original case?"

"This: If I were superstitious—if I were not wise enough to know that it is impossible, I should think in the present case, that Dr. Quartz had come to life again. I should suppose that he had risen from the grave. I should believe that he did not die, when I thought he did, for this man, with whom we have to do now, is, to all intent and purpose, Dr. Quartz."

"But he can't be the same; you have just said that."

"I know he cannot be the same; and yet he is the same."

"Nonsense, Carter!"

"I know it is nonsense. I know that this is not the same man; but I also know—or, at least, I think I know—that so far as you and I and the world at large are concerned, we are face to face with the same character; that is, with the same conditions."

"You are too deep for me, Carter."

"I mean, in a word, that we have here a man who, to begin with, looks precisely like Dr. Quartz; who possesses the same character; who is versed in the same sciences; who has the same smooth and oily manner; who is as competent, as talented, as wicked, as unrelenting, as implacable, as adroit, as skillful and as daring. We are confronted by the same conditions."

He paused a moment, and then continued:

"But there is even more than that, chief. This man seems to glory in the fact that he is—if I may make use of the term—a replica of Dr. Quartz. He boldly places a sign on the fan light over his door, and that sign reads, 'Dr. J. B. Quartz.'"

"Were those the initials of the original?"

"Yes; but wait."

"Go on."

"He begins his career—I refer to his police record—exactly as his predecessor did; by undertaking, through a lot of unnecessary trouble and expense, to call the attention of the police to his crimes. His predecessor fitted up an upright piano box like a woman's boudoir, and traveled inside of it, in company with one of his victims, three thousand miles by freight. This man fits up an entire freight car so that it will compare favorably with a Pullman, and it is certain that he spent not less than ten thousand dollars for his little joke—if it is a joke from his point of view.

"We know already that he purchased the running gear of an old car and made the rest of it over to suit his purposes; we know that he spared no pains or expense in the appointment and decoration of his car; we know that he murdered——"

"Hold on a minute, Nick. That is the very point; we don't know that he murdered anybody."

"We don't know it officially; but we are morally certain of it."

"You are. I am not."

"Very well; have it that way, then. I will say that I believe he murdered five persons—three women and two men—in order to carry out his plans."

"Well, go ahead from that point."

"Having murdered them he embalmed them with a skill which would put the ancient Egyptians to the blush; and then, with their dead bodies, he arranged a scene inside that car which would have done credit to the proprietor of an Eden Musée.[3] Nothing could have been more lifelike than the spectacle of those four corpses, seated at the table as if they were engaged in a game of cards, while the murdered girl was stretched on the bed, under a sheet, with a dagger through her heart."

"I'll grant you that. It was horrible."

"Well, my dear chief, it had a point; a point which we have not yet deciphered. In fact, it had several points."

"What were they, as you make them out?"

"We must go back to the arrival of the car in Kansas City to determine that."

"Very good. What then?"

"He shipped the car to Kansas, and purposely left it standing in the freight yard until the authorities were forced to take some action regarding it; hence, he wished the authorities to see it, and its contents."

"Well?"

"He accomplished two purposes in that."

"How so."

"He called the attention of the authorities to his own existence—that is, to the existence of a person who was not afraid to defy them, and he delivered a message, by the hands of those dead card players, to certain people for whom it was intended."

"All that sort of reasoning seems like folly to me, Carter."

"I suppose it does. It would seem the same to me if I had not known the other Dr. Quartz; but knowing him as I did, I understand this one."

"Explain."

"Chief, there was never a human being born into the world who did not have his weak point. The original Dr. Quartz had his, and it was that one point of weakness which finally compelled his defeat. If he had not possessed it, he would be alive to-day, and would have been able to snap his fingers at all the police forces of the world to the day of his natural death."

"Humph! What was his weak point?"

"Egotism. Conceit. Unlimited belief in himself. Call it what you will."

"And you think this man has it the same?"

"The freight car proves it."

"I don't see how."

"It was his conceit which built that car. He likes to do things subtly, deftly—differently from other men."

"Well, even so, I don't see——"

Nick shrugged his shoulders.

"Let us say that this man, who calls himself Dr. Quartz the second, has run the entire gamut of crime without once being suspected a criminal. Let us say that he has stolen right and left, and murdered right and left, and that the eye of suspicion has not once been turned in his direction. Let us say that he has tired of all that; that there is no spice left in the commission of crime for him, for the reason that there is no danger in it. That is the way the other man, the original Dr. Quartz, would have felt. His impulses were wicked; he loved crime for crime's sake, and he loved danger for danger's sake. He murdered because he loved to kill, while at the same time he proved to the police that he could do so with impunity. He could thrust the point of a poisoned pin into the arm or leg of an unoffending man or woman in a crowd, and an hour later, or three hours later, as he chose, that man or woman would drop dead. Dr. Quartz was never suspected. He could murder an entire family while attending them as their medical adviser, and it would be discovered later on that he had so won the confidence and love of that family that he had been made the heir to all their wealth— and yet he was so skillful that he was never suspected of the crimes.

"He grew tired of that. He amassed a huge fortune, and he could have gathered in more in the same way; but there was no spice in it.

"He desired danger. He wished to defy the police; to defy mankind, because he believed himself to be so much smarter than all other men combined. He wished to be suspected. He wanted to be pursued. He longed for the conditions which would point at him as the greatest criminal on earth, and yet to so hedge himself about with safeguards that while everybody should be morally certain that he was the greatest criminal unhung, he could laugh in the faces of the men who pursued him and defy them, because they could prove nothing against him.

"That was why he created the piano-box mystery. It was his egotism which compelled him to it. That is why this man has built and furnished the freight car as he did. It was his egotism which compelled him to it."

"I confess that I cannot understand that sort of a character."

"Nor could I—then. I do now, however. Having had to do with one, I know how to recognize the next one when I come in contact with it."

"But, man alive, why should a criminal who is practically immune from arrest, according to your theory, deliberately invite suspicion, arrest and conviction?"

"Because he is Dr. Quartz."

The chief shrugged his shoulders.

"Let me tell you one thing," said Nick. "You have set Quartz at liberty because you had no evidence on which to hold him; and now, I bet my reputation that he is laughing at you. But more; while he is laughing, he is preparing the way for another crime which will throw this one so deeply into the shade that you will forget it ever happened. Quartz has only introduced himself. Wait for his next move, chief."

CHAPTER II
The Mystery of a Murderer's Methods

"Well," said the chief, after a pause, "let us get down to the facts of the present case, and let the original Dr. Quartz rest for a time, at least."

"Gladly. It is the present case with which we have to do; not the old one. And yet if it were not for the old case—if it were not for the experience I had in that one, or rather in the several cases which grew out of it, I should be much more in the dark in the present matter than I think I am."

"Let me see," said the chief, musingly. "I will run over the facts as we know them, just for the sake of refreshing our memories."

"A good idea."

"Your first knowledge of this case came through the museum owner, Jeremy Stone, did it not, Mr. Carter?"

"Yes. He sent for me to come here from New York."

"I have never understood just why he sent for you. Will you tell me that?"

"It was purely a matter of business with him. I will have to refer again to the old case in order to make you understand."

"Well?"

"In that case, the piano box was sent by express. The box had been kept a year unclaimed. Jeremy Stone attended the sale and bought the box. When he opened it, he found that instead of containing a piano, it had been fitted up to represent a diminutive boudoir, fit for the use of any lady; in fact, that it had been made double and weighted with lead to the exact weight of a piano shipped as that was shipped.

"He had purchased the thing by accident, but being a museum owner, he at once saw the possibilities of the box as an exhibit in his museum provided he could ascertain the history of the box.

"That is why he sent for me; and his sending for me resulted in the unearthing of Dr. Quartz. If it had not been for the progressive advertising spirit in Jeremy Stone, the world might never have heard of Dr. Quartz—certainly not at that time.

"Now, in the present case, he saw in the freight car the same sort of possibilities that existed in the piano box. He determined to purchase the car, but in this case he proposed to make a mystery of it from the start. He made a great deal of money out of the piano box, and he believed that he saw a way to make still more out of the freight car; hence he sent for me.

"But there was still another reason."

"What was that?"

"You will remember that the car was billed to a person—possibly fictitious—called Z. T. Rauk. Now, if you will spell Z. T. Rauk backward, you will discover that if it does not spell Quartz, it certainly does not spell anything else. Substitute a Q for the K, and you have Quartz."

"That's a fact."

"Well, Jeremy discovered that, so he sent for me; but he did still more. He sent out letters of inquiry, and discovered that the car had no owner. The company had not thought it worthwhile to go to that trouble, but Jeremy did.

"I came to Kansas City at his solicitation. He met me at the train and told me about the car. I brought two of my assistants here with me, but I have kept them entirely in the dark so far, so that nobody aside from yourself now has any idea that they are here.

"I went to the freight yards and saw the foreman there, and I discovered from my talk with him that there were several people in the city who had manifested interest in the car. Among those were two men, who are still under surveillance— and the two women I found at the house of Dr. Quartz when I went there to arrest him."

"And those women were dazed and only half-conscious when we brought them to their senses at the police station," said the chief.

"Exactly. They knew nothing whatever about the matter which we could nail."

"And yet, Quartz made a direct charge against them when you arrested him, did he not?"

"Certainly. That was a part of his game."

"How a part of his game?"

"Why, in this way. He had no idea of having the affair connected with himself, quite so soon. Having those women in his house at the time I went there was merely a part of his own personal plot, the secrets of which we do not yet know. It was on the spur of the moment that he decided to make the charge against them. It was an accident that they were there when I went to arrest him, and it was only an evidence of his daredevil nature that he made the charge against them at the moment."

"Your reasoning may be all right, Carter, but it is altogether too far-fetched for me."

"Chief, those women are associated in some manner with the crimes, but just how I do not know. That is one of the things I have got to find out. My assistant, Patsy, is on their track since you let them go. I will know more about them before long. I have not a doubt, however, that they are victims of the machinations of Dr. Quartz, and that they were driven to investigating the car through fear."

"Fear of what?"

"That is what I don't know—yet."

"Well, let us hark back again for a moment. When the car was purchased by Stone, he had it taken to his museum, did he not?"

"Yes."

"And you entered the car while it stood there that night, waiting for me and others to go to it and examine it the following morning."

"Precisely."

"We will touch on that point again, presently. The one I wish to make just now, is that somebody hired a lot of city thugs to blow the car and the museum too, for that matter, sky high, that night."

"Yes."

"Well, the supposition is that it was the women who did that hiring, isn't it?"

"That was Dr. Quartz's charge; but we know it to be false, don't we?"

"From the standpoint of a policeman I should say that those women had no more to do with the proposed blowing up of the car while it was at the museum, than you or I had."

"Certainly not."

"Absolutely the only points you had against them was that they appeared to manifest some interest in the car while it was at the freight yards, and that Dr. Quartz made the assertion that they were concerned in it."

"Exactly."

"You and I both know that we cannot convict—that we cannot even hold people on such flimsy evidence as that."

"Certainly not."

"There was absolutely nothing at all against either of those women, Edith Peyton and her maid."

"Nothing whatever."

"We will return to them presently. Let us now go back to the car, for that is the point of issue."

"Certainly."

"Tell me about your entrance to the car, while you and Jeremy Stone were alone with it in the museum."

"There is nothing to tell more than you already know."

"Never mind that. Let's go over it together."

"Well, I found a secret door at one end of the car by which I entered it."

"Yes. Go on."

"I found four perfectly embalmed figures, two men and two women who had been wired in the positions they occupied at a card table inside the car. There was another embalmed body on the bed. The four at the table were of middle age; the one on the bed was a young woman, not more than twenty, if that. She had been stabbed through the heart after she was dead, and the dagger with which she was stabbed was still where the murderer had placed it."

"And there is not a doctor in the city who has been able to tell how any of the five persons in that car were killed."

"No; the embalming fluid, whatever it was, had destroyed all evidence of the poison used."

"But all the doctors agreed that they had been poisoned originally."

"Yes."

"Well, Mr. Carter, all that the police can see in that circumstance, is that five murders have been committed, and that the murderer took that strange method to ship the bodies of his victims out of the city where the crimes were committed, to Kansas City. But I understand that you see much more than that."

"Why, yes; I see the methods of Dr. Quartz."

"And that, according to your ideas, indicates a romance."

"Precisely."

"That is what I wish you to tell me about."

"I am afraid, chief, that you won't have much confidence in it."

"Never mind. Let me hear it."

"Well, we will begin at the creation of the car."

"Very good."

"If you recall the construction of the car, you will remember that not only was the door at the end, as I have described, but also that there were means of ventilation at the sides, with screens arranged so that a person traveling in it could have plenty of air as well as an opportunity to view the scenery in passing."

"Yes."

"Has it occurred to you that a man in constructing that car for the purpose of shipping dead bodies inside it, would not have arranged for entrance and egress, and also for ventilation?"

"By Jove! That's so."

"Doesn't that suggest that the original purpose of the car was for live people to travel in it?"

"It certainly does."

"Hence, you see that the car was not ultimately used for the purposes for which it was constructed. The car, in other words, was not built for the shipment of those dead bodies, but for the accommodation of live men and women."

"I see your point."

"Inside, it was so divided by heavy curtains, that it could easily be made into three separate compartments."

"Yes; I remember that."

"So, we will say that it was intended for a party of six—two in each compartment; but so arranged that the three compartments could be thrown into one during the day."

"Precisely."

"Now, one of the favorite pastimes of the original Dr. Quartz was to marry heiresses. He always selected a rich as well as a beautiful wife. His piano-box expedition was a case in point. As soon as he had made himself the possessor of the girl's fortune—and he frequently had to murder the entire family to do that—he quietly killed her and then looked about him for another wife and another victim."

"What a fiend he was!"

"I conjecture this case to be one in which the present Dr. Quartz has attempted to emulate his predecessor. He found his intended victim, and he built the car, we will say, for the accommodation of the bridal party, which was to consist, we will suppose, of his bride and himself, and the four people whose bodies we found in the car."

"But——"

"Wait. Something happened to interrupt his plans. At the last moment his bride went back on him. She refused to be a party to the wedding, or her friends discovered who and what he was, and refused to permit her to fulfill her contract. We will say that the car was completed and ready when the plans fell through; so the doctor worked out a most delicious revenge against them. He merely transformed the car from a bridal to a funeral car. There you are."

"But where is the motive for shipping it here? Why should he send it to the city where he lives and has his office and practice? Why should he, after committing five murders, deliberately put the police on his own trail? Why should he arrange so that everything would point directly at him, and then, in effect, pose before us, and virtually say: 'Here I am! Come and take me?'"

CHAPTER III
A Man Who Is Never Off His Guard

"My dear chief," replied Nick, to the last question, "if we could answer all such puzzles at the time they arise, there would be no need for detectives. We are face to face with a mystery which is so complex that the moment we think we have discovered a possible solution we encounter an obstacle which puts us entirely at sea again."

"I should say we did!"

"The mere facts, so far as we know them, are merely these: We——"

"That is right. State them. I would like to listen to a few facts after all this theorizing."

"I was about to do so."

"Go ahead."

"Fact 1: A car containing five dead bodies is shipped to Kansas City, and is opened there in the presence of the authorities."

The chief nodded.

"Fact 2: The bodies are found to be so perfectly embalmed, that the method of accomplishing the result is unknown to science, for there is not an undertaker, or a doctor, who can give us any information on the subject."

"Not one."

"Fact 3: Circumstances point to the association of certain names with the crimes. Those names are Dr. Quartz, Edith Peyton, and her maid, Susan Cummings. There are two other men

whose names we do not know, but who evidently had no connection with the crime itself, and were merely tools of some
other person—probably Dr. Quartz—after the arrival of the
car in Kansas City."

"Well?"

"Fact 4: There is nowhere discovered a scrap of information
which will afford us any clue to the identity of the five bodies
in the freight car. The car came from Philadelphia, but it is evident that the murdered men and women did not belong there."

"Quite so; nor the car, either. The police of Philadelphia can
give us no information whatever."

"Fact 5: Of the three names which circumstances have associated with the crimes, there is absolutely no evidence whatever against any of them. Dr. Quartz readily proves an alibi to
offset everything you attempt to prove against him, and pleasantly laughs at you. Edith Peyton and her maid are in the same
category, with the additional fact that they are either both of
weak minds, or are still under the influence of a drug which
has been administered to them to keep them silent. If Edith
Peyton does not really forget, or is not really ignorant, she
plays the part so well that we can do nothing with her."

"Correct. And the maid, also."

"Fact 6: This is an accumulation of detail, as follows: The
corpses have no identity; the car has no owner; the motive for
the murders is a mystery; the instrument of death is unknown
in each case; Dr. Quartz, so far as we know, is an estimable
gentleman; the two women, so far as we know, were as ignorant of the contents of the car as you and I were; and there is
absolutely nothing for us to go by in unraveling the mystery,
save the car itself, and what it contained."

"Now you are talking something I can understand."

"You mean, something which neither of us understands.
Now against these six facts, I have taken the following steps: I
have telegraphed my assistant, Chick, to take up the car end of
it. He is now in Philadelphia, tracing the car from that point,
backward, and I shall, myself, take up the task of working out
the identities of the murdered persons. So much for Fact 1. For
Fact 2, Dr. Wentworth, the great toxicologist and chemical

expert, arrived here last night and is now attempting to solve the mystery connected with the embalming of the bodies."

"What do you expect to accomplish by that?"

"Merely to add a nail to the future coffin of Dr. Quartz, as you will see. If he is as great a scientist as his predecessor, I will get evidence against him through that mysterious embalming fluid."

"What about Fact 3?"

"Under that head, I shall take the trail of Dr. Quartz myself; I think that will work in very well with my investigation of the identity of the murdered persons. Also, I have put one of my cleverest assistants—Ten-Ichi[4]—on the track of Edith Peyton and her maid; and Patsy[5] is working with the burglar, big Jim Gleason, who tried to blow up the car, to discover the real connection with this case of the two unknown men who went to the freight yards to see the car."

"Fact 4 is already covered by yourself."

"Yes."

"And Ten-Ichi will soon, you believe, be able to tell you all about Fact 5?"

"I do believe it; yes."

"And for Fact 6? You have already covered that ground also."

"Follow it with your eye while I go over it again: I shall discover the identity of the bodies before I am in position to go on with the case understandingly; Chick[6] will do the same service by the car, and will trace it to its owner; the motive for the murders will be revealed when the identity of the murdered persons is known; how they were killed, will develop in the natural course of events; if Dr. Quartz is an estimable gentleman; I shall find it out, and if he is not, I shall know it; Ten-Ichi will, within a week, know exactly what association Edith Peyton and her maid may have, or have had, with Dr. Quartz and with the car. There you are."

"H'm! Well, all that sounds reasonable. I can understand it much better than I can all that stuff about theorizing on what Dr. Quartz's egotism will do, and his plans for revenge. Now, about your pay for this case, Carter. The mayor——"

"I will send my bill when I have finished."

"Exactly. That is just what I was about to suggest. The mayor does not care to have any rewards offered. In fact, he agrees with me that the best thing is to keep the whole matter as quiet as possible."

Nick smiled broadly.

"Quiet or noisy, it doesn't matter to me now," he said. "I have no objection to having it known from one ocean to the other, that I am on this case. Usually I prefer to work on the quiet, but just now, I much prefer to have Dr. Quartz know that Nick Carter is after him. In fact, I shall take pains to inform him of the fact myself."

"You will? When, and how?"

"This very evening, and by going to his house and telling him of it."

"Do you mean to say that you will accuse him to his face?"

"Something very like it," smiled Nick; "although I shall not exactly do it in words."

"But you intend to go to his house."

"I do. I wish to study the man."

"Look out, Carter. He may select you for the next bit of merchandise he wishes to send across the continent by freight, or express."

"I only wish he would. I think I'd fool him. That was the game his predecessor played—and lost. The fact is, chief, I have already got a little evidence against Quartz, which I have not told you about."

"What is it?"

The detective took from one of his pockets a small velvet case which had once contained a lady's watch, and passed it to the chief.

"Look at that," he said.

"What of it?" asked the chief. "It looks like a watch case."

"It is. Open it."

The chief pressed the spring and the cover flew back, disclosing the fact that the circular bed in which a gold watch had once reposed was now filled with white wax, and that the wax had received an impression of some sort upon its surface.

"What about it?" asked the chief.

"Do you remember," asked Nick, "that when I searched the freight car in which the bodies came here, the only thing I discovered which was not put there purposely for you, or me, or somebody to find, was the imprint of several dirty fingers against the velvet plush near the secret door?"

"Yes."

"The imprint of one of those fingers—the first finger of the left hand—is very plain. I had it photographed, and then had the negative intensified and enlarged."

"Well?"

"I have put the wax in that case for the purpose of asking Dr. Quartz to give me, of his own free will, an impression of the first finger of his left hand."

"But there is already an impression here."

"That was made by my own finger. I put it there merely to show the doctor what a perfect impression the wax would produce."

"But he will refuse, likely."

"Chief, I don't care a rap whether he consents or refuses. What I want to see is the expression of his face when I ask him the question."

"What do you expect to gain by that?"

"Merely one glance at the man's thoughts. He won't refuse, but the suggestion will be a surprise to him. He knows as well as I do, that it is only in novels where a murderer is traced to his doom by the impression of his thumb or a finger. It doesn't happen in real life. The impression of my own finger looks enough like the one on the velvet near the door to convict me of the crime if that was the only thing to go by. Dr. Quartz's finger will appear much the same, and you, or I, or anybody, could determine nothing definite by it."

"Then what in the dev——"

"It is probable that Quartz has never thought of this thing. In all his studies, it may never have occurred to him to ask if a man may be traced by the impression of a finger mark. If he has not thought of it, ever, the suggestion will come to him as a surprise, and there will be one instant of hesitation while he collects his wits. It is that instant of hesitation which I wish to observe."

"I will confess, Nick, that your points are much too fine for me."

"A second's thought will convince him of the utter useless-ness of the device, and he will not hesitate after that, to grant me the impression of his finger; but, and here is the point, if his finger did make that mark near the door of the car, and if he has not thought about the pro or con of being traced by it, I will know it, no matter how guarded he may be, in that first in-stant when I ask for the impression."

"It is possible," said the chief, with a shrug; "I will not pre-tend to know."

"Men like Dr. Quartz are forever on their guard. The one thing to do with characters like his is to catch them off their guard. That is next to an impossible feat. If you wished to throw a stone through a certain window into a house, and you knew that window to be always barred with iron shutters, you would regard the feat as rather impossible, wouldn't you?"

"I should say so."

"But if you could devise some means whereby you could force the person on guard inside that window to open it for the purpose of looking out for an instant, then if you stood by, with a stone ready to hurl, you would stand a fairly good chance of succeeding, eh?"

"Sure."

"Well, Dr. Quartz's exterior is just such a window. He never opens it when there is a person near enough to him to see through it. In other words, he is always on his guard."

"And you propose, by this suggestion, to throw him off his guard for an instant."

"I think I can—provided he has not given the subject some thought. You see, he does not know that those finger marks are on the velvet near the door of the car."

"Why are you sure of that?"

"Because if he had known he made them he would have re-moved them. Not having removed them, he does not know they are there."

"He may have found out since that they are there."

"In that case, he will be on his guard, and I will not get the shutters open for me to see through; but I don't think he knows they are there. I think I will have a glimpse of the inside."

"When are you going there?"

"At once; when I leave you."

"Well, I hope you will get a look through that window. When will I see you again, Carter?"

"When I can tell you the true story of the mystery of the five murders."

CHAPTER IV
The Defiance of Dr. Quartz

When Nick Carter rang the bell of Dr. Quartz's residence and the door was opened by a servant in livery, the detective gave his own personal card to be delivered to the mysterious man upon whom he had called.

That card was engraved plainly with his own name, and, therefore, Dr. Quartz would know at once that the detective had determined to seek his interview boldly, and without any sort of subterfuge.

He was shown into the reception room, and presently the doctor came to him there.

Ha paused just inside the doorway and regarded his caller with an expression which was difficult to define; still there was a smile on his face; but whether it was one of welcome or of derision, or what it might portend, Nick could not determine.

"I scarcely hoped that you would do me so great an honor, Mr. Carter," said the doctor, in that strangely melodious voice which he could render as soft as the purring of a cat. "To what circumstance am I indebted for this call?"

He came on into the room while he was speaking, and motioned to Nick to resume the chair he had vacated upon the doctor's entrance.

"My call is due to a very natural desire on my part," replied Nick, "to ask you a few questions which I think you will not hesitate to answer."

"We can better determine that when I have listened to the questions you wish to ask," said the doctor, still smiling.

"Assuredly. You have announced yourself, I believe, as Dr. Quartz the second."

"Not at all. I have never done so. You are entirely mistaken."

"Indeed?"

"I know, of course, that there was once a certain Dr. Quartz; but there might also have been a dozen of them for all I know to the contrary. The qualifying title—'The Second'—has been given to me by others."

"Still you know to whom I refer as your predecessor?"

"Certainly."

"Did you ever know the man himself?"

"Certainly."

"Were you related?"

"He was my brother—ten years older than I."

"Thank you for being so explicit. Will you tell me how it happens that your initials are the same as his were?"

"His first name was John—or Jack, as he was familiarly called. My first name is James. Our middle initials were likewise the same. Do you care to be made acquainted with my ancestry?"

The studied insolence of the question brought a smile to the face of the detective; but he replied as coolly:

"It would give me a great deal of pleasure to know who your fathers were before you."

"So sorry that I do not feel called upon to accommodate you with the information, sir. Unless I am greatly mistaken you had ample opportunity to obtain those facts from my brother. Doubtless you have asked him the same question in the past."

"Often," replied Nick.

"The last time you called here," said the doctor, narrowing his eyes a little, and sharpening them so that they seemed like two narrow points which were reading the soul of the detective—if it had happened that Nick's soul could be so easily read—"you came here to arrest me on an entirely foolish charge, and in order to make you appear still more ridiculous, I played a little joke on you."

"You refer, I suppose, to your own charge against the two women whom I found here at that time," said Nick.

"Yes."

"One of my reasons for coming here this evening was to ask you to explain that joke."

"Was it, indeed? Are you so dense that you could not see through it?"

"I must confess that I was."

"How shall I make you understand? Let me see."

The doctor dropped his chin upon one of his hands and appeared to be lost in thought, but the detective could see that he was smiling.

Presently, with an appearance of frankness which Nick knew was assumed, he raised his head again, and with that same enigmatical smile on his lips, said:

"I think we were all more or less interested in the mysterious freight car, were we not?"

"It would appear so," replied Nick, "although you have not made public any interest you might have felt in it."

"Let us say that I was interested, then, and let it go at that."

"Very well—for the present."

"I think, Mr. Carter, that I will have to deviate from the direct subject for a moment, in order to make you understand."

"Take any course you please, doctor. I am a creature of extraordinary patience."

"So I have been informed. Very well. You must know, to begin with, that while you have been unaware of my existence, I have been quite familiar with yours."

"Indeed? You surprise me!"

"I will surprise you still more before I am through."

"I like to be surprised—pleasantly, at least."

"You are enough of a student, Mr. Carter, to understand that when a man wishes to master any given subject, he de-

votes a certain amount of study to that subject, the amount de-
pending upon two things, one of which is the difficulty of the
subject itself, and the other his own personal interest in the
subject."

"Yes."

"I have devoted something approximating ten years to
studying you."

"I certainly should feel greatly honored by so much attention."

"That is according to how you take it," replied the doctor,
coolly.

"May I ask whether it was the difficulty of the subject, or
your interest in it which induced you to devote so much time
to me?"

"Both."

"And might I inquire into the result of your studies?"

Dr. Quartz left his chair and crossed the room. From a table
he took a globe map of the world, and then returning until he
stood directly in front of the detective, he held the globe poised
in one hand while with the other he pointed at it.

"If I desired to learn thoroughly the geography of the world,
so that I would be as familiar with every portion of it as I am
with the neighborhood in which I was born, I would begin
with a map something like this. After mastering the rudiments
of this, I would take up each section by itself, by countries.
Later, I would divide the countries themselves into sections.
These I would again subdivide, and so on, *ad infinitum*. Do
you understand? In the end, I would have mastered every detail
so that I could tell you as much about the known information
of Tibet, for example, as you could tell me about—er—police
headquarters in the city of New York."

"I see your point. What of it?"

"That is something like the method I have employed in
studying you."

"But why have you studied me at all?"

"Because, Mr. Detective Carter, you succeeded in destroying
a person whom I considered the best-informed, smartest and
most intelligent man in the world."

"You refer to your distinguished predecessor, I suppose."

"I do. In the long warfare between you, you finally won. In the warfare between you and me, you will finally lose."

"Ah!" said Nick. "Then you admit that it is to be war between us."

"No; I do not admit it; I announce it."

"That fact will doubtless save both of us a lot of trouble."

"Oh, I don't know. It may possibly save you some trouble and anxiety. I had not considered you in the matter. I am glad you came here to-night, for if you had not selected to come to me, I should have gone to you."

"You might have experienced some difficulty in finding me, doctor."

"Not at all. I know every move you make, and have known them for years past. Don't forget that I have already told you of my study of you and your methods."

Nick shrugged his shoulders. There was something so coldly menacing in the attitude of the doctor, that the detective felt that the man was not boasting; and he was curious to know just how far he would go in his assumed frankness.

But he was soon to discover and to realize that Dr. Quartz was not deceiving him when he boasted of his knowledge of the detective.

"I should have sought you for the purpose of telling you a few things you do not know—for, little as you may realize the fact, there are still some things in the world with which you are not familiar," continued the doctor.

"For instance?" said Nick.

"For instance, you do not use a disguise with which I am not familiar, and you could not adopt a new one which I would not penetrate the moment I saw you. You have not made a move in the pursuit of your profession, for the past four or five years, with which I have not been in touch from the beginning to the end. I have merely looked on from a distance, to see not only what you would do, but how you would do it. You are an open book to me, Carter."

"How pleasant!"

"I knew when you received the letter from Jeremy Stone,

calling you here, and I also knew the contents of the letter. I knew exactly when you started for Kansas City and what train you took to come here. I knew when you arrived, and also that two of your assistants were on the train with you. I knew that they left the car at the opposite end. I knew of the conversation between you and Stone at that time. I know that you went to the freight yards to talk with the foreman there, one William Durland by name. I know where you took up your quarters, although you attempted to be very secret about it."

"You do seem to have been unusually well posted about my actions," replied Nick, with a shrug; "still, you must admit that all you have told me could easily have been acquired by you since it happened, and not so easily before it happened, when it would have been of more benefit to you."

"I know," continued the doctor, as if he had not heard Nick's remark, "that you have been in consultation with the chief of police to-day, and that you have told him of your intention to come here. I know that your assistants, Ten-Ichi and Patsy, are in the city now, and that each have their orders; I also know what those orders are. I know, furthermore, what your other assistant, Chick, is doing, and—— but what is the use of telling you all this? I know every move you make, often before you make it. Look at me, Mr. Carter."

"I am looking at you, doctor."

"I have told you that I am the brother of the Doctor Quartz whom you once knew. Perhaps that is true—and, perhaps I am the same man, come to life again to be your undoing."

Nick laughed outright.

"You don't expect me to believe that, of course," he said.

"I don't expect you to believe anything; I don't care whether you believe or not. You have in your pocket at this moment a red velvet watch case containing wax upon which you wish me to give you the impression of one of the fingers of my left hand. Give me the case and I will accommodate you. Does it surprise you that I know that?"

"Yes, it does," replied Nick, truthfully.

"You expected to catch me off my guard when you asked me to give you that impression, but you see I am informed in advance of your intention. I have not waited and studied for ten years, to arrive at the pleasure of this moment, for nothing, Mr. Carter."

"So I perceive."

"You do not require the impression of my finger on that wax, for I am perfectly willing to tell you that it was my finger which made the mark on the plush near the door of the freight car. We are alone, Carter, and I can tell you anything I please, and you cannot use it against me for the good reason that you can prove nothing. If you choose to go away and repeat what I have told you, I will simply deny that such a conversation has taken place. My statement is quite as good as yours before a jury, or before a court. You know that. You will always require proof, in order to convict, and that proof you cannot procure. You see, Carter, that I defy you. I have committed enough crimes to be hung a hundred times—enough to sit in all the electric chairs that were ever made—enough to spend a hundred years in prison—enough to make the records of the world's greatest criminals fall into obscurity; but you cannot prove one of them, Carter; now, or ever. That is why I have chosen to be frank with you—and to defy you."

CHAPTER V
The Victim of a Cruel Device

"May I smoke?" asked Nick, leaning back in his chair and taking a cigar from his pocket.

"Certainly. Will you have one of my cigars?"

"No, thank you. I smoked one of your predecessor's cigars once, and I did not wake up again for several hours. I have more confidence in my own."

Dr. Quartz smiled.

"Do you suppose, Carter," he said, "that if I cared to render you unconscious, I could not have done so without moving from this chair, or resorting to anything so ancient as giving you a drugged cigar?"

"I think you would have found it somewhat difficult," replied Nick.

"Let me prove to you how easily I could accomplish it. Oblige me by leaving your chair for a moment. Do not hesitate, for I assure you that I will not move from where I am seated. I merely wish to convince you."

Nick left the chair in which he was seated, and stood upon his feet.

"Now," said the doctor, "you remember, do you not, that while you were seated here, your arm was resting upon the natural place for it—that is, on the arm of the chair. Placing your own arm there served two purposes; one was, that it rested it, and the other was that it afforded you a purchase against which you could quickly and easily leap out of your chair, if I had made any belligerent move which made you think it necessary to do so. Is that correct?"

"Quite so."

"Now, if you will be good enough to examine either arm of the chair in which you were seated, you will discover that two long steel needles are protruding from it. Do you see them?"

"Yes, I see them."

"I have forced them from their places of concealment, simply by pressing a spring which is concealed in this chair. If I had pressed that spring while you were seated there, those needles would have pierced the flesh of your arms, and you would have been unconscious before you would have had time to draw a second breath."

Nick felt a shiver pass through him, although he gave no outward evidence of it.

"If," continued the doctor, "your arms had not been in the right position to have accommodated the needles you have seen, I could have pressed still another spring, and produced other needles, in other parts of the chair. So. Now look, and you will discover two in the seat of the chair, two more at the back of the chair, and two more where they would have pricked you in the head were you still seated there. Do you see them?"

"Yes."

"Do you appreciate the fact that I could easily have pricked you with any one of them, or with all of them, had I chosen to do so?"

"Yes."

"Very good. Those needles are tipped with the most delicate poison I know how to concoct. They are not deadly. They merely produce instant unconsciousness. You see, do you not, that if I wished to render you at my mercy, how foolish it would be to resort to the slow method of a drugged cigar?"

"Quite so."

"Be seated again, Mr. Carter. The needles have disappeared again, and I have no wish to prick you with them."

"If it is all the same to you, I will take a different chair," said Nick.

"Oh; any chair you please. This one in which I am seated, if you like."

The doctor chuckled when he made the remark, and Nick could have choked him gladly. But he drew forward another chair, turned it over to see that it was not connected with the floor, and finally seated himself upon it.

"This will serve my purpose," he said. "You were, I think, on the point of admitting some facts connected with your criminal record."

"Oh, I don't propose to give you detail, Mr. Carter. I am not so generous as that. My one desire is to convince you that you are as a baby in my hands; that I can, at any moment when I choose, brush you out of existence, as you would brush a spider from its web with a woman's broom. When the British Government erected Gibraltar, the place was meant to be impregnable, and it has proved so. When I prepared myself for this experience I am just beginning, I made just as painstaking preparations. You have been completely at my mercy for almost ten years and you have not, until now, known of my existence. Do you suppose, after taking all that care and trouble, that I care to put you out of the way without having my fun with you? I hope I do not offend you."

"You certainly interest me."

"Do I? How pleasant! Let me see; I believe you have elected to run me down, to arrest me, and to convict me for the murders of the five people whose dead bodies, perfectly embalmed, were found in the freight car now at the museum of Jeremy Stone; am I right?"

"You are dead right, if anybody should ask you."

"Thank you. The mayor of the city instructed the chief of police to engage your services and you have accepted the case. Am I still correct?"

"You are still correct."

"And you have informed the chief that you are positive in your own mind that the freight car incident is entirely Quartzonian, and that I, at least, possess criminal knowledge of the facts connected with it?"

"That is correct, also."

"You have sworn—or shall I say promised—to convict me of those crimes, eh?"

"Something like that; yes."

"Well, Carter, I will not say that I am guilty of the crimes you lay at my door, but I will admit that I could tell you all about the freight car, if I chose to do so. Now, with that admission from me, what are you going to do about it?"

"I am going to prove it. I am going to compel you to tell all you know, before I am done with you."

"Ah!"

The doctor rubbed his hands together in evident satisfaction. His fat face was wreathed in smiles, and his eyes sparkled with pleasure.

"That is the way to talk," he said. "Now we are getting at it. Now we understand each other. Do you know, Carter, I really thought you would be afraid to declare yourself."

"Afraid?" Nick laughed.

"Oh, I would not have blamed you had you been afraid. But, instead, you are accepting the position I wished you to assume."

"Am I, indeed? What position is that?"

"Why, of open warfare between us. We begin on even ground, don't you see?"

"How so?"

"I acknowledge myself to be the greatest criminal out of prison or unexecuted. You regard yourself as the only really great and undefeated detective in the world."

"Stow all that, Quartz, and go on with your statement."

"We meet on even ground, that is all. Have you ever watched a cat, when it has caught a mouse?"

"Often."

"If the mouse happens to be uninjured—that is, only slightly hurt—the cat takes it to an open space, and then calmly looks the other way while the mouse slowly crawls toward freedom. The cat does not appear to see the mouse until it has almost escaped, but then it leaps forward and returns the mouse to the center of the open space again; and this performance continues until the cat is tired, and generously—er—murders its victim. You have seen that, have you?"

"Frequently."

"Well, in this case, I am the cat and you are the mouse. I have caught you. I have taken you to the open space. Now, I am going to play with you. That is why I have studied you all these years. We meet on even ground, only I am much the stronger of the two because I am so much better prepared."

"You think so, no doubt."

"No; I know it."

"And yet, you have the same weak point possessed by the other Dr. Quartz."

"Not at all, Carter; not at all. You think I have; but I haven't."

Nick smiled.

"You think I have the egotism, the conceit of the other Dr. Quartz, but I assure you that you are mistaken. I possess merely the sure knowledge of my superiority. That is why I dare to acknowledge to you that I am the criminal you think me; but, my dear Carter, you will discover that I am the Gibraltar, while you are the poor fool who batters himself to pieces against the walls."

The detective still smiled and made no reply.

"Look around you, Carter; for I see that you require some further demonstration of my power, besides the needles in the chair. Do you see that open door through which you entered the room?"

"Plainly."

"It is within twelve feet of you; no?"

"About that, I should say."

"Doubtless you think that from where you are seated, you would have no difficulty in getting through that door before it could be closed. Let me see you try it."

Nick shrugged his shoulders.

"I am tired of this horse play," he said. "Have you a spring connected with that door, as well as with the chair in which I was seated?"

"Look," replied the doctor; and as the detective looked, a pair of steel shutters that were concealed in the walls at either side of the aperture, flew together with a snap, and left the two men shut inside the room. And then, as the detective was in the act of turning again to face Dr. Quartz, they flew open again, leaving the doorway as it had been before.

"You see?" said the doctor.

"Yes; I saw," replied Nick.

"Do you think you could have reached the doorway soon enough to have passed through it before the steel shutters barred your way?"

"Perhaps not," assented the detective.

"My! How grudgingly you admit it, and yet you know it to be a fact. Carter, that door and those needles are only two among hundreds of devices I have arranged for your benefit— as well as for others', for I would not have you think that I have done you too much honor. Both the door and the needles come in quite handy for others, also."

"I have not a doubt of it."

"And this house is only one of several—it is not necessary that you should know how many there are or where they are— where I could receive you with the same sort of delicate attention."

"And now," said Nick, "now that you have demonstrated something of your boasted power, and have told me so much, will you tell me why you have taken all this trouble for my entertainment?"

"Would you like to know?"

"Certainly."

"Very well, I will tell you. I have purchased a small island in the Pacific Ocean to which I mean to retire some day, and enjoy the balance of my life as suits me best; that is, among my books and instruments. In a word, in study. There, I shall enjoy the delights of vivisection[7] upon human subjects, without hindrance from the authorities, and to my heart's content. I have already stocked the place with prospective subjects, and you have no idea what a land of enchantment I shall make of it. Later, before I have done with you, I may tell you more about it; for the present, I wish to say that I intend to go there after I have done with you. But I must finish with you first.

"You see, Carter, I have promised myself that I will make you suffer a thousand pangs for every one you administered to my predecessor. I have promised myself that you shall be fooled and outwitted at every turn; that you shall first lose your reputation, then your fortune, then your friends, then your honor; I have promised myself that you shall see those whom you love best, stricken down one by one at your side, and that the corpses of your three assistants, and of the woman you love, shall finally find their several ways to a dime museum, as those now in the freight car have done; and that, finally, you shall yourself furnish for me the most interesting of my subjects for vivisection. You love a woman named Carmen——"

Nick leaped to his feet with an exclamation of anger, and started toward the doctor, but even as he did so the chair in which he had been seated flew upward behind him as if his act of leaving it had released some hidden spring.

It seemed to leap toward him, as if the whole chair were a concealed spring. Sharp spikes protruded from it, which pierced his flesh as they struck him, and in an instant more he sank to the floor, unconscious, and to all appearance, lifeless.

CHAPTER VI

The Demon Doctor's First Victim

When Nick Carter opened his eyes, he looked around him in amazement, for he was in his room, in the house to which he had repaired after his advent in Kansas City, and where he had taken accommodations, believing that he could preserve the secret of his location.

He attempted to rise, but fell back again, realizing that his nerves were still benumbed by the drug which had been injected into his veins through the agency of the spikes in the chair.

His own rooms were at least two miles from the house of Dr. Quartz, and he knew that he must have been brought there while he was unconscious; and then, step by step, he recalled all that had occurred in the reception room of the doctor.

"What a consummate fiend that man is!" he mused, while he waited for his strength to return to him. "I doubt if there is an article of furniture in that room which is not prepared to be used as a trap if the necessity shall arise. The mere act of sitting in that chair I last occupied must have released the mechanism, so that I was bound to be wounded as I was as soon as I should attempt to leave it.

"That man made no idle threats, either. He meant every word he said. And he has studied me almost as closely as he asserts.

"Well, why not? It would be like him—at least, it would have been exactly like the other Dr. Quartz to have done that very thing.

"Heaven! When one stops to consider what might have been accomplished by a man of such brain as he possesses, if only his intelligence were turned to a right use, it is appalling.

"But he adopts villainy for his pursuit, and he takes it up precisely as he would undertake the study of any science.

"What am I to conclude from all that he has said to me? Why, plainly, that he has really devoted ten years of his life— that is, one side of it—to studying me and my habits, while he has kept himself in the background, not permitting me even to know that he existed.

"It seems incredible that a man could do such a thing, and I should be the first to refuse to accept it as a fact if I did not understand how thoroughly Quartzonian it is.

"He has evidently taken pains to live near me, but to keep out of my sight. He doubtless is possessed of unlimited means, and has been able to keep a corps of detectives of his own through whom he has been able to observe.

"I could fancy, almost, that I can see the hand of Dr. Quartz in many of the cases I have had, as if he has engineered the villain in each case until he has grown tired of the game and permitted it to end.

"In ten years what could he not accomplish? He could get his own spies on the police of the cities he selected; he could worm his way into private offices through the employment of spies; he could have educated an army of assistants to do his bidding in any place where he wished to put them, and he could become, in the line he selected, almost omnipotent.

"And now, evidently the time has come when he is prepared to meet me, and to conquer me, as he believes, at every turn.

"And he prefers to do that openly; that is like Dr. Quartz.

"He prefers coolly to tell me that he is the guilty man, and then to defy me; that is like Dr. Quartz.

"He prefers to admit me to his parlor, and to show me a sample of his power, while he sits nearby and laughs in his sleeve; that is like Dr. Quartz.

"He prefers to render me unconscious at the end of our interview, and then to return me here to my own room, uninjured, in order further to demonstrate his power; that is like Dr. Quartz.

"He prefers to tell me plainly that he is actually worse than what I think him—to almost acknowledge the five murders of the freight car—to demonstrate his ability to find out my most cherished secrets, and finally to go so far as to threaten the woman I love; all that is strikingly like Dr. Quartz.

"Why, Dazaar,[8] the arch-fiend, was a joke beside Quartz; and I wonder—ay, I wonder if after all, even Dazaar was not merely a tool of his?

"Pshaw! What nonsense! And yet, to carry on that study of me, of which he boasts, he must have provided himself with human tools.

"One thing is certain. I cannot fight Dr. Quartz in the open. He is forewarned, and altogether too thoroughly forearmed for that. I must meet him on his own ground. Hello! I wonder what that is."

Nick had partly raised himself on the couch where he was lying, and he could see, resting on the table in the center of the room, a sheet of paper with writing on it.

"Quartz has left a letter for me, after the manner of his famous predecessor," he mused, rising, for now his nerves had regained their wonted energy, and no longer refused to do his bidding.

He felt thoroughly himself again, and so far as he could determine, there was not a vestige of the effects of the drug left about him.

He crossed the floor and took up the sheet of paper.

It was, as he had supposed, a message from Quartz.

It was written in a delicate chirography, almost as fine and perfect as copper plate, and was as follows:

"MY DEAR CARTER: You have accused me of possessing the weaknesses of that other person to whom we have had occasion to refer, and one of them was, I believe, that of writing too many letters for your delectation. I venture to write this one, nevertheless, and you are at liberty to use it to whatever advantage you can.

"You had the misfortune to faint away while you were in my rooms, and I have done you the service to bring you to your home, where you can receive that care of which you seem to stand so much in need.

"I trust you will have entirely recovered by the time you read this, and have no doubt that you will have done so.

"I am quite well aware that you desire nothing more than that I should say something in this letter which you could make use of but such is not my purpose. The letter is merely to assure you of my interest in your affairs, and to repeat that I will leave no stone unturned to interest myself in them.

"Some day, when I shall have completed the duties which hold me here, and have prepared the way for my continued sojourn on that island in the Pacific, of which I gave you some slight account, I hope—for a time, at least—to have the pleasure of your society and your aid in my scientific researches. I am wedded to science, my dear Carter, and the most interesting of all sciences is the study of humanity itself.

"Perhaps you will be able to read between the lines of this letter, and to extract from it that pleasant meaning which I cannot put into so many words. I hope so. In the meantime, let me venture to hope, that when you next see your good assistant, Patsy, you will remind him of my existence, and give him my remembrances.

"It is not necessary that I should sign my name, since you will know so well who penned these lines with the execrably bad pen I found on your table."

Nick laid the letter aside with a frown.

"Now, what does he mean by that reference to Patsy?" he asked himself.

He looked at his watch and then uttered an exclamation of surprise. Next, he started for the window and looked out upon the street.

"Great Scott!" he thought. "I must have been in that unconscious state many hours. This is another day. It is all of fifteen hours or more since that chair flew over and hit me, in Dr. Quartz's office. It was about nine in the evening when I was knocked over, and it is now almost noon of the next day."

He wheeled and looked anxiously around him.

"Patsy was to meet me here at midnight, last night," he mused, "and the reference in that letter can mean but one thing—one thing. Great Heaven, has he captured Patsy, and got the lad in his power already?"

For that was how it appeared to the detective, and that was the way he read the message of Dr. Quartz as contained in the letter.

"As soon as I was unconscious, Quartz brought me here," he mused. "Then he waited for the arrival of Patsy. I can see it all now. Patsy came while he was here—while I was lying helpless upon that couch, and Quartz had no difficulty in capturing him. That is what he means when he tells me when I next see my assistant, Patsy—and all that."

The detective was now thoroughly himself again, with every sense upon the alert.

Face to face with an actual incident which demanded his attention, he gave his mind entirely to it, to the utter exclusion of all things else.

His first move was to leave the room, to run rapidly down the stairs and open the street door.

His purpose in making this move was at once obvious, for he was able to tell at a glance that Patsy had been there, and also that he had not been able to leave his mark again when he went out; and also that Ten-Ichi had not been there at all.

One of his arrangements with his assistants was for each of them to leave a sign, made by a certain chalk mark, on the steps outside the house, when they entered it, so that he could tell, without entering, if either of them were there, or had been there and gone away again.

Patsy's mark was there—a figure 12, which said as plainly as if it had been written, that he had arrived there at midnight. If he had gone out again later, and could have done so, he would have crossed out the 12, and placed beside it another figure showing the hour of his leaving. The chalk mark was red; if Ten-Ichi had made it, it would have been green.

"So Patsy came here at twelve, and he was not able to leave his mark when he went away," mused the detective. "So much I know. Now to see if the lad had an opportunity of leaving me any sign concerning what happened to him inside the house."

He hastened back to his room again.

Everything seemed to be in perfect order, although he had no doubt that Dr. Quartz had thoroughly examined everything the room contained.

For a time he looked in vain for some sort of message from

the younger detective, but at last he discovered it; and when discovered, it seemed worthy of the young assistant.

The lad had evidently been bound and thrown upon the same couch where Nick awoke to consciousness, for scrawled in letters of blood against the white wall behind the couch, with bleeding finger which he had torn open on a nail in the couch covering so that he could write it, Nick found this message:

"QUARTZ HAS GOT ME"

That was all; but it was enough.

CHAPTER VII
The Woman Behind the Grating

Just as the clocks in the city were striking twelve, and thus announcing the midnight hour, two figures raised themselves over the cornice of a house three doors removed from the one in which Dr. Quartz resided, and where Nick Carter held the interview with him which had ended so disastrously.

"So far, so good," said the voice of Nick Carter, addressing his companion. "Come on, Ten-Ichi, but be silent as the grave."

He took the lead then, and the two glided swiftly and noiselessly across the roofs, until they paused in the shadow of a chimney which came from the Quartz residence.

"Yonder is the skylight," whispered the detective in the ear of his companion. "This is the first time in my experience when I have taken this method of entering a house, but it seemed necessary to-night."

"We are not inside the house yet," replied Ten-Ichi, in the same cautious voice.

"No; but we will get there. Come."

He led the way to the scuttle,[9] which was just beyond the skylight, and attempted to raise it; but it resisted his efforts.

"Fastened," he muttered. "Give me the tools, lad."

Ten-Ichi passed a small bag of tools which had been slung across his shoulders, and from this the detective extracted a brace and bit of fine workmanship. These were quickly adjusted, and in a few moments more the latter had eaten through the tin as well as the woodwork of the scuttle.

But the detective did not pause there.

Hole after hole was bored through the scuttle, and so closely together that when the detective finally desisted, and gave the tool back to his assistant, he wrenched what remained of the clinging wood loose in his grasp, and laid it silently on the roof beside him.

Next, he thrust his right arm through the opening, and after feeling around in the darkness for a considerable time, he drew it forth again, and raised himself to his feet.

"So much is done," he whispered. "Now, Ten-Ichi, I shall raise the scuttle and go down; but I wish you to remain where you are."

"Am I not to go inside the house with you?"

"No. You are to remain here. You can serve me best in that way. There may be a thousand bells ringing inside the house at this moment, to give Dr. Quartz warning of what I have already done. If he heard them, he is waiting for me, and I don't wish him to capture both of us, although I'll give him something to do to get me this time, even if he is on the watch."

"What shall I do here?"

"Wait. Wait and see what happens."

"And if I hear a scrimmage?"

"Listen with all your ears if you hear such a thing. I will shout an order. If you hear me call out the word 'Doctor!' you are to come to my assistance. If, instead, I use the word 'Quartz!' you are to make your way to the chief of police and tell him what has happened."

"All right."

"You understand thoroughly?"

"Yes."

"And you will obey to the letter?"

"I will."

"If you hear nothing at all, wait here for an hour, and then go to the chief of police. In that case, bring him here, but by the front door, and make him rip the house inside out, if it is necessary. He will have sufficient cause in case I am not back here inside of an hour."

Nick raised the scuttle then, and slowly let himself down into the darkness.

For a moment after his feet were upon the ladder under the scuttle, he paused and whispered to Ten-Ichi.

"Remember," he said.

"I will remember," replied the assistant.

Then the detective nodded his head, and in an instant more had disappeared from view into the interior of Dr. Quartz's house.

Nick descended the ladder to the floor, and then, after waiting a moment to listen, and being assured that no alarm of his approach had been given, he produced his electric search light and pressed the button.

The light revealed the fact that he was in a closet which was barely large enough to accommodate the ladder, and was, in fact, a narrow shaft, created solely to lead to the roof through the scuttle.

There was a door directly in front of him, and he found upon investigation that it was securely locked.

But locks, especially of the kind that are used in ordinary doors, offered slight obstacle to him, and in a moment, by the aid of his pick-lock, he had it opened. Then, extinguishing his light, he passed through into the uppermost hallway of the house, and closed the door behind him.

One word now, as to how the detective succeeded in reaching the roof of the house unobserved.

He was well aware that Quartz would not be caught off his guard if he could avoid it, and the moment he knew that Patsy had been captured, and was even at that moment in imminent danger of his life at the hands of Dr. Quartz, he decided that he would beard the lion in his den, so to speak; in other words, that he would penetrate to the interior of the doctor's house in search of him.

He immediately went out and found Ten-Ichi, whom he ordered to await him that night at the end of the block where his own rooms were, and then he returned to his own apartment.

There he waited till night, well knowing that one or more of the hirelings of the wily doctor was on the watch for him, but resolved to outwit them, no matter how many there might be.

To do this he remained in his room with the gas lighted, after it was dark. He also left the shutters of the window open, so that a person outside could readily see into the interior of the room.

He had already arranged a dummy for his uses;[10] and this, which represented himself, as well as he could make it do so, he placed in a rocking chair, well out of sight through the window.

This done, he calmly seated himself in another chair which was in full view.

There he remained quietly reading, and now and then nodding his head, as if sleepy, and at times really appearing to go to sleep, but in reality wide awake.

At eleven o'clock he stretched his arms, yawned and rose from the chair. Then he crossed the room until he was out of sight from the window, and dropping to the floor, seized two ropes which were connected with the chair in which he had placed the dummy.

He pulled first upon one rope and then upon the other, thus giving the chair the appearance of being hitched across the room, as a person would move it who was comfortably seated and who was too tired or too lazy to rise.

The effect was perfect.

The chair, with its contents, moved as methodically across the room to its place under the light, as if there had really been a person seated in it, and from the street he knew that it appeared as if he had fallen asleep in his chair with his book in his hands.

After that, the rest was easy.

He had only to creep from the room, taking care not to permit himself to be seen from the street, and then to make his way through the scuttle of the house to the roof; thence across the roof to the end of the block, and then down to the street by way of the water pipes, to Ten-Ichi, who was awaiting him.

He had made no effort at disguise, for the reason that he did not expect to be seen at all.

From there, he and Ten-Ichi made their way directly to the vicinity of the house where Dr. Quartz lived, thence to the roofs, and the rest we know.

But now the detective was inside the house. Nay, more; he had penetrated to the top floor through the scuttle, and before him he felt was an opportunity to unravel the mysteries of that place.

He did not wish, for reasons of caution, to make use of his light again, lest it should betray his presence there, and so he crept on cautiously, feeling with his hands along the top of the balustrade, and assisted in some degree by a faint reflection of light which sifted in through the skylight over his head.

In this way he found, one after another, the doors of the four rooms on that floor.

Each of these doors responded to his touch, and each of the rooms was vacant.

After satisfying himself of that much, he returned to the hallway and to the head of the stairs, and thence down them, to the next floor below.

Here, he realized at once that he was on different ground.

There was a light burning in the lower hall, and enough of it penetrated to the floor where he was, to enable him to see his way about, accustomed as his eyes now were to darkness.

At first, as he paused to listen, not a sound came to his ears, although he could see that there was a light in the front room of the house—he could see where it shone through a crack under the door.

As he approached it, however, he could hear the murmur of voices, although they were so indistinct that he could not even determine whether they were masculine or feminine.

He got down on his hands and knees and pressed his ear against the crack under the door, and then he felt a thrill of pleasure, for he recognized Patsy's voice on the instant— recognized it, although he could not determine a word that was uttered.

Rising, he gave a moment's examination to the door, and discovered, rather to his surprise, that it was made to open outward, instead of in, as such doors usually are hung.

He discovered also that there were bolts on the outside of the door, and with exceeding caution, lest he should alarm those inside the room—for he had no positive knowledge that Quartz himself might not be there—he shoved back the bolts and pulled the door slowly ajar.

He discovered in that instant that he was not yet inside the room by any means, for beyond the door was still another, and this one was made of iron grating as thick and heavy as that which is used in prisons.

But it was not so much the grating which arrested his attention as it was what he discovered beyond it.

He was, in fact, gazing into the interior of a room in which two persons were fastened, by chains, to the opposite walls, so that they faced each other.

One of those persons was Patsy; and the other—he could almost have sworn that she was the same young woman, come to life again, whom he had seen with a knife through her heart, on the bed in the mysterious freight car.

CHAPTER VIII
Some Light Upon Dark Events

Neither Patsy nor the young woman who was his companion in misfortune was aware of his proximity, and he dared not make a sound until he was assured that he would not be heard by other ears than theirs.

The iron door was securely locked. He discovered that at a glance, and also realized that it would not be an easy matter, even for him, to open it.

He was about to turn away as silently as before, to investigate further through the house—for he did not wish to be surprised in his work of liberating Patsy—when the young woman spoke again, addressing the young assistant.

"I hope you will have the courage to go through with the torture without a murmur, for it only delights him to see people suffer. He would smile like an angel if he could see you weep tears of blood."

"I think," replied Patsy, "that I will suffer less than you. I should rather be the victim of such torture, than to be compelled to be a helpless witness of it, when practiced upon another."

She smiled sadly across the half-lighted room at him.

"So far," she said, "I have not seen much of torture, although he has told me that it is to come. One of his theories is that he can inure the most delicate person to the most horrible sights so that they can look unmoved upon scenes which ordinarily would turn the heart of a strong man faint with horror. I have never seen anybody tortured as he says he means to torture you. Doubtless he will not compel me to see it all."

"How long have you been an inmate of this awful house?" asked Patsy.

"I do not know. I have no means of remembering time. I am either drugged, or unconscious through hypnotism, almost all the time."

"And you have not lost your reason, either. It is incredible."

"My reason? No; I have kept that; but it seems benumbed, nevertheless. For example, I feel a great sorrow for you, but it is not the sorrow I would have felt for another, long ago— before I came here. Dr. Quartz says that I am the best subject he ever had, and that I should be glad that I can do so much for science."

Nick could see that Patsy shuddered. He was about turning away the second time, when Patsy spoke again.

"How long will it be before he returns?" he asked of his companion.

"He said he would leave us together for an hour. I should say that half that time is already gone, is it not?"

"More than that," said Patsy; and then, as if in support of his statement, Nick heard the sound of approaching footsteps in the lower hall, and he drew back away from the door, closed it and shot the bolts back into place, and glided away up the stairs again, out of sight from the approaching person.

He had not an instant to spare.

Scarcely had he secured a safe distance, when the footfalls came up the stairs, and at last paused in front of the door through which the detective had just been listening.

There was sufficient light in the hall so that Nick could see him, and he drew one of his revolvers and leveled it at the human devil.

For a moment he was almost determined to shoot, and so put an end at once and forever to the career of Dr. Quartz; but for some reason he did not fire. It was not in his nature to shoot a man down in cold blood, although he felt that he would be eminently justified in doing so in this case.

Quartz undid the fastenings of the doors, after which he unlocked the iron grating, pushed it open, and entered the prison room.

He did not take the trouble to close either of the doors behind him, but continued on his way into the room, until he stood in the center of it, exactly between his two prisoners.

He paused there, and looked from one to the other of his prisoners, with an expression on his face and in his eyes which was entirely new to Nick Carter.

"I could imagine such an expression as that on the face of a sleep walker," thought the detective; and he leaned forward to examine the man the closer.

Dr. Quartz's face was as white as alabaster. The blood seemed to have entirely forsaken his cheeks, leaving them like the countenance of a corpse. His eyes, too, were dazed and glassy, and they seemed to stare upon his two victims without really sensing their presence.

"Is it possible," thought Nick, "that the man is the victim of some drug habit, and that he is now under the influence of whatever drug he takes? It would seem so. He certainly is not himself."

The oily, unctuous smile of Dr. Quartz was gone. The full lips, usually so red and so ready to smile, were stretched across his teeth as if in a half snarl, and were of the color of dirty chalk.

In fact, it was altogether a different man from the Dr. Quartz we have already seen, who stood there in the prison-like room, confronting his two victims who were chained to the wall, and who should have called forth the pity from a heart of stone.

And much to Nick's surprise, at this juncture, the young woman spoke again.

"You may talk on," she said to Patsy. "He will not hear you, or if he hears, he will not heed. I have seen him like this once before, and, oh, it was horrible! That was when he killed my cousin before my eyes, long, long ago. I do not know where it was, only that it was in another city."

"Your cousin," said Patsy. "That was the body we found in the freight car, with a dagger through her heart."

"Yes," she replied, "it must have been she whom you found, although he did not stab her—he choked her to death with his hands. Oh, my God! it was awful. I am glad that I cannot feel things as I did then. He was in just such a mood then as he is now. He looked the same as he looks now; and he turned on me, and would have killed me in the same way, only that the mood left him before he reached me, the color came back to his face, and he turned and looked at the corpse of my cousin in astonishment, as if he did not know, until then, that he had attacked her. Now, perhaps he will kill us both. I only hope that I will be his first victim. Hush!"

Dr. Quartz had turned toward her, as if the sound of her voice had disturbed him, and for a moment they all held their breath, while Nick Carter raised his revolver, ready to use in case of necessity.

But after a moment the doctor's chin sank upon his breast, as if he had drifted away again to the land of unreality; and then the young woman spoke again.

"Do I shock you with my seeming apathy to all these horrors?" she asked. "You would not wonder at it if you were aware of a tithe of what I have been compelled to see and hear ever since I fell into the power of that fiend—for fiend he is; you can never make me believe that he is human. I am used to horrors. I am accustomed to seeing murder, and talking about it. I am gradually losing my sense of perception between right and wrong, and I no longer have the quality of compassion in me, I fear. I know that Dr. Quartz murdered my father

It was a heavy weapon, and it was wielded by no light and delicate touch; but heavy as the blow was, it only staggered the man beneath it.

And even as he staggered, Nick raised his other hand and dealt him a second blow, this time with his fist, so that he and Dr. Quartz fell to the floor together, the latter underneath, the detective on top.

But the man, even under the violence of those two blows, was so strong and his vitality was so great, that he struggled as few could have done, even then.

On the other hand, Nick Carter knew what sort of a man he had tackled. He had once before had occasion to feel the strength of Dr. Quartz's muscles, and he knew that it required all his own to master him under any circumstances.

And he did not hesitate to use every art and every advantage he could employ in gaining ascendancy over the doctor.

As they fell to the floor, the detective struck him again and again, always with violence, and always as forcibly as if it were the first blow he was delivering; and by dropping the revolver from his right hand he managed to secure a pair of handcuffs from his pocket, and to force them upon the wrists of the doctor before he could prevent the act.

And still the man struggled and fought with all his might, so that Nick, even then, in order to conquer him, seized again the weapon from the floor and dealt with it another blow which was effectual, and which stiffened him out for a moment; and then Nick lost no time in fastening another paid of shackles to his ankles.

There was blood upon the doctor's face when Nick rolled him over—blood where the butt of the revolver had cut through the skin, and where Nick Carter's knuckles had made an abrasion or two; but there was also a smile on his lips, and the detective saw that he was now entirely conscious, and so again master of himself, if not of circumstances.

"You caught me napping, Carter," he said, with cool assurance. "Otherwise you would be here, where I am, and I would be there, where you are."

"It is much better as it is," replied Nick, grimly. "I think, doctor, that we will prove something against you, a little sooner than you anticipated."

"You certainly have turned the tables for the moment; but, don't forget that you are not out of the house yet."

"Oh, no, I won't forget. Don't worry."

As Nick spoke, he saw Dr. Quartz turn his eyes toward the girl who was chained to the wall, and he saw come into them that hard, determined expression which he knew indicated an effort on the part of a hypnotist to exert his power.

As quick as a flash he leaped between the doctor and his victim, and the same instant he struck the man a sharp blow across the eyes with the flat of his hand.

"Damn you!" said the doctor; but Nick did not wait to hear more, or to reply. Instead he seized the man in his arms and dragged him through the door into the hall outside; and once there, he calmly tied a bandage over his eyes, and with a third paid of handcuffs, fastened him to a spindle in the balustrade.

"I am going back inside the room now, doctor, to have a little talk with our two friends who are in there; but I shall remain where I can keep you in sight, and if you make any effort to free yourself, don't forget that I am a dead shot, and that I shall not hesitate to prove it."

"Faugh!" said the doctor. "Go there, if you like. Don't worry me by talking to me. The tables shall be turned on you before you are an hour older."

"You seem to take things quite easy," said Nick, smiling.

"Why not?"

"This is a case where the mouse is playing with the cat, isn't it, doctor?"

"Why, yes, it would almost seem so."

"And yet, you seem to keep your nerve with you."

"My nerves? They are of iron, as you will know some day. A nerve of iron and a heart of ice; that is it, Carter."

Nick turned without making a reply, and re-entered the room beyond the iron grating. Ten-Ichi, waiting on the roof, was altogether forgotten, or, if remembered, unheeded.

Nick's first duty inside the room was to free Patsy from the chains which bound him; he next crossed to the girl, and in a moment he had freed her also, for the keys which fitted the locks of the chains had been placed by the doctor upon a chair just out of reach of his victims. Tantalizingly near, but sufficiently far away to be useless to them.

Nick silenced Patsy with a gesture; then he placed one of his own revolvers in the hand of the young assistant and motioned him to stand guard over the doctor in the hallway.

Then he turned again to the young woman.

Ever since his first leap into the room when he had attacked the doctor and so summarily overcome him, she had watched the detective with a peculiar expression on her sad but beautiful countenance. She seemed, indeed, as if she were endeavoring to understand what was taking place, but had not the ability to grasp its entire meaning.

Now, when he turned to her, she greeted him with a smile which was like the expression of a pleased child—and yet Nick saw that there was sufficient intelligence in her eyes to make her a competent witness.

"Tell me your name," he said, kindly.

"My name?" she repeated after him. "I have almost forgotten it; but not quite. The doctor has refused to let me go by my own name since I have been with him."

"But you remember what it was, do you not?" asked the detective.

"Oh, yes. It was Nanine—Nanine Duclos."

"And the name of your cousin—that cousin whom you say the doctor killed before your eyes—that cousin whom Dr. Quartz choked to death and afterward placed in a freight car—what was her name?"

"Her name? It was Marie. Her last name was the same as mine, you know."

"Yes, I understand. Now, Nanine, the doctor has told you about the freight car, has he not?"

"Oh, yes, indeed!"

"Tell me what he told you about it."

"Why, the same as he told other people, I suppose."

"Never mind; tell me what he told you."

"Well, you know he was to marry Marie. All the arrangements had been made for the wedding, and he had built the car and was to have a fine time traveling in it. We lived in another city then. I don't know where it was, only that it was somewhere in the East."

"And I suppose," said Nick, leading her on as gently as he could, for she talked like a child upon whom horrors have made little or no impression, "that your father and mother and that Marie's father and mother were with you all that time, during the preparations for the wedding, were they not?"

"Oh, yes."

"I heard you say that the doctor killed them also. Did he put them in the car with your cousin?"

"Oh, yes; he said so. I suppose he did. He sent the car somewhere. You see, he did not mean to hurt Marie when he killed her. He did it in a fit of rage such as he has at times, when his face turns the color of chalk, and he goes mad. I have heard him say that some day he will kill himself in one of those mad fits. He says he cannot cure them, and it makes him wild when he thinks there is anything he cannot cure."

"What were the names of your father and mother? And what were the names of the father and mother of Marie?"

"My father and mother were George and Anne, and the others were uncle Peter and aunt Myra."

"Where did you live before you knew the doctor? Can you remember that?"

"Oh, yes. On Beacon Street, in Boston. We were all very happy then. Dr. Quartz came to us because uncle Peter was ill. The doctor cured him. After that, aunt Myra was very ill, and the doctor cured her also. And then Marie was ill. We were all ill, one after another, and the doctor was so expert that he cured us all, and my father and my uncle gave him a great deal of money. But he earned it, I have heard them say, by saving the lives of all of us."

"Your father and your uncle were rich men, were they not?"

"I suppose so. I don't know."

"You kept horses and carriages and servants; eh?"

"Oh, yes. Lots of them; and now all those things are mine. I have heard the doctor say so. That is why he keeps me here, I think, so that nobody will get my money away from me."

"I understand. Now, why does he chain you in this room as I found you? He does not keep you here all the time, does he?"

"Oh, no, indeed. I spend most of the time in a beautiful room where there are birds, and my pet cat. He waves his hands over me there, and puts me to sleep so that I have beautiful dreams and forget all the things I do not wish to remember. I am always glad when he comes to me to give me those dreams."

"And you don't remember how long it is since you have been living so, do you?"

"No; only that it is a very long time. I have lived in this house a long time. I traveled a long way on the railroad before I came here, and, oh, it was a long time after he killed Marie and the others, before we came here."

"Did the doctor ever tell you why he put all those dead people in the freight car to send them away somewhere?"

"No; only he laughed a great deal about it, and said it was a good joke, and that it would set the dogs to barking. He said that he would be there, wherever it was, when the dogs began to growl and bark, and that he would have fun in watching the leader of the pack trying to get upon the scent."

"Ah! He said that, did he? Did he also tell you the name of the leader of the pack?"

"Yes. He said the leader of them all would be Nick Carter, and that one day he would send him and his friends on the same sort of a journey."

CHAPTER X

The Man of Iron Nerve

"You have not told me, yet, why he chains you here at times," insisted Nick.

"Why, to make me like Zanoni; to make me accustomed to

horrors, he says. To make me love the sight of blood; the suffering of others; to make me like they are. And he is making me
so. While I was talking with the young man who was chained
to the wall, and whom you just set free, I found that I was anxious for the doctor to come so that I would see what he was
going to do. Oh, yes; I am getting that way. I am getting like
Zanoni."

"Who is Zanoni?"

"Zanoni, the terrible; Zanoni, the beautiful; Zanoni, the
awful; Zanoni, the witch."

"But who is she?"

"The only person in the world whom Dr. Quartz fears; that
is who she is."

"Does she live here?"

"I don't know. She comes and goes at will. She is mad. I have
heard the doctor say that. She is mad. She is the success of one
of his experiments. He says that he has destroyed her soul, and
made her like an animal, only that she still has her cunning and
her intelligence, so that she can appear in any part she pleases,
and fool all the world. You would think her a saint from
heaven, and she is a devil from hell. I have heard the doctor tell
her those very words. Ah, I tremble when I think of Zanoni.
She comes to my room sometimes, and heats an iron in the fire
in the grate until it is red hot, and then she waves it before my
eyes and says that she is going to put them out so I won't be so
beautiful. And sometimes she bares my arms to the shoulders
and pricks them with needles until they smart terribly. She is a
terrible woman; but, oh, so beautiful. And there is, somewhere, another young woman, who is beautiful, like me, and
whom this Nick Carter that he speaks about, loves."

"Ah!" said Nick, breathing hard.

"And I have heard the doctor say that he is going to capture
her and bring her here, when he has finished his education of
me, and made me like Zanoni; and that then he is going to turn
the other young woman, whose name is Carmen, over to us to
torture. But I would never torture a girl like myself, although I
know Zanoni would do so, gladly."

The girl ceased speaking with a suddenness which astonished the detective, and he saw that she was staring in terror over his shoulder at something or some person behind him.

He turned involuntarily to see what it was, only to discover, standing in the doorway, confronting him, the figure of a young and beautiful woman, whose eyes were blazing out at him like the eyes of a mad person.

"Zanoni!" was the thought which came to him on the instant; and he started forward toward her, just as he saw, beyond her shadow, the figure of Patsy creeping toward her from the hallway.

It was evident that she had entered the room without seeing either Patsy or Dr. Quartz where Nick had left them, in the hallway.

There was a strange smile of menacing power on her face, and she was in the act of raising her right hand, which contained a pistol. And Nick understood from her attitude, and also from the expression of her eyes, that she intended to use it; that she meant to fire, and fire to kill, the instant the weapon should be on a level with his heart.

But Patsy was creeping toward her, and Nick saw that he would reach her before she could fire; and at the same instant also, there came the sound of hammering against the street door. This was followed by a heavy crash, as the door fell in, and the detective remembered then the instructions he had given to Ten-Ichi, and he knew that the young assistant had gone to police headquarters and had brought officers with him to the house.

For the first time he realized how long a time had elapsed since he had descended through the scuttle from the roof.

As the crash of the falling door sounded through the house, Patsy leaped forward.

He seized Zanoni by the arms and pinioned them to her sides; and there he held her while the detective calmly stepped forward and secured her.

Strangely enough, she did not attempt to struggle. She stood quite still while the detectives bound her so that she could not escape; and just as that was accomplished, Ten-Ichi, followed by the officers he had brought with him, entered the room.

It was a strange group, which, ten minutes later, was assembled in that room with the iron doors.

Nanine Duclos was seated on the floor at one side of the room, at the feet of Dr. Quartz, for notwithstanding the fact that he had been in the hall with his eyes bandaged, he had managed, the moment that Nick ceased to talk to her, to gain his mesmeric, or hypnotic, power over her, and by the time the officers entered the room, she was completely under his control. She went to him, and she came back into the room with him, and refused to leave him, whimpering like a spoiled child when they attempted to force her from his side.

"Let her alone," was all that Nick said. "We will find a way to overcome that power later on."

Zanoni remained where they had seated her, passive, and, to all appearance, oblivious to everything that was taking place around her.

Dr. Quartz was seated in an armchair, calmly surveying the officers and the detectives who were grouped around him; and there was a smile of derision on his face—a smile which Nick could have sworn was precisely the same that the original Dr. Quartz delighted to use to show his utter contempt for his enemies.

"It is all up with you now, doctor," said Nick. "We know the story. Nanine has told me all, as you no doubt heard, and I think that hangman's rope is awaiting you somewhat sooner than you anticipated."

"The rope is not yet made that will hang me," replied the doctor, calmly.

"Nor the electric chair that will hold you, I suppose," said Nick.

"How wise you are, Carter."

"The mouse is playing with the cat; eh?"

"No; the cat has merely permitted the mouse to go a little further from its claws than was wise; but presently the cat will jump again, and the mouse will be under its paws once more."

"We will see," said the detective.

"Bah!" replied the doctor.

Nick turned toward Zanoni.

"Young woman," he said, sternly, pointing at the doctor, "do you know this man to be a murderer?"

To the surprise of all, she calmly replied:

"I do."

"And do you know that he killed the five people in the freight car?"

"I do," she replied, as calmly as before.

"You will swear to that before a court, will you?"

"I will," she said; her expression did not change while she was making these replies, and she might have been made of stone or putty for all the feeling she manifested.

"That is enough," said the detective. "Take them all away, officers."

Dr. Quartz laughed aloud.

He did not appear to be in the least affected by what Zanoni had said.

"That chap is a man of iron nerve, at least," said one of the officers.

"An iron nerve, and a heart of ice," said the doctor, laughing; "eh, Carter?"

[THE END.]

Notes

"DASHING DIAMOND DICK"

1. *concert-saloons, and free-and-easies:* Large entertainment halls. "Free-and-easies" are social gatherings (generally at a public house) where smoking, drinking, and singing are allowed.
2. *El Dorado:* A place of great wealth or opportunity, named for the legendary city in northern South America where gold and precious jewels could be found.
3. *Rialto:* A gathering place or marketplace, named for the Rialto in Venice where there was a marketplace.
4. *Doan'd you do me dot:* Exaggerated German dialect as an example of dime-novel style where a character speaks in dialect both for comic effect and to establish his station in the community. The more phonetic the rendering, the more difficult it may be to read.
5. *Greaser:* Offensive slang, referring to a Hispanic and especially a Mexican.
6. *reticule:* A woman's drawstring handbag or purse.
7. *finf und drizig:* Dialect form of *fünfunddreißig,* German for "five-and-thirty" or the number thirty-five.
8. *Teuton:* A speaker of German. Refers to Heinrich Schwauenflegle.
9. *salivated:* By context, this is a synonym for *ventilated* or shot full of holes.
10. *'tenny rate:* A shortened form of "at any rate." Colloquial dialect is used to characterize the speaker. Note other examples contrasted with the formal English of Diamond Dick.
11. *box an' rack:* The luggage area on a stagecoach. The box holds gold or the mail pouch or other valuables, and the rack holds suitcases.
12. *Nixey:* Negative.

13. *porous-plasters:* Colloquial term for porous bandages made with small holes to allow them to lie smoothly. Bertie Wade promises his bullets will put holes in Tornado Tom.
14. *hidalgo:* A member of the minor nobility in Spain.
15. *make it wounded:* Change the amount to be bet.
16. *sand in him:* Courage or grit; what a man has in him that shows he is brave.
17. *All white; a chief—free with his dust, his dukes, and his der-ringers:* Honorable or fair dealing; a leader—free with his money (gold dust), his fists, and his guns.
18. *clear grit down to hard-pan:* Slang, Dick is the real thing through and through.
19. *Keno! Ten-strike—set 'em up on the other alley:* Keno is a cow-boy exclamation meaning everything is all right. Bertie's further expressions of delight are taken from the game of bowling.
20. *billy-doo:* Colloquial for *billet-doux,* literally a short message.
21. *Chapter VII:* This chapter is written in the present tense to sug-gest the rapid passage of events.
22. *Jews' harps:* A small instrument consisting of a lyre-shaped metal frame that is held between the teeth and a projecting steel tongue that is plucked to produce a soft, twanging sound.
23. *"A chip of the old block":* A child whose appearance or character closely resembles that of one or the other parent. The phrase was originally "a chip of the old block," but by 1929 had become "a chip off the old block."
24. *a "trump" and "brick" and "whale":* "Trump" and "brick" are syn-onyms for a very good fellow; a "whale" is an expert on something.
25. *whitened sepulchre:* A hypocrite; Biblical language for one whose fair outward appearance conceals inward corruption.
26. *cry of Cain:* The warning of impending death, as Cain killed his brother, Abel.
27. *danite dogs of the Mormon Church:* The Danites were members of an alleged secret order of Mormons that acted as spies and suppressors of any anti-Mormon sentiment. In the Old Testa-ment, the Danites are descendents of the Hebrew prophet Daniel.

"OVER THE ANDES WITH FRANK READE, JR."

1. *suspensory helices or rotascopes:* Mechanical devices used to sus-pend or lift an airship. "Helices" is the plural of *helix,* a spiral

form or structure. "Rotascope" refers to the gyroscope that gave the ship stability.

2. *Begorra:* A mild oath in Irish dialect; alteration of "by God."

3. *gossoon:* Anglo-Irish word for a youth or servant boy, which may be an alteration of the French *garçon.*

4. *whitewash:* A mixture of lime and water, often with whiting, size, or glue added, that is used to whiten walls, fences, or other structures.

5. *Bejabers:* An expletive in Irish dialect, an alteration of the phrase "by Jesus."

6. *alcalde:* The mayor or chief judicial officer of a Spanish town.

7. *give them taffy:* "Taffy" is a crude or vulgar compliment or flattery; it also means "soft soap" or "blarney."

8. *stretches hemp:* "Hemp" is a cowboy term for a rope; the meaning here is to be hanged by the neck.

9. *Palanquins:* A covered litter carried on poles by two or four men.

"FRANK MERRIWELL'S FINISH"

1. *whitewashes:* Colloquial. A victory in baseball or some other game in which the opponent fails to score; also, a victory in a series of games where the opponent fails to win any of them.

2. *those fresh Harvard Willies:* The Harvard freshman baseball team. There is no evidence that the term was ever used at Harvard itself.

3. *tootsy-frooskied:* Gilbert Patten's phrase or "patter" for being inebriated.

4. *Sons of Eli:* Nickname of the Yale students, referring to Elihu Yale (1649–1721) after whom Yale University was named.

5. *a nigger in the woodpile:* A concealed motive or unknown factor that affects a situation adversely. Potentially offensive slang.

6. *coco:* A shortened form of *coconut,* a slang term for the head.

7. *three cheers and a tiger:* Applause. "Tiger" is slang for a shriek or howl at the end of an enthusiastic cheer.

8. *get his alley:* When something is "up one's alley" it is compatible with one's interests or qualifications. Frank wants to gauge his opponent's strength.

9. *sawbuck:* A ten-dollar bill.

10. *'Umpty-eight:* "'Umpty" is an indefinite number, usually fairly large. By context it refers to a member of a specific college class,

perhaps that of 1898, but not the graduating class for that year's freshmen. Frank Merriwell graduated in the class of 1901.

11. *daisy cutter:* A ball hit or thrown along the ground, a "grounder."

12. *the air of 'Oh, Give Us a Drink, Bartender':* The tune of an old drinking song.

13. *not a rainbow:* A ball that is hit too low for an easy catch. Possibly this qualifies as "Patten patter."

14. *white:* Someone who is honest and can be trusted. In this context it means purity of heart and does not refer to race.

15. *boodle:* Money.

16. *an old saw:* An old saying, especially one that has become a cliché.

17. *care a continental:* To be worth nothing—to care not at all. "Continental" refers to worthless American currency of ca. 1775.

18. *Sure, Mike:* Certainly, you can depend on it.

"THE LIBERTY BOYS OF '76"

1. *General Howe:* Sir William Howe (1729–1814) was a British general in America who defeated George Washington in a number of battles but could not force him to surrender and returned to England in 1778. His brother, Richard Howe (1726–90) was an admiral who conducted naval operations in America (1776–78) and defeated the French at Ushant (1794).

2. *Patrick Henry:* American revolutionary leader and orator (1736–99). His famous speech in which he used the words "Give me liberty or give me death" was made in 1775. He later served as governor of Virginia (1776–90).

3. *King George:* George III (1738–1820) was the king of Great Britain at the time of the American Revolution.

4. *French and Indian War:* The North American colonial wars between Great Britain and France between 1689 and 1763. The ultimate aim was domination of the eastern part of the continent by capturing the seaboard strongholds as well as the western forts and frontier settlements.

5. *General Gage:* Thomas Gage (1772–87) was a British general and colonial administrator. As governor of Massachusetts (1774–75) his attempts to suppress colonial resistance led to the beginning of the American Revolution.

6. *Colonel Smith:* Lt. Colonel Francis Smith was the British commander during most of the battles of Lexington and Concord.
7. *Major Pitcairn:* John Pitcairn (1722–75) was a British marine officer who commanded the advance guard of troops at Lexington. He was later killed at the battle of Bunker Hill.
8. *Captain John Parker:* Born in Lexington, Mass., Parker (1729–75) played a prominent role in the first battle of the American War for Independence, as leader of the volunteer American militia known as the Minutemen.
9. *Ethan Allen:* The soldier (1738–89) whose troops were known as the Green Mountain Boys. Benedict Arnold (1741–1801) was the general whose plan to surrender West Point to the British branded him a traitor.
10. *General Clinton:* Sir Henry Clinton (1738–95) was commander in chief of British forces in North America (1778–81).
11. *in my wool:* To get in one's hair; to interfere.
12. *General Putnam:* Israel Putnam (1718–90) was the officer who is supposed to have told his soldiers, "Don't one of you shoot until you see the whites of their eyes!"
13. *It is not so far to Stirling's outpost as it is to Sullivan's:* William Alexander Stirling (1726–83) was an American soldier who participated in the battles of Trenton, Princeton, Brandywine, and Germantown. John Sullivan (1740–95) was an American general and delegate in the Continental Congress.
14. *Generals Howe, Clinton, Percy and Cornwallis:* Lord Hugh Percy (1742–1817) was a brigadier general in the battles of Lexington and Concord. Charles Cornwallis (1738–1805) commanded the forces in North Carolina; his surrender at Yorktown in 1781 was the final British defeat in the war.

"DR. QUARTZ II, AT BAY"

1. *a book as big as Blaine's 'Twenty Years in Congress':* James G. Blaine (1830–93) was an American politician who ran unsuccessfully against Grover Cleveland for president of the United States in 1884. Among the books he wrote was *Twenty Years in Congress* (1884–86), published in two volumes.
2. *Jim Dandy:* An excellent person or thing.
3. *Eden Museé:* An amusement house and musical theater on Twenty-third Street and Sixth Avenue in New York City. Founded

344

in 1883, in imitation of London's Madame Tussaud's waxworks, it became the preeminent showcase for early motion pictures in America. It closed in 1915.

4. *Ten-Ichi:* Nick Carter's Japanese assistant and the son of the Mikado, who was sent to America by his father to learn detective work from Nick Carter. The name is not an authentic Japanese name but suggests the character is "tenacious" in his quest for justice.

5. *Patsy:* Patrick (Patsy) Murphy, later renamed Patsy Garvan, is Nick Carter's number-two assistant. An orphan when Nick first hires him, he grows up in the service of the great detective.

6. *Chick:* Chick Carter (born Chickering Valentine) is Nick Carter's first assistant and is a mere boy when the detective finds him and trains him to be a detective just as Nick's father, Sim Carter, had once trained Nick.

7. *vivisection:* The act or practice of cutting into or otherwise injuring living animals, especially for the purpose of scientific research.

8. *Dazaar:* Dazaar was the villain in a series of nine Nick Carter stories published earlier in 1904.

9. *scuttle:* A small opening or hatch with a movable lid in the deck or hull of a ship or in the roof, wall, or floor of a building.

10. *He had already arranged a dummy for his uses:* Readers of the Sherlock Holmes stories will remember that the detective arranged a wax bust of himself at the window of his Baker Street flat to draw the fire of Col. Sebastian Moran, in "The Adventure of the Empty House."

CLICK ON A CLASSIC
www.penguinclassics.com

The world's greatest literature at your fingertips

Constantly updated information on more than a thousand titles,
from Icelandic sagas to ancient Indian epics, Russian drama to
Italian romance, American greats to African masterpieces

•

The latest news on recent additions to the list, updated
editions, and specially commissioned translations

•

Original essays by leading writers

•

A wealth of background material, including biographies
of every classic author from Aristotle to Zamyatin, plot
synopses, readers' and teachers' guides, useful Web links

•

Online desk and examination copy assistance for academics

•

Trivia quizzes, competitions, giveaways, news on
forthcoming screen adaptations

FOR THE BEST IN PAPERBACKS, LOOK FOR THE 🐧

In every corner of the world, on every subject under the sun, Penguin represents quality and variety—the very best in publishing today.

For complete information about books available from Penguin—including Penguin Classics and Puffins—and how to order them, write to us at the appropriate address below. Please note that for copyright reasons the selection of books varies from country to country.

In the United States: Please write to *Penguin Group (USA), P.O. Box 12289 Dept. B, Newark, New Jersey 07101-5289* or call 1-800-788-6262.

In the United Kingdom: Please write to *Dept. EP, Penguin Books Ltd, Bath Road, Harmondsworth, West Drayton, Middlesex UB7 0DA.*

In Canada: Please write to *Penguin Books Canada Ltd, 90 Eglinton Avenue East, Suite 700, Toronto, Ontario M4P 2Y3.*

In Australia: Please write to *Penguin Books Australia Ltd, P.O. Box 257, Ringwood, Victoria 3134.*

In New Zealand: Please write to *Penguin Books (NZ) Ltd, Private Bag 102902, North Shore Mail Centre, Auckland 10.*

In India: Please write to *Penguin Books India Pvt Ltd, 11 Panchsheel Shopping Centre, Panchsheel Park, New Delhi 110 017.*

In the Netherlands: Please write to *Penguin Books Netherlands bv, Postbus 3507, NL-1001 AH Amsterdam.*

In Germany: Please write to *Penguin Books Deutschland GmbH, Metzlerstrasse 26, 60594 Frankfurt am Main.*

In Spain: Please write to *Penguin Books S. A., Bravo Murillo 19, 1° B, 28015 Madrid.*

In Italy: Please write to *Penguin Italia s.r.l., Via Benedetto Croce 2, 20094 Corsico, Milano.*

In France: Please write to *Penguin France, Le Carré Wilson, 62 rue Benjamin Baillaud, 31500 Toulouse.*

In Japan: Please write to *Penguin Books Japan Ltd, Kaneko Building, 2-3-25 Koraku, Bunkyo-Ku, Tokyo 112.*

In South Africa: Please write to *Penguin Books South Africa (Pty) Ltd, Private Bag X14, Parkview, 2122 Johannesburg.*